HE STARED AT HER WITH AN INTENSITY THAT MADE HER FEEL EVERY INCH OF HER S...

"Why should I get a checkup, Doct... ...d we together sometime, and then you recognized me on the field and now you have some awful, contagious disease you need to tell me about?"

"No! I can't believe—" Her face went hot. The indecency of his suggestion mixed with the indecency of her thoughts. *Oh to go to bed with a man like this.*

"Good. I didn't think so. I wouldn't forget a woman like you."

She blushed.

"So, if we don't know each other, the only other option I can think of is that you need a lesson in how to pick up men."

"Pick up men? You think I'm trying to pick you up?"

"You don't know me. You slipped a note into my bag; you got yourself caught; and now you're looking at me like I'm dinner. Your m.o. is weird, I admit, but it sure did get us alone in the park." His green eyes danced over her with open intent, pausing at strategic points of interest.

❧

"An amazing debut . . . This book has it all: humor, heart, and razor-sharp writing. Diana Holquist is a writer to watch."

—DEIRDRE MARTIN, *USA Today* bestselling author

Please turn to the back of this book for a preview of Diana Holquist's new novel, *Sexiest Man Alive.*

Make Me a Match

Diana Holquist

WARNER
FOREVER

NEW YORK   BOSTON

This book is a work of fiction. Names, characters, places, and incidents are the product of the author's imagination or are used fictitiously. Any resemblance to actual events, locales, or persons, living or dead, is coincidental.

Copyright © 2006 by Diana Holquist
Excerpt from *Sexiest Man Alive* copyright © 2006 by Diana Holquist
All rights reserved. No part of this book may be reproduced in any form or by any electronic or mechanical means, including information storage and retrieval systems, without permission in writing from the publisher, except by a reviewer who may quote brief passages in a review.

Warner Forever and the Warner Forever logo are trademarks of Time Warner Inc. or an affiliated company. Used under license by Hachette Book Group, which is not affiliated with Time Warner Inc.

Cover design by Diane Luger
Book design by Giorgetta Bell McRee

Warner Books
Hachette Book Group USA
1271 Avenue of the Americas
New York, NY 10020
Visit our Web site at www.HachetteBookGroupUSA.com

Printed in the United States of America

First Printing: September 2006

10 9 8 7 6 5 4 3 2 1

To Peter, my One True Love

Acknowledgments

A person may have One True Love, but a first book has dozens of True Authors. To Ellen, Leslie, and Liz who stayed up late with these pages too many times to count. To my agent Natasha and my editor Michele, who believed from the very beginning (with lots of revisions, of course!). And to Carol, who brought it all together. I've learned so much.

Make Me
a
Match

Chapter 1

"Cecelia? Did you hire a fortune-teller?" Jack asked.

Cecelia was glad she was sitting because if she weren't, she would have fallen into the artichoke dip.

"A gypsy?" Jack tried again, as Cecelia hadn't yet managed to speak.

Amy is here. Here, in her apartment, at her engagement party. Cecelia knew it as surely as she knew that she was going to vomit into the vase of black tulips if she didn't get a hold of herself.

Okay. She had to calm down. Maybe it wasn't Amy.

The lights of Baltimore's Inner Harbor twinkled thirty stories below. Jack, Cecelia's fiancé, knelt in front of her, his face blank and innocent. Behind him, their living room was packed with distinguished doctors (her hospital) and lawyers (Jack's firm) sipping champagne and nibbling stinky cheeses. Everything was okay. Okay, except, of course, for the fact that she had gone numb with shock.

Jack was waiting for an answer.

She took a deep breath. "No, of course I didn't, hon. A fortune-teller! Why do you ask?"

"There's a gypsy at the buffet. With no shoes." Jack leaned in and lowered his voice. "She's eating caviar out of the serving bowl." He looked around to make sure no one was within earshot. *"With her index finger."*

"Amy." The name slipped out before Cecelia could stop it. Cecelia shivered. Okay, there were only two reasons Amy would come back after ten years: she was broke, or someone was dead.

Cecelia prayed it was death. A distant cousin maybe. A long-forgotten aunt. After all, death was final. Amy appearing out of the blue with a mouth full of fish eggs meant trouble.

Jack looked over Cecelia's left shoulder. "Cel, she looks just like you only—" He paused.

"—only dressed up for Halloween?" she tried.

"Well, dressed up for *something*."

Cecelia swatted his shoulder. She knew Jack well enough to know when he was talking about sex. All right, so Amy crashed her engagement party *and* she was sexy as ever. Worse yet, Jack had noticed. Cecelia was starting to feel her fingers and toes again. She had to take control immediately. After all, she had been preparing for this moment for ten years. She could handle Amy.

"So, who is she?" Jack asked.

Cecelia still hadn't looked behind her to the buffet. Her voice was flat but firm—the voice she used to deliver a dire prognosis to her patients. "She's the one with twenty dinner rolls stuffed in her purse."

Jack looked past Cecelia again. "Her purse is huge!"

"She's the one who swiped all the silverware."

"The spoons! They're gone!" Jack looked as if he might draw a sword. Cecelia put her hand on her valiant knight's arm. Jack may have been second in his class at Harvard Law, the captain of his undergrad crew team at Yale, the best-looking man in the room by a long shot, but he didn't have a chance against Amy.

Cecelia took a deep breath. "She's the one who ruined my life." She spun around and looked right at her little sister.

A rush of affection and joy welled up inside her.

Damn, that was definitely not a good sign.

"Put down the quail egg and step away from the buffet," Cecelia said in her best bad-cop deadpan.

"Celia!" Amy cried. She licked each of her fingers, then wiped them on her burgundy peasant skirt. "Hell, Sis, you look *old*."

"You too." Cecelia tried not to stare at the tiny lines that etched her sister's face. Ten years made Amy twenty-eight to Cecelia's thirty-two. It didn't seem possible.

The two sisters embraced awkwardly, then stepped back to stare, each shaking her head in disbelief.

No wonder Jack had thought Amy was a gypsy. From her silver toe rings to her embroidered, belly-baring shirt, to her kohl-lined eyes, Amy dressed the part. All she needed was a tambourine. Actually, she didn't even need that as her silver jewelry jangled and clinked with her every move.

Of course, Amy *was* part gypsy. Cecelia was part gypsy too; one-quarter gypsy, three-quarters anti-gypsy, Amy used to say. Cecelia spread her gypsy thin, until it was barely detectable: a hint of the exotic in her almond eyes; a touch of the old country in the grace of her fingers; a shade of *something* mysterious in her olive skin.

But with her black shift, her shiny black hair imprisoned in a French twist, and her understated gold jewelry, her ethnicity was interpreted as Italian or Greek or Jewish. No one would ever mistake Cecelia for a party entertainer.

Cecelia inhaled the familiar scent of cinnamon and cloves that surrounded Amy like a cloud. "What are you doing here?" Cecelia asked, shaking off a bout of nostalgia.

"Nice to see you too." Amy touched the exquisite silk of Cecelia's dress and nodded appreciatively. "I had no idea you were having a party." Amy turned back to the buffet and scooped a finger of caviar into her mouth.

"I would have invited you if you hadn't disappeared off the face of the earth for ten years," Cecelia said.

"No you wouldn't have."

Cecelia paused. "No, I wouldn't have." An odd pressure built in her fingertips. She rubbed her hands together, trying to halt the tingling. Oh, hell. Too late, she stilled her hands. The hand-rubbing was her only tell— the one unconscious movement she made when she held lousy cards. And Amy was the one person on earth who knew it.

Amy watched Cecelia's hands with a raised eyebrow, then she looked to either side, leaned forward, and whispered triumphantly, "I came to tell you something."

Cecelia's fingers started up again. She willed them not to move but the pressure of the effort raced up her arms to stiffen her entire body. "Oh, no," Cecelia said. "This is my *engagement* party."

"Engagement! Excellent!" Amy put her knuckles on her hips and licked her lips. "Then I'm not too late!"

Ah, Amy's tell—the lips! The tingling in Cecelia's fingertips drained away, and all the pressure with it. Amy hadn't known about the engagement. Cecelia began to breathe again. "Don't try to stop this," Cecelia said.

"Why would I try to stop anything?" Amy rummaged in her bag and pulled out a tiny crystal giraffe covered with crumbs of bread. She presented it to Cecelia. "Happy engagement! So, are there gonna be strippers?"

"No!" Cecelia grabbed the giraffe. How did Amy recover so fast? Her ability to think on her feet was legendary in certain circles—circles that Cecelia wanted nothing to do with ever again. Cecelia watched her closely. "Strippers come to the bachelorette, not the engagement party. You stole this giraffe from my foyer." They were drawing curious stares, but there was a two-foot, invisible moat around them, growing larger and deeper every second, that no one dared cross.

"Hey, it's the thought that counts. So when's the bachelorette?" Amy wiggled her hips. The music of Amy's jangling jewelry made Cecelia aware how quiet her guests were growing around her.

"I'm not having a bachelorette." Cecelia crossed her long arms. They looked naked next to Amy's, which were adorned with silver bangles, a yin-yang tattoo, and a gold snake curled around her bicep.

"What about the strippers?"

"There aren't going to be strippers."

"But you said they're coming to the—"

"There's no bachelorette! No strippers!"

Betty Wagner, the wife of the head of cardiac surgery, stopped ladling punch to gape openly. Cecelia had the urge to wink at her and say, *Unless you want some beef-*

cake, Betty. My God, she was thinking like her old self.
That was bad. Well, at least she wasn't acting like her old
self. Yet. She smiled at Betty sweetly and tried to force
that awful pressure in her hands into oblivion.

"No real friends, huh?" Amy said. "Still the same old
Cel. Don't worry, hon. I'll throw you a party. The maid of
honor needs a job."

Maid of honor? Mistress of destruction was more like
it. Cecelia grabbed Amy's arm and said loudly and cheer-
fully, "I want to show you my home!"

The eyes of the crowd followed them as they moved
through the vaulted living room. Cecelia was used to admiring stares, approving of her lean, elegant grace. Now,
the stares were amused, curious. She had to get Amy to
the bedroom, slam the door, and strangle the truth out of
her.

"Hey! A gypsy!" A young surgeon, Lance Crane,
stepped into their path. "Read my fortune!"

Cecelia moaned. Lance was a consummate cardiac
surgeon and womanizer. She prayed he wouldn't notice
that her and Amy's eyes were an identical shade of
espresso brown, or that their hairlines framed their faces
into matching storybook hearts.

She didn't have to worry. Lance was staring at Amy's
cleavage.

"No. Absolutely no fortunes!" Cecelia said.

"Yes. Absolutely fortunes!" Amy put her hand on
Lance's shoulder and winked.

Cecelia swatted Amy's hand away in terror, but Amy's
lightning reflexes caused Cecelia to miss, and the
blow landed on Lance, whose eyes grew wide with
amazement.

The pleasure of smacking him thrilled through Cecelia, and her terror at Amy's appearance was replaced by a new terror. How many times on the ward had she wanted to backhand Sir Lance-a-lot (Lance had a nasty habit of performing what might be interpreted as unnecessary surgery, hence his nickname)? But she was a doctor. She did not hit colleagues. And if she did, inadvertently, by mistake, bump an esteemed fellow, it certainly shouldn't please her. She turned to Amy, who flashed her a discreet thumbs-up.

"No fortunes," Cecelia said.

"Oh, come on, Dr. Burns, let's have a little fun!" Lance spoke the last words with enough venom to halt every conversation that her sucker-punch hadn't already stopped. That Lance hated Cecelia was a given. After all, she was a cardiologist, three months off her boards and already swamped with patients she could treat with the new miracle drugs and no-operation stents. Lance had to fight for few-and-far-between surgery cases like a jackal.

"I don't *exactly* tell fortunes," Amy said loud enough to reach the far corners of the room. The crowd, which was rapidly forming around Lance, Amy, and Cecelia, leaned in. "My power is limited. I can only tell you one thing."

"I sure as hell hope it's about the stock market." Lance laughed.

Amy shot him a withering look. He shut up.

"I can tell you a name. *The Name*."

Cecelia had to hand it to Amy, she still had her touch. Lance and the rapidly growing crowd were hooked. The change in the room felt physical, as if someone had lowered the lights. Cecelia's heart pounded in the growing silence. In less than a minute, every guest had transformed into a willing member of Amy's audience.

"*The* name?" Lance asked, his voice dripping with skepticism.

Cecelia put her hands behind her back, trying to still her dancing fingers against her wrist. Pulse rate seventy-one and rising. Well, if she were going to have a heart attack, a room full of doctors would be the place to do it.

Amy addressed her audience. "You have on this earth only One True Love. A person assigned by Destiny. One person who is *The One*. Only that person can grant you the ultimate in life—*True Love*. A love like you've never experienced before." Amy paused to let the possibilities sink in.

Cecelia backed out of Amy's spotlight. Maybe she could *fake* a heart attack. But then, Lance might launch into overzealous CPR. No, he wouldn't dare. Too many lawyers around. She spotted a half-empty champagne flute on a side table and guzzled it.

Amy looked directly at Lance, her eyes dark and flashing. She slowly raised one arm, her bangles cascading down her arm like water. She pointed at his heart. "I can hear her Name as clear as day. The Name of your One and Only as Destined by Fate! Do you want to know who she is?"

Lance shifted from foot to foot. Something like a smile emerged, then retreated across his lips. Lance was decisive about everything. But now, under the power of Amy's gaze, he was frozen. Cecelia smiled; obviously, the guy was currently sleeping with at *least* two women in the room.

Then his smirk returned.

Cecelia's skin went cold. She sank back into the crowd.

"Hell, Desdemona," Lance said. "No one cares about my True Love. What everyone in this room wants to know is should Cecelia marry Jack? It's their engagement party. Let's hear it! Jack and Cecelia: are they each other's One True Love?"

The room exploded.

One hundred and twenty-seven guests clapped and cried their assent. Two of Jack's lawyer buddies pushed him forward, shouting encouragement. Jack looked sheepish, but game. He wasn't sure what kind of prank this was, but he was a good sport and would play along. Cecelia stepped gracefully into the circle. She knew she looked calm, but that was only because eight years of medical training had taught her to mask terror when she felt it.

"This is great, Cel," Jack whispered, coming to Cecelia's side. "Where did you find her?"

"Under a rock."

"Hi." Amy reached out her hand. "Amy Burns. Cecelia's little sister."

A murmur raced through the crowd. Great. Now whenever any of these people saw her, they wouldn't see a successful, serious medical professional, but a stomach-bared, gyrating, kohl-eyed gypsy with a doctor's name tag pinned to her sparkling halter top.

Jack shook Amy's hand. "No kidding. This is your sister? But I thought—"

Cecelia felt her stomach curl in on itself. He thought that her family were all practicing Sufis in India, following their guru, wearing saris, living in a commune, unable to participate in worldly things like engagement parties in Baltimore to non-believers. This was only partly untrue. Her family was certainly a sect unto themselves. Not anything as normal as Sufism, though, but followers of the religion of True Love. Their guru was standing before them now—Amy, leader of fools.

"My little sister is an actress. She loves to *pretend*. Make a scene. This is a good one, Ames. Very funny."

Amy turned to Jack, pointedly ignoring Cecelia. "Do you believe?"

"Does the magic only work if I believe?" Jack asked.

He sounded so sincere, Cecelia thought he was serious. But that wasn't possible. Not Jack. He was a respected trial lawyer, an expert in international tax code. He didn't believe in communications from the spirit world.

"Psychic powers have nothing to do with magic," Amy said, scorn radiating from her narrowed eyes. "I won't do it if you don't believe."

"Amy, no one in this room believes—" Cecelia began.

"Silence!" Amy approached Jack. She walked around him slowly, separating him from Cecelia. "Ordinary love is born of convenience, familiarity, comfort. But True Love draws from the deepest yearnings of the heart—"

"I can cut those out if you like," Lance called.

The crowd laughed but Amy ignored everyone but Jack. "Yearnings that might go against society, *against your own best interest, against the interests of the people you think you love*." She stopped circling Jack. She closed her eyes and inhaled deeply. "You believe."

Jack nodded. "Sure. I believe. I love your sister. I'm going to marry her." He moved to Cecelia and put his arm around her. Cecelia was aware of the striking couple they made—both thin, dark, tall, elegant.

"What if she isn't your One True Love?" Amy leaned close to him, her nose just inches from his.

Jack's eyes went wide, but without hesitation he said, "She is. I know she is."

The crowd erupted in applause. Julie Stone, a meek nurse practitioner, blew her nose. Cecelia let her lips curl into a gentle, serene smile. But she wished, just for a moment, that she still carried the Smith & Wesson Hammerless .38 Special that she had in her purse the last time she'd seen Amy ten years ago.

Chapter 2

They don't really believe, Cecelia reminded herself. *They think it's a game, so play along.* Amy was like a tiny clot of blood flowing through Cecelia's life, ready to become stuck and cause a paralyzing stroke at any moment. Cecelia had to take control, to remind Amy that Cecelia was the older sister, that she led the show. "Don't read him," Cecelia said, stepping between Jack and Amy before Amy had a chance to touch him. "Read me."

Cheers went up from the doctors in the crowd, but Amy's face hardened. "I won't," she said. "You no longer believe. I see—" Amy shut her eyes and put her red-nailed fingers to her forehead. "I see doubt, skepticism—"

Cecelia rolled her eyes at Amy's fakery. Sure, Amy had the power to hear the name of anyone's True Love. But that was it. She didn't have a single psychic talent beyond that, no matter how hard she tried. "Your audience awaits, madam," Cecelia challenged. "You can't let these good people down. You wouldn't want to break a promise."

Amy and Cecelia locked eyes. The promise Cecelia was referring to—Amy's childhood promise never to tell Cecelia her True Love—had been sworn in blood.

Amy narrowed her eyes. "There are times when there is good reason to break a promise."

Cecelia leaned forward and smoothed a twice-repaired rip on Amy's sleeve. Amy needed her. Cecelia didn't know why, but she was sure of it. "Watch yourself," she whispered.

Amy ignored her. "So be it. I will read Cecelia's Name. Everyone, sit!" she commanded. People found seats on the couches, the folding chairs. Some gamely sat on the carpets, tucking their expensive clothes under them carefully. A line of tuxedoed waiters formed in the back, looking like the next act in the show. Jack drifted back and leaned against a wall.

"I need silence! Bring Cecelia a chair!"

The guests handed a delicate blond-maple Eames chair head over head until it reached the front. Cecelia sat regally and the eyes of the men in the crowd roamed over her poised body. Amy might be the consummate show-woman, but no one upstaged Cecelia in sleeveless Armani.

Amy stood behind her, put her hands roughly on Cecelia's shoulders, and closed her eyes. "O Great Spirit, come to me. I need your guidance. Cecelia Arabella Burns calls on a higher power to answer life's most important question: who is her One True Love?" Amy's voice was slow and trancelike, her hands heavy and hot.

Cecelia's guests looked like children, eyes wide with excitement. They were too ignorant of anything psychic to know that this was all an act. Amy already knew the Name, had known it all her life.

Cecelia prayed that her diagnosis was right: Amy

needed a shower and a change of clothes and a place to sleep as clearly as Cecelia had all those things to offer. Amy would have no choice but to say Jack was her True Love.

But Amy was as unpredictable as, well, as a psychic gypsy annoying little sister who'd disappeared for ten years. When had Amy ever acted in her own best interest? A flutter of terror ruffled every cell in Cecelia's body followed closely by an aftershock of excitement—*her One True Love*.

No, she did not want Amy to ruin her engagement. Her life. She forced her traitorous body into calmness.

"I feel a presence!" Amy moaned. She let her head fall back. Suddenly the air filled with the smell of sulfur. Couples shivered into each other. Disbelievers met each other's eyes and shrugged. Cecelia sat stone-still, like a model in a drawing class. Images from her past flew through her brain, and she focused her mind against them. "The spirit is here!" Amy proclaimed, and everyone, from trial lawyers to neurosurgeons, looked around, as if expecting to see a sheeted ghost floating out of the marble fireplace. "I'm hearing a name. I'm getting the first sounds." Amy swayed, pretending to let the spirit overtake her.

How a room full of educated people could fall for this sideshow hoopla was beyond Cecelia.

"Cecelia Arabella Burns, your One True Love is—"

Every breath was held. Jack straightened. Cecelia saw worry in the slight wrinkling of his brow. His worry pierced her with its tenderness. Did he think she didn't love him?

"Lance Williams Crane the III!"

Everyone gasped, stunned.

Amy dropped her hands and let a huge smile take over her face.

There was a moment of silence, then Lance broke out in raucous laughter. The crowd, realizing they'd been duped, began to laugh too. Cecelia willed her face to compose itself into a good-natured smile. Jack strode through the crowd and clapped one hand on Amy's back. He grasped her hand in his and shook it vigorously. "Man, did you have us going!"

Amy, his hand in hers, stared intensely into his face. She squinted, closed her eyes, then relaxed.

Cecelia watched the interaction with dismay. Amy shot her a meaningful glance and shook her head. The indication was clear—Jack wasn't her One True Love. Cecelia's stomach did a sudden free fall, but she braced herself to withstand the emotion. Of course he wasn't her One True Love—dangerous, destructive love was not what she wanted. She was not living her life to Amy's specifications.

Amy dropped Jack's hand and beamed at the crowd. "Thank you, everyone!" Amy curtsied again and again. Cecelia prayed she wouldn't produce a hat to collect coins. "Happy engagement, Jack and Cecelia!" Amy cried. "May you have a long and happy life together! A life joined in True Love!" She bent over Cecelia and delivered a bear hug that Cecelia accepted coldly. "We have to talk," Amy whispered in Cecelia's ear. "Before it's too late."

"You gotta dump this guy," Amy said, plopping happily into the luxury of Cecelia's bed. She pulled a small diamond bracelet from her pocket and studied it.

Cecelia slammed and locked the bedroom door behind them. "That was insane. I almost had a heart attack. How did you know Lance's full name?"

"The little nurse in the back is his True Love. I had a chance to read her while Lance was being an idiot. She brushed up against me."

"Lance is Julie Stone's True Love? No way. He's such an ass and she's sweet as pie."

"Well, I read them both and there it is. I don't explain them, I just read them. This place is nice."

"Yeah, well stop reading them. At least, stop doing it on my turf. We had a deal." Cecelia noticed the bracelet. "Oh, hell. Who'd you lift that from?"

"A woman in red. Gray hair. Beady eyes."

Jack's mother. Cecelia repressed a tiny drop of happiness over the theft and held out her hand. Amy shrugged and returned the jewels.

"The rest."

"That's it."

"All of it."

Amy shrugged again and pulled out a silver cigar cutter. "From that Lance guy. So is this place yours or Jack's?"

"Okay, keep that one." Cecelia felt another flutter of pleasure and swallowed it. She was not going back over to the dark side. "Neither. Jack and I rent from an investment banker who was transferred to Hong Kong. But he's going to sell it to us. We just have to pass the co-op board."

Amy wasn't listening. She fingered the cutter thoughtfully. "You looked great up there, Cel. Oh, Cel. We're such a good team. We should be a team again. I feel like I just had the most amazing sex! Don't you feel great?"

"No! I don't feel great. I'm furious, Ames. You can't just march into my engagement party after ten years and pull a stunt like that. And don't you dare tell Julie about Lance. Or Lance about Julie."

"But why not?" Amy pulled out a handkerchief embroidered with the initials E. W. *Cecelia's boss*, Elliot Williams.

Cecelia snatched the handkerchief. "Because it's none of your business."

"Love is my business."

"Cons are your business. Don't do it. And no more sulfur capsules in my apartment!"

"Your party was dull as church. Those people needed to be shook up. Did you see how quick they bit? They were bored to tears until I came along."

"This party is supposed to be dull. My life is supposed to be dull. I want dull. I love dull."

Amy shook her head sadly. She jumped off the bed and walked around the palatial master bedroom, picking up everything, sniffing it, putting it back. "So, about Jack," Amy said. "He's sexy and hot and rich, but you can't marry the guy. You know that."

"Don't start with me, Ames. We had an agreement."

"I know. But—" She paused. Then sighed. "You're not going to like this."

"I already don't like this." Cecelia closed her eyes and recited the words she repeated by heart at least twice a day: *Amy suffers from auditory hallucinations in the form of a woman's voice at uncontrollable intervals. Recom-*

mend EEG to rule out possible neurological disorder and pursue likelihood of psychiatric disorder . . .

"It's about your Named—"

"No!" Cecelia jumped up. Her fingers were tingling again. "I'm engaged." She waved her left hand with its enormous diamond ring in front of Amy—a cross in front of a vampire.

The problem was, as much as Cecelia wanted to believe that Amy's psychic powers weren't real, her two months as a neurosurgery resident had convinced her more than ever that even the world's foremost authorities didn't know a fraction of what there was to know about the human brain. The best cerebral angiography in the world couldn't explain Amy's abilities. Although Cecelia still wanted Amy to get her brain imaged by Dr. Malhassa if she could talk her into it.

"He's the wrong guy," Amy insisted.

"He's the right guy. Jack is kind and successful, and we are very, very happy together." An image of Jack's benevolent, helpful face filled her with conviction.

"I have to tell you—"

"You promised never to tell me." Cecelia tried to control her voice, but it squeaked in desperation.

"I know, but—" Amy looked into Cecelia's eyes in the peculiar, too deep way she had.

"Don't do this. I can see you don't want to."

"I have to."

"Why?"

"Your True Love is dying."

Cecelia laughed, but it came out strained. "Oh, please. I'm the doctor here. What do you know about dying?"

"I'd say he's got three months to live."

"And on what clinical evidence do you base your diagnosis, Doctor?"

"Celia, his name is fading!" Amy spread her arms before her. Every finger had a ring. Some had two or three. None of them were diamonds.

Cecelia cracked her knuckles, an old habit from childhood. She hadn't cracked her knuckles in ten years. "Okay. So I suppose I should march out there and make an announcement?" Cecelia stood up and mimed clinking on a glass with a spoon. "Excuse, me, ladies and gentlemen, Jack. I'm so sorry, but I'm calling off my engagement. I'm ditching my life and going off to look for some random dying guy. Thanks so much for coming! Enjoy the canapés!"

"Exactly!" Amy headed for the door.

"No! Stop! For crying out loud I was kidding!"

Amy frowned. "But why not? I'm telling you, I can barely hear his name anymore. Last time that happened, I was doing a reading for a Siamese cat breeder in Omaha, and her Named was dead in thirteen days! You don't have much time, Cel. If you don't go after him now, you will never, ever experience your One True Love of a lifetime."

"Good. I don't want to."

"How can you say that?"

Cecelia sank down on the bed next to her sister. She put her hand on Amy's leg. "Ames, I'm sorry we've been out of touch. I needed time to get my head on straight after—" She paused. "After everything that happened. But I don't want to have anything to do with my One True Love. You know how I feel about that. That True Love stuff ruined our childhood. I've built a nice life without it. Look at me. Look at this place. Look at all those people out there."

Amy shrugged her shoulders. "You don't have to give all this up."

"Oh, please. You always have to give everything up."

"His name—"

"Don't tell me!" Cecelia warned.

"His name—"

"You promised never to tell me! We had a deal!" She put her hands over her ears like a child.

"His name is Finn Franklin Concord and he's dying," Amy said. "You have to find him, Cel. And you have to find him now."

"Daddy, can we go to Baltimore?"

Finn watched as Maya threw every ounce of her eight-year-old charm at him. The trouble was, since her mom died and Finn had sworn off women, it was hard for her to know how to charm. Mostly, the two of them were just straight with each other. But now, Maya threw out a tiny, chubby hip.

Finn stopped hammering the new board on the front step and blinked at his daughter. Damn, where had she gotten that move? She was an odd kid, which he supposed was mostly his fault, as the two of them spent just about all their time hanging out together in their tiny bungalow. Especially now that school was out for the summer. "What's in Baltimore?"

She didn't answer right away so he went back to hammering and wondering. He knew she wanted to get out of going to camp this summer. Her arguments ranged from "summer's for sleeping" to "I'll hold my breath and turn blue if you make me go." He was sympathetic to both lines of reasoning. But with Sally gone and him at work, she had to go. They struck a deal, sealed with a complicated handshake only they knew, that they'd both stay home for two weeks, but then it was camp time. It had been four days. Maybe she was bored already.

"My granny's in Baltimore."

"Shi-i-ips!" He slammed the hammerhead into his thumb and began a spirited pain dance, trying desperately not to swear. She watched him with big eyes, suppressing a smile. When he calmed down enough to speak, he chose his words slowly. This was dangerous ground. "Maya, you don't have a granny."

"I do. Her name's Granny Trudy and she's in Baltimore and she invited us to come and visit—"

"Granny Trudy?" Finn straightened his six-foot-two frame to its full height. He had the long, lean body of a carpenter, which is what he was most of the time when he wasn't playing hooky with his daughter.

He wiped his hands on his jeans and then wiped his face with his T-shirt. Damn, Florida was hot in the summer. "Do you know how far away Baltimore is?"

"We can drive." Maya pulled a map from behind her back and Finn's jaw dropped. She had charted their course with a yellow highlighter. Where had she gotten a yellow highlighter? A map? She didn't make any distinction between roads or highways, or even rivers. Some of her tracings went up the state lines as if they were express elevators to the next colored square. Around D.C. they would have to rent a boat to follow Maya's line into the Atlantic Ocean.

"You don't have a granny," he repeated softly.

"Or a mommy." Maya plunked down on the step he was fixing and ran her finger along the new board. The damn board looked so pure and hopeful next to the old, paint-peeling boards around it. Guess that pretty much described Maya too. She was ruddy and fresh and just-right-pudgy and pure through-and-through.

Just missing a mom.

He stared at his daughter and her cockeyed ponytail. He had no clue how to fix her hair after his wife, Sally, died, no idea that such straight, straw blonde hair would snarl and knot like it did. There were a million things like perfect little ponytails that he had taken for granted. Maya had taught him how to do it, braving his clumsy hands without crying. But he never managed as well as Sally. After a year, Maya took over, excusing him, to both their relief. Now her ponytail was eight-year-old crooked, with escaped wisps that hung over her enormous blue eyes. His stomach tightened in regret. *Can't bring back her mom, but maybe she could have a granny . . .*

"She's a rent-a-granny," Maya said softly.

Oh, boy. Finn sat down next to her on the front steps. He put his forearms on his knees and stared straight ahead. "A rent-a-granny?" He tried to keep his voice calm.

Maya jumped up and ran into the house. In an instant, she was back with a four-inch stack of letters secured with a decaying rubber band. Maya pulled the top letter off the pile and handed it to Finn.

He opened the already-ripped envelope and pulled out a piece of stationery decorated with a purple hydrangea border. It smelled like old lady—dusty rose and foot powder. The writing was tiny and cramped, like whoever wrote it had arthritis and was struggling through. The ink was purple too, running dark to light as if it came from a fountain pen.

"Dear, Maya," he read out loud. His stomach twisted. Who was this woman and why did she know his daughter? This is what happened when you had a latchkey kid who brought in the mail herself. Damn, she needed a mother. Or, a granny. He shook the thought from his mind. *We're doing just fine the two of us.*

He read: *"Your letters bring me such pleasure. I do wish that this summer, when you're done with third grade, you and your daddy could come and visit me. I could take you to the aquarium and the zoo and on a boat ride around the harbor. And I promise I'll teach you to cook my special crab cakes—"*

Finn lowered the letter. So, he couldn't cook. Regret tugged at his gut. He wanted to give Maya everything her mom was supposed to, but how could he? He made a mental note to go and buy a cookbook. "How did you find this granny?"

"An ad. In *Happy Family* magazine."

"*Happy Family*—?"

"When we were at the dentist. I memorized the number, and I called and they sent me Granny Trudy. So, can we go? Can we? Please? She really wants us to come and it's summer and school's done and she's old and she could be dead any minute."

Finn closed his eyes. Steady. "Why didn't you tell me?"

"'Cause it would make you sad."

Oh, hell.

But the kid was right. It did make him sad. Jump-off-a-bridge distraught, even. Poor kid with no women in her life had to go out and rent a granny like a car. Finn pushed his hand through his brown hair, which was too long again. It was so hard to remember the things that Sally had always remembered, like haircuts.

He looked at his daughter. Haircuts, ponytails, crab cakes—and then the real stuff: how do you tell a kid that this is a dangerous world, full of not-so-sweet grannies?

Leslie, their orange cat, pushed through the rickety screen door and rubbed against Maya's leg.

"What about Leslie?" he asked.

"She'd come too!" Maya insisted, scooping Leslie onto her lap. An edge of fear had crept into Maya's voice and she held the cat defensively, as if Finn were the one insisting she leave her cat and schlep one thousand miles to visit a stranger.

"What if this Granny Trudy isn't a cat person? What if she's a dog person?"

Maya's eyes got wide. She held the cat closer.

"I'm not saying she is a dog person," Finn back-tracked. Maya looked as if a snarling Doberman were about to push through the screen door. "I'm just saying that there are cat people and dog people and we're cat people. See? Strangers can be nice, but sometimes nice isn't enough to travel halfway across the country."

"Call her. And ask if she has a dog and see if we can bring Leslie. Call her. Please? See her number there? I really, really, really want to go."

"Even without Leslie?"

Maya considered. "She's a cat person. I just know it. You'll see. My granny wouldn't be any other way."

Chapter 3

The morning after the party, Cecelia sat at the small table in her kitchen, nursing a cup of steaming coffee. Amy was crashed in the guest bedroom, but it was just a matter of time before she got up and they had their inevitable confrontation. Cecelia had followed Amy around the party all night, watching her every move. Luckily, most of her moves involved enormous quantities of smoked fish and caviar and a forty-five-minute inspection of their engagement gifts.

Cecelia would have to check what was missing as soon as the coffee took hold. She glanced over at the table laden with gifts. Eggshell blue Tiffany boxes wrapped in white bows dominated.

"Nice haul," Amy said. She plodded into the kitchen, rubbing sleep from her eyes. Her plaid, man's bathrobe— Jack's old one—hung open to reveal a threadbare T-shirt and a pair of worn boxers—thankfully, not Jack's old ones.

Cecelia opened the morning paper and held it in front of her, blocking out her view of her sister.

"I really appreciate the bed," Amy said. She rummaged through the freezer, then the fridge, then the cabinets. It felt to Cecelia as if she were rummaging through her head. Amy clunked down, followed by an armful of food.

Cecelia willed herself not to look at the avalanche. Couldn't Amy just have a bowl of cereal like a normal person?

"Still not talking to me?" Amy pulled down a corner of the paper and peered over it at Cecelia. She put on her lost puppy-dog face.

Cecelia yanked the paper back into position.

"Where's your not-so-true love?" Amy asked.

Cecelia banged the paper shut. Amy had arrayed two pints of Ben & Jerry's, the peanut butter, and the seven-dollars-a-bottle gourmet chocolate sauce in front of her. Good. Amy was going to die of a massive coronary. That would solve a few problems. Cecelia went back to her paper. She tried to read the comics. They weren't funny.

"I got a postcard from Mom last month."

Cecelia tried not to flinch. "Oh." Her gut twisted and she struggled not to say, *Well, she always did like you better.*

"She's still with Emeril."

"Of course she is." Emeril was the first Name Amy had heard. She was five years old. At first, everyone thought Amy was adorable, making up random, pretend names in her head, assembling first, last, and middle names like normal children assembled towers out of blocks. Then, a month later, in a roadside diner on their way to a rented beach house on the North Carolina shore, Amy put her hand on the arm of their run-down waitress, closed her eyes, and said, "Joey Morris."

Cecelia still remembered that day as if it were yesterday. She was eight years old, wearing a new pair of jeans that cut her in the waist. The pink flowered embroidery circled the hems so delicately, she just couldn't let her mother take them back to JCPenney's. She was eating a grilled cheese sandwich and french fries. Her mother was scolding her for putting on too much ketchup when the waitress came with their drinks.

"Joey Morris!" Amy sang.

The waitress went white. "What did you say?" the waitress whispered. Cecelia wanted her Coke, but the waitress was frozen. Cecelia wondered if she could grab it without upsetting the whole tray.

"Joey Morris. Joey Morris. Joey Morris," Amy sang.

"How do you know Joey Morris?"

"Stop it, Amy," her father scolded. "I'm so sorry. She's just like this sometimes."

"But how does she know Joey Morris? I haven't heard that name in years."

"Who's Joey Morris?" Cecelia's mother asked.

A chill went up Cecelia's spine. Her little sister was weird. But this was different. This was spooky.

"Dun' know." Amy shrugged. She stuffed a french fry into her mouth. "I just know her name."

"That's not her name," her mother corrected, looking at the name tag on the woman's uniform. "Her name's Jenny."

"Jus' the name I hear when I touch her arm," Amy said.

"It's the name of my high school steady," the waitress said. "How could she look at me and know the name of the boy I dated all through high school?"

"Dun' know," Amy said. "I'm thirsty." She looked at the Cokes still on the tray.

"I've always thought," the waitress said, more to herself than to them, "that I should have married him. I always thought—oh, forget it. It's too dumb."

"What?" Her father leaned forward. It seemed to Cecelia that he had instantly understood Amy's odd power. Later, Cecelia saw that it took almost two years for him to form the insane plan that caused their lives to fall apart.

"No matter who I met after Joey, it was never the same," the waitress said. Tears formed in her eyes. "I've always believed that he was my One True Love."

"Joey Morris!" sang Amy. "Joey, Joey, Joey!"

"Your One True Love," their father repeated, as if it were the name of a song that he loved years ago, and had just now remembered.

After they ate, he left an enormous tip.

Cecelia hadn't touched a grilled cheese sandwich for twenty-three years.

Cecelia dumped her coffee into the sink. Its pale caramel matched the color of her silk robe, which matched the color of the highlights in her hair, which matched the granite of the counters. She watched the liquid disappear down the drain.

Amy had snatched the comics and was chuckling.

"Good morning!" Jack appeared in the kitchen doorway dressed for work. In his dark black suit, blue shirt, and shiny blue tie, he could have stepped out of the pages of *GQ*. Cecelia's eyes, though, were always drawn to his square, powerful hands.

"Good morning yourself!" Amy scanned him with undisguised female appreciation.

Cecelia stiffened. Couldn't Amy keep any information to herself? She could almost hear Amy saying, *Well, it's not like he's your True Love or anything.*

But Jack was too much the gentleman to notice. Or maybe, after last night, he was too tired. Cecelia had planned to tell Jack the truth about Amy and her family after the party. But as the last guests lingered, out came the cigars and the single malts and four of Jack's senior partners decided to stay on.

Cecelia had eventually gone to bed. Alone. The silk of the new nightgown she had bought for the evening brushed against her thighs, a small consolation for another wasted night.

Now, Jack leaned over and gave her shoulder a squeeze. "I'm off to the office. Won't be home for dinner. The Attala case is coming to a head. Then I fly out for L.A. at eight."

Cecelia gave him a sympathetic hug and planted a kiss on his cheek. He smelled like citrus. She had forgotten his trip to L.A., but it was perfect. When he came back, Amy would be gone and they'd put the entire episode behind them.

"Geez, you kids never stop working, do you? What'll you do when the babies start coming?" Amy asked.

Neither of them said a word. Jack wanted Cecelia to consider a less demanding specialty than cardiology once they were married. Maybe pediatrics, he had suggested.

Pediatricians were the lowest-paid doctors in medicine.

"Ooh, sore spot, huh?" Amy asked into the silence.

"Of course, to have kids, you'd have to have sex, which would mean spending time together—"

"Amy!" Cecelia gasped.

Jack stared wide-eyed at Amy. Then, as if detecting a comrade, he sat down at the table next to her. "So, tell me about your commune." He glanced at Amy's odd breakfast, but maintained his lawyer face, designed to lead the witness down a perilous slope.

Amy's eyes opened wide.

Cecelia jumped in. "Yeah, how come you left the Sufi compound? Is everything okay there? They can't have let you go for more than a few days, right? All that communal laundry to get done!" Cecelia shoved her chair into the too narrow gap between them and thrust her way into the space.

"The *communal laundry* can wait," Amy said, winking at Cecelia. "After all, I may be here more than a few days at the rate we're going,"

"It may be less than an hour at the rate we're going." Cecelia crossed her arms. She and Jack had sex. Maybe not as often as some people, but they were busy professionals at the beginning of their careers.

"So, is it weird to be back in society?" Jack asked Amy.

Amy grinned. "Actually, the truth is—"

"That she loves to get away from the commune once in a while!" Cecelia cried. She kicked Amy under the table. "Dress with a little flair again, do the worldly thing."

"Ouch. Why'd you kick me?" Amy inspected her shin, giving full display to her shapely bare leg and its Celticknot ankle tattoo. Good thing Jack didn't know anything about Sufis.

Jack looked up from his paper, his eyes pointedly directed away from Amy's bare limb. Then he checked his watch and jumped up. "Oh, hell. I've got to go. Maybe we can all have dinner later this week? I'll be back on the red-eye Friday night."

"Have your secretary call mine," Amy said.

"Good idea." He jumped up, kissed Cecelia on the cheek, and was gone.

Silence filled the space where Jack had been. Cecelia dried her mug, then poured herself more coffee.

Amy licked at the remains of the butter pecan. Finally, she said quietly, "What an easy mark."

"What did you say?" Cecelia had heard Amy, but she wanted to give her sister a chance to back off. *What a breezy lark! What a sneazy snark!*

"You really got him where you want him. Good work." She tapped her long, red fingernails on the table.

Cecelia felt insanely tired. "This is not a con. This is my life, Ames."

"Oh, don't pretend you're not conning him. Just because you're not in a bad part of town dressed up like a gypsy doesn't mean you're not conning that man. You're lying to him."

"I love him."

"Great. Then you're conning yourself too."

Cecelia suddenly was twenty years old again, in a dark, incense-filled room in San Francisco. She and Amy sat on the floor around a low, round table, scamming a guy who looked a lot like Jack, only with soft blue eyes and gentle, shapely hands. He was opening his wallet, pulling out bill after bill while they watched hungrily. The big mark. The one who made it possible for her to afford medical school.

"Cel? You okay?" Amy asked, her tone softened.

"Fine." She shook the memory out of her head. They had pulled the big con, each taken their cut, and gone their own ways. That Amy had obviously blown her share wasn't Cecelia's fault. Cecelia had worked like a dog to get where she was. She had invested the money in her education, and it had paid off. Now she was in a half-million-dollar co-op high in the sky. She was a cardiologist for God's sake. She didn't ever have to go back.

"Finn Franklin Concord," Amy said.

"No!" Cecelia commanded. "Look, I have every intention of telling Jack the truth about our family before I marry him. But until then, it's none of your business. You're a Sufi faithful, on a short worldly vacation to see your lapsed sister."

"Hey, you picked the mark; you pick the con. That's the way it's always worked and it's fine with me."

Cecelia felt the balance of love and hatred for her sister tip toward hatred, at first slowly, then gathering force. She didn't want to hate Amy. But if Amy came between her and Jack, then she chose Jack. "I love you, Amy, but you have to leave."

Amy shrugged. "I can't leave, Cel. See, the thing is, I don't have anywhere to go."

Chapter 4

Baltimore's Penn Station opened onto a desolate parking lot. Finn shouldered their duffel bag, hoisted the cat box (ignoring the protest of its mewing occupant), and guided a sleepy Maya through the blowing garbage. The hot, dry northern air felt good after the thirty-two-hour train ride (unexplained delays in Georgia, then a track fire in North Carolina, had held them up). Now, they were late, and Finn hurried.

After a few blocks, he stopped and put down the cat. From the pocket of his jeans, he pulled out a crumpled piece of hydrangea stationery and rechecked the address. Ten blocks from the station, she had said. Straight north four blocks, then right for six. Well, ten blocks seemed pretty far in a strange town late at night. He rehoisted the box, and started up again, Maya falling into step beside him.

He looked around warily. The only sound was the muffled footsteps of his work boots against the broken pavement. Maya's feet glided silently, as if she were not only half asleep, but also half floating.

Why had he thought this was a good idea? Right—

Trudy had sounded like exactly what Maya needed. A woman who cared, who took an interest, who would be there for her. Four good solid weeks of female companionship for Maya. Plus, Trudy had found Finn work with one of her restaurant's regulars—good work renovating a house at big-city, northern wages, while Trudy babysat Maya. It was almost twice what he made in Florida—almost too good to be true. Maya would get a granny, not have to go to camp (the horror!), and he could work without feeling guilty.

Plus, Finn liked Granny Trudy. She had explained over the phone that she ran a lively restaurant. "Lively" was her word, and Finn had liked the way it sounded in her odd Baltimore twang. They could stay free in the small apartment upstairs, all meals covered. They would have their own place—a place where they could escape the memories of Sally's sickness—a cash job, and a granny. Plus some good, hot food, which would be a welcome change from Finn's four dishes—spaghetti, hot dogs, mac-and-cheese, and grilled cheese—the red and orange food groups.

Read Street. This was it. He looked down the curving, dark road. There was no restaurant here. There must be some mistake. Row houses lined the street, curving into oblivion. Steep stairs led up to their front doors. The houses were covered in some kind of fake stone that came in all different shades, making them look like playhouses, even in the dark.

Suddenly a door opened toward the middle of the block and a man stumbled out, framed by a triangle of light. An old woman's voice shouted, "And don't come back, ya rangy bum!"

The door slammed shut. The man stumbled down the small staircase to the street, found his feet, and, to Finn's dismay, rambled toward them.

"Think that was Granny Trudy yelling?" Maya asked. Her tiny hand pulsed in his. Her voice was light as a ghost's.

He gripped her hand harder. "Nah." They started down the street. The man stumbled closer. Then, just as Finn put himself in front of Maya, the drunk lurched forward. "Whoa there." Finn easily caught and straightened the smaller man.

"Mister." Maya was at the man's side. She tugged at his coat. "We're looking for Trudy's Restaurant."

"Restaurant! Hah!" the man bellowed, looking around to determine who had spoken. He didn't seem to notice Maya below him. "Trudy ain't got no stinking restaurant," he said to Finn. "She's got a—a—" The man began to tip over again until he noticed Maya with a startled jump. Leslie growled low and fierce from deep in her box. The man regrouped and started again. "What Trudy's got is a foul temper and a boot like a rock and if you take my advice, you go find yourself a nice McDonald's, missy, far, far away from that evil woman. Get yourself a Happy Meal." The man stared at them, one after the other. Then he stumbled away.

Finn's insides hardened into a solid block of cement. But they couldn't turn back. He had canceled Maya's gymnastics camp back in Florida. Plus, he had promised Maya a granny and he wasn't going to let her down based on the boozy opinions of a drunk. "That guy was a mess. We're not going to believe anything he says, are we?"

Maya stared after the man, her mouth hanging open.

Finn tried again. "Heck, Maya, if I knew my grandkid was coming, and some guy was being drunk and sloppy in my restaurant, I'd have kicked him out too. That Granny Trudy is my kind of woman."

Maya straightened a little.

"And she hates cats!" the man shouted over his shoulder. "Despises them. Shoots 'em with her BB gun then drowns them in a bucket!"

They stood frozen in a pool of dim lamplight. The man disappeared around a corner. The street was deserted except for them and the blowing garbage.

Maya grabbed the cat box from Finn and started back toward the station.

"Wait, Maya." Finn tried to stop her but she twisted out of his grip. "Listen. This is important."

"Let's go home." She stared down the block.

"No way. We are not listening to that guy." Finn caught up with her and she stopped. "He deserved to be yelled at. I talked to Trudy—to Granny—about the cat. She knows Leslie is coming. Would a granny hurt her grandkid's cat?"

Maya got a hard look in her eyes. "God killed my mommy, so who knows what Granny might do to my cat."

Every cell in Finn's body snapped to attention. He'd follow this kid anywhere, to the edge of the earth and over it. Or at least back to Florida. Hell, they'd take off the whole summer. Go to the beach. She deserved that.

A knife twisted in his side. No, he couldn't follow her. He was her dad. He had to lead. "Look, we are not quitters! If Granny Trudy even looks at Leslie wrong, you give the signal, and we're out of there."

"What's the signal?"

Finn thought. "This." He tapped two fingers on his right cheek.

Maya mimicked the action. "You promise?"

"I promise."

"Okay." She held her fingers at the ready.

They approached the door slowly, house by tiny, narrow house, until they saw the small sign, "Trudy's."

No one looked up when they pushed through the door and into the half-empty, narrow space, which was good, because although Finn tried to hide the look of horror on his face, he didn't succeed. The place was a bar. A dark-shadowed, adult-filled bar. Luckily, Maya was too short to see his shocked expression in the dim light.

A twenty-something blonde behind the bar yelled, "No kids after ten."

Finn was preparing to speak, when he heard Maya's voice clear and strong. "I'm not a kid. I'm a grandkid. Trudy's grandkid."

The bartender and most of the dozen or so patrons stopped what they were doing and turned toward Maya and Finn.

"No shit," said a huge man who was balanced precariously on a bar stool that looked about to snap under his ample weight. "I didn't even know Trudy had a kid, much less a grandkid."

Finn realized with a start that Maya had left his side and was heading fearlessly for the bar. Two men, who probably belonged to the Harleys parked out front, watched her as if she were a small animal with potentially sharp claws. Finn hurried to catch up. She climbed up on a stool—actually climbed, using her whole body, as if she were rappelling onto a cliff ledge—and then, triumphant, smiled at the bartender. "I'm Maya." She spun around on the stool, delighted.

The bikers nodded their approval. Finn had the feeling they might start spinning too.

A chill ran down Finn's spine. He felt like someone was watching him. His eyes were growing accustomed to the dim light, and now he could make out some details: the faded pictures of baseball players from floor to ceiling in dusty frames, the boxed bats and balls on every surface.

"Two Cokes," Maya said to the bartender. "On the house!"

"She doesn't know what that means," Finn explained, putting down a five-dollar bill. Why did he feel so creepy? It was like someone was looking down on him. He tried to shake the feeling, but it was so odd.

Then he looked up. The entire ceiling was covered with a replica of the Sistine Chapel.

"Starving artists," the bartender explained, putting down two Cokes. "They'll do anything for free beer."

"Wow!" Maya looked seriously in danger of toppling backward off her stool as she gazed skyward. "It's like a church."

Finn looked around at the ragtag crowd. "Yeah, pretty much." He braced Maya so she wouldn't fall. "See, it's a copy of a famous ceiling in the Vatican. The hand of God touches the hand of man—"

"God's a lady."

Finn looked closely. Sure enough, a woman who looked a whole lot like Bette Midler was emerging from the billowing clouds, reaching her hand out to a reclining Adam.

"Looking for me?"

Finn looked down and there stood Bette Midler. Well, at least a woman who looked an awful lot like her, only she was at least seventy years old and eighty pounds heavier than the she-god above. The woman smiled. She didn't have any teeth.

"Granny!" Maya gave her a bear hug that Trudy returned warmly, inhaling the child like a woman who hadn't been hugged in a long time.

Finn checked the ceiling, but the she-god's mouth was closed. When he looked back, Trudy was behind the bar, rummaging under it.

"Maya, it is *so* good to finally meet you, honey. Your dad looks perfect. Just like you said." Trudy's voice emerged, muffled, from somewhere behind the bar.

"Perfect for the job we talked about?" Finn tried not to let his apprehension show. He squinted at Maya who shrugged in overfaked innocence. He had a bad feeling about this.

"No, no, no, no. The other job." Trudy came back, carrying something white. "Didn't Maya tell you?"

Maya swung her feet, her black Converse sneakers thumping against the bar. She wouldn't meet his eyes.

"Other job?" Finn braced himself.

Trudy unfurled—*a baseball jersey.* "Maya told me you're a mean shortstop with a slugger's bat," Trudy said. "So I left a place for you on our roster." Trudy motioned at the row of trophies over the bar. Each one shined as if it were recently polished. They all read, "Trudy's Tip-

plers, B-team, Baltimore Recreational Baseball League."
They had won ten years in a row.

"You want me to play baseball?" He could feel his
muscles relax one by one. Despite himself, he liked this
lady. He caught the jersey Trudy tossed him and exam-
ined the back. "Concord" was spelled out in block, black
letters, like the old days. *Maybe this place wasn't so bad.*
He'd have to talk to Maya about her not telling him about
this. But that could wait until later.

"I told Granny Trudy that you used to play for the
triple-A league and she said—"

"I said that's just exactly what we need for the next
four games." She held the jersey up to him. "Competi-
tion's gonna be tough. First a few whacks at the yuppies.
Then the firemen." She lifted Finn's arm and tested his
bicep. She nodded in approval. "If we win these games,
you can go back to Florida knowing that you did Maya's
Granny a great favor. I'm the coach." She said the last
words like a threat. "And we don't like to lose."

"And I'm the water girl," Maya said, mimicking
Trudy's tough-guy tone and Baltimore twang. "Plus I
packed your mitt and stuff."

"Just for the month you're here," Trudy added. "Unless of course, you decide to stay. *If* you're as good as
Maya says you are."

"He won't stay," Maya said. "Daddy thinks it's kind of
scary in here and that you're going to drown Leslie with
a BB gun."

"Maya! What stories are you making up?" Finn asked,
amazed at Maya's unfailing ability to know exactly—
well, except for a little confusion around the BB gun
part—what he was thinking.

Maya shrugged.

Granny Trudy shook her head. "Oh, we're family here. Just because we're part bar doesn't mean anything bad goes on. We're a restaurant too. Full menu. Families until ten." She looked right at Finn. "I just really wanted Maya to come and I was afraid she wouldn't if I told you it's also a bar. I don't let nobody get out of control. I rule this place with an iron fist."

Finn didn't doubt that.

"Let me see your kitty," Trudy said.

"No." Maya stood in front of Leslie's box, which Finn had set on the sticky floor.

Trudy raised her eyebrows. "You know, I was just saying that we needed a good mouse-catcher around here."

"I bet." Finn tried not to shudder.

"Oh, Leslie's the best mouse-catcher ever. Rats even, I think. Daddy, has Leslie ever caught a rat?"

"Sure. Lots." *Only in this town, the rats are probably bigger than she is*.

"Well, there we have it. She can stay. I'll even pay a dollar a mouse."

"Deal!" Maya said happily. "Only I get the money 'cause she's just a cat."

"That's my girl!" Trudy proclaimed. "Now, let's learn you your first lesson from Grandma. C'mon, your daddy looks like he could use a drink. I'll teach you how to pull a perfect draft."

Chapter 5

Two days later, Cecelia sat alone in the hospital cafeteria, her laptop open on the table before her. The cavernous room was almost empty, just a smattering of hospital staff, two droopy-eyed interns, and a huddled family, whispering in the far corner. Cecelia wore her usual hospital garb: a black Armani pants suit with a white lab coat over top, a strand of pearls, and simple gold hoops.

A woman dressed like her shouldn't do a thing like this.

After all, she was getting engaged. She didn't want to know about some stranger who was dying.

She looked down at the hospital ID tag hanging on a chain around her neck. She was a doctor. She saved people. She might have information to save this Finn, whoever he was. The future wasn't set. She could intervene.

She had taken an oath when she became a doctor to do no harm. Was erupting into some poor guy's life to tell him he was about to bite the big one doing more harm than good? After all, Amy could be wrong.

She stared at the black screen of her computer.

Amy was a lot of things, but when it came to the Names, she was never wrong.

Cecelia hit a key, and the computer flickered to life. She clicked open Google. Then, looking to either side, she quickly typed "Finn Franklin Concord" into the search engine.

Nothing.

She blinked at the "no entries found" message. Okay, so whoever Finn was, he wasn't the kind of guy who had a presence on the Web.

She typed her own name in. Seventeen entries appeared. She flashed a private smile. The Yale Bulldog Alumni newsletter, *The Johns Hopkins Medical School News*, *The American Scientist Journal* March edition, the Baltimore Tulip and Philanthropic Society.

Fortified, she returned to the task at hand.

She typed in "Finn Concord." Instantly, over six hundred entries appeared, most of them dealing with the town of Concord and two men, Finn Smith and Joe Marks. They were engaged in a ferocious battle over sewer funding.

No good.

She clicked off her computer and shut the top. After all, what was she going to do if she found the guy? Write him a letter? *Dear Finn, you ought to know that you might be dying. Please go see a doctor. Sincerely, A Concerned Party.*

That was it. A spark of hope flashed inside her.

She opened her computer again and turned it back on. She'd write a letter, but to whom?

The screen flickered to life. This time in Google, she

typed "Finn Concord" with quotation marks around the name.

Four entries appeared.

She held her breath as she read them through.

The first three concerned a lawyer in Palo Alto, California. He was listed on his law firm's web site, then again on the site of a California Bar organization, then once more in a community newspaper. He had written an editorial about how a person should be able to build as big a house as he pleased on his own land, zoning laws be damned.

Hmmm.

The fourth entry took her to a messy, long-to-load site with no graphics. She studied the screen, with its list of men's names and the odd symbols next to them. It took her a minute to realize that she was looking at the roster of a baseball team: Trudy's Tipplers. The symbols were positions: 1B, RF, C.

There he was—Finn Concord, SS. A flutter ran through her, but she shook it off. *This Finn is probably twelve years old*. She tried to follow the link back to a home page, but the site was too messy, and it wouldn't go.

She went back to Google and typed in the team's name. One hit. She fell back in her chair, closed her eyes, and tried to breathe. "Damn, damn, damn it," she whispered to herself. Damn Amy. Damn Finn. Damn Google.

Icy fear began to fill her veins like an IV. *Even if I never left this cold, hard, orange plastic cafeteria seat, Finn Concord would find me. He'd walk by the hospital and have a sudden, inexplicable urge for green Jell-O.*

Then he'd think, hospital cafeteria, and before I knew it, he'd be sitting across from me, ruining my life.

Fate was a sadistic jerk.

She checked the screen again to make sure she hadn't misread: Finn Concord, shortstop for Trudy's Tipplers, a B-team in the Adult Baltimore Recreational Baseball League.

This was the kind of coincidence that happened all the time with Amy's Names. A person's True Love was never totally out of reach. Her mother's lover, Emeril, in Bombay had been a rare exception, although he and her mother were born in the same hometown.

Amy believed coincidences happened because Fate would never give every person just One True Love and then make it impossible for the lovers to meet. That would be cruel.

Cecelia believed in the cruelty of Fate and Love. For every coincidence, there were ten instances where coincidences led lovers in the wrong direction, to the wrong person with the right name. *Or the right person who is a nightmare.*

She shivered. She scanned down the page. He was playing across town tomorrow afternoon.

Oh, God. She felt weak. I am not destined to love this stranger. I have Jack. She fiddled with her long-empty coffee cup. Why didn't this place sell whiskey? If any restaurant needed a full bar, a hospital cafeteria was it. Off-limits to the surgeons, of course.

Jack. She had to keep her mind on what was important. She loved him and he loved her. Not everything had to be a drama. Searching for a dying True Love made a good story, but a lousy life. She had seen it over and over. Okay, so maybe she was a little lonely tonight. But Jack would be back from L.A. by midnight. It wasn't so bad. *I control my life*.

She opened her word-processing program and composed her simple, to the point letter. With every efficient, crisp stroke on her keyboard, she felt a little better.

None of this was a problem.

She'd write the letters, mail them off, and make sure that she was as far away from that field as she could get tomorrow.

"I'm sorry, there's no one in Baltimore with that name."

"There has to be," Cecelia told the operator. "Try F. Concord." It was late and Cecelia had just gotten home from the hospital, grateful for the silent apartment. But Jack would be back from L.A. any minute, and she needed to get this done. She paced the formal dining room, around and around its enormous table, bare except for two white envelopes.

"I have a Danielle Concord on Charles Street."

"No. How about outside of Baltimore?"

"I'm looking at all the listings from here to D.C."

"Try Virginia." Cecelia heard the front door open and close. "Jack?" she called tentatively in what she hoped was a friendly voice, not at all tinged with terror and despair.

"Ma'am, I don't see an F. Concord. I'm sorry."

"Right. Okay. Sorry." Cecelia quickly hung up the phone. It seemed that except for playing baseball, Finn

Concord of Baltimore didn't exist. The letters were typed, printed, and sealed. But one wasn't addressed.

The footsteps came closer.

She needed somewhere to hide the letters, but it was too late.

She whisked them behind her back just as Amy appeared in the doorway.

Relief washed over Cecelia. She let her hands fall to her side. "I thought you were Jack."

"Oooh, writing to your beloved?" Amy darted at Cecelia and grabbed at the letters.

"What were you doing out so late?" Cecelia evaded her little sister. How had she seen what Cecelia was holding?

"Love letters really don't seem your style," Amy said. She faked left, then grabbed them.

"Give those back."

"Do you notice that every time we're together, we start acting like five year olds?" Amy asked. She waved the letters above her head. She was wearing a pair of Cecelia's low-rise jeans and her sky blue oxford, which she had cinched under her breasts so that her belly-button ring showed. Her black lace bra—wait, the bra was Cecelia's too—peered proudly out from behind the three undone buttons at the neck. She belted the pants with a flowing macramé cord that went below her knees. As usual, she didn't wear shoes, and Cecelia wondered if she had kicked them off at the door or if she had gone out without them.

"Yes. And I always win." Cecelia snatched back the letters. "You're in my clothes. Where were you?"

"You wrote to all the Finn Franklin Concords you

could find to tell them that they're dying, didn't you?" Amy asked. "I was just checking out the town. Man, it sure hasn't changed much since the old days. Have you been to that dive two streets over? Vintage pinball. James Bond machine—"

"Of course not."

"Do you have *any* fun? I mean, besides being pen pals with dying guys?"

No. Cecelia stared icily at her sister. "It's none of your business and those are my favorite jeans. You smell like a bar."

"No better place to catch up on a town. Anyway, letters won't get you off the hook, you know. How'd you find these Finns?"

"Google. And there's no hook to get off of. I can do whatever I please." Then pointing at Amy's attire she added, "I want those washed, dried, folded, and put away!" Cecelia knew that it wouldn't matter. The cigarette smoke and stale beer would come out, but her clothes would forever be imprinted with cinnamon and clove no matter how many times she ran them through the machine.

"Oh, for crying out loud. The Internet is totally random. You'll never find the right guy that way."

"I found two, not that it's any of your business. And one is right here in Baltimore."

Amy's eyes went wide. "No kidding?"

"He plays baseball."

Her eyes narrowed. "Professionally?"

"No. Not professionally. In a rec league. And that's all I know about him. I can't mail the letter because I can't find his address."

Amy sat down at the table and slung her feet onto its waxed, glowing surface. The bottoms of her feet were black. *She had been walking around downtown Baltimore barefoot.*

"The other Finn's a lawyer in California who thinks McMansions are every American's God-given right, damn the neighbors. It's filthy not to wear your shoes in the city."

"Did he really say 'damn the neighbors'? That sounds like your man." Amy inspected the soles of her feet and shrugged.

"My man is Jack."

"Your man is never here."

Cecelia resisted the urge to get a bucket and sponge and scrub Amy's feet. "I don't have the slightest idea what these Finns' middle names are."

Amy snatched the envelopes. She put one envelope to her forehead and closed her eyes. "California's no good. It just doesn't feel right." She switched envelopes. "But this Baltimore guy—"

Cecelia grabbed the envelopes. "Cut it out. I'm just warning them—*by mail*—that they might be sick. That's all. I'm not meeting them."

"Sick, or hit by a truck, or struck dead by lightning, or having a heart attack in front of their mailbox as they read a stranger's terrifying letter." Amy drummed her fingers on the table. "But how will you warn him without an address?"

"I don't know." Cecelia tried to hide her consternation.

"I do."

"Yeah?" Cecelia braced for the worst.

"Isn't it obvious? I think it's about time you and me

got out more. I was thinking, we could go and catch a little of America's favorite pastime." Amy jumped up and pretended to swing a bat. She had never swung a bat in her life and she looked like a drunken tennis player.

"I thought you were leaving." Cecelia braced herself for a disappointing answer.

Amy shrugged and put down her invisible bat. "I went to check out Grandma Molly's old house."

Cecelia gasped.

"Hey, it's my house too."

"It's boarded up!" No one had lived in that house, their childhood home, since Molly died six years ago.

"Well, the guy who's looking after the place let me in. He thought I was you!"

Cecelia was going to kill Mario.

"I could fix it up."

"And stay in Baltimore?" A cold dread flowed into Cecelia's veins.

"Yeah, and see a ball game with my big sis. We could buy some popcorn and Cracker Jack, slip the note into his bag, and never look back." Amy was dancing and singing, her bangles jangling.

"What you really mean is I could meet this Finn and fall in love with him."

"You're already in love with him, remember? Destiny has ordained it—"

"*If* he's the right Finn. After all, a guy with no address, no phone number, nothing except a position on a ball team is not my kind of guy."

"Is it a good position?"

"Shortstop. Although why that matters—"

"Oh, very nice. You don't want one of those right fielders. What's his team called?"

Cecelia felt dizzy. Amy was peppering her with too many random questions for so late at night. "Trudy's Tipplers."

"Did you look up Trudy's?"

Cecelia brightened for the first time in what seemed like forever. "No."

"You're a lousy detective," Amy said. She danced into the kitchen and found the phone book. She flipped through its pages. "Ah-ha. How about this? Trudy's Bar and Grill. It's just north of the train station. We could go right now."

Cecelia grabbed the book out of her sister's hands. "I'm sending the letter to the bar."

"No!" Amy cried. "You can't."

Cecelia picked up an odd note in Amy's voice. Her instincts told her something was wrong. But that was crazy. After all, Amy just wanted her to meet Finn.

"It's too risky," Amy explained. "If you send it to a bar, some drunk'll just throw it away."

Cecelia shook off the chill that crept up the back of her neck. Was there something Amy wasn't telling her? "Okay. You're right. After all, it's probably a dive."

"Well, it has a grill."

"My True Love is a drunk with no address who lives on frozen burgers cooked on a grimy grill. No wonder he's dying. He's going to get E. coli poisoning and with his alcohol-induced diabetes, he's a goner."

"This might not be the guy," Amy reminded her. "You need to meet him to know if he's The One." Amy was drumming her fingers again, waiting for the more cautious Cecelia to catch up with her. "Actually, forget you. *I* just need to meet him. I'll read his Named and let you know—"

"No!" Cecelia put her head down on the table, her forehead hot against the cool wood. Amy was taking over her life again. If Amy went alone to the ball field, she'd tell this Finn character straight out about True Love and Cecelia. It would be a mess. "Okay, I'll go. But I'm not talking to him. I'm slipping him a note."

"Whoo-hoo!" Amy slapped the table with her free hand, causing Cecelia's head to bounce. "Oh, baby. Get out the pom-poms."

"Those are for football."

Amy patted Cecelia on the back. "Oh, no. The pom-poms aren't for any game. They're to cheer you on, baby. You and Finn. I wouldn't miss this for the world."

Chapter 6

Thankfully, Amy didn't have any pom-poms; they were too crinkly to shoplift and Amy was so broke, she didn't have the $4.99 to buy them. Cecelia refused to contribute, using the money instead for a pair of flip-flops for Amy, in the hope she might actually wear them.

She didn't.

Cecelia's other hopes for Amy were also becoming less and less likely. Amy had latched on to the idea of fixing up Molly's row house. Amy did own half the house—possibly the only worldly possession Amy had—so Cecelia didn't feel right trying to stop her. Amy had no money, no skills, and a temperament not at all suited to hard physical labor. So Cecelia hoped she'd give up soon.

Another hope.

At least where Finn was concerned, she could act. She would get rid of him in a matter of moments.

The day was clear and bright—perfect for baseball in the park. Cecelia hadn't been to the park on a Saturday afternoon in months. In fact, she hadn't been anywhere relaxing for months. She was amazed by the carefree people around her: mothers pushing strollers, couples jogging, old ladies feeding the birds. Had she really been working so hard that a Saturday in the park was shocking?

Amy had pulled one of Cecelia's old baseball caps backward over her flowing hair. Cecelia wore her oldest sweatshirt and paint-stained jeans and a ragged pair of flip-flops that had seen better days. Amy carried her new flip-flops in her hand.

The stands were empty except for an old man reading the paper and a small girl listening to headphones. Amy and Cecelia climbed to the top row.

"There he is," Amy said, yanking Cecelia's arm.

"Which one?"

"The one with 'Concord' on his uniform, dummy. You want me to go down there and read him? See if I hear your Name?"

"No! Don't you dare move from these bleachers!"

A little girl turned to stare, obviously alarmed at Cecelia's tone. Cecelia smiled sweetly at her, then strained her eyes to read the uniforms.

Amy whispered, "Everything would be so much easier if I just went down there and read his Name."

"I said no."

"For heaven's sake, why not?"

"Because my fiancé is waiting for me at home. The man I am going to marry. The man I love. I'm not screwing it up with some meathead from nowhere. I already told you."

The little girl turned around again and scowled. Cecelia smiled.

There he was. "Concord" was spelled out on his uniform in black, block letters.

Cecelia watched as Finn swung a bat over his head in even, powerful circles. His arms stretched and tensed rhythmically with every circuit. "Good Lord in heaven."

"Oh, please. That man and his shoulders have nothing to do with the Lord, although they might have quite a bit to do with heaven," Amy said.

Finn Concord had light brown hair and dark eyes and a jawline just right for a ballplayer. His body was solid and muscled. Amid his bungling, mismatched, slack-bellied team he stood out like a god. Cecelia tried to find her voice. "I was just momentarily a little shocked, that's all. By his—form."

"Mmmmmm. Me too."

"His baseball form. Oh, forget it. It doesn't change anything just because he's gorgeous. I'm not getting involved with him. I'm going to slip him this note, and then I'm gone."

"This is what we romantics call love at first sight," Amy said.

"This is what we cynics call lust at first sight. You can't fall in love across a ball field. That's nuts."

"What's nuts is if you let that guy go," Amy observed. "Look, if he's your True Love, he's about to die. And you're about to get married—like death. So why not experience your One True Love of a lifetime, then he'll croak, and you can marry your lawyer. No one will ever know."

"Amy!"

Amy crossed her hands over her chest. "It sounds perfectly logical to me."

"That's because you're insane. Look, there's his gym bag." They watched Finn unzipper a tattered red duffel bag and pull out a pair of worn batting gloves. "I'm going to slip the note in there."

Finn pushed the bag under his bench.

"Yeah, if his teammates catch you, they'll probably just use you for batting practice."

Cecelia surveyed the ragtag team. Even the lone woman, an eighty-year-old Bette Midler, looked scary. "I'm not going to hand the letter to him. The bag's the only way." She paused. "Damn, this is starting to feel like a scam."

"I know! Isn't it fun?" Amy leaned back, closed her eyes, and let the sun bathe her face. "Anyway, what was so bad about our scams? Those guys deserved them. They were not good people and we made them better."

"We made them poorer."

"Poorer was better. It was what they deserved."

The third inning began and Finn's team was in the field. Amy and Cecelia, with two brand new, stiff gloves and a gleaming white ball that they had bought to get them near Finn's bag, were playing a not very skillful game of catch behind the bench of Trudy's Tipplers. They watched the action on the field, waiting for a batter to send the ball Finn's way.

The first batter struck out in three pitches.

Amy shook her head, disgustedly.

Players from Finn's bench began eyeing them suspiciously.

They continued to toss their ball, while the next batter sent a dribbler up the first baseline. The fielder scooped it easily and tagged the runner out.

Great. Two out. They were going to be there all afternoon at this rate. That, Cecelia supposed, was the idea behind baseball. But really, she had other things to get to today.

Another batter was up.

The pitcher nodded off a few signals, then began his windup. Cecelia said a little prayer.

The echoing crack of the bat surprised Cecelia as much as anyone else. The ball sailed into center field. The infielders turned, and Amy tossed her ball under the Tipplers' bench. It rolled to a stop alongside Finn's bag. Cecelia raced after it, knelt down, undid the bag's zipper, and shoved the letter inside just as the center fielder caught the ball on one hop and threw it to the second baseman.

She did it. She pulled her hand out of his bag, but it wouldn't come. Her ring was stuck on a tear in the canvas. She yanked at it as the second baseman tagged the runner out. Finn and his teammates began their slow jog toward the bench. She struggled with the threads, considering what would happen if she just left Jack's grandmother's antique 2.5-carat diamond ring behind.

Finn's teammates congratulated each other, except for a toothless woman who spat out a stream of cursing criticism.

Cecelia gave a mighty yank, and her ring broke free.

There, she had done it. She hadn't done it particularly well, but now Finn was out of her life forever.

Except that he was staring right at her.

Chapter 7

Cecelia turned her back on Finn and called out loudly, "I got the ball!" She looked around for Amy, but she was gone.

"Ames?" Cecelia hustled away from the bench, but Amy was nowhere to be seen. She risked a glance back at Finn, who was down on one knee, reading her letter.

Oh, hell. She had to get out of there. She wasn't cut out for this kind of life anymore. Next to the field was a grove of trees split by meandering paths. Panicking, she took off down a path. She ran until she couldn't see the field anymore, then she ducked behind a giant maple tree.

Okay, she was on her butt in the dirt, behind a tree, hiding from some beefy stranger in tight pants who may or may not be wielding a bat.

"A concerned party, I presume?"

Cecelia nearly jumped out of her skin. There was Finn, leaning against the tree, staring down at her. How had he gotten there so silently? That was all she needed, a True Love who was also a Ninja warrior.

"Me?" she peeped. Oh, geez. She cleared her throat. He looked even better up close—were those green eyes for real? Not that it mattered. But still, it was hard not to feel his formidable presence, especially when she was crouched at his feet. The guy was six-foot-two at least.

"I just got the strangest letter, hand-delivered from 'A Concerned Party.' I assume that's you."

"No. What? No. I'm just—"

"Just hiding behind a tree?"

She stood up. "No. I'm resting. From my jog."

He hadn't shaved and the dark stubble on his jaw made his eyes seem dark as they focused on her flip-flops. "Look. I don't have a lot of time. I need to get back on the field or a lady with no teeth is going to gum me to death. Tell me who you are and what this is all about." He waved the letter at her.

"Oh. Well. I'm a doctor."

"I didn't ask what you do. I asked who you are." He moved a step toward her.

His simple distinction gave her pause. She hadn't thought of herself as separate from her career in ten years. Who was she? She searched her brain for a suitable response. *I'm an engaged woman who is extremely turned on by the way you wear that uniform. Oh, and I just might be destined to be your True Love.* She shook her head. "I'm Cecelia Burns, M.D. I happen to be in the possession of some pertinent information regarding your health—"

She stopped. He had gone completely white. He blinked at her. For a long moment he didn't say a word. Finally, he said, "You're a doctor?" with such horror on his face, it was as if she had just told him that she was an assassin. He rubbed the back of his neck and leaned his body against the tree. He chewed on his lower lip and Cecelia tried not to notice how enticing that looked. What was happening to her? She did not pick up jocks in the park.

She was about to make up a story about seeing something medically suspect in his behavior on the field, but she couldn't escape how deadly serious his face had become, every muscle taut. "This has nothing to do with medicine," she began to explain. "That is, I think you should get a checkup. Right away." The gravity of her inane letter-writing plan began to sink in. He was worried. Really concerned. Of course he was; a doctor had just told him he might be dying.

He stared at her with an intensity that made her feel every inch of her skin. "Why should I get a checkup, Dr. Burns?"

"Because. I can't tell you. But it has nothing to do with me being a doctor."

A moment passed. He rubbed his neck some more, then nodded. "Did we sleep together sometime, and then you recognized me on the field and now you have some awful, contagious disease you need to tell me about?"

"No! I can't believe—" Her face went hot. The indecency of his suggestion mixed with the indecency of her thoughts. *Oh, to go to bed with a man like this*.

"Good. I didn't think so. I wouldn't forget a woman like you."

She blushed.

"I meant a woman so friggin' odd."

Now she really blushed.

"So, if we don't know each other, the only other option I can think of is that you need a lesson in how to pick up men."

Cecelia's hands flew to her hips. "Pick up men? You think I'm trying to pick you up?"

He shrugged. "You don't know me. You slipped a note into my bag; you got yourself caught; and now you're looking at me like I'm dinner. Your M.O. is weird, I admit, but it sure did get us alone in the park." His green eyes danced over her with open intent, pausing at strategic points of interest.

"It wasn't exactly a love letter," Cecelia protested. She crossed her arms over her chest. No one had looked at her like that in a long time. It wasn't allowed. Not in her world.

His eyes washed over her again. She had the distinct impression she had left her world behind.

"No. Not exactly a love letter. But heck, if I'm sick, then I think that a doctor is just exactly what I might need. Don't you?" He smiled at her and leaned closer. "And there you are—a doctor! What a coincidence."

"That is the most ridiculous—"

"Dr. Burns, I think I need a thorough physical." He leaned in even farther.

She could feel his hot breath. *My God, he's gorgeous.* This affirmation made her whole body feel like a cascade of tumbling molecules. Then she thought, *My lord, he's about to kiss me,* and snapped out of her lust-induced haze long enough to pull away from him.

What was she doing? She was engaged. So, he was gorgeous? Gorgeous didn't mean True Love. Gorgeous and electric and slightly smoky around the eyes meant True Lust—even more dangerous than True Love. Lust made a person make mistakes. It made a person do terrible things that engaged, co-op-owning doctors didn't do, like kissing hunky strangers in the park. She backed away from him. "You need a psychiatrist," she said.

"Me? I'm not the one picking up strange men in parks."

Cecelia sighed. "Can't a woman slip a man a note saying that he's dying without it being taken as a proposition?" Hmmm, that didn't come out exactly as she planned.

He squinted one eye.

"Oh, forget it," she said irritably.

He rubbed his chin. "Look. I'd love to forget this. But first, you have to give me a better explanation for your weirdo behavior. So, are we going to have a beer after the game to talk about your trawling-for-jocks-in-the-park problem or not?"

"That depends," she said. She had to think. This was definitely not going as planned. First, she hadn't accomplished her mission if he thought her letter was just some lame pickup prank. Second, she was letting his good looks—okay, his fiendish sexiness—get the best of her. She couldn't run back to Jack and her comfortable world until she made sure that he believed her message.

Unless, of course, she *didn't* have to deliver her message. "I know that this sounds peculiar, but what's your middle name?" she asked.

He closed his eyes and rubbed his forehead. "You think that sounds peculiar? Cecelia Burns, M.D., peculiar doesn't even begin to describe anything about the last few days. Listen, I've got to get back to the field. Meet me after the game. Trudy's Bar. I want to know what's going on."

"Tell me your middle name. Please? I won't bug you again."

"No way, Doctor." He stood up straight. "My middle name is my secret until you give me some satisfactory answers."

Suddenly a rough, gravelly voice broke through the trees. "Hey, Finn, you two-timing weasel. What are you doing? Taking a crap back there? Pull up your pants and get the hell out on that field before I send out the dogs."

"Your mother?" Cecelia asked.

He flashed her his sexy smile and she thought, *I want a man with a sense of humor.* Then she thought, *I want a man with a body like his.* Then she thought, *Get me the hell out of here before I ruin my life.*

"Duty calls. Meet me later?"

"No."

"No?"

"No. I told you everything I can. Please go see a doctor."

"Okay," Finn said. He gave her one last, long look. "You are probably the oddest person I've ever met. But don't worry. I'll see a doctor. After this strange little encounter, how could I not?" He turned and trotted back toward the field.

Cecelia took a deep breath. There, she had done it. She hadn't done it particularly well, but she had done it. She could go back to her normal life.

Except that she now had a smashing view of Finn from behind. Her hormones reared up again and she thought, *No harm in looking.* After all, she'd never have to see him again.

Suddenly he spun around.

She yanked her eyes up to the treetops an instant too late.

His smile was so wide, it nearly split his face in two. Then he turned again and disappeared down the path. She sank back down to the base of the tree and cradled her head in her hands.

"No, no, no, no, no," she said to the tree roots. She stood up and kicked the tree. "No! Damn it!" Because despite her humiliation at being caught, despite the fact that he was a stone-age primitive who was definitely not her type—despite all that, she hadn't had that much fun in, well, in ten years.

Chapter 8

The wedding gown was sleeveless, smooth satin. Not a bad start. Cecelia looked into her eyes in the mirror and thought of Finn. Oh, God. That was so wrong. She had to stop thinking about Finn. About his shoulders. Those thighs. The way he—Cecelia scowled at her reflection. *I am buying a wedding dress for my wedding to Jack*. She had to concentrate. Finn was over. Done.

She turned her back to the mirror. *Damn*. It was always something with these dresses. If the fabric dipped any lower, she'd need someone to stand behind her or she'd moon the congregation. She turned to the front again. What was holding it up? She twisted to the left, and her right boob popped out. She'd have to hire someone for the front too.

"Let me see!" Amy called from outside the dressing room. Before Cecelia could fix the dress, Amy was in with her. "Well, that certainly gives new meaning to 'to have and to hold.'"

Cecelia shimmied herself back into the bodice. "I said you could come with me only if you behaved. And behaved means *waiting outside*."

"Oh, relax, honey. This is supposed to be fun."

"Fun? This is serious. I have two weeks left to find a dress."

"Two weeks! I thought you weren't getting married until October."

"I need time for delivery, alterations, accessories. My schedule's carefully planned. Four months is exactly enough time."

"Of course it is," Amy said, as if Cecelia's careful planning were the saddest thing she'd ever heard.

"Out."

"Oh, come on. I won't peek at your underwear."

"Out."

"I can't believe you wear white cotton underwear."

"Out!"

Amy sighed and left the room. Cecelia struggled out of the peep-show dress and into another. This one was slinky and see-through. Why had she let Amy pick out dresses for her to try? And where had she found them, the Porno Bride section?

"I should work here," Amy called in through the door. "I could save people a lot of aggravation."

"Here or Frederick's of Hollywood?" Cecelia bent her right leg. There, now if she stood just like that, no one could see the outline of her crotch through the fabric. Jack's mother would have a coronary. Of course, then Cecelia could save her and she'd owe Cecelia her life, which might make for a much better mother-in-law. Of course, if Finn saw her in this dress—she caught herself. She was thinking about Finn again. About his rough hands running over the smooth fabric—

"I heard that sales lady in the showroom say that finding a dress is harder than finding a man. I could do both."

"I already have the man," Cecelia reminded her. *Jack*, she reminded herself.

"Oh, c'mon. Finn didn't change your mind even a teeny bit? I *saw* that guy, Cel."

Did he? Cecelia met her eyes in the mirror. She was overcome with the knowledge that she had no one in the entire world to talk to. If Finn *were* her True Love, shouldn't she have felt it deep down in her soul—not deep down, well, elsewhere? True Love was supposed to be pure, a force that couldn't be denied, a whirlwind as rare and memorable as a perfectly fitted wedding dress. Not a rush of teenage hormones clouding her brain.

Amy pushed open the door a crack. "So? Was I right or was I right? Is it perfect?"

"Perfect for a stripper." Cecelia whipped the gown over her head. Four more dresses hung obediently, waiting their turn. The sight of them exhausted Cecelia.

Amy came into the room and put her hand on Cecelia's naked shoulder. "Let me help you. You're wearing yourself out."

"No. I'm fine." She reached for another pouf of blinding whiteness. She stepped into it and instantly became tangled in its folds.

Amy tugged the fabric this way and that until Cecelia found the head and armholes.

"So, Finn," Amy said, "spill."

Cecelia adjusted the sleeves. Sleeves were good. Now, hopefully, this one had a back. "There's nothing to tell."

Amy stepped in to do the buttons and her closeness flooded Cecelia with its warmth. When the two of them had come into the bridal department, the saleswoman gushed with relief over Cecelia not being alone this time. "How nice that you have a second opinion," the woman had said, clapping her hands. "It's so much better than—" But the woman had stopped, unable to say the horrible words "being alone."

Amy carefully fastened each button.

"Mom should be here," Cecelia said. The words aloud were more powerful than anticipated, and she instantly regretted them.

Amy arranged the dress on Cecelia's shoulders. "She'd be all weepy and impossible over how beautiful you look."

"Right." Cecelia felt her eyes go wet with tears. She blinked them back. Her mother hadn't been around since she was twelve. Why did she care if she were here now? "It would be awful."

"She has terrible taste."

"After all those years in India, she'd want me to wear a sari."

"There." Amy did the last button and stood back.

Cecelia looked at herself in wonder. "Oh, my God."

Amy sighed. "It's perfect."

"It even fits." Cecelia looked at herself every which way. "I feel weird. Like the wedding's really going to happen. This is the first time I've felt it."

"It's the one. Oh, Cel. It's really the one."

Cecelia turned to and fro. "I won't need to alter it a bit. I must have tried on two hundred dresses."

"You found it. You look beautiful."

"We found it." Cecelia couldn't keep from grinning. Her life was really going to go as planned, despite Amy.

Amy put her arm around her sister's shoulders. "Now, all we need is a man who fits as well."

"Daddy, tell me more about that lady you were kissing in the bushes."

Finn stared at the jellyfish tank in front of him. This was the second time they'd been to the aquarium in a week, and Maya was calling the jellyfish the names she had given them on her first trip as if she could actually tell "Claude" from "Jessica." Knowing Maya, she probably could.

"Kissing?" Finn stared at his reflection in the glass. He hadn't been kissing Cecelia. Although he certainly had wanted to. Had Maya been spying on them? Or was she reading his mind again? Because just then, he had been thinking about kissing Cecelia. Kissing her like he hadn't kissed anyone in a long, long time—

Well, in two years.

"I told you, I was helping her find her ball. Which was your fault because you're the one who got me onto Trudy's ball team without telling me—"

"But you said you liked her? Right? Like, maybe she'd make a good mom?"

Finn was grateful that the low light hid his blush. Why was everywhere in Baltimore so dark? Or was he just used to the stark Florida sun? "I think Jessica is fighting with Claude."

Maya stared into the tank. "They can't fight. They don't have brains."

"You don't need brains to fight." Or brains to get involved with a beautiful woman. You just needed brains to stay away. Especially from a woman who slipped weird notes into your bag. But then, if he didn't have a brain, maybe he could stop thinking about her for one minute of his day. "You know, that lady was very nice and I'm glad I could help her. But I don't think she was stable."

"Granny Trudy says that you're lonely."

"Does she?"

"So, that means you're not stable either. You guys would be perfect. For stability-type reasons."

"Maya, it's not that simple."

"Granny Trudy says we've got to help you."

"Really?"

Maya turned away from the jellyfish and started toward the shark tank. By the end of their four weeks in Baltimore, she was going to be leading tours around this place.

"Granny Trudy and me, we think you were too direct. We think that 'cause she's a doctor and real smart, you have to be suede."

"Suede?"

"Yeah. You know, cool."

"Suave."

"Whatever."

They were walking down the ramp into the shark pit. The walkway spiraled toward the bottom while the sharks swam around on all sides in endless circles. Suave. Suede. Sexy. Suspicious. "Hey, how'd you know she was a doctor?" Finn asked.

"You told me." Maya ran ahead of him. He watched

her cockeyed ponytail bounce behind her. Despite the jolt of the very unconventional granny, he was glad that they had come to Baltimore. Maya was having a ball and Trudy, while not exactly sugar and spice, gave Maya more female attention than she'd had in a long time. Everything was falling into place.

A shark swam by and he shuddered at the cold-blooded look in its eye.

When had he told Maya that Cecelia was a doctor? He couldn't recall doing that. Maybe she *had* been spying. He'd have to talk to her about that.

He leaned onto the railing and stared into the tank. Cecelia's eyes were imprinted on his brain. It was almost like a spell. What, really, was so bad about getting involved with a woman? It didn't have to be serious. Granny Trudy seemed perfectly happy to babysit Maya every chance she had. Of course, she'd probably spend the time teaching her to break and enter, but Maya was a good kid, she'd be fine.

It could just be dinner.

A walk in the park.

He thought back to their last park interlude.

Okay, maybe not the park.

Dinner. A few drinks. A harmless experiment to get him back in the dating world. Nothing serious.

Damn, who was he kidding? A woman like her wouldn't want to have dinner with a guy like him.

Finn closed his eyes and let his head drop. Cecelia's dark, bottomless eyes. He couldn't get them out of his head. A heart-shaped face. Perfect sun-kissed skin. She looked as if below her sedate doctor's facade, there was the soul of a gypsy.

And she wanted him too. He was sure of it. He had seen it in her eyes when he caught her watching him.

And what was up with that weird note?

He looked up and startled. An enormous white shark was staring right at him. It paused mid-swim for a long moment, before it turned tail and swished away.

Chapter 9

The patient, Mr. Brush, a seventy-two-year-old litigator in a paper robe, was going to die of a massive heart attack if he didn't change his ways. Yelling at Cecelia like an irate hockey fan wasn't helping. Cecelia stood back and watched him vent, his rage filling the tiny examining room like noxious smoke. He was not going to settle for seeing a mere child-doctor, he bellowed. He was not going to trust his life to a girl, he raged. And certainly not a child-girl-immigrant who probably got her degree at East Timbuktu School of Medicine and Agricultural Science.

Cecelia took the abuse calmly, more sorry than Mr. Brush that his usual doctor, Elliot, wasn't there. He's caught in an emergency situation, she explained between bellows, trying to keep her voice soothing. Unavoidable delay to save a life, she said. This was the fourth of Elliot's patients in a row she had disappointed with her presence. She would have to start wearing her diploma around her neck to get any respect in this place.

But still, this man's direct abuse was better than the woman before him. Mrs. Steubens had been silent, tight-lipped, terse to the point of rudeness. Dr. Williams already asked me that, dear, she kept saying, looking over Cecelia's shoulder as if Cecelia had stumbled in to make small talk while the *real* doctor was delayed.

Cecelia sighed, then decided to make her move. While Mr. Brush continued to rant, Cecelia approached him slowly and firmly, like a naturalist accustomed to handling wild animals. Ignoring his flailing arms, she pressed the stethoscope to his chest. Her hand rested on his shoulder. Her head bent in concentration. His stream of invective became a trickle, then a drop, then nothing.

The rest of the exam went well. Cecelia finished with Mr. Brush (now calm as a kitten), and let herself out into the bustling hallway. She sucked in the fresh air in relief. Too many patients and every one an important leader of Baltimore society, or the mother of an important leader, or the half-cousin-twice-removed of an important leader. It was impossible to put these people off.

She closed her eyes. She had to see two more of Elliot's patients before she could go home. Home, where Amy was waiting to pester her with endless talk of True Love. Well, forget that. It had been three days since meeting Finn in the park, and she still hadn't heard from him. Not that she expected to hear from him. She certainly didn't *want* to hear from him. With any luck, he was gone, vanished into thin air as quickly as he had appeared. That was the way men like him operated.

Cecelia opened her eyes and gulped from her water bottle as she reluctantly approached the next examination room. She pulled the medical file from the holder on the outside of the closed door and thumbed through it. Male, age thirty-one, complaining of chest pains. She knocked gently on the door. "Ready?" she asked.

"Come in," a strangely familiar voice said.

She pushed open the door, saw the jeans-and-T-shirt-clad man sitting on the examination table, backed out of the room, and slammed the door shut behind her.

"Coward!" Finn called from inside the room.

Cecelia braced her back against the closed door. She stared up at the ugly, water-damaged ceiling and tried to get control over her heart.

"You told me to see a doctor," Finn called. "Well, here I am. Where's my doctor?"

She didn't respond. She couldn't. Finn was here, in her office, *and she was glad*.

That wasn't right.

And something else wasn't right.

What had she seen by his side on the table? Luggage? And what was that in his hand? She had shut the door so quickly, she hadn't taken it all in.

No, all she had taken in with a level of detail so minute, she was sure she wouldn't sleep for a week, were his dancing green eyes.

Oh, hell. Little pieces of the life she wanted no part of were seeping into her world, drop by drop. She felt them as if they were splashing on her skin.

"Oh, ow, Doctor! Chest pains!" he called through the closed door.

Emily, the senior nurse practitioner, walked by, stopped, and gaped at Cecelia.

"It's okay. I've got it," Cecelia assured her.

Emily continued to stare, unassured, her hands crossed over her immense bosom.

Right, Cecelia had to go back in there.

She took a deep breath, then opened the door a crack and slipped in. She didn't want Emily to see the very well-built cause of her distress sitting inside.

Except he was no longer sitting. Finn had jumped off the examination table and had his back to her.

"What are you doing?" She walked around him. What she thought was luggage was a picnic cooler.

He pulled out the foot-extension platform to make the table longer, and began unpacking the cooler onto the red-checkered picnic blanket he had spread. "You look like hell," he said. "Take a break."

"What in God's name do you think you're doing?" Was that a 1989 Bordeaux he was unpacking? Her fingertips tingled. She flexed her hands to dislodge the pressure.

"I'm just picking up where we left off. I was thinking that if I had wanted to pick *you* up in the park that day, I'd have had a full picnic waiting—wine, cheese, bread, Frisbee." He pulled out a red disc and piled it onto the examination table on top of a crusty loaf of French bread.

She couldn't speak. Fear and anger shouted inside her, drowning out a tiny voice that said, *This is nice*.

This was not nice. This was irresponsible. Nicely irresponsible. Oh, to be irresponsible for just a few minutes. Have a glass of wine. The pressure building in her hands began to spread up her arms. One sip.

No. Nothing. It wasn't possible. *You can't have it both ways*, she reminded herself. She tried to focus on the problem at hand: getting this impossible, irresponsible man out of her office before someone discovered him.

"Listen very carefully: I was not trying to pick you up in the park."

"Okay. Forget the pickup. Let's be friends." He scooted himself back up on the table next to the meal and sat casually, his legs slightly splayed, swinging loosely from the knee. He poured the wine and offered her a glass. "Last time I saw you, you were an uptight wreck, just like now. You need to relax."

"I'll relax after I'm fired for fraternizing with patients!"

"Just one sip, to deal with those awful humans you call patients." He held up his hand to stop her rebuttal. "Oh, I know, they're sick, they're dying, yada yada yada. They still have no right to yell at you. I heard that jerk through the wall. He was so rude, I almost busted in there to tell him a thing or two."

"Don't think you can charm me," she said, already charmed but trying to fight it off.

He grinned, shaking his head at her. "Wouldn't dream of it. Cheese? I have a really nice Stilton." He unwrapped a wedge of cheese. "That guy deserved a punch in the jaw."

"That guy was the head litigator for the United States Defense Department and very sick. You might have killed him."

"Good. No one should yell at you that way and live."

His words stopped her cold. All the air went out of her and she found herself completely empty. Light. Weightless. When was the last time Jack had offered to beat up an unruly patient? (Never.) When was the last time he had noticed she was tired? (Never.) When had he ever packed her a picnic? (Never.) When had his shoulders stretched to infinity—

Oh, God. She had to be careful. "What are you doing here?"

"See, I may be dying." He handed her a poppy cracker with cheese.

8,412 kinds of cheese in the world, and he had picked her favorite. Fate? She eyed him suspiciously.

He urged the tiny cracker toward her.

French Bordeaux (her favorite). Now the Stilton. And those shoulders, those hands, those eyes. It was all so right that it was creepy—creepy in the way that only things connected with Amy's Names could be creepy. Like the time they were in Austin, Texas, and the woman who didn't have a single hair on her entire body found out her True Love was Jacques LaMier, the world's pre-eminent wig-maker.

Except that Finn was so wrong. She could never be with a man who was so irresponsible that he put her job in jeopardy with a lame pickup prank. A man with no address or phone number who played recreational baseball for a bar (probably a drinker). He was a loner, a drifter— a personification of every man she had ever known—and despised—in her childhood.

Plus, if he was the right Finn, he was dying.

A wave of sympathy overcame her. This picnic was hands down the nicest thing anyone had done for her in years. Irresponsible, but nice.

He held out the cracker. She hadn't eaten since eight that morning. One cracker wasn't adultery. One cracker wasn't betrayal. There was nothing in the Hippocratic

Oath against snacking. She took his offering. "So, you're here for a checkup?"

"Right. And while you give me the checkup, you're going to tell me why you slipped me that note. The truth this time. Here, I'll say it for you. The truth is this: Finn, I was trying to pick you up. I'm living a boring, uptight, stressful life and then you came along—"

"I am not risking my job and my fiancé all in one fell swoop for—"

"Fiancé?" He stopped cold.

She held up her ring.

He looked stricken. "I never get those left-hand right-hand things straight." His voice had changed, gotten lower, quieter.

"Left hand. Ring finger. Engaged. To be married."

He put his wineglass down. He looked so confused, she felt guilty as if she'd been leading him on. Which she hadn't.

"Why were you trying to pick me up if you're engaged?" he asked.

She rolled her eyes. "For the last time, I wasn't picking you up."

He stared at her a long minute. "Boy, do I not get you."

Now she was the one who felt confused. The Stilton, the Bordeaux, the way he made her feel—she realized that she thought that he *did* get her. But he didn't. Of course not: he had no part in the world she had worked so hard to build for herself.

They both stood, looking at the floor, as if they had just broken off a serious relationship. What was wrong with her? He was a stranger.

"Engaged," he said under his breath. "I better go." He

stuffed the spread, along with everything else, back into the cooler. The Frisbee jutted up, refusing to let the lid close. "I feel like an ass."

She watched him pack the cooler and she felt as if he were putting away tiny parts of her. Okay, she had to get a hold of herself. This wasn't about imagined longings for an inappropriate stranger. This was about possibly saving his life. He might be dying and she had him here in her office. She couldn't let him go. "Wait. Stay."

He stopped packing and took a deep, troubled breath. "Why?"

She sighed. "I really am afraid you're sick." The office reflected white and pure around her. The sterile room, her white coat, her proper, pressed clothing, were a cold contrast to his messy, hastily packed picnic, his jeans, the faint hint of stubble on his face.

He crossed his arms over his chest. "Why?"

"I'll get Dr. Sutter to do an exam," she said, hoping that she could duck more questions.

He looked irritated. "No. If I'm staying, I want you and I want answers."

I want you. His ambiguous words combined with his intense green eyes made her break out in a cold sweat. No man had said those words to her in so long. Not even Jack. He said things like, "Should we meet at seven-thirty in the love nest, chick-a-dee?"

Jack.

"I'll make you a deal, Finn Concord. You want the truth? I'll give it to you. But only if you let me check you out."

"The whole truth."

"And you tell me your middle name."

"Are you always such a weirdo?"

"Yes."

He stared at her long and hard. "All right Doctor, you win. But I want the whole story, start to finish."

She tossed him a paper gown. "Strip."

He smiled ruefully. "I thought you'd never ask."

Chapter 10

She turned her back to him, trying not to listen to the soft swish of denim sliding over skin. The paper gown rustled as she watched a ghostly outline of him reflected in the chrome paper towel holder, a blur of movement and color. She silently repeated the ancient Hippocratic Oath she had memorized when she became a doctor: *Whatever houses I may visit, I will come for the benefit of the sick, remaining free of all intentional injustice, of all mischief and in particular of sexual relations with both female and male persons, be they free or slaves . . . or hot recreational league shortstops.*

This was not helping.

"Okay, Doc. I'm ready to go to the ball," he said.

She willed her face into an impartial mask, then turned. "All right, let's go," she said. This was a routine checkup, so why were her hands trembling? She placed her stethoscope on his chest and leaned in. He smelled like vanilla. She loved vanilla on a man.

"Geez, you look worried already, Doc."

She pushed aside her thoughts. She had to stay in the moment. "Your heart sounds fine. Normal—in a medical sense, anyway. You weren't really having pain, were you?"

"No I just told them that to get in here."

She retreated to the safety of his chart and scribbled some notes. Keep it business.

"It wasn't easy to get in here. Did you know your office takes only private insurance? No HMOs, no Medicaid or Medicare?"

"I see you managed," she said.

"Yeah, but I lied."

"Why does that not surprise me?"

"Good thing I'm not really sick."

She leaned against the counter and crossed her arms. "We'll see about that."

"Let me ask you a question. If someone came in here, someone really sick, but she didn't have the right insurance—"

She? Cecelia felt a twinge of jealousy. Which was ridiculous.

"Would you help her?"

"I'd send her to the right agencies—"

Finn held up his hand to stop her. "If all that's no good. If the agencies don't work. If she needed *your* help. What would you do?"

"Well—" Cecelia took a deep breath and approached him. She took his wrist in her hand and counted his pulse. Sixty-seven—perfectly normal. Why was she the only one whose pulse was racing? "You have to understand the way medicine works, there's no such thing as free— it would cost me. I'd have to take a loss, see? Pay the hospital, the nurses, the pharmacy, the lab. We even have to rent the operating rooms if it were something serious."

Saying "she" made Cecelia wince. Who were they talking about? "It would be impossible."

His eyes turned to glass.

She felt a pang of impatience. Nondoctors never understood. "People always wonder why doctors don't do more to help people, but the way the system is set up, it's not possible. We're cogs in the machine. Why do you think American doctors are always going abroad to help people? There's a joke, that the only border Doctors Without Borders won't cross is the border into the U.S. The system here is so broken, we can't help if we wanted to. Blood pressure."

She reached for his arm, then drew back with surprise.

She felt the power of the tattoo etched onto the skin of his upper arm as if it were carved into her own. A crying angel knelt on one knee, weeping openly, its body wracked with grief, its wings folded over in pain, its head in its hands. It was the most moving, beautiful tattoo she'd ever seen. Actually, it was the only moving, beautiful tattoo she'd ever seen.

He watched her react. "An angel cries when someone dies who shouldn't have," Finn said. His voice seemed to come from another world. "Someone innocent who couldn't get the help they needed."

She couldn't find her voice.

"Not that you'd care about someone innocent dying, Doctor. I mean, unless she had private insurance."

She again. Someone he loved had died. Cecelia shook herself from the image's spell. She tried to concentrate on taking his blood pressure. She calmed herself by the rhythmic whoosh of his blood as it pulsed through his veins. Everything so far was normal. This wasn't a dying man. This was not her True Love. In twenty minutes, this man would be out of her life forever.

He stared straight ahead at nothing.

"Breathe," she commanded.

He obeyed.

She listened through the stethoscope, watching his back expand and contract. She jotted some notes on his chart, then dabbed at his arm with alcohol-soaked cotton and unwrapped a syringe from its plastic enclosure.

She jabbed him with the needle a little harder than she needed to, realizing only then that she was mad at him for his smugness about her life. She worked hard for a living, damn it. She did her charity work outside the office.

Or was she just jealous of a dead woman?

He didn't even flinch.

They watched his blood fill the tube.

"Okay, now that I've given blood, it's your turn," he said. "Tell me about the letter."

Okay, do the exam, try not to think, just talk.

She leaned over with her otoscope and looked into Finn's ears. Nice ears. Clean, smallish. Oh, hell, even his eardrum was kind of sensuous. "You're not going to believe this, so I'm just going to tell you straight out. Look away from the light." She put the otoscope away and picked up the ophthalmoscope. She pulsed the light until she found the small beam, and peered into his eyes. "My sister is a psychic. She can hear the name of a person's True Love."

He looked directly into the beam of light. "Ouch!"

"Hey, I said look away from the light," she warned, clicking off the beam.

He blinked the flash from his eyes. "Did you just say your sister is a psychic?"

"Look *away* from the light."

He looked back at the spot on the wall, his mouth drawn down in a frown. She flicked the beam back on and continued to inspect his eyes. They were just eyes and she was just looking for abnormalities. She was not looking at their incredible, indelible green, the green of a forest after a rainfall.

He looked right at her, shooting a ray of his own directly into her eyes. "A psychic? Like a seer?"

She shook herself back into the present. Cecelia put the scope away and pressed her fingers up and down his neck. "No, a hearer." Thyroid, parathyroid, she tried to ignore the warmth of him. "She has the power to hear a person's True Love's name. Open your mouth." Cecelia inspected his throat, or at least she meant to. Instead, she drank in the warmth that flowed to her hand, which was resting lightly on his shoulder. "Okay, lie back."

"Not until you stop talking like a crazy person. You slipped me that note in the park because a ghost told your sister the fortune-teller that I was dying?"

"Yes. Well, it might be a ghost. She doesn't really know where the voice comes from."

He settled back on the table, shaking his head in disbelief. The frown was on his lips again. She pressed on his flat, chiseled stomach. The guy must do a hundred sit-ups a day.

"Are you really a doctor?" he asked.

"Oh, for heaven's sake!" She stopped the exam. "Why is it so unbelievable that a doctor can believe in a psychic?"

He stared up at her. "Is there a hidden camera in here? Are we on TV?"

"No."

He tried to sit up again and she pushed him down. "Let's just finish this."

"So, according to some ghost, I'm dying and you're marrying your True Love?" he asked.

"No. My True Love is named Finn Concord."

A coughing fit overcame him.

She crossed her arms, waiting for him to get over the thrill of discovering he might be her one and only.

Only he wasn't stopping. He was going a little green around the gills.

Oh, great, he was going to die of asphyxiation right here in her office because she told him he might be destined to love her.

She whacked him hard on the back.

He sputtered to a stop, caught his breath, then managed, "So your fiancé's name is also Finn Concord?"

"No."

"Okay. Let's get back to that in a minute." He bit his lower lip. He coughed again. "So did the ghost say what I was dying of?"

"The Name Amy hears is fading. That means death. No more info."

"Did this ghost go to the same medical school you did—?"

"Mr. Concord!"

"I hope his bedside manner is better than yours—"

"Enough! You asked, I'm telling." She felt her face go hot.

"So, you wrote letters to warn all the world's Finn Concords that they might be dying."

"Yes. I found you on the Internet. But I couldn't find your address. So I came to the game to give you the note so you could get help."

He ran his tongue inside his cheek. Then he shook his head in consternation. "And you believe that your True Love is named Finn Concord, but you're marrying another guy?"

"Right."

Suddenly he brightened. "Oh, I get it. You don't want to marry a dying guy."

Cecelia sighed. "No. I'm marrying another man because I'm not interested in True Love."

He blinked a few times, then cocked his head. "That is the dumbest thing I've ever heard. I mean, after the psychic bit."

Cecelia rolled her eyes to the ceiling. "Everyone thinks that they want to know the name of their True Love. Then Amy tells the upstanding citizen that his One True Love is a junkie, or the die-hard Republican that his True Love is a Communist. My favorite was once down in Georgia, this Klu Klux Klan Grand Wizard came to Amy, and she had to tell him that his True Love was a black hairdresser named David."

"Or, what about the time the serious, high-living doctor discovers that her One True Love is a dying, tattooed construction worker living over a stranger's bar with a little kid?"

Cecelia's hands froze. Living over a bar? *With a kid?* Her eyes flew to his left ring finger of their own accord.

Nothing. Of course nothing, she would have noticed *that*. He must be divorced.

Or—of course. His wife died.

She felt a stab of guilt in her gut. *She*. He had been talking about his wife. Her diplomas framed on the wall stared down at her, accusing. *Nice job, Doc*. "Lie back on the table. We need to finish this."

He lay back. She manipulated his arms to test their range of motion. Nice arms. Strong. It made her crazy that he thought she was a rich, loony, carefree doctor with nothing better to do than pester strangers in the park. "My sister's psychic powers ruined my life," she said. Was she telling him or reminding herself?

"How so?" He looked past her at a spot on the ceiling.

"It didn't take long to figure out that my mom and dad had chosen the wrong mates."

He nodded. "Ouch."

She had gotten to the part of the exam that was decidedly private. Her hands hovered, then withdrew. "I'm skipping the next part."

"If I die of testicular cancer, Doctor, it'll be your fault."

"Tough beans." She felt down his legs. Manipulated his feet. "Sit up. You're healthy as an ox. Get dressed."

"Aren't you going to leave the room first?"

"Not if you want the end of the story. I won't look." She turned her back on him. That was better; it made it easier to finish her story and she didn't want to stop. It felt good to finally tell someone.

"My mom left my dad and moved to Bombay with my littlest sister to find her One True Love. Then Amy and I got dragged around the country for six years while my dad searched for the perfect Jane Smith. You can't imagine how many Jane Smiths there are. Most of them are hideous."

"So he had to meet all the Jane Smiths to know which one was his True Love? That's a lousy ghost you guys got."

"All Amy gets is the Name. That's it. Sometimes a middle name—" The blur of him buttoning his jeans in the reflection engrossed her and she lost the thread of her story.

He hadn't put his shirt on yet, and she tried not to notice. He wasn't dying, so he wasn't The One. Her stomach pulled at her. She felt empty. Surely, she couldn't be disappointed that this impossibly unsettled man wasn't her True Love? Her hormones were getting the best of her.

He pulled his T-shirt over his head. The image of his bare stomach, his expansive chest, his muscled arms raised over his head, would be engraved in her memory forever.

"That's quite a story," he said.

"I know. It's bizarre. But it's true. I've watched the power of the Names. I've seen amazing things. Terrible things. Which is why Amy promised me in the very beginning never to tell me the Name of my One True Love."

"She didn't tell you as a kid?" He shook his brown bangs, and she wished he'd make the same motion again and again. She could watch it forever. God, she was drinking this man in like a desert wanderer at an oasis. Could she be that desperate for—for what? She rubbed her hands together to stop them from tingling.

"No, people get their Names later. It's odd. But the Names seem to have a set of rules all their own."

Finn tied his work boots. "But you don't care about the Names?"

"There are other things in life that matter more than True Love," Cecelia insisted.

"Right. Like this." He motioned at the room around him. "A medical practice that only helps people who can pay the big bucks. Or that mega-diamond on your finger?" He shook his head. "You're even more whacked than I suspected, Doctor. Listen, not that you give a damn, but am I going to live?"

"Unfortunately, yes. You're healthy," she managed to get out.

"Excellent." He grabbed his cooler and headed for the door. "So since I'm not dying, I'm not your True Love."

"Right." *Unless you get hit by a bus on your way home.*

"Well, that's a relief."

She wasn't sure if he meant that it was a relief that he wasn't her True Love, or that he wasn't dying. She didn't want to know. "Wait," she called after him. "We had a deal. Your middle name?"

He looked back at her. "You know what, Dr. Cecelia Burns? You don't deserve to know my middle name. Because, really, what difference does it make? A woman with your hang-ups would never condescend to be with a guy like me. And I would never condescend to be with a woman who thinks that love—and people—don't matter."

Chapter 11

The sun outside beat down so fiercely, Finn was
blinded by the darkness inside Trudy's Bar. He stood in
the doorway as shadows became shapes that became the
outline of Trudy and Maya perched on bar stools, playing
cards. When he got closer, he saw Trudy was teaching
Maya Texas Hold 'em. They were playing for real money.
Looked like Maya was winning.

When she saw him, she spun around happily on her
stool. "So? Are you two in love?"

Finn sat on the stool next to his daughter. He spun
around too, trying to gather his thoughts. Cecelia's crazy
story about the Names, the way he felt when she touched
him, the prophecy of his imminent death—his head was
swimming. All he wanted was to come to Baltimore to
make his daughter and her adopted, chain-smoking
granny happy.

Trudy didn't look up. She scowled at her cards.

"The woman is insane," he said finally.

Maya jumped down, expertly selected a pint glass, and
pulled a draft Bud into it like a pro. She snapped a nap-

kin onto the bar, winked, and slammed the beer onto it. "How was that, Granny? Did I do it good?"

"Perfect. I'm going to make something of you yet."

"How do you like the head on that pint, Daddy?"

"It's perfect, but I'm not so sure I like it," he said, shooting a scowl at Trudy. "Couldn't you get shut down for that?"

"I know all the cops," she said with a shrug.

Yeah, I wonder why? He sipped the cold beer. Damn, it was a perfect pour.

"Tell us more about the doctor lady," Maya demanded, like a mini-bartender fishing for a good tip, her elbows on the bar, her face in her hands.

"She says that I'm her True Love as destined by Fate."

Trudy looked up. "She said *that* and you didn't get laid?"

"What's 'get laid'?" Maya asked.

"It's a card game grown-ups play," Finn said, glaring at Trudy.

"Which you obviously suck at," Trudy said. She gathered the cards and began to shuffle them.

Finn watched her expert fingers work the cards. Her hands flew like lightning. A chill ran through him. Every word he had seen on that purple hydrangea stationery was written in a gnarled hand. With a purple pen. *I do hope that when you're finished with third grade . . .* That wasn't the way Trudy talked. And this lady probably never saw a hydrangea in her life. "Maybe I *was* a little hard on the doctor. I'll write her a letter. Trudy, can I borrow your purple fountain pen?"

"I don't have a purple fountain pen. What would I do with a purple—?" She stopped shuffling and squinted at him. Then she started shuffling again. "Oh, that pen. I threw it out. Ran out of ink." She held his gaze, and Finn shuddered. He recognized that look, but from where?

Then he remembered. The shark at the aquarium. Trudy was a shark. He was in a shark tank. Right now.

Maya had gone back to her stool and was spinning again. "Granny Trudy? When are we gonna make those crab cakes you promised?" she asked.

Trudy gave the little girl's stool a spirited twirl. "Soon, honey. How 'bout tonight? We'll put them on the appetizer menu."

Maya spun giddily, gripping the stool. "Hooray!" she shouted.

Finn shook off his foreboding. He was going crazy, that was all. It made sense, since everyone he met in this weird, dark town was slightly off-center. He couldn't let his creepy premonitions ruin it for Maya. He just had to stay away from that doctor. *Psychics*, my foot. She was making him believe in things that weren't there.

Amy sat in the corner of the bar, her back to Finn and Maya, her Ravens cap pulled down low.

This guy was smart. Well, that was good. Cecelia wouldn't go for a dumb guy, no matter how much he looked like a young Harrison Ford. But maybe he was too smart. And this just had to work. It was her last chance.

She sipped her whiskey as she watched Finn's reflection in the Orioles mirror behind the bar. She wondered, again, for the millionth time why she needed Cecelia. Well, the damn spirits weren't giving her any clues about that, that was for sure. Amy had thought when she left Cecelia ten years ago that she'd go out on her own. Hell,

Cecelia didn't need her anymore, so she certainly didn't need Cecelia.

But then, it turned out, she did. The Names Amy heard so clearly all her life started to fade the instant they had parted. Every year, the voice grew a little fainter. Now, it was almost gone. Sometimes she could get a whisper of a Name, a few syllables; sometimes, nothing.

Cecelia was the key. Hell, the first time they were together in ten years, at that overstuffed engagement party, the Name for that horrible Lance and the little nurse Julie came clear as day. Her powers were back. For an instant. Now, with Cecelia mad at her, they were fading out again. It all revolved around Cecelia. But why?

She finished her whiskey and studied the bottom of the glass as if it might reveal an answer. Why didn't matter, all that mattered was what to do about it.

"On the house," Trudy said, sloshing a fresh whiskey on the table. She leaned in close to Amy, not looking at her, while she washed the table with a gray rag. "Your hot shot sister's blowing it big time with handsome over there."

"That's what I was afraid of. What happened?"

"Guess she got all high-and-mighty on him. Plus, he thinks she's bonkers." She scrubbed at a permanent spot on the table. "Seems she believes in spirits."

"We've got to get them back together." Amy sipped the new whiskey. Getting Finn and Cecelia together was mandatory. If Cecelia never experienced True Love, she'd never see that it was all that mattered. And if she didn't see that love was all that mattered, she'd never join Amy in the psychic business again. And if she didn't join Amy, then Amy couldn't hear the voices—

"Maybe he's the wrong Finn."

Amy had the strange sensation she was in a confessional, the way Trudy wouldn't look at her. "Hell, I don't know. That's the thing. I can't be sure until I can get up close and concentrate on him. Which would definitely be too risky now." Amy looked over at Finn. He and Maya had gone to the back of the bar and were engrossed in a spirited pinball game, each manning one flipper.

"If he was the right one, wouldn't Cecelia have known?" Trudy picked up the empty whiskey and put it on her small, round tray.

"Cecelia? Hell, she wouldn't know if she had an orgasm without some kind of blinking monitor. That's the trouble. She's a block of wood."

"So, now what? I need him around for one more ball game—we gotta nail those firefighters. Not that they're not my heroes. God bless them. Just I wanna rip their hearts out on the ball field and Finny's got a hell of a bat—"

"Can you think of anything besides baseball?"

Trudy shrugged. She looked up at her trophies as if they were her children. Then she looked at Maya with just as much affection. "Well, what about the kid? Maya will do anything for her granny—and her daddy. That girl wants a mom so bad, she can't stop talking about it. I've been sitting with her for days hearing about how awesome Cecelia would be for a mom and how her daddy was off in dreamland all day thinking about her. Little girl even tried to stop him from putting that god-awful cheese in the picnic basket. Lord and heaven that cheese reeked!"

Amy traced a scratch in the ancient table. Stinky cheese—how did he know Cecelia loved that stuff? Was he the one? She had to think. "Okay, the kid came up with the rent-a-granny idea, maybe she can figure out what to do about this little setback. You talk to her."

Maya glanced over at them, as if she heard her name from clear across the bar. After a beat, she recognized Amy and waved happily.

Amy scowled at her.

Maya put her free hand over her mouth in giggling horror and glanced at Finn. He was absorbed in the pinball game, shouting at her, "Flip, flip!"

"I can't pay you for this," Amy said, polishing off the second whiskey.

"Pay me when we get Cecelia to join you in your little scams again. I remember when you two were girls—"

"I already told you, we're not going to scam people this time. We're going to go legit."

"In that case, I want the money now. Four dollars and fifty cents. Plus tip."

Amy rolled her eyes. "We're gonna make money. With Cecelia's class act, we can get a whole new kind of client. The big guys, who will pay for real info. So no more cons. I've got it all worked out."

"Except for the part where Cecelia quits her doctor's gig and joins you as a psychic's assistant." Trudy began to move around the bar, picking up empties and straightening napkins.

Amy scowled. When Trudy put it that way, it did seem unlikely. But True Love changed everything. Amy was sure of it. It had the power to change Cecelia. It had the power to change the world. This was amazing stuff they were dealing with.

True Love.

If she could get Cecelia in here so that she could hear that damn voice and find out who Trudy's One True Love is, then she'd stop being such a skeptic. That lady could use a little love. Get her off her baseball obsession.

But she couldn't tell Trudy her One True Love. Not without Cecelia. Hell, why couldn't she do this without Cecelia? It was enough to drive a person to drink. She eyed her empty glass greedily, but Trudy was across the bar now, talking it up with some regulars.

Suddenly she felt something brush her leg. She pulled back in terror (Rats! Mice!), then realized the something was Maya. Under her table. Grinning.

"Psst. Down here." Maya giggled.

"You can't talk to me here!" Amy hissed. She looked at Finn, who was pounding away at the pinball game.

"Daddy didn't like Cecelia."

Amy let her head fall back. "That's talking," she pointed out.

The girl shrugged.

"I know about what happened. Trudy told me. We have to fix it."

"You told me your sister was beautiful and nice and rich."

"She is."

"Just not the nice part."

"She's nice. Underneath. Didn't you ever know anyone like that?" Amy rolled the empty whiskey glass around in her fingers, her eyes on Finn. If he found Maya under her table, the gig would be up. Stupid kid.

But she needed the stupid kid to come up with a plan.

Maya was silent. Amy glanced under the table to see the girl playing with her neon green shoelaces. She looked so tiny down there. Amy closed her eyes. Her life was hanging in the balance, and it all depended on a child.

"Shirley Jinx," Maya said.

"Who? What? Oh, hell—your dad's moving away from the game. He's looking around."

"Shirley Jinx, Mrs. Nelson's second grade. She was like Cecelia. Okay. I know what to do. I can help her."

Finn turned toward the back of the bar.

"Go," Amy urged. "Now!"

Maya raced out from under the table and flew around the side of the curved bar just as Finn turned and moved down the bar toward her.

The kid is good.

Maybe Maya could pull it off. Maybe Amy's plan would work. Maybe she'd have money to pay for her drinks again.

She put her head down as Finn passed.

It was awful not having money. And she deserved money. Okay, so she had blown almost all the loot she and Cecelia had gotten off the last big scam. But she had spent every last cent of what was left of it searching for men named Finn Concord. She finally found this one with the help of a team of private detectives and endless psychic consultations. For four months she had hung out in his boring, conservative town, watching him, trying to figure him out, spending all her cash.

Until that day in the diner, when she had finally sat next to Maya and her chocolate milk shake. The girl opened right up, let her story pour out between huge, sucking slurps of milk shake inhaled through a straw with all her might, as if she had to replace everything she let out. "My dad needs a new wife and I need a new mom," she had said. Amy would never forget those words. It was like the moment when the skies opened and the sun came streaming through the gap in the clouds, except it was Florida, and the damn sun never stopped. A new mom. Cecelia. It was gorgeous.

And what a plan that kid came up with! A rent-a-granny in Baltimore. And Amy knew exactly who could play the granny. One call to Trudy, Amy's old buddy, and everything was set. Too bad "granny" had flubbed the pen thing. But her recovery was decent, for someone who'd been out of the con game for two decades.

And too bad Cecelia had flubbed the seduction.

Amy watched Finn find Maya. She bounced out from behind the bar as if she'd been playing hide-and-seek all along. He shook his very cute head at her and they went back to the pinball game, Maya skipping the whole way.

How could Cecelia have let that man get away? Look at the shoulders on that guy. He just had to be the right Finn, especially since the Finn Franklin Concord she had found in California wouldn't even return her calls.

Amy willed Trudy to come back with more whiskey.

Trudy didn't.

Okay, no time for sitting around, anyway. If Maya could work her end of the deal, then Amy still had some work to do on her end.

She had to get Cecelia to realize that Jack wasn't The One.

Or maybe she could help Jack to realize Cecelia wasn't *his* type.

Oh, the things she did for True Love.

Chapter 12

Cecelia, Jack, and Amy fell into an awkward silence around the twelve-seat dining-room table. They passed each other the grated cheese, the pepper, the wine. Cecelia had made spaghetti with capers and broiled onions. She had tossed a salad. She hadn't eaten a meal with Jack since before their engagement party ten days ago. How was that possible? Oh, right, they were always working. Jack had been out of town three times in the last two weeks, and she had been doing fourteen-hour days. Now, seeing how awkward it was for all of them to be together, Cecelia wondered if she hadn't been avoiding him on purpose.

If she could stop thinking about Finn, she wouldn't feel so tense. It was as if the guy were at the table with them, sitting next to Jack, passing him the salad, straightening his tie. It had been like that ever since he left her office in his self-satisfied snit. Everything she did, she felt him looking over her shoulder, making snide comments. "Couldn't use ordinary lettuce, huh? Gotta have that arugula at $7.99 a pound. You know, there are kids starving in East Baltimore . . ."

She watched Jack eat with obvious pleasure. The man liked arugula. Appreciated it. Jack understood that when you worked hard and took risks, you were entitled to really good lettuce.

Cecelia sighed. She was sitting at the dinner table with her fiancé, but silently defending herself to a man she was never going to see again. She tried again to shake Finn out of her head. She remembered her teacher, Dr. Manx, in her first year of medical school. He told them that he was about to reveal to them the most important thing they'd ever learn in medical school. "Every action you take in life," he lectured, "is done for someone. Make sure it's the right someone. When you're in the hospital, don't do things for the nurses. Don't work hard to please the fellows. You'll only be a good doctor if you act at all times for the patient."

Cecelia tried to see her life through her old teacher's lens. Who was she trying to please? Certainly not Finn. She was not going to live to please a stranger who couldn't stand her. That was crazy.

She stuffed a bite of lettuce in her mouth. It didn't taste as good as she remembered.

"The meal is excellent," Jack said.

"Thanks, hon." Cecelia patted his hand.

He smiled at her.

This is my fiancé. I am going to act to please him. He likes fancy lettuce. I like fancy lettuce. Case closed.

She looked across the table at Amy, who was inspecting her lettuce critically, obviously shocked by its peppery bite. Was the woman ever going to leave? A fleck of spaghetti sauce dotted her chin. Cecelia felt Amy's words echo in her head, *I can fix up Molly's old place . . .*

She was never going to leave.

"So!" Jack said merrily, trying to cut through the discomfort that filled the room like fog. "Tell me about your mom and life at that commune. Cel never talks about it." He used a spoon and fork to eat his pasta, every wound-up strand a perfect, compact bite.

Cecelia met Amy's eyes. "That's because it's extremely boring."

"Liar." Amy helped herself to more wine, sloshing some on the tablecloth. She tried to blot it up with her white cloth napkin. "It's fascinating."

Jack looked from sister to sister.

Cecelia felt her blood come to a slow, even boil. What was Amy up to?

Amy crammed a wad of spaghetti into her mouth, chewed, then sucked in the loose ends.

Cecelia snuck a look at Jack, who was watching Amy's eating habits with amazement. Or was he amazed at the dirty laundry she seemed compelled to reveal? Cecelia would have to tell him everything, the sooner the better, because Amy sure couldn't keep a thing inside. But not now. She was going to tell him on her terms.

"Are there any other siblings?" Jack asked.

"Well—" Cecelia said just as Amy said, "Yes."

Jack stopped chewing.

Cecelia felt terribly sorry for him. He came from a family that owned horses, for heaven's sake. How could he understand a family that set their only pet, Fred the gerbil, free into the heat vents of the Stallings Welfare Hotel so he could search for a better life elsewhere?

Or a family who couldn't find Jasmine, their youngest sister, who disappeared ten years ago? Cecelia's stomach took a nose dive. Jasmine was one of the reasons she and Amy had split up back then. A sixteen-year-old sister, gone. She'd be twenty-six now. And they had been too young to know what to do, so they had done nothing. Pretended she had never existed. She came out of the blue from India, and returned to—where? Cecelia pushed it out of her mind.

Conversation ceased. Cecelia tried not to listen to Amy's slurping.

The noise stopped abruptly, midstrand. "I never showed you that postcard Mom sent me," Amy said.

"No!" Cecelia cried.

Jack turned to her, his mouth a perfect O.

"I mean, we're eating. Show me later," Cecelia said lamely. Her blood was roiling, overheating her body, causing her heart to pound. Amy was out of control, and there was nothing Cecelia could do about it without alerting Jack to her panic. Why hadn't she just told him everything before?

"I'll go get it," Amy said merrily. She jumped up from the table and disappeared down the hall into the guest room, chewing a hunk of bread, crumbs falling behind her.

Cecelia shrugged at Jack. "She has no manners." As if that were the problem.

"I like her," Jack said. "She's the only family of yours I've ever met. She grounds you. Puts you in perspective."

Cecelia looked out at the night sky. She didn't want to be grounded. She wanted to stay right where she was on the thirtieth floor.

Jack shook his head. "You two have more in common than you think."

Cecelia scowled, "I don't think so."

Jack took her hand. "She's your sister."

She's the Antichrist and she's up to something. Cecelia's fingers tingled in Jack's warm, solid hands.

Amy bounded back into the room waving the postcard. "It's the Hindu god Shiva," she said, pointing to the picture on the front of the postcard. It looked a lot like an aging hippy blissed out in the lotus position. His skin was purple and he sat on a jeweled cushion. "Shiva, the god of destruction," Amy read from the back of the postcard.

"Mom's a kidder," Cecelia said, snapping the card out of Amy's hands before Jack could see it clearly. She flipped the card to the writing. The familiar script made her woozy with longing. She hadn't seen her mother in twenty years. "Mom never sends me postcards," Cecelia said before she could stop herself.

"She only sends them to me in emergencies," Amy said. "Hardly ever."

Cecelia felt Amy's "hardly ever" like a dagger in her side. Hardly ever was so much better than never. Never was, well, never.

"Anyway, after the way you responded to the last postcard she sent you, you can hardly blame her," Amy said.

"That was fourteen years ago," Cecelia protested.

"But who's counting?"

"She wanted money. There was no way I was going to send her money after she left us."

"She didn't *just* want money. And you didn't have to be so mean."

"I did. Someone had to take care of us. You were too young and Daddy was hopeless. You'd have given her our last penny." Cecelia stopped, alarmed that she had fallen into her life story. She glanced at Jack. His eyes were wide with shock. She watched in horror as his face recomposed itself into its lawyer's mask.

"Of course I would have. If she needed it," Amy retorted, clearly enjoying herself.

The two sisters glared at each other.

"You could give away a few pennies now," Amy challenged.

Cecelia blanched. "I am not rich, Amy. I have school loans—"

"What did you do with all the money we made—?"

"Stop!" Cecelia cried. She had to hold herself back from vaulting over the table and fastening her hand firmly over Amy's mouth the way she used to when they were kids. Jack did not have to know about the cons they used to pull to get by. Especially about the last con, the big score, the one that changed everything. The one that made Jasmine run away. *Don't worry about me. I don't want my cut. I'm going somewhere quiet for a while*, her note had said. Cecelia could still see the man they had conned, his kindly blue eyes warm with trust, hands that couldn't hurt a fly. After all, Cecelia was posing as his One True Love, and he had bought it hook, line, and sinker. Cecelia had taken the money and gone right to work. The premed courses were a breeze. She blew through the MCAT. Her whole life, she had known that she had the aptitude to do it, and now she had the cash and the time. When she had gotten into Johns Hopkins, there was no looking back. She was launched. Her big break. As if it were all meant to be.

Jack was completely still, as if trying not to break a spell.

"We made a lot of money those last few years," Amy told Jack merrily. "After we ditched Dad and Jane. After we figured out the perfect—"

Cecelia pushed her chair back. "No more!" She leaned forward over the table, looming over Amy. "Not another word or you're out! And this time, never coming back." Cecelia knew she was blowing it. Jack with his photographic memory was taking in every word as surely as if there were a tiny court stenographer tippity-tapping away in his head. Amy was out of control. She was about to tell Jack everything. And Jack didn't have to hear *everything*. It was the past. Gone. Over.

Cecelia sat back down and carefully folded her napkin on her lap. She could handle Amy. "What we had wasn't that much, Amy. It seemed like a lot because we were kids and we were so used to being poor. But medical school was a fortune. I still had to take out mammoth loans—"

"You could have fooled me." Amy expanded her arms to take in the palatial apartment.

"We don't own this place, Amy. I told you that before."

"We don't own it *yet*." It was the first word Jack had spoken since the fight had broken out, and both of them startled at his voice. "This place belongs to an investment banker who's off in Hong Kong. He's willing to sell, but first we have to get married."

"You have to be married to live here?" Amy shook her head in disgust. "What is this, Communist China?"

Cecelia was relieved for the change in subject. "No.

But we have to meet the income guidelines of the co-op. If we're not married, our individual incomes would each have to meet the guidelines. Which is a bit of a stretch."

Amy's eyebrows reached for the ceiling. "So that's why you two are—"

"No," Cecelia cut her off. "Stop. Before you say something you deeply regret."

Amy nodded. Her smile said, *No problem, my work here is done.*

Cecelia continued to stew. She was not marrying Jack for his money or for stability or for this apartment. It was just a side effect of their love.

She imagined Finn sitting next to Jack, ignoring the good wine and throwing back a beer while he shook his head sadly at her.

"So," Jack said brightly, trying to break the mood. "Shiva, huh? He doesn't look destructive. Actually, he looks high." Jack had picked up the postcard.

Cecelia watched horrified as Jack studied the card. She had forgotten all about it. She had to calm down. She was slipping, making mistakes. Cecelia's fingers were beyond tingling, they were on fire. She wrung them together, ignoring Amy's satisfied grin. She had let Amy manipulate her. She had played right into her hand. "Getting high *is* destructive," Cecelia said, snatching the postcard from him. He straightened in astonishment at her uncharacteristic grabbing.

"Since when?" Amy protested. "I remember—"

"We're not going down that road." Cecelia cut in.

"Oh, do tell!" Jack leaned forward. "Cecelia is probably the straightest person I know."

"Hah!" Amy snorted, obviously warming to the delightful new path the conversation had taken. "I could tell you stories." She picked an onion off of Jack's plate and ate it.

"Not if you want to stay in this apartment, you can't," Cecelia warned.

Amy leaned toward Jack and fake-whispered, "I'll meet you later on the balcony. Bring the wine."

"I can't wait."

Cecelia ignored them and tried to focus on her mother's words. The familiar handwriting brought tears to her eyes. She fought them back and read: *Dear Amy, Please find your sister. I am worried about her. I think she needs your help.* Cecelia felt her cheeks go hot. "I'm the emergency?"

Amy shrugged. "You know how she is."

Their mother was prone to feelings and hunches that someone needed help. But this time, her mother was wrong, she didn't need help. *Please, honey, remember that an act of destruction is an act of creation. Without destruction, there can be no creation. Say "hi" to your father and Jane for me if you see them. Love, Mom.*

Great. It was official. Amy had come to destroy her.

"So, is a Sufi a kind of Hindu?" Jack asked. He had his lawyer face on, totally blank.

"Nah. Mom just likes the art," Amy said.

"What's the emergency?" Jack asked.

"She needed money," Cecelia said.

Amy rolled her eyes. "Mom is a bit of a psychic—"

"She's kidding! Mom's a free spirit; she's half gypsy. So how is the Comso case coming, honey?" Cecelia tried desperately to steer the conversation back to solid ground.

"So that makes you a quarter gypsy at least," Jack marveled. "A gypsy named Cecelia."

"Her middle name is Desdemona," Amy said.

Jack's eyes widened.

"She's kidding!" Cecelia cried. "Anyone ready for dessert?"

"Dad was Irish," Amy explained. "And a true romantic. He would do anything for love. Mom was a wanderer too. And Jasmine—"

Cecelia let the dishes she was carrying smash to the table with an alarming crash. They were startled into silence.

Finally, Jack spoke. "Who's Jasmine?"

Cecelia glared at Amy. "Jasmine was an innocent soul until Shiva got her." She picked up the postcard, and tore it in two. "Which is why I no longer have anything to do with our mother."

Amy snatched the pieces out of Cecelia's hand. "Or me."

"Or you," Cecelia said, aware of her viciousness, but unable to stop. She grabbed the torn card back and ripped it to pieces. She tossed the pieces on the floor.

"Hey!"

"That's what I think of Shiva. And Mom." She tried to deliver a stare to Amy that let her know that she was on the list of people she would have nothing to do with. "Now, who's ready for dessert? I made an apple pie."

Cecelia left the ward just past noon. The day was clear and warm, and she decided she'd walk for her lunch hour. She needed time to think. Amy had really gone overboard the night before. If Jack hadn't run off to his Thursday night drinks and cigars with the partners after dinner, she would have told him everything.

As it was, he didn't get back until after two in the morning. Cecelia pretended to be asleep, although sleeping with everything Amy had said floating in her head was beyond impossible. She had to get Amy out of her apartment and into Molly's old row house as soon as possible. But the place was a mess. Totally uninhabitable. Amy couldn't live there for weeks.

The elevator door opened onto the bustling lobby. There was nowhere worse than a hospital lobby. The combination of the brisk-walking staff and the shuffling, hesitant patients and their families was unbearable. It was as if two films were running on top of each other, one at hyperspeed and in color, the other black-and-white and slow-motion. She had the sensation that the staff could walk right through the patients as if they were ghosts.

"Dr. Burns?"

Cecelia looked down to see a small, chubby girl of around eight or nine. The girl swung her leg around on the fulcrum of her big toe. The girl looked familiar somehow. Had she treated her mother, her father? Cecelia tried desperately to place her.

"I'm Finn's kid," the girl said.

Cecelia's eyes went wide. Of course, she looked just like him, in a blonde, beefy way. But around the mouth, they looked exactly the same. Lord, this girl had a beautiful mouth. "Call me Cecelia."

"You're my daddy's Truest Lover."

"Don't call me that." Cecelia walked out of the awful lobby into the warm afternoon air. The girl fell into step beside her. Cecelia felt an urge to take the girl shopping, buy her something pink and flowery to replace the tomboy jeans and T-shirt that she obviously preferred.

At least straighten her ponytail.

"You hurt my daddy's feelings. You owe him an apology," the girl said in a pretty decent imitation of an annoyed grown-up.

Cecelia stopped. She looked at the girl closely. "Shouldn't you be in day camp making lanyards and playing capture the flag?"

"A doctor just like you killed my mommy, so it's not going to be so easy for him to love you unless you apologize."

Cecelia felt her mouth drop open. She wasn't sure what part of that sentence to address first. She began walking again briskly down the sidewalk, the girl keeping pace at her side. Was she supposed to apologize for killing Finn's wife? "Did your daddy send you here?"

"No. He'd be mad if he knew."

"Is that because it's wrong to be here behind your dad's back?"

The girl harrumphed, as if dealing with idiotic adults took every ounce of her patience. "No. It's because he's your perfect boyfriend and he's too dumb to know it."

They passed a small park, where normal children ran after balls. Cecelia looked at Maya. "He is not my boyfriend," she said carefully. "In fact, I don't think he even likes me."

"Well of course he doesn't like you. No one likes you. But I'm gonna help you with that."

Cecelia opened her mouth, but nothing came out.

"We're gonna start with your clothes."

"Funny, I was thinking the exact same thing about you."

Maya looked at her clothes and shrugged. "You're too fancy for him. And too—pinchy."

"Pinchy?"

"Yeah. You know. Mean-looking."

Cecelia blinked again. "I can't be that mean-looking. You're not afraid of me."

"I'm not afraid of anyone. But if you want to get my daddy—"

"I do not want to get your daddy." Geez, hadn't she already had this conversation with Finn? They passed an empty storefront and Cecelia stopped to look at her reflection. She did not look mean. She looked—professional. The little girl standing at her side reflected in the mirror too. They were ridiculously incongruous, like two strangers in an elevator, on their way to two very different floors.

"So. First, we get you out of your witchy clothes."

"Black happens to be very chic, young lady."

"Whatever. It's scary. Then, we let down your hair so you don't look like a skull-head. And you have to lose that vampire-lady makeup."

"Now stop right there!"

The girl stopped. She bit her lip. "Sorry. But if you're daddy's True Lover, you have to learn to get him to love you and he needs to love you because I want him to be happy. So you have to go home and put on pretty clothes and wash your face, and then you can apologize to him for being so mean. Then, since he's your True Lover, you can play cards."

Cecelia was speechless.

"So you can get laid!" the girl explained as if to a two year old.

Cecelia bit her lip in consternation.

The girl took a crumpled piece of paper out of her pocket. She thrust it into Cecelia's hand. It read: "Fisher man's Warf, sushy restorant, 20 minets. Meet my Daddy. No whichy clothes."

Cecelia was aghast. The nerve of this child. As if Cecelia were going to go to a smelly fish market to apologize to a jerk who couldn't stand her. Apologize for what?

She looked up from the paper to see the girl heading downtown. "Where are you going?"

"To Granny Trudy's."

The bar from the ball team. She thought back to the address she and Amy had found in the phone book what seemed like ages ago. The girl was going the wrong way. "How did you get here?"

"Bus. But I don't have enough change to ride it back. I lost my allowance to Granny T. at cards and I just had enough in tips to get here." The girl began walking the wrong way again.

Cards? Tips? The girl looked so tiny, weaving through the grown-ups, her head proudly lifted.

Cecelia looked at her watch. She caught up with her. "C'mon." Cecelia hailed a passing cab. She couldn't let this child get lost in the city. Baltimore was a town of hundreds of tiny neighborhoods with invisible borders. Go one block the wrong way, and you were suddenly somewhere very different than where you had been before. "We're going to take you to your daddy."

Chapter 13

Here's fine," she told the cabdriver. She gave him a ten, and they emerged into the fish-laden air. Homeless men on cardboard boxes held out their hands to her. She ignored them, and herded Maya ahead of her into the block-long open market through the rough-wood swinging door. Vendors of every kind shouted out prices and haggled with shrunken old ladies over shrimp counts. Asian grocers bagged apples and bok choy while mothers juggled babies on their hips, their strollers overflowing with the makings of dinner.

Maya—the girl was named "Maya" Cecelia had learned on the way down—suddenly cut right, then left. She shouted out, "Daddy's at the sushi stand!" And was gone.

"Maya!" Cecelia almost slipped on the shiny wet cement floor trying to catch up with her. She definitely wasn't dressed for this place, with her two-inch heels and power-doctor Armani black pants suit.

Where had Maya gone? Dumb kid. She had no idea how dangerous a city could be.

Cecelia searched up and down the stands, giving wide

berth to the angry-looking piles of crabs. She collided with a man mopping down the floor with filthy water. He gave her an appreciative whistle, which she studiously ignored. Okay, if she couldn't find the kid, at least she could find the sushi stand. Who in their right mind would eat raw fish in a place like this?

There was Finn on a bar stool, chatting with the sushi chef. She stopped, mesmerized by the side of his face. A curious roiling began in her stomach. She hadn't felt like this since she had hid behind the bleachers in seventh grade to spy on Danny Michaels at football practice. She ducked behind a mound of clams and watched him. This was ridiculous. He was such a beautiful man. *Lust isn't love*, she reminded herself. *Just because I want to take him home means nothing*—anyway they needed to find Maya.

The sushi man handed Finn a plate of sliced sushi roll. Finn took it, bowed his head to the chef, and popped a piece into his mouth.

She marched up to him and tapped him on the shoulder at the exact instant she spotted Maya, ducking behind a display of packaged chowder crackers.

Finn turned, saw Cecelia, and leaped off the stool. His eyes were wide and blazing. He waved his hands in front of his face, forcing her away.

"Don't get all crazy. I came for a reason." She was shocked by his visceral reaction to the sight of her. Had she been that awful?

Finn shook his head and continued to gesture.

What was wrong with him? Was he too upset to even speak to her?

The sushi chef handed Finn an opened beer. Finn

grabbed it gratefully, bowed his head quickly to the chef, and guzzled almost the entire thing. He gasped for breath. "Macho man," he croaked, pointing at his chest.

Cecelia just stared. Was he serious? Sure, his shoulders were amazing and his tanned, muscled arms were nothing to scoff at, but really. She glanced back to where Maya had been, but the girl was gone.

"Wasabi. Too much wasabi," he explained weakly, his eyes tearing up. He finished the beer. "It's a sushi roll Kaiya makes. It's called Macho Man. You gotta try it. Whew, that was a rush."

Cecelia tried to fight off the rush she felt watching him. She was here on business. "I brought Maya."

Finn looked around, confused. "Maya?"

"Your daughter? Only she ran away from me when we got in here. I just saw her spying, so don't worry, she's okay. I'm sure she'll turn up in a minute or two."

"Why—? What—? How—?" He looked around suspiciously. "Never mind. I don't think I want to know. Maya was supposed to be with her grandmother. I'll have to talk to that lady." He turned his back to the market. "If we pretend that we don't care where she is, she'll come over."

Now what? Cecelia couldn't exactly leave until the girl showed her face again. She sat on the stool next to Finn, trying not to look around for the girl.

"Nice day," he said.

"Yeah. Unseasonably warm."

"Yeah. Warm. But I hear it's gonna rain soon."

Silence.

Cecelia rolled her eyes. This was unbearable. Not doing anything made Cecelia restless. "Maya told me about your wife," she blurted.

Finn's eyes widened.

"Well, not everything, but she told me the basics. I hadn't realized. I'm very sorry. I wouldn't have spoken so bluntly if I had known you had a—history."

Finn shrugged and went back to his sushi.

Cecelia felt adrift. If there was one thing they didn't teach at medical school, it was how to say, "I'm sorry." She breathed in. "The picnic, it was a really nice thing to do. It was kind."

He picked up a piece of sushi with his chopsticks. The sushi was huge and messy and looked just exactly the way sushi belonging to a tattooed construction worker should look. He offered her the piece, but she refused. He popped it into his mouth. "You don't eat much do you?"

"I do. I just run every morning, seven on the dot. Three point two miles. It keeps the weight off."

He nodded, but didn't say anything. She watched him eat the fish, but this time he just grimaced and swallowed.

She took a deep breath. Where was that kid? How long did she have to sit here? She couldn't stand the silence. "I knew that someone had been sick," she blurted. "I realized that when I was talking to you. But I just—"

"You just rambled on like a bureaucratic, no-soul robotron." He looked her square in the eyes.

She blushed. Maybe they could go back to silence. Or discussing the weather.

They sat wordlessly while the market bustled around them. He popped another sushi and swallowed it with no problem. The sushi man nodded his approval from his side of the counter.

She risked a glance around for Maya. "Maybe she left."

"She's here. We have to wait."

Right. Wait. She watched the sushi man, Kaiya, put together an avocado and tuna roll. She wasn't used to waiting. She was used to action. She watched how peacefully Finn sat, as if his daughter hadn't gone AWOL in a public place. As if he didn't have a care in the world.

She decided to try it. She tried to clear her head. Relax her body. Just breathe in the fishy stench. Suddenly she was struck with a memory so vivid, she almost fell off her stool.

"You okay?" Finn asked. "You look like you saw a ghost."

"I was just remembering that I used to come here with my sister," Cecelia said.

"The psychic?"

"Yeah. We lived in Baltimore when we were kids. Came back for a few years when we were teenagers. We used to steal apples from that guy. I can't believe he's still alive. See the short fat man at the vegetable stand over there?"

"The sweating, dirty guy?"

"Yeah. He was an awful man. Terrible racist. Oh, hell, I haven't thought about him in years."

Finn was looking at her as if she had grown horns. "You want me to believe that *you* used to steal apples?"

"We used to steal everything that wasn't super-glued and alarm-tagged. We didn't have much, ah, guidance. But we only stole from bad people." She couldn't believe the words she was saying—as if stealing were ever okay. She sounded like Amy.

"But now look at you. You couldn't steal an apple from Hitler."

"I could so."

He smiled a devilish smile that nearly knocked her off her stool again. "You couldn't. You'd be too afraid of your social standing. How would it look, after all, to the folks at the country club?"

"I don't belong to the country club," she said. Okay, so Jack did. But that wasn't the point.

"Then steal an apple."

"No. Back then we had to. Now, it would just be wrong. And what if your daughter is watching?"

"She'd like you better for it. Come to think of it, I probably would too." He shrugged. "Anyway, you can't do it."

"I could. But I'm not."

"Right."

Silence descended on them again. It felt okay this time. Like they had come to some sort of understanding, although Cecelia wasn't sure what it was. She watched the vegetable man arrange grapefruits. It *was* the same guy. She and Amy used to slip away from him down these crowded aisles, just the way Maya had slipped away from her. They could snatch a whole dinner in minutes. Tiny, darting hands. They would take it home and arrange it the best they could on plates. Then they'd pretend their mother was calling them. *Cecelia! Amy! Dinner! Wash your hands!* It was no good not having a mother. Just too hard. A wave of compassion for Maya washed over her. "Tell me what happened to Maya's mother."

"She needed an aortic valve. But she couldn't withstand the operation—too weak. Some experimental guys had a new procedure for a nonoperative valve insertion."

"The team in Atlanta."

"Right. She qualified for the trial, but our place in the study kept getting taken by, well—"

"By people with connections."

"Right." His face hardened. "Anyway, finally, we got in, but before we could get there, well, it was too late." He looked as if he had swallowed another dose of wasabi.

"I'm sorry."

"Well, I should apologize too," he said. "It's just that doctors set me off sometimes." His eyes were unfocused, as if he were seeing into the past. "Anyway, we're even. I didn't know about the fiancé thing. And you didn't know about Sally."

"Not quite even."

"Right," he said. "I apologize for Maya too. I'll talk to her. I don't know how she found you. I never should have told her that True Love stuff."

Cecelia smiled. "Yeah, well, it is a nice fairy tale for a kid. Except I'm pretty sure she thinks I'm the wicked witch."

"Uh-oh."

"She said I was scary-looking."

"You are a little—formidable."

Cecelia felt the color rise on her cheeks.

He ate the last sushi and he handed the empty tray back to the chef. "Well, let's go."

"What about Maya?"

He leaned in and whispered, "Behind the broccoli." He left a twenty on the counter. They made their way over to the vegetables as if nothing were amiss.

"You're not so bad, Doctor," Finn said loudly. "Even if you're not my True Love but a wicked witch in disguise."

"She's not a witch, Daddy, she just looks like one," Maya cried, emerging from behind the oranges.

"Oh! Look who's here!" Finn put his hand firmly on Maya's shoulder, trapping her in his grip.

The vegetable seller came over and said to Cecelia, "You should watch your daughter! Sneaking around here like a thief. I would've called the police if she wasn't so—so—"

"White?" Cecelia supplied. Her fingers itched. The apples were gorgeous—shiny and huge.

The man scowled at her. "This is a dangerous place, missy. There's all kinds of bad sorts here. I gotta look out for myself. I don't have time to worry about watching out for kids with lousy mothers."

Maya beamed up at Cecelia like an angel.

Finn squeezed her shoulder harder.

Cecelia took one last look at the fruit. She shook her hands, rubbed them together, then quickly followed Finn and Maya toward the exit.

They snaked their way out of the market, then stood awkwardly on the sidewalk.

"Thank you for bringing her," Finn said.

"No problem," Cecelia said.

"You should thank me for bringing *her*," Maya complained.

Finn tightened his hold on Maya's shoulder. He steered the girl away.

"Bye, Cecelia!" Maya called. "See you soon!"

"Bye, Maya," Cecelia returned. But she wouldn't see her soon. In fact, she'd probably never see the girl, or her father, again. She turned back for one last look, and froze, stunned at what she saw: the homeless man had a lap full of beautiful apples and he was waving happily at Maya, who winked back at him, before taking Finn's hand and skipping merrily away.

The next morning, Cecelia pulled on her running shoes, went into the kitchen, and found her mother's postcard taped together and stuck on the refrigerator with a smiley-face magnet. She pulled it off and reread it. Just when everything was going so right, why did her family have to bust in and try to ruin it?

Jack came into the kitchen dressed for weekend work, khakis and a light blue shirt. He went to the fridge and got out the juice. "Your mother's worried. I've got to tell you the truth, I'm a little worried too. Why didn't you tell me about any of this, Cel?"

"About any of what? That my family is nuts?" She reread the postcard. *I have a feeling your sister needs help*. What if her mother didn't mean her? What if her mother meant Jasmine?

"Your family, they're not Sufis, are they? Why did you make up a story? I would have understood the truth."

Cecelia stood dumbly with the card in her hands.

Jack shook his head and guzzled the juice, glanced at his watch, then came to her and wrapped her in his arms. He rested his chin on her head.

She buried her head on his chest. "Amy is leaving soon. It doesn't matter. None of it matters." The vision of Jasmine's face formed in her mind so clearly, she closed her eyes, hoping to hold on to the vision for a moment, as if somehow it might contain a clue as to where Jasmine was.

"It matters to me," Jack said. "Your family is a part

of you, whether you like it or not. You can't pretend
they're off in a commune. That scares me. You need to
tell me things. We never see each other. There's never
time to talk."

"I know. But tonight, you're coming with me to the
Baltimore Physicians Gala. Right? We can talk there. I'll
tell you everything. I promise."

Jack winced. "I can't go. The Barker case—I've got to
work all weekend. I forgot all about the dinner. Darn it.
I'm sorry." He let her go.

Cecelia looked at her watch. Why did a Saturday seem
like any other day to them? "I've got to get my three miles
in before eight, then go in and catch up on paperwork."

"You could take Amy tonight."

Cecelia imagined Amy breaking up her colleagues'
marriages, cracking sulfur capsules in the gilded Rain-
bow Room of the Hyatt Hotel, slipping silverware into
her purse. "I don't think so. I'll just go alone. It's okay.
Elliot bought a table. I'll have friends to sit with."

"Sorry, sweetums. But we will talk soon. Work this
all out."

"Right. Soon."

He kissed her gently. "Soon."

And, as usual, she watched him go.

Cecelia emerged into the brisk morning air. She loved
this time of the morning. Everything seemed possible.
Everything, of course, except speaking to her fiancé. This
was getting bad. The conversation she had with Finn the
day before seemed deeper and more real than all the con-
versations she'd had with Jack in the last year. Had they
had a real conversation in the last year?

"You're late." It was Finn, running up beside her. He was wearing gray sweats, gray sneakers, and a wool cap pulled down over his ears despite the warm summer morning. He looked like a hoodlum. He fell easily into her stride.

The shock of seeing him nearly threw Cecelia into the gutter. How did he find her? Then she remembered, at the market, she had told him she ran every morning at 7:00 A.M. "How did you know where I lived?"

"Phone book." Finn smiled a perfect smile.

"Don't even think you can keep up with me," Cecelia said, quickening her pace. Guilt jolted through her with every footfall. What would Jack think?

"Oh, I don't know, I've been known to hold my own on the streets." He matched her pace easily, punching at the air like Rocky Balboa.

"Now I know how you're going to die. A heart attack on the third mile trying to keep up with me," she teased. She tried not to notice the jolly little elf who seemed to be doing a jig in her stomach. *I am not happy to see Finn.*

"Is that all? Three miles?" Finn threw another one-two punch into the air. "Good thing I've already done two to warm up."

She ran faster, but he matched her pace. They ran side by side for a while before she found breath enough to ask, "What are you doing here?"

"Hitting on you."

She missed a step and almost tripped.

"Whoa," he said, catching her. "Careful there, Doctor. I was just kidding. I thought we established that the romance was off. Something about a ring. But I could use a running partner. And when you said you went running in the morning, well, so do I."

She kept her eyes straight ahead. A running partner beside her, in pace with her, felt like a gift. Was she that lonely?

No. She shouldn't be with him. Yesterday, it was for the welfare of a child. But this? This was for that damn dancing elf.

A person wasn't supposed to feel giddy around another person by their mere presence. A person wasn't supposed to notice that other person's legs—

They reached the park and turned down a tree-lined path. She quickened the pace again. *Maybe if I lose him, I can go back to my normal life. Maybe I can outrun them all. Maybe it's all a test.*

"I hate to pry, but you looked upset when you came out to play this morning," he said. His voice was easy, as if he weren't running at all.

She increased the pace. "We shouldn't be doing this."

"Running? Oh, no. All the experts say exercise is good for you—"

"You know what I mean." She tried not to smile. *I am a serious doctor. The elf is an invader.*

"I don't. Talk to me." His voice was low and serious.

They were sprinting now.

He shook his head. "You can't run away from life, Doctor."

Did this man understand everything about her? Well, one thing he didn't know: she was a champion runaway artist. The best. She pushed her body forward with all her strength, but he followed easily. Their feet hit the ground in tandem. A hill loomed ahead and she cursed, but pushed on, even faster. Her legs felt like they were going to collapse. Pain zipped up her side. There, that was more like it. More like what she deserved.

She deserved the pain for flirting with a hunky stranger just moments after being in her fiancé's arms.

She ran faster. He kept up easily, his breath even beside her.

She deserved the pain for having spent years scamming innocent people who only wanted True Love. Who was she to enjoy True Love when she had denied it to so many?

She upped the pace again, her lungs straining.

He pulled a little ahead of her. "Cecelia. Stop."

She deserved the pain for wanting more than a poor gypsy wanderer could have: medical school, a career, a future. And now, to add to all that, she wanted this man. Wanted him desperately, here, now. Well, you couldn't have everything. That wasn't the way life worked. You chose and she had chosen and this man did not fit.

He was a full stride ahead of her now. "Slow down."

They reached the top of the hill and began the long descent to the fields and playground that lay below. The slope steepened. A jagged hole in the pavement loomed. She noticed it just as he reached out and touched her shoulder. The shock of his firm hand on her heaving shoulder threw her into confusion. *Why does his touch feel so right if he's everything I fought against—?*

Suddenly her foot caught. Her body flew forward and she put out her hands to catch her plunging body. A sharp pain radiated up her arm, and she cried out. She collapsed on the cold sidewalk, aware of the piercing heat radiating from her hand.

A shard of glass stuck out of her palm like the sail of a tiny sinking ship.

Chapter 14

Finn was at her side in an instant. "We gotta get that out." He took her hand.

"It's superficial," she said. She wasn't sure if she meant the wound or her feelings for this incredibly beautiful man. "I need—" she began. *I need you to tell me that it's okay. To tell me that I'm okay.*

Before she could finish her sentence, he steadied her hand and expertly extracted the glass. "Stay put. I'll be right back."

She held her hand gingerly. Good. He was going. Breathing room. Her body was reacting to this man like it was beyond her control.

What was it with her and this guy and parks?

Okay, pull yourself together. Stay in the present. She looked around her. The playground was below them. A solitary father shouldered a cranky baby. A pickup basketball game raged full guns farther off, the men's shouts and the ball slapping the concrete, echoing to where she still sat in the middle of the path. A hot-dog vendor served steaming coffee in paper cups and donuts. His hot dogs spun patiently in their rows, waiting for lunchtime.

Finn jogged over the grass and down the steep slope. He stopped at the hot-dog stand. The man handed Finn a bottled water, some napkins, and two hot dogs. Finn raced back up to Cecelia. He put the hot dogs carefully by her side.

"Ah. The ancient Chinese hot-dog remedy."

"Hell no. I'm not getting our breakfast all bloody. Hold still." He poured water on the cut. When the blood cleared, they saw that it wasn't too bad. Cecelia held a wad of napkins to it and they walked the rest of the way down the hill. They collapsed onto a bench.

Finn offered her a hot dog. "For strength."

"Those things are filthy. Plus, it's not even eight in the morning. They're probably raw."

"Breakfast of champions." He bit into one.

It smelled divine. "Oh, hell. So long as I'm covered with blood and hanging out with a stranger in the park, I might as well."

She accepted the hot dog.

"I don't have to be a stranger, you know."

"I'm engaged."

"So what? I just want a running partner. Although now, I'm not so sure about you as a running partner. Don't pull a stunt like that again."

How long had it been since anyone had made her feel so relaxed? She thought back to the time Jack had tried to teach her golf, a pastime they were planning to share. But she didn't have the patience. And of course, he didn't have the time.

"So, ask me something," he said.

She tentatively nibbled at the end of the hot dog. It tasted better than she remembered. "I don't have to ask, I know exactly who you are." She took a bigger bite. She could eat five of these things.

"If you know so much, then go ahead. Tell me who I am." He leaned back and stretched out his legs, his food already gone.

Cecelia tried not to notice his calves. She loved runner's calves, long and lean. "You've got no address, no phone, so you're a drifter."

"We're here to visit Maya's grandmother."

She hesitated, momentarily silenced. "So, you're barging into my life for a few days and then you're disappearing back to wherever you came from."

"Wrong again. One of the regulars at Trudy's offered me some carpentry work. Trudy set it up. I start on Monday. We might even be here for the whole summer."

"Your sneakers are circa 2002, so you're broke." She finished the hot dog and longed for more.

"I love these sneakers. I wouldn't replace them if I was a millionaire."

"I knew that too."

He smiled. "You want another hot dog?"

"You're disgusting."

"And you're hungry."

"All right, but I'm buying." She fished into her sock and pulled out a sweaty five-dollar bill.

He made a face. "I can't eat after touching that." He trotted off to the hot-dog man. This time, he came back with four. "Pre-breakfast special today."

"That's gross."

He handed her two. "You can do it." He ate half of his in one bite.

She bit into hers. It was better than the first. She swallowed, then said, "I bet you ride a motorcycle. A Harley."

"Kawasaki. Until I sold it to pay off some of Sally's medical bills. We had some pretty lean times after she died. But we're back on our feet now."

Without thinking, she handed him her last dog. He ate it in three bites.

They sat in silence. The combination of the sun and her full stomach made her sleepy. She closed her eyes.

"Now I'll tell you all the stuff you forgot to ask."

She opened one eye.

"My wife died two years ago and I miss her like hell. Every minute of every day, I feel her gone, right here." He put his open palm over his chest. "Maya feels the same. Whatever goes on in the world, it doesn't matter compared to that hole that's left. That's the most important thing about my life. And the second most important thing is protecting Maya. I'd do anything for that kid. Anything. She lost her mom—and you of all people should know how awful that is. So you can ask me about my crummy shoes and my ordinary job, but that really says more about you, Doctor, than it does about me."

Cecelia sat up. She felt strangely grateful for his stinging criticism.

He shrugged. "Sorry. But you were starting to piss me off."

"Well, I certainly won't risk pissing you off again," she said. She tried to keep her voice light to hide the tender spot his words had hit. Was Maya right? Did no one like her?

"Now I'll tell you about you," he said.

"I think you already have."

"You work all the time."

"I'm a doctor. That's what we do."

"Yeah, but you work because you have no friends. You don't let people in. That's why you're marrying a guy who barely knows you."

"You've never met Jack. You don't know anything about him."

"Neither do you."

Cecelia sat up. "Tell me again why you're here."

"If I don't make friends with you, my daughter isn't going to speak to me again. She thinks that because of all this True Love crap, you're going to be her mother."

Cecelia lay back and closed her eyes again. "Well, that was honest."

"Plus, you're just weird enough to keep me interested."

She smiled. Something about being called weird by him felt good. It was better, at least, than what he had said before.

He gave her a funny look. "Want to hear something truly weird?"

She sat forward. Something about his face had changed, as if he'd aged in the last few moments. She felt the urge to touch the worry lines that had emerged on his forehead.

"It was back in Florida with Maya. I'm nailing new boards onto our porch, thinking about how hard it is to work and take care of her. About how my house is driving me nuts, because Sally died there. I see her everywhere."

"See her? Your wife?"

"Not weirdo psychic seeing. I mean I think about her all the time. Her stuff's all over the house. I'm thinking, we've got to get out of there. Then, Maya tells me about this pen pal granny she hooked up with who wants us to come to Baltimore. We go around about it for a while. I have no idea what to do. So I say to myself, 'Sally, if we should go, give me a sign.' " He stopped to see how she was taking all this.

She tried to encourage him with her eyes. "I don't think that's weird."

"No. You wouldn't. So anyway, bam, the phone rings. It's my boss. The next project's canceled—a city job that was going to keep us going all summer. He's laying off the whole crew. It's gonna be hard for me to get work with a new crew, because I had this sweet deal with my boss where I could get Maya off to school or camp or whatever, and then show at the site. But no one else is gonna be that soft. So there's Maya with her big blue eyes and a map with this crazy line she drew to Baltimore. What can I do? I call this granny in a daze. I mean, I'm on autopilot. I hardly know what I'm saying. But this lady offers me a carpentry job with one of her regulars, and tells me she'll take care of Maya. She offers us a place to stay, and tells us she'll feed us." He got a far-away look in his eyes. He said softly, "It was like a sign."

"Maybe it was."

He shook his head at what he obviously considered his craziness. "A sign that I'm losing it."

Cecelia said quietly, "It's not nuts. Your wife could be looking out for you. And Maya."

He seemed to consider this. Then he snapped back into the present. He jumped up, and looked around nervously. "Hey, you wanna race?"

Cecelia looked at him doubtfully. "Race?" The hot

dogs formed a lump in her stomach. "To see who can throw up first?"

"Exactly," he said.

"No thanks. I think I'll just sit here until a crane comes to take me away."

"Suit yourself. But I have to get going. Me and Maya are taking the train to D.C. today. Get her a little historical perspective on this great country." He started a slow jog away from her. Then he stopped. "Hey, Doctor. I had fun this morning."

"Was it the bloody hand or the toxic hot dogs?"

"The conversation and the spandex." He let his eyes roam quickly over her.

"In that order?" She felt the blush rise and hoped her face was already red from the exercise.

"Yeah. In that order. Especially if you keep scarfing down those disgusting hot dogs."

She watched him jog away. Suddenly she felt so alone, she couldn't bear it. *She liked to talk to him.* He was almost at the edge of the park when she sprung after him. "Finn—wait!"

He stopped.

She approached him warily. A voice in her head told her to let him go, but she didn't listen. "What time are you getting back from D.C.?" she asked.

"Dinnerish. Why?"

"You wanna go somewhere with me tonight? As friends?"

He looked her in the eyes long and hard, as if looking elsewhere might be dangerous. "You think that's a good idea?"

It was a terrible idea. The worst idea she'd had in ages.

What was she doing? "I'm sure. It's a big, boring doctor's fund-raiser. It'll be—"

"Awful?" He moved a step toward her.

"Yeah," she managed to get out. She felt like touching him. Just a lock of hair.

"Maya will be delighted. But your fiancé—"

"He has to work," she said quickly. "Plus, we'd be going as friends." The air had become charged between them. If she moved, the entire park might ignite.

"Running buddies."

"Right. Nothing more." Their eyes locked. "Every tourist should see the incredible view from the Hyatt."

"Right. The view," he said. "Pick you up at—?"

"Seven-thirty. Meet me at the Hyatt on the waterfront. Oh, hell. You need a tux."

"Don't worry. I'll manage. That's why they have rental shops—for bums like me. See you tonight. Buddy." Then he turned away again and disappeared over the hill before she could change her mind.

What on earth had she just done?

Chapter 15

What had been in those hot dogs to make her think this was a good idea? Cecelia walked into the ballroom with Finn in a very nicely fitting tux at her side. It would be fine. He was a friend. It was okay to spend some time with a friend at a work-related social event just so long as she didn't notice how that tux fit—

Cecelia gasped.

Finn grinned. "You didn't tell me to wear my head scarf."

Cecelia couldn't speak, her confused feelings for Finn were replaced by pure horror.

The room was decorated like a giant gypsy carnival. Well, a gypsy carnival under six sparkling faux-crystal chandeliers, on top of a purple Stainmaster rug, and populated by five-hundred middle-aged doctors and their spouses. Despite the obvious impossibility, someone had gone to elaborate trouble to transform the top floor of the Hyatt into an exotic den of unbridled gypsy lawlessness.

Whoever had chosen this theme had obviously never met a doctor.

Or a gypsy.

Red and gold batiks hung from golden trellises around the outskirts of the room. Huge mirrors tiled in glittering colored glass were propped strategically to reflect red and purple lights, giving the room a sundown-at-the-Casbah disco glow. Each table was draped in a bloodred cloth with a huge hookah at the center blowing smoke.

"Think they're real?" Cecelia asked hopefully, indicating the opium bongs.

Finn grabbed a purple drink off a passing waiter's tray. "No, but this is." Finn handed her the purple drink. Its stirrer was topped with a tiny crystal ball.

The poor waiter was dressed as a badly imagined snake charmer. Other waiters wore eye patches and swords, as if the differences between gypsy and pirate were too small to make a difference.

She gulped the drink gratefully and glanced at Finn. "You're laughing at me."

"Me? No. I would never do that." He grabbed another drink. This time he broke off the crystal ball and tossed it into the pipe of the nearest hookah. He took an enormous gulp. "I thought maybe the party fund-raiser bit was a lie and you really wanted to introduce me to your gypsy family—ouch!"

Cecelia had stomped soundly on his rental loafers with her two-inch heel. "This is just the kind of stereotypical nonsense that makes me cringe whenever people think about gypsies." She wished she hadn't worn bright red tonight, that her dress didn't have such a swishy skirt, or at least had sleeves. She checked her hair to make sure it was securely plastered to her head. A waitress in an *I Dream of Jeannie* costume passed. "Aunt Betty," Cecelia whispered to Finn with a wink.

She felt his laughter to the tips of her toes. If this were so awful, why did he still make her feel so good? Her fingers began their familiar tingle. She felt certain that she could stop them by taking his hand—

The band, dressed as gypsies, began to play a twangy horah, jolting her back to reality.

She was surrounded by her professional associates, escorted by a man who was not her fiancé, and she had almost taken his hand. She rubbed her hands together to stop their throbbing.

Finn studied her hands with concern. "You cold?"

"No."

"You wanna split before the urologists start belly-dancing?"

"Maybe we should."

Finn turned toward the doors.

Play it safe or take a risk? Cecelia looked around her at the crowd—these were the people she was going to spend the rest of her life with. She looked at Finn and every molecule of her being said, *This is the man.* "Let's stay," Cecelia cried a tad too loud. The people around them turned to look. "I'm having—fun." There went her fingertips again. *Fun.* The sensation floated up her arms. In her head, she heard the echo of her words to Amy at her engagement party just a few short weeks ago: *This party is supposed to be dull. My life is supposed to be dull. I want dull. I love dull.*

And now she didn't. She wanted to see what would happen. It was as if a layer of her skin had been exposed to the air and she didn't want to cover it up again. Not now. Not yet. Just a few hours of fun. Then she'd go back to her regular life.

"Dr. Burns!" Elliot, the senior doctor in her practice, floated to her side with his wife in tow.

That lady looks pinched, Cecelia thought, remembering Maya and her wonderful descriptions. "Elliot! Julia! I'd like you to meet—"

"Finn Concord," Finn interrupted. He reached in and shook both their hands. "I'm visiting Baltimore to do a little construction work and Cecelia agreed to show me the sights. We're old friends."

"Construction?" Julia said dryly. "How fascinating."

Cecelia felt a sudden kinship with Finn; the two of them against all the snooty uptightness that Julia and Elliot represented. She had the sudden urge to pick Julia's purse. It would be so easy. She could see the outline of the tiny wallet in the black silk bag—

Julia asked, "Where's our dear Jack?" She looked Finn up and down like she wanted to eat him.

"He had to work." Cecelia held her hands behind her tightly, as if they were two naughty children. She saw Finn through the eyes of her colleague's wife: he didn't belong here. He was too rough, too textured, too inexcusably gorgeous. "Excuse us please." Cecelia smiled her sweetest, con-woman smile at Elliot and his wife. The smile felt odd on her lips. She hadn't smiled it in years. "I want Finn to see the view of the waterfront before the sun goes down." Cecelia grabbed Finn and pulled him into the crowd.

"I think she liked me," Finn said.

"I think if we stood there one more minute, she was going to eat you," Cecelia said. Why hadn't she anticipated how Finn's raw, rough good looks would fit into this pale, stiff crowd? What had made her think she

could disguise him here as anything less than what he
was—the most virile man she had ever known? She
found a pirate-gypsy waiter and grabbed two more
glasses of the purple concoction.

Finn scowled at the oversweet drink. "I don't suppose
they have a keg going."

"Just gypsy hooch."

They made their way to the windows. The city spread
below them. "Nice view," he said.

Cecelia glanced up at him. He was looking at her, not
the view. She looked away quickly, trying to avoid the
electricity shooting between them. They were friends.
Running buddies.

The band stopped and the leader announced dinner.

"You ready for the show?" Cecelia asked, not at all
sure that *she* was ready to face her colleagues with Finn
at her side.

"A bunch of overstuffed doctors don't scare me."

"Forget the doctors," Cecelia said, a jolt of something
that felt suspiciously like jealousy running through her.
"It's their wives you should worry about."

The table Elliot had bought for a five-thousand-dollar
donation to the cause (what was the cause of this fund-
raiser anyway? *God, don't let it be gypsy orphans . . .*)
seated ten. Thankfully, Finn and Cecelia had seats across
from Elliot and his wife, putting them as far away as they
could get at the circular table. Finn chatted politely with
the other doctors. Sports made all differences irrelevant
when it came to small talk.

Camille Debirsh, the only other woman doctor in the
practice, sat next to Cecelia. She was a hot-shot cardiol-

ogist, an ecophysiologist known for difficult, obscure diagnoses. Her reputation for being blunt and to the point was legendary. So Cecelia didn't know why she was shocked when Camille leaned over and whispered, "Where did you find him and whatever did you do with Jack?"

Cecelia straightened. If she had claws, they would have emerged from the soft pads of her hands. She whispered back sweetly, "He's just an old friend. Jack had to work."

Camille smiled coldly. "Well, then you don't mind, do you? Can't hog all the eligibles."

Cecelia realized with horror what Camille meant. "No. Oh, no sure. He's, ah, all yours." *Bitch. No—not bitch. Good. I have a fiancé. Finn is just a friend.*

Camille manhandled Cecelia aside with an adept hip check. Before Cecelia fully realized what had happened, Camille had taken her seat and she had her hand on Finn's shoulder. "Finn? I'm Dr. Debirsh. You can call me Camille."

Cecelia had never seen this side of Dr. Debirsh. Finn's green eyes were dancing in his head from Camille's feminine attention. Or maybe, they were spinning from her overbearing perfume. In any case, the man looked like everything anyone could ever want in a man and Camille looked determined to get it.

Finn smiled his million-dollar smile. In an instant, they were engaged in a spirited conversation about baseball. How did Camille know anything about baseball?

Cecelia sank back in her seat and sampled her beet and walnut salad. Elliot's wife stared her down, so she perked up and started a conversation with Joe Ridley, the most boring nurse practitioner in the practice. As they talked, she snuck glances at Finn and Camille. They looked intimate. Their faces too close for friends. But what did she care? She had Jack and she was going to marry him. Anyway, this would be good. Bringing Finn had been a dumb way to start rumors. And she had been feeling peculiarly close to him in a way that would certainly start rumors if she let it show. Now she'd be protected from gossip. And reminded that he was just a friend.

Joe told her about his pet iguana.

Gossip sure would liven up this place. She watched Camille touch Finn's shoulder and a bolt of hot, raging jealousy ripped through her. *Killing Camille sure would liven up this place.*

She nodded at the long list of dietary needs of six-foot iguanas. Lettuce. Corn bread. She wanted to grab Finn and kiss him like he'd never been kissed before. Tomatoes. The occasional carrot. *He is just a friend.*

She could not be jealous of a man that she couldn't have. Better that Camille move in now, save her the agony.

Finn laughed at something Camille said and Cecelia felt a superhuman urge to vault the table, scoop Finn up, and disappear with him.

Something stirred deep inside her. She tried to shake it off, but it was too strong. She smiled sweetly at iguana man. "Corn bread? I had no idea iguanas were vegetarians!" she exclaimed in mock fascination while she shot her right arm out to emphasize her amazement. Her purple drink went flying, right down the front of Camille's dress.

Camille gasped and turned to her, purple liquid dripping down her lap.

"Oh, I am so sorry!" Cecelia dabbed at the clingy drops on Camille's bare arm. She thought that she saw Finn smile. "Let me help you."

Camille ignored Cecelia's offer of help, arched her eyebrows, smiled between narrowed lips, then turned back to Finn. "Oh, dear. Can I borrow your napkin?" she asked, patting herself provocatively. "What a mess! And to think that this fabric goes completely see-through when wet!"

Cecelia stared at Camille's back in horror. The woman wasn't wearing a bra.

Cecelia had to get out of there. She excused herself and raced for the hallway. She was pretending to check her cell when Elliot appeared. He came straight for her and she clicked her phone shut. "Elliot."

"Cecelia." He held up one hand. "I'm going to say this quickly. And if none of it applies, then pretend this conversation never happened."

She started to protest, but he held up both hands and shook his head. "We are a prestigious practice that depends on our doctors upholding our values. Now, Ellen told me about a patient who wasn't referred through the usual channels—"

Ellen was their receptionist. Cecelia thought back to Finn showing up in the office. Nothing got by these guys.

Elliot was still speaking. "—and that was why we chose to ignore a first-time transgression. But now, this man. Cecelia." He shook his head sadly. "Jack is a good person. He knows the right people. I'm sure your friend is a fine man too. But, well, his accent, the way he moves, the cut of his hair, *construction work!* I know that this sounds unfair, but we have standards to uphold—"

"Elliot. Finn is just a friend—"

"Yes. I know. That's why I'm saying that you should forget this conversation if it doesn't apply. I know that you're one of us, Cecelia. I've always known that. I just, well, never mind. I've got to get back in there before Julia lets the waiter take my dinner away." He put his hand on her shoulder and smiled coldly before he walked away.

Cecelia was still seething as she returned to the ballroom. Elliot, ensconced beside his wife, raised a glass to Cecelia across the table. Finn sat beside an empty seat, idly playing with his bowtie, leaning back as if he didn't have a trouble in the world. Camille must have gone to clean herself up. Maybe she'd drown in the bathroom.

The dessert was being cleared and the music began. It wasn't the typical eighties dance tunes these bands usually played to get the crowd going, but real gypsy folk music. She felt as if two worlds were pulling at her. *It is time to choose.*

She sat down. The vast space of the empty seat gaped between Finn and Cecelia.

"The curry chicken was—" Finn began.

"Awful," Cecelia finished. Elliot's not-so-friendly warning rang in her ears. *These people can take one look at Finn and know he doesn't belong. But what about me? Do I belong?*

Finn leaned in. "Fascinating friend you have."

"Liar," Cecelia whispered.

Finn lowered his voice. "Jealous are we?"

"I am not jealous," Cecelia whispered. "I just think she's boring, that's all. Very nice, but uptight."

"Not like you," Finn said.

"Not at all like me!" Cecelia protested. "I'm—I'm a hot dog eater!" she finished, ridiculously proud. Fate hung in the air. It buzzed around her. Her anger at Elliot's speech clouded her judgment. She was no longer in control.

They sat in silence a few beats, the room buzzing around them.

Finn nodded at Jim Perry, a retired pulmonary special-ist across the table who was eyeing them suspiciously. "Wonderful music!" he said loudly to Jim. Then quietly to Cecelia he whispered, "Name me one thing about you that makes you less uptight than Camille."

"You," Cecelia said before she could think. Then she quickly corrected herself, "I have a *friend* like you."

"Oh, I don't know," Finn said as he leaned back to make room for the returning Camille. "Maybe you two have that in common."

Cecelia smiled sweetly at Camille. Finn's teasing made Cecelia aware of how similar she and Camille did look. The way they sat, the way they pulled back their hair, the way they held their shoulders erect. Was it some-thing they both picked up at medical school? *Mannerisms of the Female Doctor 101*? Or had Camille always been regal and possessed, while Cecelia copied her and women like her subconsciously, internalizing their move-ments so jerks like Elliot wouldn't know she wasn't one of them?

She caught a glimpse of herself, reflected in the metal of the hookah at the center of the table. In the distortion of the curved metal, she looked like a stranger, a stranger buried in mannerisms. But she could feel her old self, the one that wanted to throw one arm loosely around Camille's shoulders and whisper, sweetly and with a smile, *Back the hell off, bitch*.

The music came to a slow, arrhythmic stop. Then started up again with the trancelike notes of a Turkish folk song Cecelia recognized. To her horror, six belly dancers appeared on the dance floor, their hips swinging, their snakelike arms carving the air.

The dancers began pulling aging doctors onto the floor as the rhythm quickened. They tried to get the old men's potbellies rolling by circling their waists with their scarves. What idiocy. She could dance better than these women. Not that she would. Although it would show Finn a thing or two about how she was nothing like Camille. Not that she had to prove anything to Finn. Or to hide anything from Elliot.

Finn's head was bent toward Camille's and they were deep in discussion.

Cecelia tried not to huff. Her fingers were tingling. She noticed Camille's purse slung over the back of the chair. She shouldn't. The dancers prowled the tables, pulling unsuspecting diners to the dance floor. Human sacrifice, unless you counted the orthopedists, whom Cecelia considered semihuman based on their despicable bedside manner. She rubbed her hands together furtively. She was not like these doctors. She was from another world. If they knew—if Finn knew . . .

A dancer passed her table, drawing all eyes to her bared, concave stomach. Cecelia's hand darted into

Camille's bag, then back out, satisfyingly competent after all these years. She glanced at her booty.

It was a condom. Ribbed. Extra-large.

Why had she done that? She palmed the condom in horror. Okay, so now she had proven to herself that she could still go back to her old world. She was more than just a doctor, she was a gypsy. She looked down at the condom. She could be both and stay hidden. Live in both worlds.

If she quit pick-pocketing her colleagues.

Something fluttered over her bare shoulder. It was a scarf. One of the dancers leaned over her and pulled her to her feet. Cecelia resisted.

The woman continued to pull.

Cecelia slipped the condom into her purse.

Finn did a double take, but Camille put her hand on his arm and pulled him back into their conversation.

Cecelia felt a curious urge to dance. Why not? It wasn't like she couldn't dance. Show this crowd a thing or two. *She could live in both worlds*. She relented and let the woman pull her to the floor. The woman demonstrated her moves, swinging her hips gently to and fro as they worked their way between the tables back to the dance floor. Cecelia fell into the rhythm and the woman nodded her approval. She tossed Cecelia a scarf.

Cecelia closed her eyes. The music beat an irresistible rhythm, at first matching the pulse in her veins, then seeming to come out of her veins, as she became the instrument. She swayed to the sound of her own heartbeat. This song was so familiar. What were the words? Her mother had taught her dances to this music from their scratchy, warped record collection. Her mother must have spent a hundred hours teaching her to flick her hips just so. The trick was to keep the rest of the body still. Move the hips slightly, so slightly. Nothing vulgar.

She pictured her mother, twirling through the living room, back when everything was good. Tiny Amy would shake her body dramatically. But Cecelia's mother would wink at Cecelia and whisper that she had a gift, the grace of a cat, the only cheetah in South Baltimore. She conjured the animal's glowing eyes, its luscious grace.

Her hair tumbled onto her shoulders. The dancer behind her gave her a mischievous smile and tucked the clip she had stolen from Cecelia's bun into the bra of her costume. Cecelia closed her eyes again. The music was the thing. The flow of it. How long had it been since she had danced? Forever since she had danced like this. She kicked off her heels (closer to the earth—where was the earth? Thirty stories below, under the parking garage?). She was vaguely aware of one of the other dancers gathering her shoes like treasures.

There was a time when she and her mother danced every night. After dinner, they'd rush to clean the dishes, then, hands still dripping, race for the record player. Balance books on their heads to keep their bodies upright. Put tiny bells on their hips and try to ring them cleanly. It was a million miles away. She had been such a child. No hips. No chest. Just the soul of a gypsy in love with her mother and the way she moved. Who cared that they had split a watered-down can of soup between three of them for dinner again? Who cared that life as they knew it was about to end in the most chilling of ways, at the hands of Amy and her relentless power.

The tempo increased. Cecelia let her hips follow. No,

the musicians were definitely following her now. Her mother could move like a jeweled angel. Her whispered words of praise echoed in Cecelia's head. Sweat streamed down her face. The whirl of the dancers around her spurred her on. She urged herself into the stream of their spirit. To dance was to join. To dance was to remember. To dance was to forget.

The music built to a furious crescendo. To dance was to be. That was all. Just the luxurious wonder of being.

Then, it slowed. Slower. Slower. Until it stopped on a single ringing note. Cecelia froze on cue, in synch with the band of gypsies.

Silence surrounded them.

Cecelia opened her eyes.

A thousand eyes blinked at her.

She was at the center of a semicircle of dancers. They clinked their finger cymbals in tribute and bowed low.

Then the applause began. The male doctors stood, one after the other. Their wives followed reluctantly. The female doctors clapped mutedly from their seats, their spouses sitting obediently at their sides.

Cecelia, gasping for breath after her exertion, looked around her in wonder.

What had she just done? Where was Finn?

And then she saw Jack, standing behind Finn and Camille. He looked at Cecelia like she had sprouted a second head.

A dancer returned her hair clip. Another, her shoes. They surrounded her, peppering her with questions and praise.

By the time she got free of them, Jack was gone.

Chapter 16

Cecelia found Jack in the hotel bar, his tux jacket slung carelessly over the back of his chair, sipping a single malt. His slumped shoulders instantly sobered her from the intoxication of her dance. Or was it the intoxication of the gypsy liquor she'd been throwing back all night?

Or the intoxication of Finn?

She slid into the seat next to Jack's, struggling to clear her head. He seemed not to know her. She touched his shoulder, but he didn't respond. Something inside her curled up and retreated. *I hurt the man I love.*

"I got off early," he said. "I thought I'd surprise you. Guess I was the one who got the surprise."

She struggled to calm her still-dancing nerves. Why had she danced that dance? What had she done?

"Camille told me you came with another guy. Who is he?" Jack's voice was soggy with defeat.

He is my One True Love; he is dying; he is a man who set me free; he is my destiny; he is nothing; he is Camille's. The vibration of the music from the ballroom called to her, and at the same time frightened her. She could still go back to her comfortable world. "He's a friend—"

Jack's voice was tight and cold. "A friend I learn about from Camille? A friend you take to dinner behind my back? A friend I don't know?"

Yes, she wanted to scream, *there's so much you don't know*. But that was her fault, not his. Cecelia took a deep breath. "I met him in the park when I was out with Amy. I wanted to hook him up with Camille. I think it worked." The easy lie elated and terrified her. She could get her life back to normal with a few well-chosen words. But did she want to? She put her hand lightly on the wooden table between them, her fingertips pulsing with the rhythm from the ballroom.

"What's going on? You're not yourself."

I'm a gypsy. My destiny is set. I'm in love with another man. I'm in love with you. "I have to tell you about Amy."

Jack held up his hands like a man in a sinking rowboat, hoping to keep at least his fingertips dry. "Please."

Cecelia's loose hair brushed her shoulders. The heat of the dance radiated from her face. "Amy is a psychic," Cecelia began.

Jack blinked.

Cecelia told him about Amy, her power, and their past—about everything but Finn.

Jack continued to blink.

When she was done, Jack looked at his now empty glass, refusing to meet her eyes. Finally, he said in his courtroom voice, "You believe your sister is a psychic." The words sounded absurd coming from his mouth.

"I've seen proof," she countered, too emphatically, like a talking head on a toothpaste ad. It did sound absurd and for a moment she saw everything clearly: she loved Jack because believing in Amy wasn't possible in his world. If she joined him, she was free of Fate. Of her destiny. Of Finn.

Jack must have read her silent concurrence, because his voice quickened. "You—a doctor of medicine— think that your sister can defy the scientific laws of nature and intercept—what? Thought rays? Ghosts? Spirits?" Jack glanced toward the door, as if he were expecting someone more rational to show up to provide a more plausible explanation.

"It's hard to say what she hears." At that moment, she both loved and despised Jack for his ruthless pursuit of empirical evidence. *Finn is my One True Love?* It depended on what world she inhabited. *It is up to me to decide.*

"If you believe that Amy can hear the Name of your True Love, is it me?" Jack's lawyerly mind cut right to the chase.

"She never told me." The truth flooded her, but she tossed the lie like a rickety raft, keeping them afloat between two islands—one civilized, one a dense jungle.

The erratic drumbeat of the folk music continued to pulse from the ballroom. In the face of Jack's astute rationality, it sounded ominous.

"Why didn't Amy tell you?"

Cecelia drew in a breath. "Amy and I made a pact that she would never tell me unless I wanted to know."

"But why?" He took her hand.

"Because—" Cecelia focused her full attention on Jack. Her hands nestled in his. She closed her eyes. Was this her life? She thought of her dance—wild, irresponsible. She felt the warmth of Jack's hands—calm, strong. She didn't have to go back to the painful memories of that dance. Not if she chose civilization, safety. Not if she chose Jack. "Because I want to be normal."

The music stopped and the silence made Cecelia aware of her pounding heart. She opened her eyes.

Jack nodded, as if this were the first thing Cecelia had said that made a lick of sense. He motioned the bartender for another scotch. When it came, he sipped it thoughtfully.

"Here's how I see it, Cel." Jack looked right at her and his directness filled her with shame. "I think that we control our lives. The concept of One True Love means that life is predestined. That's not the kind of world I want to live in. I control my world. You control your world. Maybe it's true that some people read the future, but other people make it." He paused. "We're the sort of people who make it."

Cecelia wanted to be that sort of person. With every fiber of her being, that was what she wanted. The wounds that the dance had opened in her felt like they could close again. In one concise statement, Jack had made her future clear: she could accept Fate or defy it. She gathered her hair and pinned it to the back of her head. No more dancing. No more purple drinks. No more gypsy wildness. No more lies.

No more Finn.

Jack stared past her out the doorway of the bar. Suddenly his eyes grew wide. Cecelia turned and looked, just catching the blur of Finn and Camille hurrying by. They fled breathlessly, almost floating across the square of light. Then they stopped, and drifted back, dead into the porthole of the doorway. Camille bent demurely to fix a strap on her shoe, her dress falling distractedly low to reveal remarkable cleavage. She steadied herself with a proprietary hand on Finn's shoulder. He stared down at her, no doubt mesmerized.

And then, they floated off again. Gone.

Cecelia's head swayed with the narrowness of her escape. She had almost left her kind, rational fiancé for a stranger who thought Camille was worth going home with.

Cecelia had chosen the right man.

Jack's hand still covered hers. He was wearing the gold cuff links she had given him for their first anniversary together. Cecelia's heart pounded. She touched his arm. *Here is good. Here is safe.*

Finn chose Camille, and she chose Jack. Everything was back to normal and Cecelia felt infinitely relieved.

She and Jack had decided to return to the banquet. He gathered his coat, she her bag. He pulled back her chair like a gentleman, let her precede him. But before they got out of the bar, he said, "Of course, now you have to ask Amy who your One True Love is."

Cecelia stopped dead. *But the worlds don't cross.*

"Before we get married. You have to know."

"Jack, it's not necessary—"

"I can't marry you if you don't know."

Cecelia's stomach clenched. They had stopped just inside the door of the bar, and people had to excuse themselves to push by. "What if it's not you?"

"Then you'll decide what to do. If you believe in Amy, there isn't any other way."

There was no music, no first-time lovers running off on fanciful whims. Just pure rationality leading to the unavoidable solution. Amy would tell them Cecelia's True Love's name. They could take it or leave it.

But if it was so rational, why did it sound so nuts? Amy would say Finn was her True Love—

If Jack believes.

If Jack didn't believe, then Amy could say anything. It didn't matter. In Jack's world, Amy was make-believe. Not a liar, but an actor. A game player. A clown. "Okay. I'll ask her."

"I love you, Cecelia." Jack stared deeply into her eyes.

It was almost over. Jack knew that Amy was a psychic and he still wanted to marry her. One last lie and they'd be past it all.

And Finn? Well, Finn was probably in line at the drugstore, buying a replacement condom.

Chapter 17

Finn stood in the line at the drugstore, waiting for the stooped, wrinkled woman ahead of him to choose her lottery ticket. Camille's red Maserati glimmered through the plate-glass windows of the store, and everyone in the place stared from it to him.

He couldn't wait to change back into jeans. He rubbed the back of his neck, trying to relieve the tension that this crazy night had implanted deep in his skull. He never should have said "yes" to the gala. In the park, eating hot dogs, he'd thought that maybe he and Cecelia could be friends. But the minute he picked her up in that dress— God, that dress—he knew he was kidding himself.

Then when Jack showed up, it was like a bucket of cold water was thrown over his head. *I am falling in love with an engaged woman. Not smart.* He had to get out of there immediately. Sure, he could have slunk away, walked uptown in the warm evening air. But the best way to get out and to protect Cecelia's reputation was to leave with another woman. So when he had complained of a headache, and Camille had offered him a ride home, it was the perfect solution to make Cecelia look blameless.

After all, he must have really been nothing more than a friend if he left with another woman. Even if he felt like a cad.

Problem was, now he had Camille on his hands.

The lady in front of him finally chose her last scratch-off game—she went with the Baseball Buzz and not the Sand, Surf, and Scratch—and moved to the next counter to scratch. Finn nodded at the clerk.

Camille revved the engine outside.

"Extra-large, huh?" the clerk asked, eyeing Finn's selection, then the car outside. "Looks like you're in for quite a night."

"There's tonight. And then there's tomorrow morning," Finn said, paying for the extra-large bottle of Tylenol. *And then there's the rest of my screwed-up life.* They exchanged money for the receipt.

Finn opened the bottle, tossed the wad of cotton in the trash, and downed four pills. The lady with the lottery tickets tossed the used tickets in the trash too. *Guess she should have tried the Sand, Surf, and Scratch. Choices are hard.* Finn offered her a Tylenol. She shook her head and shuffled away.

"Good luck!" the clerk called after Finn, laughing. "Let me know if you need backup."

Finn shot him a weary smile. *I must look like an asshole in this tux.*

What a night. Cecelia and that dance. Oh, hell. It had taken every ounce of his energy to keep his head turned to Camille. If he had watched that dance, it would have been over. He'd have to ruin Cecelia's life and pursue her, fiancé or no fiancé.

Which was why he didn't look. Kept his eyes trained on Camille.

Camille.

He pushed through the door into the cooling evening air. He crumpled his six-foot-two frame back into the passenger seat of the low-riding sports car. "Thanks for stopping here."

Camille shrugged. "Hey, it's not every day a guy tells *me* that *he* has a headache. Especially when I wear this dress."

Finn smiled. "I appreciate the ride. And the dress. I'm just beat and my kid's probably waiting up. It's just a few more blocks and to the right."

Camille gunned the car down the deserted street, past boarded-up storefronts, graffiti-covered empty lots. "So how do you know Cecelia?" she asked, not so sweetly.

"I don't really. Not much." *Not enough*. Finn knew his answer wasn't what she was fishing for, but he needed another extra-large bottle of pills for that story. Then a thought occurred to him. When Jack had entered the room, his eyes had been on Cecelia. But then they quickly turned to take in Camille. Something had sparked between those two. "How well do you know Jack?" he asked.

She slammed on the gas pedal hard. Finn braced himself against the side door as they peeled down the street, then careened right onto Trudy's street. She screeched the car to a stop in front of the bar, took a deep breath, then smiled at Finn. "I don't."

Finn took in her angry lips, her flashing eyes. "Hot damn. You're sleeping with Jack!"

Camille smiled ruefully and shrugged. "Guess we both got dumped."

For the first time that night, Finn liked her. *She's on my side*. He was still just drunk enough to enjoy the dim lights of the bar that danced on the hood of the fancy car, the irony of the situation, the night air. He offered her the Tylenol.

She grabbed the bottle, dumped three in her palm, and downed them. Then she handed the bottle back and cut the powerful engine. They were engulfed in the silence of the dark night. "Cecelia is an odd bird," Camille said, leaning back in the black leather seat. "I wouldn't blame you for being in love with her. She's gorgeous. She's smart. She'll be rich soon enough."

He was about to deny that he loved her. But he couldn't get the words out. "And she's engaged," he said. "I know I'm old-fashioned, but that really kills the buzz for me." *Do I love Cecelia?* Oh, hell, he hoped not. Maybe it was just lust. Lust he could walk away from.

Camille's eyes were closed. "Theirs is not a marriage that should happen."

"Who are we, the marriage fairies? We decide who gets who?"

"Why not? Maybe we're the best ones to decide. Jack was cheating on her."

"With you," Finn reminded her.

"Right. But that little affair was over almost before it began. The minute I met you."

"Sorry to let you down," he said.

"Oh. It's no big deal. I don't do men for the long-term; just the occasional treat. And now that I see where you live, I don't think you're really my type."

"Hey, you should see the inside. It's amazing."

"Are you inviting me in?" She smiled at his wide-eyed shock. "Relax, Boy Scout. I'm just kidding."

"So Jack came to the gala looking for you?" he asked, quickly changing the subject.

"I was going to stay at that boring party just long enough to hobnob, then meet Jack in the lobby. But instead, you caught my eye. Too bad you turned out to be such a Boy Scout."

"Could we cut the Boy Scout stuff?"

"Right. Okay. Too bad you turned out to be in love with Cecelia."

Her words knocked him in the gut. All the wind sucked out of him. *In love. With Cecelia. Who's engaged to another man. Who is cheating on her.* His mind skipped back to the first part. The realization hit him full on. He was in love with Cecelia. "I might love her." He took two more Tylenol. "That is not good."

"What's good have to do with love?" Camille asked.

"Like I said, I'm old-fashioned. I just want her to be happy."

"Bullshit. You want to fuck her brains out, Boy Scout."

Hell, this woman certainly wasn't turning out as uptight as Cecelia had painted her. Finn pursed his lips to hide his smile. "Well, yeah, of course. But not if it ruins her life. If she chooses Jack, then that's her choice." Even if he's a *two-timing schmuck*.

"And you're not going to try to change her mind?"

"No. She already made a choice. So did Jack."

"Don't you get lonely?" Camille asked into the darkness.

Finn nodded. "Every minute of every day. But it's not enough of a reason to ruin someone else's life."

"I see it as brightening up someone's life. Even if it's just temporary."

"Guess we can agree to disagree on that."

Camille nodded. "Friends?"

"Friends. Scout's honor."

They shook hands.

Finn hesitated.

"What?" she asked.

"Friends if you break it off with Jack." There, that was the least he could do for Cecelia.

She rolled her eyes. "Broken. Not that there was much to break. He looks good, but he's a little boring in bed—"

Finn held up his hand. "Too much information."

Camille laughed. "Anyway, after that dance of Cecelia's, I bet he might be re-interested in his chilly fiancée."

"Hey—she's not chilly—"

"Careful," Camille interrupted. "Your true feelings are showing."

His true feelings *were* showing. They were, in fact, growing before his eyes into giant green monsters, ready to tear down buildings, swat down airplanes, roar into the silent Baltimore night in pursuit of Cecelia. He had to get his mind off her. "You want a beer?" Finn asked Camille. She suddenly seemed incredibly sad to him.

"Is that a proposition?"

"A beer and a game of cards. Oh, and you can meet my daughter and her granny. That's all I have to offer."

Camille tossed her keys in her purse and reached for

her door. "You know what, Boy Scout? Somehow, tonight, that actually sounds good."

"Is the bimbo gone yet?" Trudy asked Finn. She ducked behind the bar. Only a few regulars were left, scattered around the tables. Max, Finn's supervisor, was paging through a newspaper at the far end of the bar. "Maya's upstairs sound asleep," Trudy said, before he could ask. "She knows where to find us."

"Yeah, I saw her sneaking down and looking at me a few times already." He smiled to himself at what Camille, a cardiologist, would think of Trudy calling her a bimbo.

"So? The date didn't work out, huh, Romeo?"

"It wasn't a date. I knew all along Cecelia was engaged." *To a cheating bastard.* Finn's stomach tightened uncomfortably. What was he going to do now? Would Cecelia even believe him? He thought back to his conversation with Camille. *He loved Cecelia—*

"Is that why you brought home Bambi?" Trudy broke into his thoughts.

Finn shook his head. "Her name's Camille. She's all right. She gave me a lift after my date left with her fiancé."

They fell into silence, Trudy wiping down the far end of the bar. Finn thought he heard her mutter, "Idiot," under her breath, but he was too tired to address it.

Max, Finn's foreman at the end of the bar, looked up. "Hey, Finny. Look at this!" He shot the paper down the length of the empty bar between them.

It was opened to a page with an article on a fabric show at the Baltimore Convention Center. "You think I need curtains?" Geez, Finn had always suspected that under Max's tough-guy exterior, there was a softer side.

Max had been married forever—a devoted husband and father despite his bluster.

"No, dummy. Flip the page."

Finn turned to the next page. It was filled with ads for local bars and the bands they were hosting. "You want to go hear some music?" He looked at his watch. It was 1:30 A.M.

"Look at the one down in the corner. How about that?" Max said proudly.

Finn saw it. His face dropped.

Trudy snatched the paper from him. She looked at it, then tore the entire paper in two and tossed it in the trash. "Finny isn't interested in bands in bars. Right, Finny? He's got a kid to raise."

Finn was taken aback by Trudy's abruptness—and her superhuman strength. After all, she'd been the one shooing him out at every opportunity, telling him she'd babysit, to go and have a good time. Trudy never had anything against bars.

Max said, "Yeah, but did you see the name of that band? The Finn Concord Five. You moonlighting on me with a secret band, Finny?"

Finn felt something tug in the bottom of his stomach. There was another Finn Concord in town. If Cecelia were here, she'd think the new Finn Concord might be her One True Love. After all, since he wasn't dying, he was the wrong guy. But maybe this one—

Oh, hell. He was slipping into treating this gonzo True Love business like it made sense. It was cracked. Some guy in a band wasn't Cecelia's One True Love.

"Listen," he said, loudly enough for Trudy and Max to hear, but not meeting anyone's eye. "Say there was this woman. And you thought you might be falling in love with her. But she's got a fiancé. But you know he's cheating on her. Would you tell her?"

"Is she hot?" Max asked.

Finn sighed.

Trudy picked up the phone from behind the bar. "I'll tell her. What's her number?"

"I didn't mean right this second," Finn protested.

Trudy shrugged. "If you really loved her—"

"I'd wake her up at two in the morning?" He shook his head. "Okay. There's more. Say you knew that this woman believed something totally whacked—but she really believed it—"

"Example," Max demanded.

Finn looked around him. "Okay. Say she believed that I was a pretty nice guy, she liked me fine. But a psychic told her that her One True Love was named Max Toledo and she believed it."

"Hey! That's me!" Max leaned forward. "Did you say she was hot?"

"Stay with me here," Finn said. "Do I have an obligation to tell her about the cheating fiancé and also to tell her about you? Tell her where you are? Introduce you?"

"Hell no!" Trudy boomed. "What the hell kind of dumb-ass obligation would that be?"

"A moral one," Finn explained.

"Moral? Grow up and go get her, you chicken-shit."

"Hey, wait a minute," Max protested. "What about me?"

"Screw you. Why should Finny worry about a schmuck like you?"

"I'm not worried about Max." Even as he said it, a

nagging thought tugged at him: was he messing up Cecelia's chance at True Love? No, he didn't believe in the psychic bit. Why did he have to keep reminding himself of that? "I'm worried about living with myself for the rest of my life knowing that I lied to her."

"You didn't lie. You just withheld some information that was mumbo-jumbo voodoo anyway." Trudy leaned right into Finn's face. Her breath scorched his cheek, so he felt every word. "Don't tell her, Finny."

When Trudy got that look in her eye, let her gums show, every word she said came out like a threat. His body tensed. Couldn't Maya have found a sweet, tender granny who baked cookies and knitted socks? A granny who told him to do the right thing, no matter what his narrow self-interests were?

Max put a twenty down on the bar, then came to stand behind Finn. "If you really love her, tell her. Let her decide. Then you can live with yourself for having done the right thing."

They both stared at Max with wide eyes. Max turned beet red. "I mean, you're still the boss, of course."

Finn felt as if an angel were perched on one shoulder, a devil on the other. That the angel was forty pounds overweight and stunk like Bud while the devil was his kid's pen pal toothless gin-drinking granny made the image a little odd, but still, it somehow served.

"Go home, Max. You're drunk." Trudy's eyes were hard, her voice otherworldly.

Finn shivered.

Max shrugged and thumped Finn hard on the back, as if that would reassert his manly credentials. Then he looked around to make sure no one else was listening, and leaned in close. "Maybe I *am* drunk. But I've been married twenty-seven years, and if there's one thing I've learned about women it's that you've got to tell them the truth. All the truth. Always." Max straightened, thudded Finn again, then turned to go.

Finn watched Max make his slow, careful, wobbly way out of the bar.

Great. Did he listen to the drunk or the she-devil?

He looked up at the ceiling. The saints and angels stared down at him. *Sally, I think I love Cecelia. What should I do?* He closed his eyes. If Amy could talk to spirits, then he could talk to his dead wife. It wasn't like he expected her to talk back.

Tell her everything.

His eyes popped open.

Maya was on the stairs in her pink bunny jammies.

"Maya? Did you say something?"

She rubbed her eyes. She was half asleep. "Daddy? Is the witchy lady gone?"

First Camille was a bimbo, now a witch. Poor lady had no idea how bad a night she was having. "I'm coming up, buddy. Let's get you back in bed." He glanced back up at the ceiling and shivered. What the hell had that been? Finn got up and went toward Maya. Then he stopped. He spotted another copy of the day's paper, open to the horse racing, abandoned on an empty table. He stuck it under his arm.

"What are you going to do, lover boy?" Trudy hissed, eyeing the paper.

"Why do you care about my love life?"

"I don't give a shit about you and your loveless life. I'm representing the kid."

Finn's stomach tightened. *Touché*. He ought to give the lady more credit. His voice softened. "The band's not playing until Wednesday. I have a while to figure it out. I'm gonna sleep on it." He caught up with Maya on the stairs and turned her sleepy body toward the top.

"Alone," Trudy called after him as he ushered Maya back to bed. "You're gonna sleep on it *alone*—for the rest of your life if you're not careful, you stupid, ignorant fool."

Chapter 18

Amy was practicing pulling aces out of her sleeve at Cecelia's dining-room table. One thing about her gypsy-chic was that she didn't usually have sleeves and if she did have them they were see-through. So she wore one of Cecelia's sweaters. The thing was pure cashmere, like wearing a kitten. It must have cost a bundle. Not that Cecelia cared about money. No, she might be an idiot about love, but at least she understood how to make money.

Well, hopefully, Cecelia was finally catching on about the love thing too. She sure had come home late last night. Amy felt sure she had finally connected with Finn at that doctors' dance. The dress Cecelia wore was on the right track, anyway. No woman wears a dress like Cecelia had worn to that banquet without having naughty intentions.

Amy smiled and dealt a few hands, keeping the aces firmly in place. The cards had to be positioned just so, then she could shrug one into her down-turned palm—damn it always got caught on the hem.

The buzzer rang. Amy jumped. The clock on the wall

said it was two in the afternoon; no way workaholic Cecelia or Jack could be back so early.

She went to the intercom and picked up the receiver. The doorman's voice came through. "Ma'am? I have a little girl here to see you?"

Amy froze. "Little girl? Chubby little girl?"

Silence. Then, "Well, um, okay, you could say that."

"Looks like she's casing the joint?"

"That would be her, ma'am."

Shit. What was Maya doing here? She wasn't ever supposed to come here. "Send her up. Quick. But first check and see if you still have your wallet."

Amy put the phone back on the intercom and waited. The doorbell rang and Amy dashed to answer it. She bundled the girl inside. "What are you doing here? Do you know what will happen if Cecelia sees us together? She'll suspect. And once she suspects, it's all over. Do you understand? All over. No mommy. Right?"

Maya walked by Amy as if she weren't there. The girl's eyes were wide as she took in Cecelia's palatial apartment. She petted the velvet chairs, then went straight for the balcony and pressed her entire face up against the glass doors. Yuck. Amy would have to wash that before Cecelia came home. Why were children so sticky?

"Wow. I can see heaven from here," Maya said.

"Well, good." *That's probably the only view you'll ever get of it at the rate you're going.* "What are you doing here?"

"Daddy got laid."

"No kidding! Oh, I knew we could do it. All right Cecelia!" Amy danced a celebratory jig.

"It wasn't Cecelia. It was some other lady. She has witchy fingers and hairs *on her hands.*" The memory of the horror made Maya shudder.

Amy stopped dancing. "Damn. Another woman? We have to get rid of her."

"You're gonna kill her?" Maya's eyes grew wide.

Amy began pacing, her chin in her hand. "What? No, of course not. You watch too much TV." She looked at the calm child. "I mean, not unless you have any ideas."

"We could throw her off of here," Maya said, indicating the balcony.

"Good thinking, but no. We're going to have to keep her alive. Sit down and tell me everything."

"Okay." The girl perched on the edge of an enormous stuffed chair. Amy couldn't remember ever being that small. "Daddy took me on the train to C.D.—"

"D.C."

"D.C.B.A . . . I can do the whole alphabet backwards—"

"Don't."

"Okay." Maya searched for her train of thought. "We got ice cream and mine was chocolate—"

"Wait. I didn't mean tell me absolutely everything. I meant everything about your dad and the hairy witch."

"Oh." Maya looked at the ceiling and took a deep breath. "Okay. He had a date with Cecelia. He looked like a prince. Then when Granny Trudy was teaching me to pull aces out of my sleeve—"

"Can you do it?"

"What?"

"The aces." Amy tossed her the deck.

Maya dutifully stuck a card up her sleeve. She looked

to her right and said, "My, it sure is hot lately," just like a tiny, airy southern belle. By the time she said "hot," the ace of spades was cradled in her palm.

"Amazing."

"I know. Granny Trudy says I'm a natural. So, I'm doing the trick and he comes in with this witch." She paused so the awfulness could properly sink in. "She got all mushy with me and touchy and yicky and then Granny Trudy says it's way past my bedtime. Not like she cared when we were practicing the aces. And I can have a sleep-over with her if I want—"

"Granny Trudy said that? I'm going to kill her."

"Oh, no, I love Granny Trudy!"

Amy scowled. "I won't really kill her." Amy took the cards and tried to pull the ace as flawlessly as Maya. Damn, that girl was good at cards, but lousy with romance. "Go on."

"Granny Trudy snores, but she makes a good breakfast."

Amy shook her head. "You're supposed to stick by your dad. If you let other women in, then Cecelia can't get in, and then she can't be your mommy."

Maya considered this. "Shit."

"Language!"

"Ships!" She rolled her eyes like a tiny grown-up. "I didn't know True Love worked like that."

"Well, it does. Just one woman fits, see? So then what?"

"So then, Granny and me we went upstairs. But I snuck down later and they were getting laid."

"Downstairs? On the bar?"

"Yup."

"Oh, gross. Remind me not to order lunch there again."

Maya looked pained. "It was gross. Totally gross. I almost threw up. Then, the first chance I got, I came here."

"Which was bad. What if Cecelia was here?"

"Is she?" Maya looked around, alarmed.

"No, dummy. I wouldn't have let you up if she were here. Now—"

Suddenly they both froze. A key turned in the lock.

"Shit! Hide!" Amy and Maya both jumped up.

"Language!" Maya scolded as Amy shoved her into the broom closet. The moment the closet clicked shut, the front door swung open and Cecelia walked in.

Cecelia had spent the morning at the hospital, but she couldn't keep her mind off the night before. After Finn and Camille had disappeared into the steamy night, she and Jack had returned to the gala. If she planned on repairing her reputation, it must be done immediately, with Jack at her side.

She and Jack didn't talk about the reasons they went back and endured the uncomfortable small talk and sideways stares of the soused, suspicious doctors. They didn't need to—they understood what was required. The exquisite relief of that unsaid knowing had kept Cecelia lively throughout the ordeal. She had made the right choice; this was the man who understood her and her world. The craggy rocks of society couldn't touch their smoothly sailing vessel.

Whether Cecelia consciously had been avoiding going home to Amy or not, the delay worked. Like old times, Elliot and Julia gave her and Jack a ride home. Elliot gave her a fatherly nod of the head as they climbed out of his BMW. It had given Cecelia a creepy feeling, but she shook it off. Decisions had been made, and she was sticking by them. By the time they arrived upstairs, Amy was sound asleep in bed. She and Jack were too exhausted to do anything but follow her example.

Now, the next day, she had to talk Amy into lying to Jack. Unfortunately, Amy was antsy and unfocused. She stood. She sat. She licked her lips ferociously. But Cecelia didn't care what scam or lie or plan she was interrupting. She needed Amy to concentrate on the most important psychic reading of Cecelia's life.

"C'mon," Amy pleaded, "let's get out of this stuffy apartment. We'll talk about this over Chinese. I'm starved."

"Stop being so jumpy. We're not going anywhere until we talk this through. I only have twenty minutes before I have to get back to the office." Cecelia's impatience was rising. She had explained about Jack's demand that she learn the name of her One True Love. Slowly and patiently she had taken Amy through the whole awful conversation, and now all Amy could think about was food?

"Let's go talk in the kitchen."

Cecelia let her head fall back. "No. This is important. Sit down and look me in the eyes and tell me you'll do it."

"Forget it." Amy sighed, plunked onto the couch, then swirled herself so that her feet stuck up in the air and her head hung over the bottom cushions. "I will not lie for you, Cel."

"Why are you whispering? I can barely hear you. You said that it was my con, I call the rules. So, I'm calling them. I want you to tell Jack he's The One."

"Listen to yourself," Amy whispered. "You just admitted it. You know, if I had a dollar for every marriage based on convenience and appearance and material gain, I'd be rich! The Baltimore police might call me a con artist, but it's women like you who are the liars and the cheats."

"That is so unfair. I love Jack." Cecelia tried not to think about why Amy might be involved with the Baltimore police already. Was that why she kept licking her lips?

"Shhh."

"What is the matter with you? I will not 'shhhh.' Just because Jack's not the love of my life doesn't mean that we can't love each other." Was Amy in so much trouble with the police that she thought the place was bugged?

"Let's go jogging. I've been wanting to start jogging—"

"We are not jogging. We're working this out. Jack will be home in a few hours. What is the matter with you?" Cecelia was instantly sorry for her exasperated words. She watched Amy's eyes grow hard.

"What's the matter with me!" Amy hissed. "You love Jack? Love like what? Like cousins? Like buddies? Oh, that's a rich thing to base a marriage on. Face it, Cel, you want the guy because he's rich and successful and safe. That's not love. Tell him the truth."

Cecelia wanted Amy to sit up in the chair like a normal person. She was sick of everything topsy-turvy. Marrying a good man who she loved was a betrayal, but chasing after a man who had no future and was probably sleeping with her colleague was okay? "Sit up. And stop whispering. I can't hear you when you whisper."

"I have a hangover. I can't talk. My head's about to explode," Amy hissed. "If you love him, you wouldn't lie to him."

"Lovers lie to each other all the time. That's how real life works, Amy."

"Ouch! My head!"

Cecelia rolled her eyes. She had to rein in her frustration, or she'd never get anywhere with Amy. She whispered fiercely. "This is real life. It's not a novel or a Hollywood movie. Plus, he doesn't believe. It's like Santa Claus."

"Santa Claus? Oh, no, we're not talking about Santa Claus." Amy looked around nervously. Suddenly she jumped up and switched on the radio.

Cecelia switched the blaring music off. What was wrong with her sister? "It's exactly like Santa Claus. If a kid believes, the Santa at the mall tells the kid, 'I ate the cookies. I brought the gift.' But if a kid knows that there's no Santa, the fat guy in the cheap suit can say, 'I see you've been very, very naughty this year.' It doesn't matter what he says, it's all a game."

Amy stared out the window at the endless sky. "Remember the year that we didn't get any gifts?" she asked, her voice so low, Cecelia could barely hear her.

Cecelia surprised herself by matching Amy's tone. "No. We always got gifts."

"No we didn't. Remember, right after Mom left and we were on the road with Dad, in that moldy hotel outside of Tampa?"

"He had found Jane Smith the meter maid. The wrong Jane Smith, thank God. She was awful. Why wouldn't Dad ever see how awful these Janes were? She would give tickets twenty minutes before the meter ran out and then argue with people like she enjoyed it. But Dad was convinced she was his One True Love! How can you remember that? You were too little."

"I believed in Santa, Cel. Dad told us that Santa had brought us the right Jane Smith and that was the only present a person needed—"

"Daddy would never say that." Cecelia felt a strange tugging in the bottom of her gut.

"Of course he would. All he cared about was True Love. He didn't just *say* that little girls didn't need presents, he *believed* it. He was such a damn romantic, he thought that that fat, farty old meter maid was the world's best gift to his daughters."

Cecelia tried not to remember. She was done with all that. Her father's obsession with True Love had ruined more than that one Christmas.

"I tried so hard to be good," Amy went on. "I tried extra hard to use the Voice to get Daddy the money he needed to make Jane see that we were her perfect little family."

"I remember you being an extra suck-up kiss-ass," Cecelia said. "You were all, 'Yes, Daddy, no, Daddy.' I wanted to kill you."

"That's what you remember? Wanting to kill me? You know, Cel, I think that you need to open your eyes a little and look at the bigger picture. It wasn't my fault." Her voice ratcheted louder.

They sat in the silence. Cecelia closed her eyes. Suddenly the bigger picture appeared in her mind fully formed like a scene in a movie—the nubby, brown overwashed bedspread, the spicy vapor of industrial cleaning fluid, the moon-shaped water rings that stained the hotel tub. She had sat on the edge of the tub and traced them with her finger, thinking of her mother and wondering where she was. "I was sure that Mom sent us presents that year, but that they were lost because we traveled so much. I imagined all sorts of dolls and games waiting for me—for us—back in Baltimore. Just as soon as Dad found his True Love, we'd go home and get them."

Amy sat down. Cecelia sat beside her.

"We always had each other," Amy said.

Cecelia swallowed hard. "Yeah, who needs Santa when you've got an annoying little sister?"

"An annoying little sister who's trying to save you."

Cecelia closed her eyes. "I don't want to be saved. Lie for me. It's not like you haven't done it before."

Amy sighed. "Does this have anything to do with Finn?"

"Finn?" Cecelia's eyes popped open.

"Did something happen last night that you're not telling me?"

"No."

"I don't believe you. Did he go off with another woman?"

"How did you know that?" Cecelia cried. "No. Wait. He didn't exactly go off with her. I mean, I don't know if he did. Jack showed up—"

"—and Finn took off with another woman."

"I don't know. And you know what? I don't care. I'm marrying Jack—"

"I wish you would stop being so rigid about that."

Cecelia's blood rose, heating her face. Amy was impossible. She'd just have to lay down the law. "I have to go. Tonight, I'm coming back with Jack and we're having a séance at which you will break sulfur capsules and howl at the moon and tell him that he's my One True Love. And if you don't, then you're leaving. I'm kicking you out. For good. Are we clear?"

"Finn got laid by another woman and you're angry."

Images of Finn and Camille, framed in the doorway of the hotel bar, flooded her. "I don't know if he—"

Suddenly the closet door flew open and Maya exploded out.

"Well I know! He did get laid! Twice! And I'm glad. Because I don't want you to be my mommy anyway! You're a great big liar and you don't even believe in Santa!"

Maya's face was red and wet with streaming tears. She flung herself past Amy and Cecelia and ran for the door while they sat, openmouthed, the reverberation of the slammed door echoing around them.

Chapter 19

It started as a tiny light that Cecelia swatted away like a firefly. But the light returned, brighter. She closed her eyes against it. But it was no use. It lit the outside of her eyelids, demanding to get in. The whispering. The radio. There was only one way that little girl could have gotten in her closet. "I'm an idiot."

Amy shrugged.

"A moron." Cecelia opened her eyes and she let the light blind her. She hoped she'd never see again. She fell back onto the couch. "Trudy's Bar. Trudy Dubois. She used to run that pawnshop in Fell's Point where Dad would go when we were kids and things really got bad. He pawned all of Grandma Molly's silver there."

Amy shrugged again. "I like to keep in touch with old friends."

Cecelia was going to throw up. "Trudy isn't Maya's granny. How did you—?"

"Rent-a-granny. The kid made it up." Amy twirled her hair around her finger. She was licking her lips furiously. She didn't meet Cecelia's eye.

Maya is in on the con. "Tell me everything. Straight.

Now." Cecelia was falling off a cliff, the world whizzing by her.

Amy sighed. "I wanted to bring you your One True Love. I searched everywhere for Finn Franklin Concord. It took five damn years." She paused, apparently for Cecelia to commend her hard work.

Cecelia urged her on with cold, hard eyes.

"Right. So, I found Maya's dad. Who, by the way, is one good-looking man. You should be glad—"

Cecelia held up a warning hand.

"Right." Amy shrugged. "So I met Maya. We got to talking every Tuesday when she'd get herself a milk shake at this diner, and she let me in on her mommy fantasy." She paused again.

Cecelia shook her head. *Fantasy*. It was all a fantasy. A con. A lie. A story. "You used a little kid."

"It was for everyone's benefit! I saw that if I could figure out a way to convince the kid to get her dad to come to Baltimore, you guys could meet. So I tell the kid that I know who her daddy's One True Love is. I tell her all about my powers. I tell her that I can make her daddy the happiest man alive. And, Cecelia—I tell her all this because it's true. It is! I wasn't conning her! You know that!"

Cecelia scowled. "Go on."

"So one Tuesday, the kid's slurping away on her milk shake, and she says, 'If I had a granny in Baltimore, we could visit her.' Which was when I thought of Trudy. So I told her that I knew a lady who could be *like* her granny for a while. And Maya says, 'Hey, you mean, like, I could rent her?' Bam! It was like a lightning bolt had struck us both! It was brilliant. Free chocolate milk shakes for a month for that kid! So we worked out the whole rent-a-granny plan. Trudy was delighted about the whole thing. Trudy believes in True Love and doing good deeds, you know."

Cecelia felt every drop of her blood drain out of her body. "The baseball. That was it, wasn't it? Trudy was always a baseball nut? You didn't have the money to pay her for her part in the con so you told her Finn could play for the bar's team." Cecelia felt dizzy. Why hadn't she seen it before?

"Well, okay. Whatever. But don't you see? It was all meant to be! The rest, as they say, is history."

"The rest is repulsive!" The cells of Cecelia's body were floating away one by one. She could barely speak. "You and that little girl are conning Finn. Conning me. My God. You're corrupting a minor. That's—that's just so wrong on so many levels."

"Oh. That's rich. You can lie to your fiancé but I can't put together a tiny con to unite two lovers who are meant to be. *And* find a child a mommy." She paused, then raised her chin proudly. "*And* help a ball team—"

Cecelia covered her ears with her hands like a child. She had trusted Amy. But Amy had brought Finn to Baltimore; she had brainwashed the child; and Cecelia had strolled right into Amy's trap. "Get out. Go. I can't stand that I didn't see it sooner. You're making that child into a tiny con artist—"

"People are what they are, Cel. Destiny."

Cecelia froze, her skin ice. Her voice came out strained and high. "Is Finn in on this?"

"No. Of course not. He's for real. He just wants to

make his kid happy. He'll do anything for that brat! What an easy—"

"No." Cecelia held up her hand like a traffic cop. "Not another word. Go. Don't be here tonight. Don't be here for another ten years! Twenty this time! I'm telling Jack that you're gone. When I come home tonight, I want you and everyone who is in my closet and under my bed and lurking in a stinking bar gone." Cecelia fought desperately to stay in control. She carefully gathered her purse, took one last long look at Amy, who was wearing Cecelia's jeans, her bracelet, even her lipstick—well, it was a small price to pay—and then raced out of the apartment to catch a tiny, weeping con girl.

A semicircle of concrete steps led from the shopping mall to the promenade along the waterfront. Cecelia spotted Maya sitting on the top step on the far side of the curve. All around her, campers in matching yellow T-shirts darted and romped. They were Maya's size, but they looked like creatures from a colorful, happier world. *The Planet of Happy Childhood.*

A blond boy chased a brown-haired girl around Maya. He caught his prey by the shoulder, then yanked her pigtail. The girl shrieked in pain and delight.

Cecelia had never had a pigtail pulled.

Actually. She never had a pigtail. It was ballerina buns even back then.

Maya never looked away from the horizon.

Cecelia started toward her, then stopped. She sank on to the steps across the arc from Maya. What could she say? Sorry the glass slipper didn't fit? Sorry the clock struck twelve and you saw my rags? Sorry, so, so terribly sorry about Amy. She doesn't look like a wicked witch, but then they never do in the real world.

Oh, hell. Tears rose in Cecelia's eyes and she forced them back. Maybe she could explain to Maya that at least she had a cool dad. All the family Cecelia had was Amy, and she stank.

Maya still stared, her elbows on her knees, her chin in her hands. She had stopped crying, but her face was puffy and red.

Cecelia stared at the spot on the horizon that fascinated Maya. There was nothing there. Not a fishing boat or pleasure yacht, just the hazy line where the distant dips and curves of Federal Hill across the harbor met the sky. The heat of the concrete soothed Cecelia, and she leaned back on the steps. She closed her eyes, allowing the summer sun to massage her face. She stayed like that for— how long? A minute? An hour? A lifetime? When she opened her eyes, she saw that Maya had assumed the exact same position across the arc of the stairs, her head resting on the step, the sun healing her swollen face.

If only Cecelia could send thought rays zinging around the curved steps, like at one of those magical childhood places where you could whisper into one side of an arc and your voice would travel, ghostlike, to the other end. What would she say?

She studied the curve. Maya's ear was against it. Who knows? She put her lips close to the step and whispered, "It'll be okay."

Maya didn't budge.

Good thing that she didn't hear. After all, wasn't that just another lie?

Life certainly hadn't been okay for Cecelia. How

many weeks, months, years, had Cecelia spent, scheming, praying for a perfect mother after her mother left? The Jane Smith her father ended up marrying was awful—lazy and stupid. And her dad was thrilled. It was a hard lesson that the happiness of someone you love didn't necessarily correspond with your own happiness. All those years she was buoyed by the hope her dad's Jane Smith would be a saint, able to fix their broken family, be a mother to her. Her hope had carried her through.

Maya still hadn't moved. She looked as if she might never move. Live there. Become a statue. A perch for the overeager pigeons. She was a real girl once, people might say. But they'd be wrong. Maya had been robbed of her childhood the moment her mother was taken from her. Then fleeced again by Amy's manipulations. Then rung dry by overhearing the adult world's take on the okayness of living a life of lies.

Or was that Cecelia's life she had just described?

Cecelia whispered into the step, "It'll suck, but it'll be okay."

Suddenly Maya turned and looked right at Cecelia across the fifty yards of concrete and crowds. She narrowed her eyes. Then Cecelia heard her voice, clear as day, "No, *you* suck. But I'll be okay."

Cecelia's eyes widened. Had Maya really said that? Or had Cecelia imagined it?

The girl stood, smoothed her shorts and T-shirt, and walked away.

Wherever those words had come from, they were true. Maya would be fine. Cecelia watched her weave through the scampering children, her head high, more than a child.

Well, that was best, really. Maya and Finn could leave Baltimore, go back to sunny Florida where boys could pull Maya's pigtails and Finn could get on with his life.

Or, he could marry Camille and Maya could join the kids romping around the waterfront in a bright yellow T-shirt.

Camille would make Maya a fine mother.

Cecelia shuddered at the thought.

She had to forget about them. Forget about everything and get back to the way her life was before Amy.

How hard, after all, could that be?

Chapter 20

Amy made herself a cheese sandwich, then sat down at the kitchen table. She stared out over the water. She'd go to their grandmother's house in North Baltimore. Start fixing it up. No big deal. Cecelia would come around, eventually.

But she might as well have some lunch first. After all, maybe Cecelia would relent and let her stay. Cecelia would realize that Amy was bringing her True Love. Then Amy would explain the whole truth—how her powers were fading more and more every day, and she needed Cecelia's help, although she didn't know why. They would laugh about that awhile. Crazy mixed-up spirit world. Then Cecelia would agree to help Amy get her powers back because Amy had brought her the most beautiful thing in the world—True Love.

She heard a key in the door. She looked around her guiltily, then rationalized that she was only sitting at the table eating a sandwich. That was okay. Cecelia had said to go, now. But "now" could mean right after a sandwich; even Cecelia wouldn't deny her lunch.

But it was a man's footsteps that neared the kitchen.

"Amy?" Jack called, his voice oddly rough. "Are you here?"

What is this, Take the Day Off from Work to Torture Amy Day?

Jack appeared in the doorway in full lawyer regalia. His tie was metallic gold. "Thought I'd come home for lunch for a change," he said. He was in a dark gray suit with a dark blue shirt. He carefully placed his briefcase on the floor and came into the kitchen. "I see I'm just in time. How are the cheese sandwiches in this joint?"

"Oh, especially tasty today. Although, I understand this place does a pretty mean canned soup."

"Can't beat chicken noodle," he said. He sat down across from Amy and made no effort to get any food. He wrung his hands, and Amy thought of Cecelia. Did he always have the same tell as Cecelia, or had Jack unconsciously adopted Cecelia's?

"I have questions," he said.

She looked toward the door. How long would Cecelia be gone? She'd flip out if she saw them together. No, she'd be at work till dinner for sure. "Shoot."

"If you know the name of people's True Loves, why are you alone?"

"You must be a lawyer," she said, taking a particularly challenging bite of her sandwich and answering through the mouthful. "Okay, here's the deal. I can hear everybody's Name but mine." She swallowed. "Believe me, I've spent hours, days even, staring at myself in the mirror, trying to call a name up. I used to leave pictures of myself around, hoping that one day I'd glance at one and the Name would come to me."

"You'd trick your spirit guide or whatever it is that talks to you?"

Amy hadn't thought of it exactly that way. Con the ghosts. Well, why not? "I guess."

Jack shook his head. "Okay. Question Number Two: Why won't Cecelia let you tell her the Name of her True Love?"

"I shouldn't get involved." Amy pushed her sandwich away. She wasn't hungry anymore. Then she pulled it back. This conversation sucked, but really, it was a good sandwich. And Cecelia might throw Amy out the second she stormed back, so she should eat.

"I'm losing her," Jack said. "I don't know what to do. I'm looking for advice, Amy. I need your help."

He did need her help. Poor guy was about to marry the wrong woman—ruin both his and Cecelia's lives in one fell swoop.

No, she couldn't. She thought back to Cecelia's raw fury at their harmless little granny scam. Cecelia would never forgive her if she helped Jack too. And she needed Cecelia. (*Why? Why? Why?*) "Cel always hated the Names. She blamed them for everything rotten in our childhood. It's not about you, if that makes you feel any better. It's about me."

"Amy, tell me Cecelia's Name."

She squeezed her eyes shut. "I can't."

"Then you've told me. By not telling me, you've told me." His jaw twitched.

Amy felt his trap close around her. She licked her lips. "It's not that simple."

"I think it is." He got up from the table and started to

pace. "Not that I believe in your magic—but Cecelia does."

"It's not magic."

"I think it's nuts—no offense."

No offense. Was he kidding? She had spent a lifetime being teased and bullied and mocked because of her powers. If he didn't believe, then to hell with him. He asked, after all. She didn't force anything on him.

Jack leaned in close to her. His voice was a whisper. "Make me believe, Amy. Convince me."

Oh, she did want to convince him. She loved convincing non-believers. She could convince him—blow his mind. She had heard his Name at the engagement party. She just had to remember it.

Anyway, Cecelia would kill her. Amy struggled to find a reason to deny him. "This isn't about great sex, is it?" she blurted. "Men sometimes think that True Love will be an incredible erotic experience. It can be. But that's not what it's about."

"That's not what I'm about."

"Jack, this is a mistake. You can love Cecelia even if she isn't your One True Love. There's all kinds of love." Amy's stomach sank. What nonsense.

She should tell the truth. Then, she could get rid of Jack. Then, Cecelia would consider Finn. Then, if he *was* the right Finn (Amy still couldn't read Finn without Cecelia around—and the three of them together hadn't happened since the ball game, when Finn was too far away) Cecelia would finally know True Love. She'd forget about her silly, contrived life of penthouses and doctors, see there was no greater calling in life than helping people find their One True Love, and join Amy in her quest.

They'd have their old life back and Amy's powers would work again like before. Amy was sure of it. Things had been good when they were together, bad when they were apart.

And here was Jack, handing it all to her on a platter.

"Make me a believer, Amy," he repeated.

Amy let her future play out before her. She could deal with Cecelia. It was love that mattered. Everything else was secondary. Love was the key.

Cecelia's image conjured itself in Amy's head. Her set brow, her scowling lips. She'd never give up her fancy doctor's life. "I can't, Jack."

He hesitated. Then his blank lawyer face was replaced by angry, flashing eyes. "Amy, prove your power to me or leave. You're destroying Cecelia. You're destroying us."

"Funny. You're the second person who's kicked me out today." Amy closed her eyes. Okay, maybe she could do it. She was, after all, doing this for Cecelia. "Hell. I'll try. But this might take a while." Amy took his hand in hers and was shocked by the warmth of it. Well, this was her sad fate, wasn't it? Holding hands with men who would never be hers. Uniting lovers, yet always alone. Oh, if Cecelia only knew how good she had it.

Amy took a deep breath. Could she get a first letter? Anything to help her remember the name she had heard at the engagement party?

Maybe being in Cecelia's apartment, with so much of her essence around, would make the voices work. She prayed for a clue, then cleared her mind.

She closed her eyes.

Chapter 21

Cecelia opened the front door and was struck with a chill. "Jack? I'm home!" she called.

Silence greeted her. A full silence. The kind that made her shudder. She looked around for signs of Amy. The silver candlesticks that had been in the center of the dining room table were gone. Good. Amy had left with everything she could pawn.

Cecelia breathed a sigh of relief. It was her and Jack now. Back to normal.

But why wasn't Jack answering? She had seen his briefcase lined up neatly in the closet. Maybe he was mad that she was so late. Cecelia had gotten stuck at the hospital with a patient coding just as she was putting her white lab coat on the hanger to leave. Now it was past eight o'clock.

She heard noises from the bedroom.

She called a hearty "Hello?"

No answer. She felt the chill again, but shook it away.

She lined her shoes carefully in the closet.

Her skin was clammy.

Something was wrong. She felt it to the core of her

bones. She tiptoed cautiously to the bedroom, aware of the absurdity of her stealthy approach. The door was open. She peered in and froze.

Jack sat on the side of the bed, his head hanging. He had an envelope in his hand. He looked up, and stared at her with the same look he'd had at the banquet. As if he had no idea who she was. She came gently into the room.

He handed her the envelope.

She didn't open it. Instead, she sat down next to him, too concerned with his pallor to investigate his offering. "What's wrong?" It wasn't possible that he had talked to Amy; Cecelia had noticed on her way through the apartment that three crystal vases on the front mantel, Jack's collection of antique boxes, and the small Chagall print from the hall were all missing. Amy had definitely left for the long haul.

Jack looked at her for a long moment and shook his head. Then he stood and walked stiffly to the end of the bed. He pulled a small leather duffel bag off the floor.

Cecelia tried to swallow her panic. "What's going on?" Did Jack move the Chagall print? How would Amy have known its value from among all the art that hung on the walls? Her fingertips began to tingle.

Maybe Amy was so angry with Cecelia, she had gone to Jack. Maybe she had showed up at his office and told him all about Finn.

"I talked to Amy," Jack said.

"No!" Cecelia jumped up. Hearing it was worse than imagining it. "Where is she?" Cecelia had the creepy feeling that Amy was under the bed, flat on her back, the bottom of the box spring just brushing her nose.

Cecelia sat back down heavily on the bed.

"But that's not why I'm leaving," Jack said as if Cecelia hadn't spoken.

"Leaving?" All the breath went out of her. "But—"

Jack held the bag in one hand. In the other hand, he turned his keys over and over as if they were worry beads. He nodded at the envelope in Cecelia's hand.

Cecelia looked at the envelope for the first time. She didn't need to open it to know what was inside. Was that what this was all about? Hope filled her. "Jack, I can explain."

"I don't want to know."

She tore open the envelope and the condom she had stolen from Camille slid into her hand. Extra-large. Ribbed. Maybe it would be harder to explain than she first thought. How had Jack found this? "I took it from Camille's purse." The thought repulsed her and she tossed it onto the bed where it smoldered between them.

Jack's face stretched like a rubber band at the mention of Camille's name, then quickly snapped back.

Cecelia shook off the image of his momentarily distorted features. Of course he was shocked. She was admitting to petty theft—value of stolen possessions under fifty dollars, punishable in the state of Maryland by a thousand dollar fine, if she remembered it correctly, although she doubted that would soothe Jack's concern. "I don't know why I did it. I was feeling weird at the banquet, and I stole it."

She might as well have said she murdered a waiter and chopped him to bits, judging by the look on Jack's face. "I come to the banquet and you're there with another man. Then, I'm looking for my passport and I find a condom in the drawer. Then, all this talk about True Love—"

"What happened with Amy?" Cecelia asked, trying to keep the panic out of her voice. *His passport?* Her skin was alive with ten thousand needle pricks and her life was seeping out the holes.

He turned away from her. "I can't stand the lies anymore. My lies. Your lies. I'm going to Cincinnati. And then. I don't know."

"Ohio?" Cecelia struggled to understand. *His lies?* "What about work?"

"Can you for one minute think about something other than work?" he boomed.

Cecelia shrank back, stunned. Jack didn't yell. She felt what he must have felt when he saw her dancing: I don't know this person. Maybe Jack longed to yell. Maybe Jack, the real Jack, was a raging, screaming maniac, fed up with the rules and restraints of his logical mind.

Then he said quietly, "I was having an affair with Camille. Our engagement isn't right. I'm going to find my One True Love."

She wished he'd yell again. Yelling was better than this quiet, certain news. She felt the ring on her finger. "*Was* having an affair?"

"Was. Now I'm going to Cincinnati. My One True Love is an old friend. We'll talk when I come back."

Come back? Jack had cheated on her. Just when she had gotten rid of Amy. And Maya. And Finn. She felt flat.

"Look, Cel. It's not working." He began pacing, like a lawyer in a courtroom. She stealed herself for his evidence. He pointed at exhibit A, the condom. "That's the condom my fiancée pick-pocketed from her senior colleague—my mistress. This crime was committed right before her obscene dance for her colleagues *and* for her mysterious date who turns out to be her One True Love—according to her newly appeared psychic sister." Jack pulled his bag onto his shoulder. Case closed. "I'll be back in three days. You have my cell."

Jack and Camille.

Jack and his One True Love.

"Who is she?" Cecelia asked. When Amy pulled a Name from someone's past, it was almost impossible not to believe. *She's not going to be what you expect*, Cecelia wanted to warn him. But you couldn't warn people. They had to learn for themselves.

"Sharon Pranks. I told you about her once."

Cecelia felt like laughing. Sharon had been Jack's date for the senior prom. "The cat lady? The kitty doctor?" She tried to keep her amusement out of her voice. "The *vegan*?"

"She's a veterinary acupuncturist with a specialty in feline oncology. I spoke to her this afternoon."

Cecelia let the news wash over her: she was being left for a woman with a cat fetish and a serious belief in the evil powers of cheese. *Jack loves cheese.*

He loves me.

Loved.

Camille.

Why did she feel so flat? Shouldn't she be furious?

"I'll call you." Jack's footsteps retreated down the hall. The front door opened, then slammed shut like a gunshot.

Silence.

She fell back onto the bed. The condom was cold

against her bare arm. She picked it up. The extra-large circle under the foil wrapper seemed to be saying, *OOOOOOOOps!*

Extra-large? For Jack?

She had to admire Camille's sense of hope.

Cecelia threw the offending square into the trash.

She wandered into the living room and slumped onto the couch. She noticed a tiny white jewel box on the coffee table where the tiny gold candy bowls used to be. Damn Amy. Had she left anything of value?

She opened the white box despondently, not caring what was inside. A turd? A diamond? The key to the meaning of life? There was no note. No signature of the person who left it. She rooted in the cushioning cotton, and pulled out a tiny, painted statue of Shiva, the god of destruction.

Well, he had certainly done his work, hadn't he?

She put the dancing god in the center of the otherwise empty mantel, went back to her bedroom, and crawled under the covers.

Chapter 22

Jack and Camille. That, Cecelia could understand. But Jack leaving her for True Love. She burrowed deeper under the covers, becoming fetal. She had been tossing and turning in bed for two hours, trying to make sense of what had happened and how she felt about it.

She replayed their relationship, over and over, moment by moment. Each memory was illuminated by a small light of hope—the hope that because they had so much in common, they would be able to one day love each other in the passionate, intense way that Amy preached. But now she saw that her hope was a candle, melting away with each day.

They would never have loved each other that way.

She pulled the covers tighter over her head and curled up, making herself as small as possible. She thought that she and Jack understood each other. They had given up passionate, destructive love for something more real, more lasting, more stable.

Except that now, she was the only one who had given it up.

She was completely alone in the world.

The empty bed stretched forever around her. She couldn't get warm. Each organ inside her twisted into a tight knot. She named them one by one: pancreas, spleen, right kidney, left kidney—

Cecelia threw the covers off her, letting the cold accost her skin. The things she had worked so hard for surrounded her: real wool carpets, tastefully painted walls, a master suite that could have housed four families *and* their farm animals.

She pulled off her ring and stared out at the view of the harbor, but it was shrouded in fog. She didn't want love to matter. She had built a safe world where love didn't matter—*and now she had nothing but stuff.*

She left the window and paced the room. If love mattered, then her parents had done the right thing to divorce. If love mattered, then her father had done the right thing to drag them all over creation to find Jane. If love mattered, then of course Jack should have left her.

If love matters, then Amy holds all the cards.

True lovers had to have a gypsy soul. To find True Love, nothing else—nothing!—could matter. Not jobs, not homes, not even children. She felt a dull ache in the pit of her stomach.

She was dead tired of wandering. A gypsy life was too hard.

She opened her jewelry box and carefully put the ring inside.

Jack had decided that love did matter.

He had become like Amy.

Jack, of all people, had become a gypsy.

*   *   *

Two nights later, her cell phone rang, startling Cecelia out of a deep sleep. She fumbled for the receiver.

"Jack?"

"Cel. It's Finn."

"Oh." She rubbed the sleep from her eyes. The clock glowed 10:46 P.M. Why was Finn calling her? Was Camille on call tonight?

"Meet me. Can you get away?"

She struggled awake. He was whispering. Of course, he thought Jack was sleeping by her side. "Why? Is something wrong?" His voice sounded odd. Tense and nervous.

"Just come. 2102 Renny Street."

"Renny Street? Where is that?"

"I don't know. I've never been there. Joe's Pub. Just meet me."

"Why?" she asked wearily. Jack was gone. Amy was gone. At least someone was calling her. She was strangely grateful.

"There's a band," Finn explained, still whispering.

Poor guy, she should put him out of his misery of thinking he was tempting her out of her marriage bed.

Then she thought of Camille.

She didn't say a thing.

"They're playing in ten minutes. How quick can you get there?"

"You want me to come to a bar in the middle of the night to see a band? Um, let me see—no."

"The band is called the Finn Concord Five."

Now she was awake. She sat up in bed, the covers pooling in her lap. She was still fully dressed in her work clothes, which were wrinkled and stale. She hadn't washed her face, and her makeup felt heavy on her skin.

"Are you there?" he asked.

"Is Camille busy tonight?"

"What? Who?"

He didn't remember Camille? How casually did he sleep with women?

"I saw an ad in the paper for this band—"

"The Finn Concord Five."

"Right."

She climbed out of bed and looked in the mirror. Old mascara raccooned her eyes. Her wild black hair stuck out at alarming angles. She tried to smooth it to no avail.

He cleared his throat. "Will you meet me?"

She imagined the scene. A sweaty, dark club filled with drunk college students. In the back, on a tiny stage crammed with a drum set, stood a long-haired, ripped-jeaned, twenty-year-old gyrating over an electric guitar. *My One True Love is a shaggy dude in a lousy band.* The claws of her past gripped her tight, squeezing, tearing. A musician. A wanderer. Of course. The claws were pulling her back to her old life.

Does True Love matter?

She wandered into the living room and picked up the tiny statue of Shiva. She turned it over in her palm. Amy believed that True Love was everything. Amy possessed the single-minded blindness of a true believer: she did what she thought was right. Amy was—Cecelia took in a huge gulp of air to help the repulsive thought sink in— trying to help.

Finn was too. Only he had no idea what he was dealing with.

The Finn Concord Five.

Finn broke into her thoughts. "You know what? Forget it. It doesn't make any difference. I just thought I'd do you a favor and let you know."

Cecelia fell back in her bed. Maybe this was what she deserved. All her lying. All the scams of her past. It made sense that karma was paying her back. *A shaggy dude with a bass guitar is my One True Love.*

Cecelia paid the cabdriver, then stepped carefully onto the trash-strewn sidewalk. She looked around her in disgust: was this Finn's idea of a joke? She checked her watch. She was supposed to meet him in half an hour, the earliest she thought she could pull herself together. But instead she had thrown on dirty jeans, washed her face, and arrived early. She wanted to meet this new Finn without having to face the old Finn. Now, she wished desperately that he was there. Neon lights blinked all around her, beckoning her to "Girls! Girls! Girls!" A man with a dragon tattoo covering his entire face, the reptilian nostrils lined up with the human, stood in the doorway of an adult bookstore. Could you really tattoo an eyelid? He nodded at her and opened the door.

No thanks, my destiny is waiting for me—a shaggy dude in a band playing the back room of a strip club. I'll come back for my pornography later.

She felt ill. She was on the sleaziest street in Baltimore. And yet, somehow, it made sense. Karma. She was getting paid back for the sins of her past. Paid back with a sleaze-bag True Love who played guitar in the back rooms of scummy strip joints.

She spun away from the doorman, and retreated down

the street. This was a mistake. A huge mistake. Just because Jack decided to throw his life away for love didn't mean she had to. She would devote herself to work. Or to finding another man. No. Who needed a man? Work— that was the answer. More work.

She felt so empty, she was sure she'd float away.

She turned and walked back down the street. She searched the signs: Live Girls, Girls, Girls XXX, Peep Shows 50 cents, Manny's Adult Emporium.

Then, there it was: a small sign with a red pulsing neon arrow pointing down a row of steep stairs—"Joe's Pub." *Joe's Pub and Boobarama*, it should have read. Next to it was another sign, handscrawled in black marker: "Finn Concord Five, 11:00 P.M., five dollars."

Her stomach heaved. It was eleven-thirty.

An obese man at the top of the staircase barked at her, "You gonna block my action, lady?"

"Me? What? No. Sorry." She hurried away. She couldn't go down there alone, and Finn wouldn't show up for at least twenty more minutes. What was she going to do? Every stinking bar, every sleazy guy, every booze-soaked mark from her past, came back to her in a rush. This was just the kind of place that she and Amy had ended up after they left Jane and their dad. Sure, they had never been strippers or dancers; Amy's power protected them from that fate. But still, they had to seek out their desperate prey on streets like this.

She felt a chill down her back. The ghosts of the past were swirling around her. She had to sit down.

"Come, sit with me, dear," a voice beckoned her.

She spun around. An old woman dressed in gypsy's rags looked at her. Rather, the woman turned her face to her, but her eyes were so clouded, they were almost entirely white. Each muted pupil roamed in a different direction. The woman stood in the doorway of a storefront that was decorated in red velvet and Christmas lights. "Fortunes Revealed," a sign blinked in half burnt-out orange letters—Fortunes _eveal__.

"Oh, no, I'm okay." Cecelia backed away from the woman. She could just make out the faint shadow of a pupil under the woman's cataracts.

"Don't worry, dear-y. I won't take your money. Just sit down. I'll get you a glass of water until you feel better."

The woman was lying. She'd do everything in her power to take Cecelia's money. But a seat and a glass of water sounded good. She nodded and let the old woman lead her into the storefront parlor.

The blind leading the blind.

"There, there. You sit. I get you water." The old woman felt for her chair behind her. She sat down heavily, then clapped her hands. A bored teenage girl appeared wearing headphones. The old woman said something in a language Cecelia didn't recognize, and the teenager slumped away.

The woman regarded Cecelia with first one eye, then with the other, moving her head to make them rotate. "You are making a big decision. Those are hard. It's best to sit. Go about things slowly."

Something about this woman soothed her. "Are you blind?"

"Only my eyes."

Cecelia laughed out loud. "I'm the opposite." How

had she misjudged Jack so badly? How had she let Amy crawl back into her life?

"Oh, no. You are beginning to see. You have taken off your ring. You've given up a lot. That is good. Your journey has begun."

Cecelia looked down at her hand. The room was so dark, even she couldn't see tan lines from the missing jewelry. She searched the woman for her trick. Was there a microphone in her ear? A spy feeding her information?

The teenager reappeared with a glass of ice water in an enormous goblet. Cecelia gulped it down.

"You've taken the biggest step already. You've let go of some of the things standing in the way."

"In the way of what?"

"True Love, of course."

Cecelia fell back in her chair. "Oh, for God's sake, there's more to life than love," she muttered.

"He's coming for you."

"Who?"

"How odd—he's to be underground. Is he dead?"

"Finn put you up to this, didn't he?"

"Who is Finn?"

"You tell me."

The woman laughed. "You have to follow your passion."

Cecelia pulled a twenty out of her wallet and put it on the table. The woman's eyes rolled deliriously in opposite directions, but her hand darted out to grab the money, like a tiny animal (with excellent eyesight) snatching its dinner.

"Is the new Finn I'm about to meet The One?" Cecelia

felt her insides shift. It couldn't be—and yet, there it was: the truth she had been avoiding ever since Jack had left her: she wasn't here to be punished for her bad karma. *I am here to get a piece of True Love too.* Sure, she had promised herself to never care. Convinced herself that she didn't deserve it. But now with Jack gone, she wanted it. Just for a while. If he could have it, so could she. One little nibble of love, and then she'd go back to her responsible life.

That wasn't so dangerous. Was it?

That wasn't so greedy. Right?

After all, she wasn't like her mom, or her dad, or any of the others who had let themselves become consumed by love. She could handle a little bit and not become a junkie. One taste of The One. She'd open herself to him for a moment, feel the rush, then get her life back on track.

The fortune-teller's eyes wandered.

"Well?" Cecelia asked. "Is he The One?"

Suddenly both of the woman's eyes focused on Cecelia. "The One? My dear, don't be ridiculous. Nothing is predetermined. The future is entirely up to you."

Finn stared at the cardboard sign in horror. He had asked Cecelia to come to the sleaziest street in Baltimore. Why hadn't Trudy warned him?

Right, she had warned him. Over and over. *Don't do it!*

A little more information would have helped, though.

Joe's Pub sounded okay. Like a place with a roaring fire and brats and kraut. Now he saw that naked lap dancers might be more like it. Why hadn't the ad read "strip joint"? He looked up and down the street. Cecelia was nowhere in sight.

Every sign on the street was neon, flashing, and insistent: "XXX, Bare Naked," "Peep! Peep! Peep!" Every sign, of course, but one: "Finn Concord Five, 11:00 P.M., five dollars."

He studied the sign in a state of abject terror. The Finn Concord Five had to be a band, right? What else could they be? He looked up and down the revolting street. Hell, in a hole like this, they could be naked contortionist midgets for all he knew.

He tried his cell phone. But Cecelia's number rang and rang until her automated message service picked up. He clicked the phone shut. What could he say? Forget it? He knew she couldn't forget a Finn Concord.

Plus, he wanted to see her again.

Okay. Calm down. Maybe this was okay. After all, she couldn't believe that a midget contortionist was her One True Love. Another Finn Concord was about to be eliminated from the running.

This new Finn, whoever he was, was going to make him look awfully good.

But what if she believed that this Finn Concord was The One? That would mean Cecelia would leave that rat-bastard Jack. She'd never have to know the guy was cheating on her. She'd be the one doing the running off. *Jack*, she'd say, *this is Finn. He's short but he's flexible* . . .

He could save her from so much hurt.

And lose her at the same time.

He watched a mob of drunken college students stumble by. He looked at his watch. It was almost three minutes past the time she should have shown up. Maybe she was inside already. Maybe she had come early and he missed her. He looked up and down the street. No Cecelia.

Oh, hell. Was she sitting in this crap-hole alone?

He hurried down the steps. He had to get her out of here.

Chapter 23

Could she possibly get any lower? Cecelia watched Finn Concord gyrate on the tiny, backroom stage for a rowdy crowd of drunk college students. He wailed something that sounded like "baby you my llama." Cecelia tried not to listen too closely. Every so often, he'd grab an obliging fan's beer and slosh it in its plastic cup all over himself and the stage. Then he'd chug what was left of it to the hoots and cheers of the crowd.

Suddenly he spit beer out all over the audience and yelled, "I only drink Bud, assholes!"

Just weeks ago, I was sipping red wine at my engagement party.

She needed a drink. She went to the bar and ordered a beer, trying not to meet anyone's eye. It was almost midnight. Finn should be here any minute.

She finished the beer.

Maybe he was waiting outside. She *had* come in early. She turned back to her beer and the naked pole dancers.

"What's a nice girl like you doing in a joint like this?" Finn slid onto the empty stool next to hers.

"I have no idea," she said. Liquid relief spread through her veins at the sound of his voice.

Finn watched the man on the stage. "Maybe this is just his stage persona," Finn tried. He moved close to her, shielding her from the rowdy crowd. "He's probably very nice in person."

The deafening music was popping the bubbles in her beer. They watched the Finn on stage gyrate.

"Or not. Let's get out of here. Big mistake," Finn said. He took her arm.

Cecelia shook her arm free. Was he kidding? She stared at him in disbelief. She wasn't leaving. In fact, she had given the manager of the band—a lanky woman with blue hair—a note for Finn. It read, "I need to meet you. Please find the woman in the gray sweatshirt at the bar. It's urgent."

"Cecelia. When I called you, I didn't know this place was—" He nodded to the half-naked pole dancers.

"Well, the musical entertainment more than makes up for it." She winced at the chaotic music. The band reached a deafening crescendo, then fell silent. After a beat, the silence was filled with raucous applause.

He shouldn't have called Cecelia. Finn saw that now. She believed in the worst when it came to True Love, so of course she believed that the low-life jerk on the stage was her destiny. He should have known that she'd think that. Maybe he had only been thinking of himself when he called her. He'd wanted to see her so badly.

No, he had decided that this was the right thing to do. Of course, that was before he had known he was inviting her to sleazeball alley. *Nice second date, Finny.* Anyway, it was too late. It was done.

The applause died out and the audience rushed the bar.

Cecelia's eyes followed the sweaty lead singer as he greeted a bevy of rabid fans with elaborate hand slaps and head butts. "Finn Two," Finn had taken to calling the straggly musician—if musician wasn't too optimistic a word for the soaked, drunk man-child. Finn Two couldn't have been a day over twenty-five. Finn wished the guy would pull a shirt over his spindly, protruding ribs.

Finn Two began arguing with the bartender for free drinks. He gave the bartender the finger, turned, and checked out the scene.

Finn watched in amazement as Cecelia signaled him over with a determined nod of her chin and wave of her graceful hand.

To Finn's astonishment, Finn Two sauntered toward them, looking for all the world like a child Mick Jagger. Finn felt the urge to throw himself between them. But what if the guy *was* her True Love? Who was he to stand in the way of fate?

Oh, hell, he refused to believe in that nonsense.

Finn Two licked his lips. "Hey," he said to Cecelia. "Didja like the show?"

He didn't seem to notice Finn, which was remarkable, because Finn was sure he was foaming at the mouth, his teeth bared. What had made him think he could handle seeing Cecelia again? As if he were a selfless monk, calling her to introduce her to another Finn Concord.

"Like it? Ah, right, sure. It was very—" Cecelia paused.

"Entertaining," Finn supplied, trying to ease her distress. He had to shake off the urge to gather her up in his arms, kiss her despondent lips back to life, then pull out a sword and slice this guy's head off. Was that why he really called her? Because he knew deep down Cecelia's True Love couldn't be a guy in a band?

Oh, hell, he had to get a hold of himself. Not only was she engaged, but he was leaving town just as soon as his construction gig with Max was done. His crazy thoughts of maybe staying around awhile longer—for Maya of course—had ended abruptly the day after the gala. Maya had suddenly turned moody and weepy, and wanted to leave on the first train. Trudy had tried everything to cheer her up, even took her to play duckpin bowling yesterday, some ridiculous game he didn't understand that seemed to exist only in dark rooms in peculiar cities like Baltimore. But even that didn't help. She was despondent and wouldn't tell Finn why.

"Come here often?" Finn Two asked Cecelia, ignoring Finn.

Cecelia stared at the gyrating, bored dancers. "All the time."

"So that's an interesting name for your band," Finn said. He rolled up the sleeves on his shirt, baring his tanned muscles. He hit his fist into his palm. *Just testing, buddy*.

Finn Two looked at him like he had a raging skin disease. "Why? There's five of us. 'Finn Concord Seven' might have been interesting. Everyone wondering where the other two had gone." He laughed a snickering, grunting, drunken laugh.

"Probably passed out from a heroine overdose in the gutter," Finn mumbled. He turned to Cecelia. There was something so desperate about her tonight, but Finn couldn't put his finger on it.

"So, are you two from a record label, or what?" Finn Two asked.

Cecelia giggled nervously.

Good God. Did she just giggle? Finn stared at her, amazed. Cecelia was actually considering this punk. She was flirting with him. What was wrong with her? Right, she believed her flaky sister. That was how this all came to be. "We're not from a record label," Finn said.

Finn Two leaned in close to Cecelia. "Oh. Then you have something else in mind?" He regarded Finn suspiciously. "Threesies?"

Finn and Cecelia were both so shocked, they couldn't speak. Finn took a step forward, an animal rage rising in him. He wanted to skin the asshole alive. Wring his scrawny neck. He'd give them the Finn Concord Four and a half. Finn Two backed off, but Cecelia's eyes were blank; her shoulders slumped.

Then Finn looked down at her finger and saw that her ring was gone.

What had she said when he met her in her office with his picnic basket? Left hand. Ring finger. Yep, it was gone. Had she left Jack? Had she found out about Camille? *Is the engagement off?*

He positioned himself between Finn Two and Cecelia. He towered over them both. "Thanks for coming over, but I see now it won't work out. So scram. She's with me."

"I am?" Cecelia asked, surprised.

"Yes." He put his arm around her. "You are. And we're getting the hell out of here."

Chapter 24

Finn Two shrugged and wandered back to the stage.

"C'mon," said Finn.

Cecelia blinked up at him.

A rush of repressed feeling swamped Finn. "Where's your ring?" he growled. Then he cleared his throat. He tried to look distracted, as if his every fiber didn't hang on her answer.

"Jack left." Her voice was flat, as if she were telling a stranger the time.

I'll have to buy that putz a beer. Finn cleared his throat again. "You told him about Amy?" His body had gone haywire as every ounce of restraint flowed out of him like water, leaving him a dried husk, ready to ignite at the slightest spark.

"Amy told him the name of his One True Love." She threw her head back and downed what was left of her beer. She looked to the stage and sighed.

The second set had started, but it sounded pretty much like the first. He had to get her out of this dive. But first, he had to make her realize that she deserved better. "Jack is not your True Love and that man," he said, glancing over his shoulder with distaste, "is not fit to be the True Love of an ape." Finn grabbed her arms and gave her a gentle shake.

She straightened and moved away. He had to get a hold of himself.

"How do I know that? He might be," she said slowly. "That's what scares me."

Finn sucked in his cheeks, resisting the urge to scoop her up and carry her off. He couldn't be expected to restrain himself when she was being such an idiot. "That Name bull—" He stopped at the alarmed look on her face. He took a deep breath and tried slowly. "How could you believe Amy over the reality of how you feel about me? I mean, how you feel about that guy? Tell the truth—he makes you want to puke."

"True Love doesn't always give you what you expect."

"Expect!" He was furious with her. How could she be such an idiot? Didn't she see that there was something between them? Didn't she see that guy was a moron who didn't deserve to touch her shoe? She wanted what she didn't expect? Well, he could give her that. Without warning, he took her arm. He turned her to him and kissed her. Soundly. Roundly. Warmly.

She tensed and pushed away. Then, slowly, relaxed. She melted under his pressure. Softened. Her lips parted, and he tasted her deeply, drawing her in.

He cupped his hand under her head, deepening his hold on her. Her hair was silk under his rough fingertips. She was moving toward him, through him. He held her, just held her, his lips pressed to hers while the incredible rightness of her poured through him. To move was too much. To kiss was too much.

Then, all at once, it wasn't nearly enough. He ran his hand down her back and she shuddered under his touch. He pulled her to him by the small of her back and she came willingly. He bit at her ear, her neck. My God, this woman. He had been a fool. He was never going to let her go again.

She responded to his touch, his kiss, with her entire body. Her mouth opened to his, her hands ran through his hair, the length of her pushed against him, urgent and demanding.

"Cecelia." He moaned her name.

She pulled back and they looked at each other, Finn struggling to overcome his shock at the power of what had just occurred. Amazingly, life still went on around them, continued outside of her lips, her hand.

Well, most of it did.

They heard a thud, then a groan. Finn Two had passed out facedown on the stage. His band, now the Finn Concord Four, played on without him.

"Well."

"Well."

Her hand went to her lips, which buzzed with electricity.

"So."

"Right."

"I better get home," she said. "Work tomorrow morning." *That kiss*. And his body beneath her hands. Never before—

"Me too. Work."

She tried to shake off the tremor of him. "Um, so Camille—?"

He waved his hands in front of him. "Nothing. Oh, hell. No. I left with her so that Jack and your colleagues wouldn't suspect. She just gave me a ride home and we had a beer and played some cards."

Cecelia suddenly remembered the odd conversation she had with Maya ages ago, when Maya showed up at her work the very first time. *Then, since he's your True Lover, you can play cards . . . So you can get laid!* The little girl must think that "getting laid" had something to do with cards. Finn never slept with Camille. Cecelia felt her whole body electrify again. "I believe you. It's just that—" She stopped. *Don't ruin it. Just forget everything but him.*

"What's wrong?" His green eyes bore into her, their heat filling her every cell.

"Before we"—She took a deep breath. *Just take him home*—"get involved." She had to do this right. If she was going to start with him, she couldn't make the same mistakes and live a life of lies. *God, those incredible eyes and that kiss.* No. Calm. Truth. *Shoulders.* Deep breath. "Finn, there's something you have to know."

Methodically, tersely, like she was summarizing a complex case for first-year medical students, she started from the beginning. She explained how Amy had created the whole granny setup with Trudy in order to get him to come to Baltimore to meet his One True Love, and how Maya had gone along because she was worried about him and wanted a mommy. She got to the part where Maya jumped out of her closet when he seemed to understand what she was saying.

"Holy shit!" Finn jumped off his stool. "I have to get back to Maya. I can't believe I left her with a con-woman stranger liar. I trusted that lady. I can't believe that she— that your sister—that I. That you—" He shook his head as if maybe the truth were a small animal that he could dislodge.

"No. Not me—" She knew this moment so well. The moment where the conned finds out he's been had. In this moment, everything that happened before would be changed. He'd spend hours, days, running every moment through his mind, wondering how he missed all the clues. She felt so sorry for him.

She felt so sorry for herself.

"I have to go. I'll. I don't know. Call you." He was halfway up the stairs.

Cecelia still felt his lips on hers. "Okay," she said.

But she said it to no one; he was gone.

That night Cecelia got home to find a message on her answering machine from Jack. He was staying another week in Ohio. He'd call when he got back. She felt something odd in her stomach—it was warm and full. It was happiness. She felt glad for him.

And sad for herself. Not because he was gone, but because she was alone.

There was another message too. A man from the co-op board. The preliminary meeting was this month. They needed her and Jack's paperwork by Thursday. They were sure it wouldn't be a problem.

No. No problem, she thought, a tear rolling down her cheek.

No problems here at all.

The next morning, Cecelia stood in front of the steep steps that led to Trudy's, but she couldn't move. What if Finn was still here? What if he wasn't?

A breeze startled her. How long had she been standing here? She had to get back to the hospital. She had patients scheduled all afternoon. Do this quick, then go. In a rush of resolve, she darted up the steps and into the darkness.

She was blinded by the dimness. She made her way carefully into the narrow space. Her eyes adjusted, revealing the almost empty bar. A woman was behind the bar—Trudy. The shock of the past knocked the breath out of her. *Karma.* She recognized her now as the woman from their childhood pawnshop—only a hundred pounds heavier. No wonder she hadn't recognized her on the ball field. Cecelia could almost hear the old woman's heart abnormalities from where she stood.

In the back, a heavy man with a cigarette hanging out of his mouth played pinball.

This place was a cardiologist's nightmare.

She made her way carefully to the bar and sat down.

"He ain't here," Trudy said, not looking up from the glasses she was drying with a grayish towel.

Cecelia was startled that Trudy recognized her too. Suddenly Cecelia remembered Trudy's living room. How could she have ever seen Trudy's living room? Then she remembered: Trudy had taken care of them. Babysat sometimes when their father was on another Jane Smith quest and their Granny Molly was on one of

her extended trips abroad. Trudy had been—oh, hell—
like a granny to them.

Well, it didn't matter. Now she was a con woman and
Finn was gone. That was what Cecelia had come to find
out. Now she could go. Her heart constricted and she
scolded it: stupid organ. He wasn't right for her. He was,
in fact, everything she never wanted in a man—a man
from her old world.

She turned to go.

"He's at work." Trudy had scribbled an address on the
back of a napkin. She pushed it toward Cecelia.

My perfect man is still here! Cecelia took the napkin
as carelessly as she could manage. She glanced at it
quickly but she didn't recognize the street name.
"Thanks." She put the napkin in her purse. Her skin was
already tingling at the idea of seeing him again.

Trudy was grinning at her like a toothless monkey.
"Sexy man, huh?"

Cecelia blushed. Trudy always had been a bit of a
mind reader. "You know who I am?"

"Of course. The smart one in that crazy family." She
smiled, as if to say, *Who's the smart one now?* "Hear
you're a fancy doctor."

"Hear you're working with Amy."

Trudy showed her gums. "Always a pleasure that one.
And the little girl is something. I begged them to stay. But
Finn was too mad. I'll miss them until he comes around.
I'm pretty sure he'll come around. He's too good to Maya
to keep her from her granny—"

"You're not her granny," Cecelia reminded her.

"I wish I were," Trudy said wistfully as she swiped at

a decades-old stain on the counter. "And he is a fine-looking man. Ooh, if I had my molars—"

Cecelia tried not to let that image form. "Where is Maya?"

"Where else would she be? She's with Amy. Helping her clean out an old house or something."

Where else? Cecelia slid off the stool and made her way to the door. She pushed the door open and paused. Something felt so weird about this place. Then she looked up to the ceiling. The replica of the Sistine Chapel shone down on her.

"No one ever gets out the door without looking up," Trudy said, laughing. "No one. Not even Dr. Cecelia Burns."

Chapter 25

Cecelia told the cabdriver to pull up a block away from the address scrawled on the napkin. She paid, then walked cautiously up the street. She wished she had changed out of her work clothes. Her witchy clothes. Ahead, a group of men swarmed over a town house like ants—on the roof, the walls, in and out the front door. She recognized a few of the workers from the baseball team. When she got closer, she spotted Finn in front of the house, smoothing stucco on the front facade.

She stood on the pavement before Finn. She didn't know what to say. She wanted to leap into his arms and scream, *you stayed!* But that might ruin his stucco job.

He looked up and saw her. He looked at her a long, hard moment. She willed him not to turn away.

He said, "Hey, Max. I'm taking ten," without looking away from her.

A stout man with a clipboard nodded but didn't look up.

Finn carefully wiped his trowel. He balanced it on the porch edge, came to the sidewalk, and said, "Wanna see something cool?"

"Sure." She fell in beside him on the sidewalk. A sheen of white dust had settled over his hair, his face, his ripped jeans, his work boots. He looked like a ghost beside her.

They were silent except for her black pumps clicking authoritatively along the sidewalk, echoing through the empty streets, reminding her how out of place she was by his side.

They turned a corner, then another. They walked halfway down a street of small formstone-covered houses, and then she saw it.

"My God!" Cecelia took in the tiny postage-stamp yard before her. It was stuffed with more lawn ornaments than she'd seen in her entire life. Six flamingos towered over an army of garden gnomes. Two windmills were surrounded by all sizes and species of woodland creatures. "How did you find this?" A plastic owl winked at her from its perch in a small, flowering magnolia.

"I like to walk." There was a white scrolled bench in the center of the garden. A sign in front of it read, "Come in and Stay a While. All Welcome." He opened the gate. "My office, madam."

"We can't."

"Sure we can. I do all the time. In fact, I fixed Mrs. Sawatsky's front porch railing last week." He motioned toward the porch. "We're buddies." He led the way and she strolled around the garden in awe. Three plaster squirrels begged her for seeds. The windmills spun. Cecelia felt as if they were the only people on earth. Well, the only nonplastic people.

They worked their way down the side yard, which was equally stuffed with oddities. Finally she managed, "So?"

"So." He petted a plaster deer. "I told Trudy and Maya that I knew about the scam. They admitted everything. Not that they were the least bit sorry. Well, maybe Maya was a little sorry, in a self-righteous, eight-year-old sort of way."

"Turns out Amy came down to Florida after a detective had found me and a psychic agreed that I was the one." He sidestepped a plastic pooch that began barking "Jingle Bells" when they passed. "Amy pounced on Maya in a diner I used to let her go to for her chocolate milk shakes every Tuesday after school. I knew I shouldn't have let her drink those things." He shook his head ruefully. "Anyway, after a couple of weeks they became friends." He paused at the irony of the word. "They cooked up the granny scheme just like you said they did. But, Cecelia, you didn't tell me that Trudy cared about you. She said she knew you, took care of you, wanted you to be happy and to find True Love. It all sounded sort of fun and harmless."

"She thinks whiskey at 10:00 A.M. with a couple of cigars is fun and harmless." Cecelia wandered around the side of the house, halting at the stunning array of bunnies. Maybe the plastic ones multiplied too.

"Funny thing was, I knew something was wrong. Deep down. But I just wouldn't let myself see it."

"The person getting conned always knows. That's why the con works. The person wants to believe so badly, they go along even though they know." They moved into the backyard, which was just as small as the front. It was filled with knee-high plastic houses, an astonishing number of multicolored mushrooms, and one normal-sized shed pushed up against the fence. The shed looked like a castle next to its tiny yard-mates. Stone paths of alarming neon colors meandered through the chaos.

"I wanted Maya to have a woman in her life. Someone who'd love her unconditionally like her mom did. Someone who could make a damn ponytail."

Cecelia felt a tingle of excitement. *I could make a ponytail.*

"Maya and I moved out of Trudy's place. Maya wanted to stay but I said no. I said she could still see Granny—I mean Trudy—if she promised to keep everything honest. No lies. We got a room on the twentieth floor of the Belvedere. We're leaving just as soon as I get my next paycheck and get some kind of camp arranged back home."

"How's Maya taking all this?" They were at the center of the garden on a three-foot bridge that arched over a nonexistent stream. Giant plastic koi goldfish frolicked in the grass below them.

"Pretty good." He paused. "Actually, she blames you."

"Ouch."

"Yeah. I assured her that I won't have anything to do with you."

"What!"

He punched her lightly on the shoulder. "Kidding. Sort of." He paused. "Not really."

Cecelia blanched. Amy had said Finn would do anything for his kid and she wondered how true that was. "Heard you got a new babysitter." She strolled off the bridge and under a tree. At least the tree was real.

"I figure Amy owes me big time."

"Finn." Cecelia turned to him. "Last night—"

"I know." He touched her cheek with the back of his hand. "It was kind of sudden. I'm sorry."

She felt him fading away from her. "I'm sorry you're leaving."

"Yeah, well I'm sorry too. I was starting to like it here. But we can't stay in a hotel. Payday is Friday, and then we catch the first train out."

It was Tuesday. "Right. Well. I don't blame you." She bent down and patted a duck in a raincoat. Damn the truth. No. She had to keep on telling the truth. "I'll miss you."

"I'll kind of miss you too." He looked at her long and hard. "A good-bye kiss?"

She pulled back. "The baby woodchucks!"

"Oh, I'll keep it Disney." He leaned in and kissed her gently on the cheek. "How could I not in this place?"

Damn the woodchucks. Even Snow White got kissed on the lips. She corrected his kiss so that it found its mark. He was leaving. Damn him. She pulled him closer. The warmth of him spread to the tips of her toes. She couldn't let him go. Not when he kissed like this. Touched her soul. Every cell of her. She felt her whole being meld with his. Closer. Warmer.

Oh, God. A kiss like this—

He released her just enough to murmur, "I can't believe I'm gonna leave without ever properly running my hands through your hair."

She pulled him to her lips again, then reached back and yanked out the clip that held her hair to the back of her head. Her hair tumbled past her shoulders. Hell, if he was leaving, what was the harm? She didn't have to worry about who he was. He was just a make-believe handsome prince in an enchanted garden.

She felt the corner of his mouth raise half a centimeter as he pulled his fingers through her hair, catching the ends in his fist like a drowning man.

"You're gonna leave before I get to do this?" She pulled his hand to her lips and kissed it. He tasted like sweat and plaster and man.

He released her hair and cupped her chin in his hand and she nuzzled against it. "I'm gonna go just as soon as—" He found her mouth again and took her lower lip between his teeth.

"Sure. Right after—" She put her arms up and down the length of him, feeling the powerful muscles in his back respond to her touch.

His lips were against her neck. Biting her ear. Nibbling her hair. She was desperate for him. He couldn't leave before—no, that was impossible.

He pulled back and met her eyes. Then he nodded toward the shed.

All seven of the dwarfs watched them, grinning. Well, except for Grumpy, but what did Grumpy know about needing someone so bad that you'd swallow all the poison apples in the forest to feel his kiss one last time even if you were already drowning in the fact that you'd never see him again? She followed him to the shed. The door was unlocked. "Mrs. Sawatsky—?"

"She plays bridge at the community center on Tuesday mornings."

"I love that woman." She pulled him into the shed.

"Sorry, guys," he said to the dwarfs as he shut the door behind them. "Keep your eye out for the wicked witch."

*   *   *

Inside the shed was tiny furniture. A child's table with
toddler chairs. A small bed big enough for a few dolls.
They crashed through the useless furniture, giants oblivi-
ous of their destruction, ending up against the far wall of
the doll-like house. The cold metal of the wall behind Cecelia made the hard warmth of him in front of her even
more desperately necessary.

He kissed her neck feverishly, tearing her out of her
suit jacket. Out of her shirt. Her pants. Her panties hit the
floor and there was no turning back. She clawed off his
clothes in a frenzy, not aware of anything but the pure ex-
panses of skin exposed. She ran her hands down his back,
pulling him closer, closer. She needed him closer.

He pressed her against the wall with his full length, pin-
ning her hands to her sides. "I want to make love to you."

"Yes."

He spun around, so that his back was against the wall.
He pulled her onto him, wrapping her legs around his
waist, supporting her easily, cupping one hand under her,
the other behind her back.

She was floating, lost, nowhere. She felt him push inside her and she gasped with the shock of it. The perfec-
tion of it. Closer. Closer. She pushed into him and let her
head fall back. This was crazy. It was impossible. It
was—she let out a cry as her body rocked with his—it
was too fast. He filled her in a way no man had ever
filled her.

She muffled her cry on his shoulder and collapsed into
him. Her breasts against his chest, her arms limp around
his shoulders. He rocked into her, and she felt him climax
with a final thrust.

They stood that way, together, not moving, not sure what it was, exactly, that they had done.

Ten minutes later, they crept out of the shed, slightly disheveled and grinning. Now he knew why all those gnomes looked so happy. *They know what goes on in this place.* Cecelia's grin matched the gnomes' and Finn considered taking her right back in there so that her smile would never wear off.

He checked his watch. No. The only place he was going back to was work. He was going to have his pay docked if he didn't get back to the site—and he needed that pay. Plus, he had to figure out what the hell he had just done. He promised Maya they were going back to Florida. He promised Maya (and made her promise him) that they weren't going to have anything else to do with Cecelia and Trudy. And as soon as he didn't need Amy for babysitting, he'd be done with her too. Then, he was going to get himself and Maya as far away from this crazy family as possible.

At least, that was the plan before she blew his mind in that shed. Hell, that was cataclysmic. And they had been standing in a shed surrounded by children's furniture. Just imagine—

No. Don't imagine. Oh, hell. A woman like her—

He glanced at Cecelia, and was shocked by the change in her. Her smile was gone, replaced by a look of utter confusion. "What's wrong?"

"That was good," she said, plunking stiffly down onto a small bench.

"I know." He wiped a smudge of white plaster powder off her cheek.

"No. I mean scary good." She was staring into the distance, an actress reading stiffly off cue cards. "Too good."

"There's no such thing as too good." He sat down next to her. Every cell in his body joyfully ricocheted off every other cell in a riot of electricity. He wanted her all over again just to soothe the panic out of her eyes. A similar panic began forming in his gut. *Oh, hell.* He could see what was wrong in her eyes—she was terrified that her One True Love was him.

"I think you're it—my One True Love," she said. She looked down at the white powder covering her. She rubbed her hands over her sleeves, down her front. The powder wasn't budging.

He shrugged. "So, what's wrong with that?"

"We have great sex and then you die."

He felt endlessly relieved that she wasn't miserable because he wasn't an overeducated stiff. He was thinking the worst of her, which wasn't fair. Especially after what had just happened in that shed.

My God, what had happened in that shed? He felt the sensation of it course through him all over again. "It's reassuring to know you care. But I'm not gonna die."

She rubbed furiously at the dust clinging to her. Maybe she *was* worried because he wasn't an overeducated stiff.

"You can't believe that voodoo stuff. Something else is bugging you."

She considered for a moment. "Okay. Maybe it is. Maybe it's more like, we have great sex and then you leave."

"I can't stay here," he reminded her. He took a deep

breath. Might as well get this out in the open. "And you don't want me to stay."

"What?" Her eyes flashed.

"You think you do. Because you're lonely. Jack left. Amy left. And we just had life-altering sex. But face it, I don't fit in your world. I'm in construction. I'm working like mad to take care of my wife's medical bills. I have a kid who is going to end up in juvie lockup at the rate we're going. Look at you."

She looked down at her black suit. The white dust hadn't budged. "Don't do this, Finn. I'm not that same person you met three weeks ago."

"I have to do it, Cecelia." He took a deep breath. "We're not really meant for each other, no matter what the stars or spirits or whatever say. Even if the sex was—" Worth dying for? Worth living for? Worth risking his kid for? Oh, hell, was it more than sex? Did it matter? Or did getting Maya away from here matter? He was starting to lose his resolve. "Couldn't we just say what we had is great sex between two lonely people? Isn't that enough?"

Her voice was small. "We fucked in a shed. No, that's not quite enough." She was so white and still, she looked like she was going to turn to plaster herself, never leave the garden.

He looked at the fairies hanging from the trees and shuddered. "C'mon. You know it's not like that. What just happened was good. But life isn't about that. Life is the real world." He put out his arms but all he could encompass in their sweep were the elfland creatures. "Well, you know what I mean. And more importantly, it's about Maya."

"Right." She wrapped her arms around herself. Maya.

"I have to get back to work."

"Me too."

"I'm here till Friday. We'll talk."

"Right."

He gave her hand a squeeze, then let it drop. "I'll walk you back to the site," he offered.

"No. Thanks. I'm just going to sit here a minute and think. I'll call a cab." She didn't actually know where she was, but she'd deal with that later. Right now, she just wanted him as far away from her as possible so she could think.

He gave her one last long look, then threaded his way carefully between the statues.

He didn't trust her. Well, why should he? After all, he'd been conned by his kid, by Amy, by Trudy. And, in a way, by life when his wife died. He'd be a fool to trust her. But she had changed. She was sure of it. She remembered his words in her office what seemed ages ago: *A woman with your hang-ups would never condescend to be with a guy like me. And I would never condescend to be with a woman who thinks that love—and people— don't matter.*

She was a new person. Now all she had to do was to prove it.

Chapter 26

Cecelia called her office and told them she had a family emergency. She reached Elliot on the golf course, seventh hole, and he reluctantly agreed to cover for her.

She took a cab to her grandmother's old house. The street was exactly as Cecelia remembered it: dirty, gray, and noisy. Cecelia asked the cabdriver to let her off on the corner. She hurried past the toddlers drawing with chalk on the sidewalk. She smiled at two old ladies who stared back with stony suspicion. She counted down the row houses, just like she used to do when she was a kid, one, two, three, alley, four, five, six, alley.

Then she paused.

There it was. Graffiti-splattered plywood covered every window. The roof sagged. The gutters hung askew.

Her grandmother's house.

Grandma Molly had been dead for six years, seven in October; no one lived there anymore. Cecelia had closed the house up until Amy showed up again, so they could work out what to do with it. A handyman looked in on it every month, setting traps for rodents and keeping the furnace alive.

Cecelia paid the bills and didn't go near it.

But now, as she climbed the crumbling, concrete steps, she knew that Amy was inside. With Maya. And she had to talk to them both.

She stared at the old wooden door. Its owl-head knocker was rusty with disuse. She was about to try the bell when the door flung open.

Amy, wearing Cecelia's jeans, her polo shirt, and green rubber gloves, stood before her. A long, red scarf tied back her black hair. "I thought it was you," she said. She turned and went back into the dark hallway.

Cecelia followed her. A single bulb hung from the ceiling, throwing a harsh, shadowy light. Cobwebs strung everywhere, so massive they looked as if they were put up by spider carpenters to hold the place together. Spiders. Cecelia shuddered, imagining the eyes of thousands of creatures watching her from their hidden perches. "Please tell me that you didn't sleep here," she said.

"Well, all the four-star hotels were booked."

Cecelia wiped dust off a photograph hanging on the wall. She jumped back, startled to see a younger version of herself staring back at her. She wiped more dust. "Remember this day?"

Amy craned her neck to see the picture. "Oh, sure. I remember. Grans insisted that we see an Orioles game and I caught that foul ball."

"I caught it. You knocked it out of my hands."

"Whatever." Amy walked to the kitchen and Cecelia followed. This was obviously where Amy had decided to start cleaning. Half the floor was dingy gray, the other half was almost black. Amy stuck a mop into a bucket of black water and halfheartedly swished it in circles.

"Ames? What are you doing?"

"Moving in."

"You can't live here unless you're a spider. Or a rat."

"Why are you here, Cecelia?" Amy asked. She stopped mopping and rested her chin on the handle. Then she let the mop handle fall into Cecelia's arms. "To help?"

"I'm looking for Maya. I need to talk to her." Cecelia caught the mop. "This place is haunted."

"So? Don't tell me you're afraid of ghosts?" She put her hands on her hips. "Maya's upstairs sleeping. Apparently, she didn't get much shut-eye last night 'cause she was up till dawn crying."

Cecelia pushed the mop, painting a streaky, greasy smudge on the floor. She lugged the dirty bucket to the sink. She sloshed out the repulsive mess, then filled it again. Well, it wasn't like she didn't have to bring her suit to the cleaners already anyway. The water that came out of the tap was brown.

Amy leaned against the counter, watching Cecelia rinse the bucket. "Do you remember when we all lived here?"

"Sure. Do you?"

"I remember little things. The space under the stairs that we used as a clubhouse. The time we crawled out on the roof."

"You crawled on the roof," Cecelia corrected.

"Right. And you told on me."

They listened to the water fill the bucket. "Where's the soap?" Cecelia asked.

"What soap?"

"No wonder nothing's getting clean," Cecelia shut off the water. "Amy, this house is a five-year project."

"I've got time."

"Yeah, but you need more than time. You need carpentry skills and tools and—"

"Money," Amy finished.

Cecelia nodded.

"I'm gonna get a job."

Cecelia shook her head. "Well, that's a first."

"No. I really am. I've got a lead. I'm going to be a waitress."

"A waitress? You've never—"

"Doesn't matter. It's a Mexican place. They think I'll pass."

"Pass as a waitress or as a Mexican?"

Amy frowned. "You know, this is where I found my power."

Cecelia remembered the day as if it were yesterday. Was that why she never came back here?

"C'mon. I want to show you something." Amy took off up the back stairs that led out of the kitchen.

Cecelia stood, rooted to the spot. She didn't want to go up there.

"C'mon," Amy called from somewhere above. "Just don't wake up Maya."

Cecelia swallowed her fear. What was she afraid of, anyway? She climbed the narrow, twisting stairs. Cobwebs hung everywhere, reached down, and brushed against her skin. She shuddered.

When she got to the top of the stairs, Amy was gone. Cecelia walked cautiously down the creaky hallway. "Ames?"

"In here," she called quietly from their childhood bedroom. They had shared it for almost six years. Cecelia stood in the hall, frozen. What was wrong with her? She didn't believe in ghosts. It was the middle of the day. There was nothing to fear.

"Cel?" Amy poked her head out. "Look at this." Then she pulled her head back and another head poked out.

Lucy the talking bear. When Amy was little, she used to pretend that the voices in her head came from the bear. A five-year-old's brilliant rationality. "Hello, Cecelia," Amy said in a high, squeaky voice, pretending to be the bear. "You look so well after all these years."

Cecelia groaned.

Amy made the bear wave.

Cecelia threw her purse at its head.

"Ouch!" Amy pulled the bear back. "Watch it. Maya's sleeping in the next room."

Cecelia retrieved her purse, then slowly moved into the bedroom. "I always wondered what happened to that thing. Let's burn it."

"No!" Amy hugged it to her chest. "Never!"

Cecelia flopped down on the dusty mattress. "This is creepy."

"Nah. Your place with all that green fuzzy furniture is creepy. This place is nice."

Cecelia looked at the wall behind the bed. The wall between their room and their parents'. "Remember how thin that wall was?"

"We could hear everything!" Amy flopped down next to her.

Cecelia tried to remember what she had heard. All she could remember was tiny Amy, sharing a bed with her, sweaty and crabby, singing herself to sleep with the names that flew through her head. "Did you hear them have sex?" Cecelia asked.

"EWWWW!" Amy threw Lucy at Cecelia. "Yuck! No! Don't you remember? The fighting?"

"No."

"No? They were like cats and dogs. It never stopped."

"You mean after you told them their Names? Right before Mom left to find her One True Love?"

Amy sat up and looked down at Cecelia. "No, dummy, I mean always. They always fought."

"You just don't remember when they were happy. You were too young."

Amy raised her eyebrows. "Cel, we lived with Grandma because Dad couldn't get a job. He was such a dreamer, he never fit in with the real world."

"Not always. That was after Mom left. After the Names."

"We ALWAYS lived with Grams," Amy said, "even before Mom left. He never had a job. He was an unemployed tinkerer who slept in his childhood bedroom between his mother and his kids. Cel, he was a mess. That was why Mom left. He couldn't deal with the real world."

Cecelia closed her eyes. She tried to remember it that way. But it didn't fit. Amy had it wrong.

"Don't you remember the sound of Mom crying? She would cry and we could hear her. Don't tell me you don't remember that?"

"I remember," Cecelia said softly. "But it was after."

"I'm sorry, hon. It was always."

Chapter 27

When she heard footsteps enter the room, Cecelia jolted awake. She looked at her watch. Four in the afternoon—she must have fallen asleep.

Amy was gone and in her place Maya stood at the foot of the bed.

"Don't do that! You gave me a heart attack," Cecelia complained.

"So. You're a doctor. You could fix a heart attack." Maya sat down heavily on the bed and pulled Lucy the stuffed bear into her lap.

Surely, I don't have to tell you that doctors can't fix everything. Cecelia tried to decide where to start. The girl looked so young with that bear in her arms. "You were sleeping too, weren't you? You have bed head."

"So do you."

Cecelia felt her hair. "Yeah. You want me to do yours?"

The girl considered. "I like your house. It's creepy like you." She moved toward Cecelia and turned her back.

Cecelia rummaged in her purse for a comb. She pulled it through Maya's hair as gently as possible. Her hair, which only seemed mussed on the surface, was actually a rat's nest of tangles. "I wanted to talk to you about that."

"Yeah?" She let her head tense and relax into the rhythm of Cecelia's strokes.

Her hair was so thin and delicate. And so perfectly blonde. "Grown women would kill for this hair." She moved to Maya's side. "I'm going shopping this afternoon. If you want to come and help me buy some better clothes—"

Maya turned to her. "If you're my dad's True Love then that means my mom wasn't."

Cecelia turned the girl back and continued to comb. "Well—" *When one True Love dies, another is formed . . . a person can have two True Loves . . .* No. The truth, she was working on the truth. "That's true."

"I don't mind. Because Mom and Dad had to get together to have me. If a person can have One True Love then why can't they have one true kid? Right? So they had to get together to have me and then Mom went to heaven and can be reborn and this time she'll find her One True Love and be happy." She paused. "And healthy."

Cecelia considered this. "Sounds logical."

"So it's okay if you're my dad's One True Love. I mean, if you get new clothes and promise to stop butting into my business."

"You want a bun?"

"I want a ponytail."

"Right." Cecelia shuffled through her purse for a band. "I had to tell your dad about Granny Trudy. He had to know. See, I'm trying a new thing that is working really well. You should try it. It's called telling the truth. That's what I do now. Always. Tell the truth. It's because of you, you know." She found a much too big plastic clip. It would have to do.

"So now I don't have a mom and I don't have a granny. And I have to go back and have a boring summer at stupid camp while Dad works. So thanks a lot. Great time to get honest." Maya struggled with her pocket and produced a worn, yellow elastic band.

Cecelia considered Maya's interpretation of her future as she captured Maya's hair and expertly trapped it in the hair band. She pulled it tight and Maya flinched slightly. "Perfect." She admired her work. "I think your dad wants to stay in Baltimore."

"Oh, yuck! You kissed him, didn't you? He promised—" Maya jumped up and went to the mirror over the dresser. She wiped it clean of dust and nodded her head approvingly at her hair. "He promised he wouldn't do that."

Guess I shouldn't go into what else he did. Cecelia felt strangely thrilled at Maya's perfect ponytail. "I really want you to try this truth thing with me. Especially with your dad."

"Okay. I don't like you."

"Oh. Well. That's truthful. Good."

"But you make a good ponytail."

"Well, there's that."

Just then, the doorbell rang. They heard Amy's footsteps in the hall below. Amy's voice floated up the stairs.

Cecelia could make out a man's voice, low and urgent. She strained to hear better. It was probably Mario, the man who took care of the place. He must think that Amy was a squatter.

"C'mon." She made her way down the stairs, Maya following. The kitchen was almost as dirty as it had been a few hours earlier, except now, the whole floor was dingy and streaked. Cecelia hurried through the kitchen and down the hall.

Then she froze.

Finn saw Cecelia and froze too. "Oh. Hi."

Amy looked from Cecelia to Finn to Maya and then back to Cecelia. "Well. Looks like we've got a party."

Amy held the door open and he came in. "Nice place. Refinish these floors and fix that plaster, and it'll be almost inhabitable." He got down on one knee to inspect the floors. "Hey bugger," he said to Maya when she squatted down next to him. "Mouse hole. See it?"

"We put steel wool in it," she said.

"And then you patch it up. That's my girl."

"Yeah, well, easier said than done," Amy said.

"Nah. It's easy. I could do it for you."

Cecelia blanched. "No." *Yes!*

Finn tapped his fingertips over the plaster on the wall. He paused at a spot and pushed. His fingers sank into the rotted wall. "I'd have to replace most of this framing."

"Daddy, we're leaving."

Amy rubbed her hands together. "You're hired."

Finn wiped the plaster onto his already stained jeans.

"Daddy." Maya put her tiny hands on her nonexistent hips. "Can we talk?"

"Sure. C'mon. We'll sit on the steps outside."

Maya followed her daddy out with her chin in the air. Proud to be the woman with the upper hand.

* * *

Cecelia was in the kitchen, whacking down spiderwebs with a broom when Finn and Maya came back in. Finn had a funny look on his face and he'd gone a bit gray around the gills.

"So." He leaned against the counter.

"So," Maya picked up. "Daddy wants Amy to tell him who his One True Love is so that we know if it's you or not and we can quit messing around."

Cecelia dropped the broom. It clanked to the floor. "He doesn't look like that's what he wants."

"I do," he said.

"See, Daddy doesn't believe. So I said, what's it matter if Amy reads him or not? See, it's like Santa Claus: if you really believe—"

Amy walked into the room. Everyone fell silent.

"What?" She looked from face to face.

Maya huffed. "Daddy wants you to read about his One True Love."

Cecelia felt slightly ill. "Let's go into the living room." She had to sit down. There was an old couch in there.

They all followed her into the dusty, huge room. Spiderwebs hung from every surface. The windows were still boarded except for one that Amy had torn the plywood off. Dirty sunlight streamed in, lighting the dense dust floating in the musty air.

Cecelia flung herself onto the couch and sat on her hands to stop their tingling. If he was her One True Love, then that was good. Right? They had something going on, something electric. But then, her life. A man like Finn and a girl like Maya in *her* life. And then, there was the part about her One True Love having only days to live.

"You look a little gray, there, Cel," Amy said. "I won't do it unless it's what you want."

A chill raced up Cecelia's spine. Was this what she wanted? Or did she want Jack to come back and Amy to go away and this house to get boarded back up so the rats could play? *And then Finn wouldn't have to die*. She shuddered in the icy air. The curtains, the spiderwebs, the whole world was still, waiting.

I might be sitting in the same room as my beloved, my One True Love as assigned by Fate. She regarded Finn. Everything she ever wanted—stability, respectability, distance from the underbelly of life—would be gone if he were the one. He'd never fit into her world.

He'd be a dead man.

And if he wasn't The One—what then? Would she go to California and find that lawyer named Finn? Wait for Jack? Be alone?

Or, have really great sex with Finn until Friday when he split, even though he wasn't her One True Love? Just fun sex. To celebrate the fact that he wasn't condemned to death—or to loving her forever.

"Cel?" Amy asked. Her voice shook.

Hell, Amy was nervous too. Why was *she* nervous? Finn tapped his foot too fast against the dingy floor. His lips formed a straight, tense, white line. Cecelia looked at Maya, and she felt the hairs raise on the back of her neck. The child looked like she was watching a horror movie. *The Revenge of the Idiotic Grown-ups*.

"Are we doing this or not?" Finn asked. "Maya and I are starving and I promised her a movie tonight."

"With popcorn," Maya added. At least one person in the room seemed to know what was important.

"I don't have to tell him if you don't want," Amy said.

"You can't not tell me," Finn said.

"Tell him," Cecelia said. "Go on. We've come this far."

Chapter 28

Amy took a deep breath, then stared at Finn. Really stared. She put her hand on his arm and drew him in deeply with her eyes. She snapped her eyes shut. She squeezed them tighter and tighter. Then she opened them again.

Amy dropped his arm and got up. She strode to the ancient fireplace and squatted before it.

"What's wrong?" Cecelia asked.

"I can't get a signal." Amy said it so quietly, Cecelia wasn't sure she had heard her right.

"What do you mean you can't get a signal?" Finn asked.

"I can't hear the name. I'm getting a voice, but it's faint."

"This is ridiculous," Finn said.

"Give her more information," Cecelia said. The disappointment of not knowing seeped into her stomach like a poison.

"Daddy, this is spooky," Maya put in.

Finn paced the room.

"Is there something that could be blocking you?" Cecelia asked Amy.

"Maybe it's this house. There's too much interference," Amy suggested.

"Yeah. This place is starting to give me the creeps," Maya said.

"No, it's him. He's giving off—something."

Finn looked annoyed. "All right, I don't know what kind of game you two are playing."

Amy cut in. "It's not a game." She looked horrible. Sweaty and white.

Finn looked at Amy long and hard. "Franklin," he said. "My name's Finn Franklin Concord. And me and Maya are going to go see a movie."

"Don't go!" Cecelia heard herself cry.

Finn stopped.

"Is your middle name really Franklin?" Cecelia asked. Her whole body went cold.

Amy was doing her stare again. She put her hand on his shoulder.

"You know, my whole life, I hated that damn name. I have a funny feeling I'm about to hate it even more." Finn tried to back away from Amy, who was rocking, trancelike beside him.

"Shhhh!" Amy whispered. "I'm getting a voice."

Everyone froze.

"It's coming. It's getting louder." Suddenly Amy snapped her eyes shut.

"This is nuts." Finn started to walk toward the door.

After a dramatic pause that seemed to last an eternity, Amy's eyes opened. "I've got it!"

Finn stopped in his tracks.

"Who?" Finn and Cecelia both cried at once.

Amy fell onto the couch, clearly exhausted by her efforts. She shook her head at Cecelia.

"What?" Cecelia cried.

"He's not The One." Amy's voice was small.

Cecelia went numb. She blinked. She snuck a glance at Finn. He'd be gone within ten minutes, off to search for his True Love. No one could resist the pull.

He shook his head, pursed his lips. "Who is my True Love?"

Amy, who had closed her eyes, remained completely still. "Do you know someone named Cindy Reidel?"

Cecelia held her breath.

He paused. He narrowed his eyes. Finally, he said, "Yeah."

Cecelia let out the breath that she hadn't realized she was holding.

"Well, that's her. Cindy Reidel."

Cecelia locked herself in the ornate upstairs bathroom and splashed ice-cold water on her face. She met her eyes in the mirror and stared into them accusingly. *Stupid, stupid, stupid*. She had let her guard down for an instant, and somehow Finn had snuck in. Now, just as quickly, he belonged to another woman.

What was wrong with her?

Maybe she just wanted somebody.

"Cel? It's me. Your not-true Love," Finn called in through the door.

"Bug off," she said. She ran the water harder. It splashed in the old marble basin with a satisfying surety. She watched it swirl down the drain. She had thought that he was The One. The talks they had over the last few weeks had been so natural, so honest. And then there was that shed. And his middle name was Franklin. But he was still the wrong Finn Franklin Concord. There must be another one.

"Um, Cel? Listen, I think we should talk this over. Figure out what to do."

"That's easy. You should go off in search of Cindy Reidel."

"You know, I'm not very happy about this either," he called through the door.

"Really?" She marched to the door, but didn't open it. "Why?"

"Sex. I thought we'd be good together."

Thank God he couldn't see her smile through the door.

"Although, I suppose the good news is that I'm not dying."

Oh, hell. She opened the door. She turned her back on him and walked back into the bathroom. She sank down onto the edge of the claw-foot tub. "Congratulations. Not being tied to me is the best thing that could happen to you."

He came into the room and leaned against the tiled wall. "You really believe this psychic mumbo-jumbo?"

"Don't you?"

"No. I just couldn't figure out any other way to get you to open the door. C'mon now. You're a doctor. You know that spirits don't exist."

"I told you before. I've seen the Names in action."

"Ridiculous."

"I envy you." Cecelia ran her finger along the tub's cold enamel.

He strode to the sink and shut off the running water. It didn't shut off all the way, and dripped into the basin. He fiddled with the handles. She listened to the rhythm of the drops. It was the slow drip of life. Her life, dripping away.

"If it's not true, how did Amy come up with the name Cindy Reidel?"

"Amy hung out in my town for months, Cel. It's a tiny place."

"Who is she?"

"Oh, for crying out loud, I'm not going there. Forget Cindy. This is about us." He gave up on the sink and sat down on the edge of the tub next to her. "I changed my mind. I think we should be together." He paused. "This place is a mess."

"Yeah."

"I can help you guys fix it up." He stood and began a survey of the room. "Truth is, there's nothing for us back in Florida. I could use the better-paying work here. And Maya likes it here. Don't ask me why, but she changed her mind about you. Something about the way you did her hair." He turned on the tub, watched the water flow, then shut it off.

Maya likes me. Cecelia was shocked at how important this suddenly seemed.

"Plaster needs work. Plumbing's about to blow. Chimney's coming down if a feather lands on it. Probably have to gut most of the walls." He paused. "I'd do it in exchange for a place to stay plus expenses and forty dollars an hour."

Cecelia considered him. Now that she knew that he wasn't her True Love, he was just a guy—okay, a guy with whom she happened to have awesome sex, but still. Nothing to do with her. What harm would it do to let him fix the place up? As mad as she was at Amy, she hated the idea of her living in this squalor. It would take time and effort to find a decent contractor this late into the summer. "Thirty dollars an hour. But you can't stay here. The rats and spiders would eat you alive."

He shrugged. "Nothing I'm not used to. Thirty-five dollars."

She watched him look out the window. Hell, she couldn't help it. She still felt drawn to him in a way that she couldn't describe. "You and Maya can stay at my co-op for a few weeks until this place is okay enough to live in."

He met her eyes with a questioning gaze.

"We'll hardly even see each other. I work all the time," she explained quickly. "Plus, Amy will be there too." She had already decided that she couldn't let Amy live in this dump, no matter what awful things she had done.

He hesitated.

"Okay. Forty-five."

"Forty dollars." He smiled. "Apartment mates." He put out his hand to shake.

She took it, ignoring the zing of energy she felt at his touch.

It obviously didn't mean a thing.

Right?

Chapter 29

Cecelia cuddled into her giant bed. Finn was on the couch in the living room. Amy was back in the guest bedroom with Maya.

Cecelia stared at the ceiling. She looked out the huge plate-glass windows at the blinking lights of the city and the harbor spread out below her.

Oh, hell. She couldn't sleep.

She threw off her covers, slipped her feet into her slippers, and padded to the kitchen. A little warm milk and a magazine would put her out.

Finn shifted on the couch. His leg hung over the edge.

She went to the fridge and got out the milk. While it heated in the microwave, she watched his silhouette.

"Quit staring and come on over here," he said into the darkness.

"I'm not staring," she lied. "I just couldn't sleep."

"Me neither. C'mon. We'll see what's on."

He sat up and she could see the tapering outline of his torso in the dim light. Guess he forgot his jammies. She wondered if there was anything on under the sheet that pooled in his lap. God, she hoped there was. *She hoped there wasn't.* She padded into the living room and stood at the edge of the couch. "We have nothing in common," she said finally.

"We don't have to have anything in common to watch TV together." He pulled in his legs to make room for her.

She plopped down on the far end of the couch, as far from him as possible. She clicked on the TV and the blue light bathed them in an eerie glow. They watched the channels click by. Talk shows, infomercials, old movies. She tried not to look at his powerful body. "So where are you from?"

"All over. I grew up in Virginia."

"Sounds nice."

"It was."

"Do you miss her?" She stopped flicking and they both watched Esther Williams swim. She could hear her own breath.

"My wife? Sally? Like crazy."

Cecelia didn't want to know any more. He was here. He was real. Esther Williams pulled herself out of the pool, water streaming down her body.

"C'mere," he said. He held out his hand.

"Me?"

"No, Esther. Yes you. C'mere," he repeated.

She could snuggle. Snuggling wasn't bad. After all, Maya was sound asleep in the back room with Amy. She crept to his side of the couch and he put his arm around her. She let her eyes fall shut as she took in his warmth, desperate for it.

They watched the screen. Esther was now dressed primly, talking to an actor Cecelia didn't recognize.

Finn pulled her closer.

Being held made her woozy with regret. What was she doing with her life?

"Are you crying?" he asked.

"No," she snuffled. Oh, hell. She was crying. "I wish that I didn't believe in Amy," she said.

"So don't."

"I can't just not believe."

"Why not?"

"It's real, Finn."

In answer, he put his hand under her chin, raised her face to his, and kissed her. She let her lips fall open and his tongue danced over them, so softly she wasn't sure if she felt his touch or just his breath.

"This is real."

She put her hand on the side of his face. He was real. His kiss was real. Her longing was real.

"Believe in yourself," he whispered.

Was it really that easy? She closed her eyes and let the world dissolve around her. His warmth enveloped her, his touch aroused her. She pulled him closer.

He kissed down her neck, along her collarbone. He turned her to him, and shifted so that his weight was above her. "Believe in this," he said as he returned to her lips. This time his kiss was harder, more insistent, the roughness of his face awakening her skin, her desire. His hand was firmly on her hip, bracing her.

She pushed against his hand, suddenly urgent to feel more of him. But he held her apart from him, continuing his searching kiss over her lips, around her eyes, down her neck.

"Finn." This was crazy. She was hot and blind from his kisses.

"Shhh." He traced her lips with his finger, then let his weight settle next to her. "Just listen. Close your eyes and listen." He snuck his hand under her pajama top and she shuddered at the sensation of rough skin on smooth. He cupped her breast and sighed and she sighed.

She didn't want to listen, she just wanted to feel. She let her hands roam his shoulders. Down his tapered back. He wore a pair of boxers, and she slipped her hand under the waistband and pulled him to her.

"Cel." His voice came from a million miles away. "Do you have protection?"

"I'm on the pill."

He turned her face to his. "Is that enough?"

"You weren't asking that in the shed." She wanted him so badly she could feel her desire like a separate being, controlling her. "Yes."

"Are you sure?"

She wasn't sure of anything. He was the wrong Finn. Amy wanted her to have True Love, if he was the right one, she would have said so. He was the wrong Finn and she didn't care. "Yes."

"Hold on." He jumped up and suddenly she was alone, cold. She repositioned her clothes and watched him fish through the pockets of his jeans. He came back and stood before her.

He took her breath away.

As he unrolled a condom, she tried not to peek at its size. Then, suddenly, he was back with her and she was warm again, enclosed again.

"Where were we?" he asked.

She shimmied out of her shirt, then he helped her out of her pants. They dove under the comforter for cover.

"Here," she said, settling down again. "We were right here." Don't think, she reminded herself. She could think later.

He ran his finger up and down her stomach. "Here is good."

"Yeah. Here is good." She closed her eyes and felt his weight on her. He started kissing her all over again and she melted into him.

"Cecelia?" he asked.

"Hmmm?" she said. Then she saw the look in his eyes and said, "Yes, now."

He pushed her legs open with his thigh, and she let her head fall back. *Yes. Now. Please.* She hadn't realized how badly she had wanted this, waiting for it. A lifetime.

He pushed inside her all at once. She rocked into him. This man. This place. This was good. It was all good and nothing else mattered but the rhythm of them, moving together. They were underwater, submerged in desire, in each other.

"Finn." She needed him closer. Stronger.

He responded to her movement, her words, her every breath. He was exactly where she needed him to be but it was too much. His knowing, his power, his surety, overwhelmed her. Her toes curled into the liquid warmth of him.

"God, Finn."

He was part of her, above her, controlling her. She gasped into him. He tensed, prolonging her, teasing her. She lost track of time, of herself. Then, with a slow, small cry, she came into his final thrust, feeling him climax too.

"Cecelia," he whispered.

She shuddered at the power of what they had just done. My God, what had they just done?

"Cecelia Burns," he whispered again. He stroked her hair.

She clung to him, unable to pull him close enough. "What?" she whispered back. With him it was like nothing else. It was like magic.

"Nothing," he said. "Just your name. I'm just hearing it, in every cell of my body, that name."

And for that moment, she let herself believe.

Chapter 30

Cecelia came in the door from a grueling day at work—three codes in two hours, one which was clearly a DNR (Do Not Resuscitate by order of the family). The nervous medical student on duty had called the code anyway, and Cecelia didn't arrive until they had the poor ninety-seven-year-old woman intubated and hooked up to every machine in the ward.

It made her think of Fate. Of how maybe Fate had intruded into the family's plans for the sick woman, how maybe Fate had needed this old woman to live a few days longer. Just as it needed Finn to live. To not be her One True Love so that he could take care of Maya, get the happiness he deserved.

She'd have to let him go, eventually. The fact pulled at her. He had to be happy and being with Cecelia was keeping him from the ultimate happiness.

She thought of the amazing time they had last night, on that couch. *The ultimate happiness*. No sense in rushing anything. They could have their own sort of happiness for a while. That wasn't a crime.

Amy plodded down the hallway in her bathrobe and

slippers, eating cold Chinese food out of the carton with her fingers.

Cecelia peered around Amy. "Where's Finn? Where's Maya?"

"Man, this is no fun," Amy said. "Look at me—I'm lazing about. It's seven at night and I haven't even gotten dressed today. You're so damn happy that I can't even get you mad at me anymore."

"Mad?" Cecelia barely looked at her. Where was Finn? She'd been waiting all day to see him. "Why should I be mad?"

"Slippers! Jammies! I took the day off. Doesn't that piss you off?"

Cecelia patted Amy's shoulder distractedly. "No. You're right. I'm too happy to be pissed off."

"Oh? And why are we so happy, my little fleshpot?" Amy asked. "Did my big sis get her mind blown last night with a very naughty man—"

Cecelia couldn't help herself. "A very sexy, knowledgeable, naughty man—"

"Why thank you! You're pretty sexy and knowledgeable yourself, Doctor." Finn sat up from where he'd been lounging with a magazine on the couch. He was freshly showered and wearing a T-shirt and jeans.

Cecelia felt her face go red. "Where's—?"

"Maya's having a sleepover with Granny Trudy."

"*Granny* Trudy?"

"Yeah. I think she'll always be Granny Trudy whether I like it or not." Finn held up his hands in surrender.

"I don't suppose anyone made dinner?" she asked. She let herself fall into a lime green slipper chair across from Finn. She pulled off her sensible hospital flats. She had been seeing patients from seven in the morning until six-thirty at night and she hadn't eaten all day.

"I can order in," Amy said brightly.

"Or we can just eat the leftovers. How did you get that Chinese food? Did you use my credit card?"

"I started an account—"

"Amy!" Cecelia fell back in her chair. Now that she had located Finn and gotten her fix, she could muster some anger at her little sister.

"In my name!" Amy protested. "I got the job. Starting tomorrow I'm a waitress at Santa Anna's. My name tag says 'Maria.'"

Cecelia blinked in surprise.

"It was that or Juan. They only had two tags."

Cecelia turned to Finn. "But you, lounging around, you're supposed to be fixing up Molly's place." She pointed an accusing finger at Finn.

He smiled at her and her whole body reacted. *Forgiven.*

"I worked from 6:00 A.M. until 5:00 P.M., lady. Hard physical labor. We contractors got you cardiologists beat by a mile."

Oh, right. He *had* been gone in the morning when she'd left. All this sex was making her stupid.

"Anyway, I'm making dinner tonight," Finn announced. He jumped up.

Cecelia watched him walk into the kitchen and thought, *who needs dinner?*

Amy winked at Cecelia. "*And* he cooks!" she whispered.

Cecelia ignored her sister and followed Finn into the kitchen. "What can you make?" she asked dubiously.

"Ah," Finn said. "Vat vould dee lady desire?"

Cecelia leaned back on the counter. *You.* "Oh, are we French? Well, in that case, how about omelettes with wild mushrooms in a cream sauce?"

"*Non*. Eet is not my specialty." He crossed the kitchen and pinned her to the counter with the length of his body. *His specialty.*

"Cheese soufflé with a baby greens salad?" His body was warm against her.

"*Non*." He guided her face to his and nipped at her lower lip.

"Leg of lamb with—"

He kissed her full on the mouth, stopping her words. She opened her lips to his. Warmth, then heat, then fire. He pulled her closer and she didn't resist.

"—with sex?" She gasped.

He kissed down her neck. "Ah, that vee only serve on Mondays." He pulled back and let his eyes travel the length of her. "Today, eets the vorld's best grilled cheese sandwich."

Cecelia's body went rigid.

"Vat's wrong? Dee mademoiselle does not like le grilled cheese?"

"I haven't eaten grilled cheese in twenty years."

He frowned at her serious tone. "Why not?"

"It's a little hard to explain." Cecelia sighed. She could eat a grilled cheese. It wasn't as if she were a little kid. "Okay. Grilled cheese tonight, but I'm making wild mushroom omelettes for you tomorrow morning."

"You won't have time to make omelettes tomorrow morning." He stroked her cheek.

She pulled back.

"What's wrong?" he asked.

"Is it the tenth?"

"*Oui.*"

She looked at the calendar hanging by the phone. "I'm supposed to be at an appetizer tasting for the wedding tonight."

"Don't you think that's a little ridiculous?"

"But I have an appointment that I didn't cancel." Cecelia looked at the man in her kitchen. "Right. I guess it's a little ridiculous."

Finn opened and closed the cabinets. "There's really nothing in this place." He smiled a very wicked smile. "Let's go to the tasting together."

"You mean pretend that we're a couple getting married?"

"Why not? It's a free meal."

"Me too!" Amy came into the room. "I am the maid of honor, after all."

"No way. It'll be a hundred happy couples and us."

"We're a happy couple."

"A happy threesome," Amy corrected.

"Exactly," Cecelia said. "No way."

"C'mon," Finn urged. "I worked eight straight hours dragging drywall up three flights of stairs. I don't really want to cook or shop and neither do you. Maya's at Trudy's all night. Let's do it."

He took her in his arms and she thought, *I'll do anything you say, buddy, just keep on holding me that way.* "Okay. But I'm not pretending anything."

"Right," Finn said. He looked at her long and hard. "I'm not either."

*   *   *

Cecelia would never have come if she had known it would be like this. Couples wearing white baseball hats that said "Bride," "Groom," "Worst Man," and even "Jilted Ex-Lover," filled the vast room. Chippendale dancers strolled by in their tuxedo pants and suspenders (and only pants and suspenders), stopping here and there to pose for pictures with giddy brides.

A woman with an oversized smile handed Cecelia a huge pen with a loopy, droopy white feather spiraling off the back. The pen said "Your Name and Date Here" in gold letters down the side. Another woman handed her a white and gold notebook with a pad of paper. Then she reached into the bag of hats. "Bride I presume?" the woman asked.

"Sure," Cecelia accepted the hat and stuffed it into her purse. She shouldn't have come.

"This is the time we have scheduled for your makeup consultation and your hair consultation if you choose to indulge," the woman said, handing Cecelia slips of gold paper. Then she gave Amy and Finn their hats. Amy got a hat that said "Maid of Honor." When the woman wasn't looking, she switched it for a hat that said "Still Available." Finn accepted an "Eligible Bachelor" hat, then stuck it immediately into the nearest potted plant.

"This is worse than the gypsy fiasco," Cecelia whispered to Finn as they entered the crush of people in the room. "I thought it was just an appetizer tasting." Waiters circulated with huge trays. Each tray had a number on it. Cecelia checked her pad of paper—right, she was supposed to check off what numbers she liked so they could be served at her wedding.

Her wedding. Emptiness engulfed her. My God, was

there still a part of her that wanted to plan the wedding? She looked around the room at the endless sea of happy couples. She took a roast beef sliver on a cracker off a tray and tried it. A little salty, but not bad. She wrote the number down on her pad with the quill pen.

"What are you doing?" Amy asked.

"Nothing."

"You're planning a wedding! Oh, goody goody. You know, I always said, forget True Love and just go for great sex." Amy grabbed three doughy poufs off a passing tray and stuffed two in her mouth.

Finn, who had been investigating an enormous ice sculpture imitation of Rodin's Kiss statue, joined them. "It's only four thousand dollars. What do you think, honey? Should we get it?"

Cecelia wasn't in the mood to joke. In fact, she was feeling sick. She was hanging out with the wrong man for great sex. She had to stop, to let him go. "I've got to get out of here," she said to them.

"Not before your makeover!" Amy cried. "Unless, of course, you want to give your appointment to me."

Cecelia handed all her paraphernalia over. "I'm going to the bathroom," she told them. "And when I come back, we're leaving."

Finn started to say something, then stopped. Cecelia pushed through the crowd of couples, surprised that tears were already in her eyes.

Chapter 31

She stared at herself in the bathroom mirror. This was pathetic. She was hanging out with a gorgeous guy for great sex, but he wasn't her One True Love. She let a solitary tear drop.

Okay, she had to get herself together. As soon as this was over, she had to make up her mind: Finn or True Love. Being with Finn was fun—hell, it was a lot of fun—but maybe it was time to get serious. Jack wasn't coming back. At least, not back to her. So, the next step was obviously to go to California and find that lawyer named Finn.

She splashed water on her face and rejoined the crowd. A waiter passed and offered his tray. Salmon, dill, a dab of créme fraiche on a sliver of French bread: the appetizer would have been superb if Cecelia hadn't stuffed it in her mouth the exact moment that she saw Jack across the room. On his arm, her grasp light and sure, was a pale woman in a pink dress. Her thin brown hair, under her "Bride" cap, was needle straight. She didn't wear a trace of makeup. On the other side of Jack stood his happy mother. Her hat said, "Warning: Mother of the Groom."

Cecelia spit the salmon into a napkin.

She stood stock-still. Jack didn't see her. She was, after all, just one shocked face in a sea of smiling happy ones. Happy couples in jeans or casual work clothes surrounded her. They nibbled off heaped trays, kissed, put food into each other's smiling mouths, kissed, scribbled notes onto their menu handouts, kissed, met each other's eyes with knowing glances, kissed.

Cecelia turned back to the bathroom. It seemed acres away, impossible. Just when she decided to make a break for it anyway, a giggling bridal party scurried through the bathroom door, and she knew it was hopeless. She'd just have to discreetly throw up behind the pillar.

No. She'd get a hold of herself.

Where were Finn and Amy? She scanned the buffet, where Amy was tucking filled napkins into her purse. Finn, his arms crossed, didn't eat anything at all. He had his back to the buffet, probably looking for the hot dogs and keg.

Cecelia looked back at Jack and his pink lady. He was feeding her a mushroom cap stuffed with something that must have been delicious because she shut her eyes as she chewed. Jack watched her with such tender concern, Cecelia knew they weren't going to see her. They weren't going to see anybody. Her dread was replaced with fascination.

Jack ate his mushroom cap and the pink woman stared up at him, expectant, as if the mushroom held the key to the universe. Jack's mother checked something off on her paper, but she, like the rest of humankind, was outside the love bubble that enclosed Jack and his new fiancée.

Jack murmured something into his love's ear. She

smiled and took his hand in hers. She was so tiny, so wispy; Cecelia felt for a moment that maybe Amy had conjured her.

A waiter in all black offered Cecelia something brown on a tray and she ate it without tasting. She had come on a whim, a lark, for fun and free food. But Jack was here for real. She had come with a man who couldn't possibly be part of her future. Jack had come with a woman who obviously adored him as much as he adored her.

And they were planning their wedding.

Regret spread through her into every cell. She didn't want Jack—but she wanted some of that True Love. And she didn't want to deny it to Finn.

She looked to the other couples. They were playing the part of rapturous engaged young people. Their moves were too obvious, too scripted. Their smiles and hugs bellowed, "All this *and* we're having awesome sex!"

But Jack and his True Love were different. Jack pushed a lock of hair off her face and she looked up. He kissed her gently and she squeezed his arm, then looked away. It was a dance, and only they could hear the music. They were the real thing. True Love.

She was happy for them.

"Is that Jack?" Finn was beside her.

She nodded, but she didn't look at Finn. She felt hidden at his side.

Jack and his entourage moved toward the buffet.

"Amy—" Cecelia and Finn both said at once.

Then they both said, "Shit."

But it was too late. Amy was hugging Jack, then his mother, then his new fiancée.

* * *

"They probably want her to be their maid of honor," said Cecelia.

Finn laughed—then grew serious. "They're looking over here."

"Oh, God." Cecelia put on a merry smile and waved. "I'm going to pass out."

"I have a better idea." Finn waved too and put his arm around Cecelia.

She continued to smile, but she said, "I don't want to play games, Finn."

"Who's playing games?" he asked. He drew her closer. "I love you."

Her smile fell. "What?"

"Cecelia, I know you don't believe in me, but we've got something. Can't you feel it?"

"Sure. I feel it. It's great sex. It's fun. I love it. But it's not—"

Suddenly he was kissing her. A thorough, complete kiss that rocked her to the soles of her feet. "It is," he murmured, then kissed her again.

She let herself fall into his kiss. Jack, the pink lady, Amy, Jack's mother, were forgotten. Why had she cared about them again?

"We're not like the other couples here. Can't you feel that?" Finn murmured, not letting her go. "You have to stop believing in Amy and believe in me. Believe in yourself."

"Cecelia?" Another voice was beside her.

Finn let her go.

"Hello, Jack," she said, turning to the voice. Her lips still tasted of Finn.

"Can we talk?" Jack asked.

*   *   *

They were alone—as alone as they could get in a packed room, which meant pushed up against a radiator on the wall farthest from the buffet. Jack shook his head at her in wonder. "You found him. I'm so happy for you!"

Cecelia stared at Jack. "I found—?"

"Your True Love! Look at the two of you. The minute I saw you guys together, I could tell. It was like you were in a bubble and the rest of the world was outside it. Isn't it amazing? Can you believe that we almost missed it?" He was giddier than she'd ever seen him. Come to think of it, she'd never seen him even the slightest bit giddy.

"Sharon—" he began.

"The cat lady from Ohio?" Cecelia asked.

Jack laughed. "Yes! That's her." He waved to her and she waved shyly back. "She has changed my life in so many ways," he went on. "I was living such a lie, Cel. I mean, no offense. But it wasn't just us. It was everything. Everything that I thought mattered, didn't matter. I quit my job."

"You did what?"

"I quit. I'm moving to Ohio. I'm so happy."

"Ohio?"

"Sharon has a cabin on a lake and I'm going to write a novel, Cel. I've always wanted to write a novel and now I'm going to do it. A lawyer-crime thriller. It's inside me. I can feel it straining to get out. I can't believe how much of my life I've wasted."

"Who are you?" Cecelia asked. "What have you done with Jack?"

"He's gone. He was no good."

Cecelia felt oddly calm. *It was all meant to be.* "I'm glad you found your One True Love," Cecelia said.

He laughed, then pulled her into a bear hug. "I'm so happy that we both found it, Cel. Before it was too late." He thumped her back. He let her go and held out his hand. "Friends?"

His eyes sparkled; his face glowed. Whatever he had found, it made him a better person. Maybe that's what love was, finding the person who brings out the best in you and eliminates the worst. She and Jack together had amplified each other's weaknesses for money, for power, for status. "Friends," she said.

She felt content. Happy even. After all, nothing between her and Jack had changed; friends were all they had ever been.

Chapter 32

The doorbell rang.

Cecelia bolted up in bed. She grabbed the clock. It was six o'clock in the evening. She had to be back at the hospital at seven. She and Finn had just fallen into bed for a quick, well, a quick screw. Ever since the appetizer tasting and meeting Jack, she and Finn couldn't keep their hands off each other. She felt like it would end any minute, and he'd run off to find his real True Love.

In fact, when she had gotten a little free time, she had Googled Cindy Reidel. Sure enough, there was one in Finn's hometown of Lakeford. She didn't find much about her—only that she was having an art show at the local community center. But finding her was enough to make her feel sick to her stomach. There was a woman waiting for him, although she didn't know it yet. She couldn't stand in the way of him finding his One True Love forever.

But for now, she couldn't get enough of him. "We must have fallen asleep." Finn was stretched out next to her. He looked as sated as she felt.

"I'll get it," Finn said, tumbling out of bed and pulling on his jeans. "It's Maya and Amy back from the aquarium."

Cecelia rolled into the warm spot he left behind. *Heaven.* It had been ten days since she'd seen Jack, told him that she didn't mind him and Sharon (the pink woman) using their date, their church, their caterer. She had joked that Sharon would still have to get her own dress. That was when Jack invited her to the wedding.

She wasn't quite there yet.

But then, where was she?

She was having fun with Finn and right now that was enough.

Amy would never ring the doorbell. She has a key.

She jumped out of bed, yanked on her clothes, and hurried down the hall, smoothing her hair.

She stopped. Two women and a man stood at the door, gaping at Finn. Actually, the man stared at her. The women seemed transfixed by Finn's bare chest.

"Hello?" Cecelia pulled her T-shirt down. "Can I help you?"

"Are you Cecelia Burns?" one of the women asked Finn's left pectoral. She was wearing a tweed suit.

"Yes." Cecelia's hand flew to her lips. Were they still swollen from Finn's passionate kisses? Not that the women would notice. They were still working their way across Finn's bare torso.

Get your greedy eyes off that nipple, she wanted to tell them.

"*Doctor* Cecelia Burns?" the man asked, as if what he really meant was, *harlot and fornicator Cecelia Burns?*

"Yes," she answered.

"So you must be—" The second woman glanced at the

paper in the man's hand. "Jack Peterson, Esquire?" The woman licked her lips.

Oh, for heaven's sake.

"No," Finn answered. "Finn Concord, shortstop, Trudy's Tipplers B-league." Finn held out his hand.

Both women tried to take it at once.

Finn smiled.

Cecelia shot him a dirty look.

"We're the co-op board," the man said. "Here on *business*."

The women with him cleared their throats and looked at the floor. "I'm Justin Smeeds. This is Julie Bordens. And this is my *wife*, Cindy Wilson." He seemed to be trying to remind her.

"Cindy—what was that last name?" Finn asked. "Reidel?"

"Wilson," Cecelia growled.

"Right. Wilson. Very nice to meet you," Finn said.

Cecelia had an incredible urge to bite his shoulder.

"We need some information before the board meeting on Wednesday." Mr. Smeeds looked past Cecelia and into the apartment. Cecelia maneuvered to block his view.

"We've written you several letters. There hasn't been a response. We just have to see that everything's in order. Up to standards."

"Oh, yeah! Is that the chow?" Amy approached from the elevator, coming up behind the crowd in the hallway. She held a huge shark balloon on a stick. "Wow, a whole delivery crew. Do we have to tip all of them?"

"This is my little sister, Amy. Amy, this is the Towne Towers co-op board. Where's Maya?"

"Oh. Hello." Amy smiled broadly. "She's chatting

with the doorman. I think he owes her some money on last week's baseball pool."

The co-op board's eyes went wide.

"Just a little friendly pool, nothing serious."

"Do all three of you live here?" the co-op man asked.

"Yes—" Amy began.

"Of course not!" Cecelia cut her off, just as Maya appeared.

Her balloon was a huge, floating jellyfish complete with silvery tentacles. Cecelia wondered how Amy could possibly have stolen such enormous booty.

"Chow?" Maya asked. "Oh, hell, do we have to tip them all?"

Cecelia blinked at the child. She was mini-Amy. Repeating her words exactly, a tiny con woman in training.

"I have here that your marital status is engaged, to Jack Peterson," the man said, eyeing Maya.

"Scratch that," Amy said merrily. She pushed past the man into the apartment, pulling Maya with her

"Ames! Really!" Cecelia scowled at her.

The man scratched out Jack's name. Cecelia blanched.

"There aren't any animals here?" the tweed woman asked.

"Depends what you mean by animal." Amy winked at Finn.

Maya quickly put her hands behind her back. Cecelia caught a glimpse of a tiny goldfish sloshing in a plastic bag.

"Perhaps we should come back at a more appropriate time." The man backed away. "Here, I'll leave these forms with you. Doctor." He handed Cecelia a packet. "The meeting is Wednesday at six. We'll need all your financials before then. Of course, we anticipate the financials of you and your fiancé—er, of whomever—will meet the building requirements."

"It'll just be my financials," Cecelia said, closing the door. "But don't worry, they'll be fine. No problem." She wondered if they'd be fine. She'd have to check the building requirements. She looked to the enormous stack of mail piled on her table. She was getting irresponsible, lax. She had to get her life back on track.

"Very good then," the man said, just before Cecelia clicked the door shut on the outside world.

She thought she heard the women sigh.

Cecelia had never been to Elliot's house. It was out in the suburbs, embedded in a maze of almost identical houses. She stopped her BMW in front of a brick colonial with white columns and got out. Number 1334. This must be it.

Hopefully, this would be easy. Since she didn't have a pay stub that showed her income anywhere close to what the co-op board required, her plan was to get Elliot to sign a letter that indicated how quickly her income was projected to grow just as soon as she became a more established doctor. The numbers were a bit exaggerated—

Elliot's wife, Julia, opened the door with a warm smile. "Hi, Cecelia. I'm so sorry you had to come all the way out here. Did Jack drive you?" She tried to peer around Cecelia, who quickly shut the door.

"It's no problem. It's my fault, anyway," Cecelia said, stepping into the immaculate foyer. "I should have gotten Elliot to sign these papers last week. They're for the co-op board."

"Oh, I know, dear. Elliot told me all about it. He's upstairs in his study. Why don't you run on up and I'll bring you some tea."

"Oh, no. That's okay. No tea. I'll just be a minute."

Julia shrugged. "Okay. But you just call down if you change your mind." She pointed Cecelia up the stairs. "Second door on the right."

Cecelia walked quickly through the house. The place was a museum. She knocked gently on the door. "Elliot?"

"Cecelia. What a pleasure! Come in." Elliot was sitting behind a huge mahogany desk tapping away on a laptop. "I'll just be one second."

Cecelia walked around the room. Medical books and journals lined the walls from floor to ceiling.

He clicked his laptop shut and came around the desk. "You can borrow anything you like." He stood by her. "Although I'm sure you've already read most of them."

She reached into her purse. "I'm so sorry to bug you at home like this. I drew up these financial papers for my co-op board, like you suggested. I need you to sign them."

He ignored the papers. "Is that all you need?"

"Excuse me?" She felt a chill in the room that hadn't been there before.

"I'm hearing rumors, Cecelia. Rumors that you're seeing someone. A—" He paused as if the words were too unbelievable to utter. "A construction worker?"

Bile rose in her stomach. All she needed was his signature, then she could get out of there and keep her co-op and forget that this ever happened. "The papers, Elliot?"

He looked at the papers in her hands and smiled. "It's

very important that the doctors in our practice see eye-to-eye."

"Elliot—just say it straight out. Are you saying that if I'm dating a construction worker, then you don't want me in your practice?"

"Dr. Burns, don't deny that you've changed. Look at you, in my house in the middle of the night? That's not the Dr. Burns that we took on. Asking me to lie about some papers? You've been dressing more and more provocatively at work. Your hair is always down. Your way of moving—"

"I have changed," she cut him off. Her blood was boiling. "I've changed a great deal." She looked around Elliot's immaculate, huge house. If she said much more, she'd never have a piece of all this. Was she really ready to throw it all away?

He put his hand on her shoulder and she bristled under its weight. "I don't know why you're so hostile, Cecelia. Relax. I think you're slipping. It happens to the best of us. You need to assure me that you'll come back over to where you were. Be the upstanding doctor we hired."

Cecelia looked at the papers in her hands. No signature, no co-op.

The papers aren't an "exaggeration." They are a lie. I am done lying.

The silent house echoed nothingness. She took a deep breath, then ripped the papers in two. She held out her hand to Elliot. "Thank you, Elliot. Thank you so much for making everything absolutely clear."

He shook her hand weakly, obviously confused.

But before he could ask her any questions, she was

down the stairs, out the door, and on her way back to where she belonged.

Cecelia climbed into the warm bed next to Finn.

"Mmmm." He gathered her in. "How'd it go?" he mumbled, half asleep.

"Great," she said. She pressed her body into his.

"Mmmmm. You're so cold," he said.

"That's your department," she reminded him. She kissed him as she rolled on top of him.

"No wonder you're cold, you're naked, Doctor."

"Hmmm. Starting to wake up, are we?" she asked.

"Parts of me," he said, pulling her into him. He slid his hands down her back. "Wow, I'll have to start sending you off to other men's houses in the middle of the night more often." He squeezed her thigh. "Did you get the papers signed?"

"No."

Finn opened his eyes for the first time. He peered at her in the dim light. "No?"

"I think I need a new job," she said into his neck. "And a new place to live."

"What happened?" He tried to sit up, but she remained soundly on his chest.

"Oh, Elliot just made clear what I already knew." She slid her hand down the length of him.

He groaned.

She smiled.

"So what now?" he asked, but his voice was weak.

"Now we shut up and make love." She kissed his neck, drinking in his warmth, his skin, his taste.

"Am I going to have to offer Mrs. Cindy Tweed sexual favors to get you into this building?" he asked, rolling over her to claim the dominant position.

"You do and I'll kill you."

"That's why I love you," he said. "Such a romantic."

And then he pushed inside her and they didn't say another word.

Chapter 33

The next day at the hospital, Cecelia watched Dr. Parsia, the director of the East Baltimore Neighborhood Clinic, talk to a group of nurses in the hall. After last night, she knew that she could never work with Elliot again. She had felt powerful marching out of his house, ecstatic driving home. Making love with Finn just added to her sense that her life was falling into place. She flipped her file closed, took a deep breath, and headed toward Dr. Parsia.

"Dr. Parsia?" Cecelia asked, stepping into her path. Her heart was racing. Dr. Parsia had a reputation. She didn't deal with the difficult population her clinic served without learning to cut right to the punch.

"Dr. Burns." She nodded curtly.

"Do you have a minute?"

"Sure," Dr. Parsia said. She didn't try to mask the curiosity on her face. "Let's sit down."

"I'm thrilled," Dr. Parsia said when Cecelia was done explaining that she wanted to join her clinic. "But are you sure?"

"Yes. I've never been more sure about anything."

"We can't come near your present salary. Your lifestyle is going to have to change significantly." She eyed Cecelia's three-hundred-dollar pumps.

"I know. That's fine. I'm reassessing my lifestyle anyway."

"Well, then let me speak to our board. I'll get back to you next week and we can get the wheels rolling. I've always admired your work, Doctor. I'd be thrilled to have you join us."

When Cecelia came home from work, Amy, Finn, and Maya were glum-faced at the door.

"What?" Cecelia was too tired to deal with another trauma. The stress of talking to Dr. Parsia had taken everything out of her. Now she just wanted to relax.

Finn handed her a thin envelope. "This was pushed under the door."

Her name was scribbled on it. The return address was a logo for the building. "This year's Miss America is . . ." She tore the envelope open. "Not me." *We regret to inform you that your application to buy unit #3472 has been declined. Unfortunately, we must uphold certain standards . . .*

She crumpled the paper into a ball and tossed it in the trash. "Doesn't matter. Right? Because we can move into Molly's place soon."

"We can move in now. That is, the plumbing is in and the electric is laid. If you want drywall—"

"Okay then, let's do it." Cecelia looked out at the harbor. She'd miss this view. Oh, hell, she'd miss everything about this place. "It's not like I can afford this place any-more, anyway," she told them.

They stared at her apprehensively.

"I quit the practice today. I'm finishing up there in a few weeks and then, hopefully, I'm going to work for the East Baltimore Neighborhood clinic."

Finn took her hand. "That's—"

Amy cut in "—incredibly stupid. How are we going to pay for everything."

Cecelia smiled her sweetest smile. "Well, how's that waitressing going?"

That weekend, Cecelia began moving her things into her old bedroom of her grandmother's house. Amy and Finn were stripping ancient wallpaper from the living room while Cecelia took a breather on the couch.

"Remind me why you're not helping us again?" Amy grunted.

"Because I'm paying." Cecelia collapsed on the couch. A cloud of dust rose up around her. "And this is my one day off this week *and* I have rounds at six-thirty in the morning tomorrow—"

Maya raced into the room. She screeched to a halt, looked from face to face to be sure she had everyone's attention, and then she announced, "There's a man here."

Cecelia stood up and wiped her hands on her paint-stained jeans. "Did he say who he was?"

"Yeah. But it's really weird. He said that he's Finn Concord. But he's not. How could he be Finn Concord if you are, Daddy?"

*   *   *

Everyone stumbled into the hallway to look at the man in the doorway. He was tall and blond, wearing an impeccable, perfectly fitting dark blue suit. He peered into the dim hallway doubtfully. "Cecelia Burns?" He looked from Amy to Cecelia, happily, as if either woman would be equally satisfactory. His blue eyes twinkled out of his too tanned face. "I stopped by the address I had, but the doorman sent me here."

Cecelia emerged from the silent group. She put out a hand. "I'm Cecelia Burns."

He shook her hand carefully. "May I come in? There's something I'd like to discuss with you." And with that, he carefully reached into his suit pocket and took out the letter that Cecelia had sent him ages ago—or was it just a few weeks?—telling him to please go see a doctor, he might be dying.

The adults shuffled into the living room, sending Maya upstairs to watch TV. Cecelia sat on the couch. California Finn sat down across from her on a chair and put her letter on the table between them.

"Exhibit A," he said good-naturedly. His fingernails were buffed to a lustrous shine. He leaned forward, smiling pleasantly as he waited for her to make her case.

Finn paced behind the couch, deep in thought.

Amy stood by the fireplace and watched.

"So you're Finn Concord, the lawyer from Palo Alto?" Cecelia asked.

"The very one."

"How did you find me?"

"Well, it wasn't easy," he said. "Took a while. But then I put two and two together." He pulled another letter out of his jacket pocket. Cecelia snatched it up. She recognized Amy's scrawling handwriting instantly. She read Amy's plea for him to contact a Dr. Cecelia Burns in Baltimore, as soon as possible. *I can't tell you why, please just trust this letter and find her.* Cecelia tossed the letter back onto the table. Her stomach had formed itself into a tight ball.

"I was looking for all the Finn Concords," Amy explained. "This guy wouldn't call me back."

"The only reason I didn't toss these letters into the trash was that they were so odd. But then, this week, I had business in Baltimore and I thought, what the hell?" He leaned back in his chair and crossed his ankle over his leg. He didn't seem the least bit uptight at the strange circumstances. He was so confident, so sure of himself. She thought back to Finn reading her letter in the park. He had reacted so viscerally, so intensely.

He was still pacing.

California Finn wove his fingers together into a steeple. "So? What makes you think I'm dying, Dr. Burns?"

Obviously, he thought this was some sort of prank. Well, that was better than him thinking she was trying to pick him up. She glanced at Finn.

"It's rather odd—" Cecelia began.

"Cecelia, can I talk to you a minute?" Finn interrupted.

"I don't think we've met," California Finn said. He stood up and put out his hand. "Finn Concord."

Finn shook his head. "Nice to meet you, Finn Concord. I'm Finn Concord."

For the first time, the lawyer flinched. But he quickly regained his composure and smiled.

A laugh came from near the fireplace. "It's weirder

than you thought, huh?" Amy asked California Finn. "You two kids talk. I'll entertain Mr. Concord here with some parlor tricks until you come back." She crossed the room and sat on the armrest of California Finn's chair. "I'm Amy, resident psychic," she said, putting out her hand as Finn pulled Cecelia out of the room.

Cecelia followed Finn into the dark hallway and before she knew what was happening, she was in his arms. He kissed her long and hard. When he finally released her, she was woozy from the waves of desire that crashed through her body. "Jealous are we?" she asked.

Without a word, Finn kissed her again, harder. He pulled her to him fiercely, as if he might never get the chance to kiss her again. Then his kiss softened, melted, becoming pure warmth.

"Oh, my," she said weakly when they parted. She didn't dare make another joke. She couldn't handle another kiss like that without having to get naked.

"I'm leaving," he said.

She laughed, then realized that he was serious. "Finn, you don't think he's—?"

"Cecelia. If he's your True Love, you have to know."

The seriousness of his tone radiated down to the pit of her stomach. "You don't believe."

"And if he's your True Love, you'll stay with him. You'll forget me and stay with him."

Cecelia's whole body tensed with desire and fear. "No. I don't want him. I want you." She was light as air, floating outside her body. This couldn't be happening. "He might not be The One," she reminded him.

"If he's not, I'll wait at Trudy's," Finn said. He called to Maya up the stairs.

She yelled down irritably that she needed a minute.

"You deserve True Love, Cecelia. I love you, but you have to consider him. Promise me you will."

"Why?"

"You believe. It would ruin us, destroy us. You have to know. Find out. Take it seriously. Really think."

Cecelia blanched. He was so honest with her. It was time to be completely honest with him. "Then you have to call Cindy Reidel."

"Maya!" he called up the stairs.

"I looked her up on the Internet. She's a painter. It would be a better life for Maya."

Maya bounded down the steps. "Uh-oh. Is blondie the right Finn?"

"No," Cecelia said. Then she thought of Cindy, her easel set up on the beach, Maya building sand castles nearby, Finn up on a ladder cleaning the gutters of the seaside cottage. It was a better life than a city with a workaholic mom. "Maybe."

"Then why are we leaving?"

"Because I'm hungry," Finn said. "C'mon, let's go get a burger and play some pinball."

"And make that phone call," Cecelia said, her heart clenching.

Finn shook his head. "You're nuts. C'mon, Maya. Let's get out of here."

Maya shrugged. But before she let Finn pull her away, she whispered to Cecelia, "I wouldn't blame you or anything. That guy is totally suede. Just don't forget us, okay?"

Cecelia melted at the vulnerability in Maya's eyes. "Hold on. I forgot something." She ran to the hall closet and pulled out a bag. "I've been meaning to give you this."

She handed Maya the shopping bag. Maya reached in and pulled out a simple yellow sundress.

Cecelia was liquid with regret for letting this child go. "It's just for—" For what? Cecelia tried to keep the tears from her eyes, the quaver from her voice. "Just if you want it. If it's your size."

Maya nodded. "Maybe. I'll try it on."

Cecelia swallowed hard. "Good."

"Good," Finn cut in. "We gotta go."

Cecelia nodded. She stood and watched the two of them go down the front steps, Maya carrying Cecelia's present. Finn's hands empty at his side.

Chapter 34

Good, good, you got it!" Amy clapped her hands. Cecelia came back into the living room in time to see California Finn make an ace of clubs disappear with a flick of his wrist. She went to the couch to join them.

"Ah, she returns," California Finn said. "Watch this." He did the trick again. He smiled like a little kid.

"So, where were we?" Cecelia wanted this over with. She didn't want to think about any of it anymore.

Finn stacked the deck and put it down onto the table. "You were about to tell me why you were sending me threatening letters by federal post—a felony, I might add."

Cecelia blanched.

California Finn laughed. "Okay, shoot. What's going on in this crazy place?"

"You want me to tell him?" Amy asked.

"No. No. I will." Cecelia watched California Finn carefully. He looked nice enough. Harmless, even. But he was a lawyer. She had to be careful. "Right, well, I guess I'll just start from the beginning."

She told him the story, while he listened like judge, jury, and hangman.

"That is definitely the most interesting story I've heard in a long time. And I'm a criminal lawyer, so I hear a lot of stories," California Finn said when she was done.

"Well, it's true. So, like I said, I hope I didn't cause you too much trouble."

"Me? Oh, no trouble at all. Actually, it was exciting. A mystery. I've been enjoying it."

"So, now I suppose you want Amy to tell you your Named?"

He went white. "No."

The two sisters caught each other's eye. Amy shrugged.

"Really?"

"Well, here's the thing. First, I don't believe a word that you just said."

"We're not lying—"

"I know you're not lying. I believe that *you* believe what you said. Defendants always do. But I don't believe in any of that psychic bullshit." He smiled sweetly, as if he'd just told them he loved their taste in decorating. "Second, I can see that you two believe this mumbo-jumbo hook, line, and sinker. So if you tell your sister that I'm her True Love, I'm a little nervous that I might never get rid of her. Not that I would want to get rid of you, Dr. Burns. It's just that I'm not really a commitment kind of guy."

He's not my True Love. Cecelia glanced at her watch. She could jump in a cab and be at Trudy's in five minutes.

"Let me read you," Amy said.

"Why, Ames? Let him go," Cecelia said. She was beginning to feel claustrophobic in the house.

"Okay, what the hell," California Finn said suddenly. "Although, you don't have to touch me, do you? I don't want to be getting all touchy-feely here."

"Just for a minute."

"Well—no chanting."

"Shut up and be still," Amy commanded.

Cecelia wanted to leave. But morbid curiosity had the best of her. She was so sure that Amy would say "no," that she almost felt calm.

Amy shut her eyes. She began to rock. California Finn fidgeted in his chair. Cecelia marveled over how shiny his shoes were.

Suddenly Amy's eyes popped open. "Hot damn!" she said.

"What?" Cecelia and California Finn asked in unison.

"Cecelia, meet Finn Franklin Concord, your One True Love as prophesied by Fate. Finn, meet Cecelia Arabella Burns, the soon-to-be love of your life."

"Well, this is awkward," Cecelia said to California Finn. Or should she call him True Love Finn from now on? They had both jumped up at the news, more in alarm than happiness. Cecelia felt an odd twitch deep in her stomach. She felt—blank. It was as if Amy had told her something about a stranger, not about the deepest yearnings of her heart. *Amy has just declared my One True Love. Amy is never wrong.*

So why did Cecelia feel like laughing?

Amy looked from one to the other of them like a delighted yenta.

"Fairly awkward. Yes. It is." Finn clasped his hands behind his back, then in front. Finally, he let them fall helplessly to his sides. "I'd always thought meeting my True Love would be more, um, romantic."

"I could light a fire," Amy suggested.

"That chimney is about to come crashing down," Cecelia said, looking to the badly leaning stone construction. Why did she feel so calm? She watched Amy closely.

"I'll just leave you two kids alone," Amy said, getting up to leave. She licked her lips.

"No!" they both cried.

They looked at each other sheepishly.

Suddenly Cecelia's mind cleared. *Amy licked her lips.* "No," she said more firmly. "You're not going anywhere."

"What's wrong?" Amy asked. "You don't look too good."

Cecelia shook her head. "No? Well, I feel great. Really great. I feel better than I've felt for a very, very long time." She stretched her arms over her head and smiled. She could run a marathon. She could swim the Atlantic Ocean.

"I have that effect on women," California Finn said doubtfully.

Cecelia patted his shoulder. "You're not my True Love, Finn."

"No?" He seemed delighted. He coughed, then modulated his voice to sound more concerned. "No?"

"What do you mean?" Amy countered. "He is. I heard your name, Cel. I heard it loud and clear."

"You're lying," Cecelia said.

"Why would I lie about a thing like that?" Amy licked her lips again.

"You lick your lips when you're lying. Why are you lying?" Cecelia's voice rose.

Amy cried, "I am not lying. I know."

Cecelia shook her head. "This man and I are not destined for anything but grief. Finn is waiting for me at Trudy's and he's The One."

"You don't have powers!" Amy said.

"I do, though, Amy. I have the power to see through you. I don't need voices in my head to know that you're lying."

"Hey," California Finn said. "Let me know if you need a lawyer."

"The last thing I need is another lawyer," she said. "In fact, the last thing I need is another man. I already have one and I'm going to get him."

Chapter 35

Amy and Cecelia glared at each other in the fading light of the day. Neither one moved.

"So, I think I'll just go make a few phone calls, then," California Finn said. "Holler if you need me."

Neither woman noticed as he hurried out of the room.

"Why are you conning me? It's me, Cecelia. Your sister. I thought you wanted me to find my True Love. Why didn't you tell me that Finn was The One?"

Amy shrugged. She let her fingers run over the ripped, brown upholstery of the couch. She said something so quietly that Cecelia only heard a trace of her voice.

"What? You lost what?"

"I lost my powers!" Amy shouted at the top of her lungs. She slammed both her fists down on the back of the couch.

Cecelia jumped back in surprise.

"I can hardly hear a thing anymore, okay? The voice is barely a whisper! I haven't been able to make out a name clearly in years! All I get are faint whispers, snatches of sounds. Now are you happy? Is that what you wanted to know? Of course you're happy! You always hated that I had the power and you didn't. Now we're even!"

Amy without her powers. Who was she without her powers? Her anger at Amy's lie was struggling against concern for her sister. No. The anger won out. *We're not exactly even.* Then, it came to her. A perfect plan for revenge. It appeared in her head fully formed. She filed it away for later. Now, she had to convince Amy that she was taking it all in stride. "Where did you get the name Cindy Reidel?"

"She used to come into the diner where I met Maya down in Florida. She was a regular at the back table. It was the first name I thought of."

"Why didn't you just tell me you were losing your powers?" Cecelia asked.

Amy sank onto the faded chair. "I thought that if we got back together, I'd get my powers back. It was working too. Every time I'm with you, I can hear the Names loud and clear."

"You lied about everything!"

Amy got a horrible look on her face, as if she had eaten something sour. "Cel. When I came, all the Names were fading. Yes, I made up the part about Finn being about to die. But when I'm with you, I hear all the Names loud and clear."

Cecelia waited.

"Except for Finn's. Your Finn's."

Cecelia's stomach clenched. *My Finn's.* "So you think he's dying." She could hardly get the words out. Amy's never wrong.

"Cel—I can hardly get a sound. His Name's almost gone. Every time I'm with you and I read you, it's a little fainter. I didn't want you to have to be with a guy who's really dying."

"I don't believe you." Finn dying. Her One True Love. She thought about all the time she had wasted. She wanted to bolt out of the room and run to Trudy's. Tell him to forget the phone call. Forget everything but her.

Amy looked miserable. She didn't lick her lips. "I was trying to spare you. When I brought him to Baltimore, I thought *all* the Names were fading. It wasn't until I got around you that I knew it was just his. I thought it was a mistake. I kept waiting for his name to come back—"

"You can only hear the Names when I'm around?" Cecelia tried to take it all in.

"It's really weird."

California Finn came back in.

"So," Cecelia said quietly. "You can hear the name of *his* One True Love?" She had to get to Trudy's. But how could she face him, knowing there was something horribly wrong.

"Loud and clear."

"Good. Then tell him quick so he can go home. He ought to at least get something out of this craziness."

"So?" California Finn leaned forward on the couch. "If she's not my One True Love, then who is?"

"Well, I might not have heard exactly right."

Now what was wrong? Cecelia felt so incredibly tired. She wanted to go and find Finn. To tell him that she loved him. That she had always loved him. That she always would love him, until—it was too awful to contemplate. She tried to focus on the present. "Oh, hell, just tell him, Ames. He doesn't believe in it anyway."

"Is that true?" Amy asked. "If you don't believe, there's no way I'll tell you."

"Oh, for God's sake!" Cecelia looked at her watch.

"Make me believe," California Finn said good-naturedly.

Amy frowned. "Okay. Here's the thing: your Named sounded like Jonnie Something."

Finn jumped up. "Was it Jonnie Busso?"

Amy nodded. "Yeah, Busso. Do you know the guy?"

"He's my boss." Finn clapped his hands. "Oh, I just knew it."

"You're gay?" Cecelia asked.

"Oh, I knew it was Jonnie since the first time I saw him—May twelfth, 2005, three forty-five, by the elevators. He was wearing his blue cashmere sweater that I love so much. I've got to get back to California. It was nice meeting you all. We'll just forget your little threatening letter. Okay?" He grabbed his jacket and headed for the door.

"So you do believe?" Amy called after him.

"Yes! That was amazing! Yes! Yes! Yes!"

"Good. Tell your friends," Amy said.

He opened the door, then paused. "It really was nice to meet you two. And you—" He pointed at Cecelia. "You must go scoop up that green-eyed Finn. He was a dream!"

Cecelia and Amy stood awkwardly in the creepy living room.

"Go get him," Amy said.

"You were really losing your powers?" Cecelia asked.

Amy slumped onto the couch. "Yeah. Except when I'm around you. How screwed up is that?"

Cecelia tried to keep her mind focused on revenge. Laying the foundation for the con. It didn't take much. Just a few words. Then she could go and get Finn. "I know why your powers are fading." She tried to keep her face neutral.

Amy sat up. Her face was pure shock.

"If you had just told me in the first place, then I could have explained everything. Up front. Saved us all a lot of trouble."

"Yeah, well, what fun would that have been?" Amy licked her lips ferociously and twisted her rings on her fingers.

Cecelia waited a beat, enjoying Amy's twitching. Finally she said, "Jasmine."

"Jasmine?" Amy tensed at the mention of her younger sister's name. "Jasmine has been gone for ten years."

"Remember Mom's postcard? *Your sister needs your help.* It wasn't me; the sister that needed help was Jasmine. The day you and me split up ten years ago was exactly one week after Jasmine took off. That was when your powers started fading. Somehow, something is trying to get us together. And why would we get together except to find Jasmine? It's not me who's bringing your powers back. It's Jasmine. She must be near."

Amy seemed to consider this. Her face went whiter and whiter. She sucked the insides of her cheeks for a long moment. "You think she's alive then?"

Cecelia shrugged. "I don't know."

Amy's eyes went wide. Her mouth dropped open. "What if she's—"

"Dead?" Cecelia asked. "Hell. You're a *psychic*, Amy. Dead's never bothered you before."

Cecelia climbed the rickety steps from Trudy's to the second floor. Her heart was pounding. How could such a healthy man be dying? She felt as if she were entering a patient's room. But Finn wasn't a patient. She had no medical knowledge to share, no cure. For the first time, she understood the Victorian notion of not telling a terminal patient the end was near. Telling without also plotting a course of action seemed too cruel. But she had to tell him. *No lies*.

A door on the landing was slightly open, and a small orange cat slithered through the gap and blinked at her.

"Is Finn here?" she asked the cat, scratching its ears.

"That depends who's asking," Finn said. He appeared in the doorway in jeans and a ripped T-shirt.

"Your One True Love as destined by prophecy," Cecelia said. She tried to keep her voice flat. *Don't run into his arms until you tell him everything*, she commanded herself.

Finn smiled and held the door open. "Oh. And I thought it was just you."

"It is just me. I'm your True Love. Amy lied." She walked past him and into the tiny apartment. "Where's Maya?"

"She went to the movies with Trudy. Then they're having a sleepover."

I love that Trudy. The carpet was old, threadbare, industrial grade, and public-bus blue. The furniture was a mishmash of clawed-up castoffs. There was nothing on the walls. "You knew I'd come."

"Of course. I've been waiting almost an hour. You were the only one who didn't know." He took her hand and added affectionately, "Stupid."

She fell onto the couch, each individual spring making itself known. She paused, delaying the inevitable conversation. "Did you call her?"

"Cindy Reidel in Florida? I did."

"What did she say?"

"She said congratulations on finding you and when I get back I better redo her porch swing and fix her wheelchair ramp."

"Wheelchair—"

"Well, she is eighty-six. She broke her hip twice in the last three years. Poor Cindy."

"You could have told me she was an old lady!"

"And ruin the fun?"

They sat side by side. He held her hand.

"What happened to the lawyer?" he asked.

"He was gay. Amy called it."

Finn shook his head in awe. "Why did Amy lie about us? Why did she say you weren't my One True Love?"

Cecelia held her breath. *The truth*. She walked over to the small dingy window. What if Amy *was* wrong? Cecelia had checked Finn out. He was fine. Amy could be wrong. "It's complicated."

"Well, we have all night. C'mon. Sit down."

She sat and Finn grabbed her legs and swung them onto his lap. Before she could react, he pulled off her shoes and began rubbing her feet.

She relaxed into the sensation.

He bent to her and softly kissed her lips.

Cecelia let the waves of sensation pulse through her.

How did he always know just exactly how to touch her? Oh, right, destiny.

Finn rubbed farther up her ankles, to her calves. Gentle, sure strokes. Then he traced delicately up and down her thigh with his finger. Cecelia tried to control the shock waves his finger was causing. *The truth.* She watched his finger sneak under the waistband of her jeans. "Wait. I want to tell you everything." She said it, but she wasn't sure she meant it.

"You talk," he said, concentrating on moving his hand farther inside her jeans in slow, searching circles. "I'll explore."

"Amy's losing her power. All the voices are fading." She willed his hand closer to its mark.

"If all the voices are fading, then I'm not dying?" He didn't seem to care about the answer. He kissed her again, still moving his hand deeper, closer.

"Finn."

He pulled his hand out of her jeans and she thought, *Oh, hell* as he stared intently into her eyes. "Cecelia. From the minute I saw you in the park, I knew you were the one. From the minute I made love to you, I knew that I'd never make love to another woman as long as I lived. I don't want to hear another word about Amy. This is between you and me."

She looked into the smoky depths of his green eyes. No Amy. Forget everything but the two of them. "Good. We'll both shut up."

He kissed her again, as if starting from the beginning. His finger began to sneak back toward its goal.

"Oh, hell." She sat up.

"You're talking," he reminded her.

"I know. But I have to say this: when I'm around, Amy hears all the names clearly. Except yours. Yours is still fading. You're still dying."

Without missing a beat, he said, "Good, then let's make love like we might never make love again."

"Finn!"

"Oooh, I think I'm dying! Tend to me!" He threw himself back on the couch, his hands over his heart.

Cecelia swatted him.

He grew suddenly serious. "Cecelia. I'm not dying. Stop with Amy. Believe what you see." He took her face in his hands and kissed her so thoroughly, she felt light.

He was right. She knew it with every cell in her body. No more Amy. Amy, after all, was a proven liar.

Without a word, Cecelia opened the buttons on her shirt one by one.

Finn pushed back the shirt. He let his hands trace the lace of her bra. Then he pushed down the lace, and traced her nipple with his tongue.

She leaned back as he gently teased her. He emerged just long enough to murmur, "If I did have to die, this would be the way to go." He thoroughly kissed her nipple until she was moaning with pleasure.

"You'd better not expire until you're done, mister."

"Then we better hurry." He eased her out of her shirt, tracing her collarbone with his fingertip. "I love you, Cecelia Burns."

She felt his words to the core of her soul.

He undid the clasp of her jeans and she wiggled out of them. He took her hips firmly in his hands and pulled her onto his lap.

She pushed against him with her hips. She was lost in

the feel of his rough jeans through her panties. She took his face in her hands. "I love you, Finn Concord." The words were like lightning, illuminating them both.

He scooped her into his arms. "I'm not having the last sex of my life on this awful couch. C'mon. I'm taking you into the bedroom."

She clasped her arms around his neck.

"Sorry, Leslie." He shut the door on the cat. "This is between Cecelia and me."

Chapter 36

Cecelia awoke to the bass of the jukebox thumping in the bar below. *I'm lying in a cot over a beer bar listening to* Bad to the Bone *and I've never been happier in my life.*

Finn was sitting in a chair by the window, staring out at the blackness. She watched him in the dim light. He was her One True Love and she'd love him no matter what. She'd love him, as the song went, until the day he died. She'd stay beside him, always, *in sickness and in health until death do they part.*

She shook off her feeling of dread. People said those words all the time, and yet they said it without thinking. Bad things happened to other people. They didn't happen to good people. She curled deeper into the sparse covers.

He turned when he heard her stir. "Hey."

"Hey yourself." She pulled herself out of the rickety bed and crossed the room. "There's something we need to talk about."

"This better not be about Amy." He took her into his arms.

"No. It's about my other sister."

He traced her collarbone with his finger. "Another sister? I don't think I can take another Burns sister."

"I think I need to find her."

"Where is she?"

"That's the thing; I don't know. When I was immersed in my second year of medical school, Jasmine came back from India. We hardly knew her. She left with my mom for India when she was two and came back when she was sixteen. We were supposed to look after her."

"You guys? The con women with the helpless dad? How'd that go?"

She shrugged. "Not so well. I was too busy with school. Amy let her in on our cons, but she was a disaster. She was really shy. In fact, she could hardly speak without blushing. She was an interesting person. But I was way too busy to get to know her." Guilt tugged at her, but she shook it off.

Finn leaned in and kissed her neck.

"Actually, I guess I was pretty jealous of her. She grew up with my mom. Amy and I didn't treat her so well. We weren't mean. We just weren't as nice as we could have been." Cecelia let her mind wander back to her timid sister. She was so quiet. Sometimes they would forget she was there and talk about her as if she weren't. "When she left, she left a note. It said she'd be fine. Not to worry. And we didn't. That was the awful part. We should have worried, gone after her, found her, but we didn't."

Finn pulled her into his lap. "Okay. So how do you find a missing sister?"

"I don't know. I've got to figure that out. I guess I hire a detective." Cecelia's stomach tightened. What if

Jasmine wasn't okay? What if something had happened to her?

"Okay," Finn said. "Hire a detective. But not now." He let his hand slip under her hair. "Now, you're busy."

"Am I?" she murmured, letting her head fall back into his hand. "Hmmmm . . . I suppose I am."

Cecelia raced home the next morning to change before her 6:30 A.M. rounds. Her message machine blinked at her insistently.

The first message was the co-op board. They needed her to vacate and empty her apartment by next week. The investment banker in Hong Kong had a new buyer. The prospect actually cheered her. Get done with the past. All of it. She'd move into Molly's house. They all would.

A family.

The second and third messages were from Ellen, at Elliot and Stan's office, asking her to please call. She deleted them both. Whatever they wanted, it would have to wait.

The next message was from Dr. Parsia. She wanted to confirm their meeting tomorrow to discuss final details about Cecelia joining their East Baltimore Neighborhood Clinic. Cecelia grinned. All her past, exorcized. She could start again, all over, a new life with Finn and Maya.

The next beep was followed by Elliot's familiar voice: "Cecelia? Listen, Ellen's been trying to get in touch with you. We got a bad blood test back for one of your patients. Somehow, it slipped through the cracks. He didn't have a proper file. But we finally hunted it down, and we can't locate him. The address he gave is phony. His name

is Finn Concord. We're screwed if we don't get a certi-
fied letter to him on this pronto. Call me. Bye."

Cecelia stopped the machine and replayed the message. With each word, her heart sank lower. She felt
numb. *Amy's always right.*

She called back Ellen, but slammed down the phone in
frustration when she realized it was too early, the office
was closed. She considered waking Elliot, but what
would he remember at six-thirty in the morning about a
blood test?

Okay, she had to pull herself together. If it was a bad
blood test, it wasn't an emergency. In fact, maybe it was
nothing.

Or, maybe, it was destiny.

Five hours later, Cecelia sat in her office reviewing
Finn's test. Extremely high white blood cell count. Sure
sign of infection. But what kind? He could have been sick
when they took the blood, but fine now. A high white cell
count could mean nothing—or everything.

She would just redo the test. That was all. It was stan-
dard practice in an asymptomatic case. False positives
were common. She'd see Finn later tonight. She'd just
get him to go to the lab to draw some blood.

There was nothing at all to worry about.

So why did she feel like crying?

No. She wasn't going to cry. She had work to do. Important work. She picked up the phone and dialed.

"Hello, Edison Detective Agency," said the deep voice
on the other end of the line.

*   *   *

Amy brought the strawberry margarita to the woman at table number six. "Here you go. Your food'll be ready in a minute."

"You don't look Mexican," the woman at the table said.

Amy shrugged. *And you don't look like the strawberry margarita type.* But she restrained herself. These old, lonely diners turned out to be the best tippers at Santa Anna's, the restaurant where she waitressed five nights a week. The place was almost empty at this late hour. Plus, Amy never minded a conversation, especially about herself. "I'm half Irish, a quarter Swedish, and a quarter Roma. You know, gypsy."

The woman nodded. "I could tell there was something spiritual about you."

"Nope." Amy flattened her round tray to her stomach mashing her black flounced skirt and her red and green blouse. What a stupid uniform. "Nothing going on here but what you see. Guess the Swedish won out."

"That's not true," the woman said. "I can see that you used to have a power. What happened?"

Amy studied the woman closely. She was over seventy, bent, her knuckles gnarled and chapped. She wore a dark, woolen dress that was worn shiny at the elbows. "Who are you?"

The woman sipped her margarita. "I never come in here. Don't do well with the spices. Then today, I say to myself, go in. Have your dinner there. I don't know why. But I follow my hunches."

Amy watched her last customers slip out of their red booth and toss some money on the table. She glanced around for the manager, who was nowhere in sight, then sat down opposite the old woman. She leaned forward and whispered, "I lost my powers. All of them."

The woman nodded. "I know. I can tell. You have that look about you. Do you know why you lost them?"

"Maybe. I don't know."

"So you know. Good. Then you also know how to get them back."

"I don't!" Amy cried. She crouched into her seat, then said more quietly, "I've tried everything. I've lit candles, said prayers. I've tried to right the wrongs that I did. Honestly."

"Really?"

"What do you mean?"

The old woman closed her eyes. Her lids were as thin as onion skins. "Jasmine Burns."

Amy's eyes grew huge. "How do you know that name?"

"I have a power too. One that I've never lost."

Amy's heart was racing. "Tell me."

"I can look at a person, and hear the name of the one she's wronged."

Amy was white as a sheet.

"I can hear the name of your worst enemy."

"But, but, she's—" Amy couldn't say it.

"What, darling?" the old woman cooed.

"She's not my enemy. She's my sister. And I'm afraid she might be dead."

Finn jostled the pinball game in the back of Trudy's and it lit up like a Christmas tree. The score zinged up by the thousands. If he could just keep this ball going, then he wouldn't have to look at Cecelia, and if he didn't look at her, maybe she'd quit bugging him about his blood and go away.

"Finn"—Cecelia leaned in, obscuring his view—"you're not listening."

"I told you. I don't listen to Amy's nonsense." He plowed his left hip into the game to keep the ball from rolling down the alley. It was a delicate balance, maneuvering the thing enough to up his score, but not enough to tilt it. Trudy taught him everything he knew, although Maya still kicked his butt at this game. Granny was withholding secrets from him, he was sure.

"But it's not Amy, it's a blood test."

The ball ricocheted off a side bumper and shot right between his flippers. Game over. He glanced at Cecelia and saw the desperation in her eyes. He fished in his pockets for more quarters. "I feel fine."

"Finn." Cecelia rummaged through her purse. She came up with four quarters. She clinked them onto the glass. Then she glanced at Maya, who was drawing a picture at the bar, and leaned in close. "Twelve cc's of blood. Just come to the hospital tomorrow and I'll draw it—"

"No." He ignored the quarters and headed for a table in the back. He threw himself into a chair.

Cecelia shook her head impatiently. "You're like a little kid." She scooped her quarters into her hand and followed him. She sat down in the chair next to his.

Finn felt his stomach sink. "I'm not like a little kid, Cel. I'm like a grown man with a little kid. I can't be sick. That's all. Because if I am, there's not a damn thing I can do about it." He was trying not to become exasperated at her. But she had no idea how hard Sally's illness had been; dealing with the system, losing to the system. *Don't ever get sick,* a kindly nurse had said to him one day. *And if you do, stay away from the hospital.* It was the best advice he'd ever gotten and he was going to live—and die—by it.

"How can you not want to know?"

He watched Maya. One of the bar's regulars had given her a set of colored pencils and she was lost in her drawing. She was pretty good, actually. "Maya's been through enough."

"But I can help."

"No one helps if it's a lost cause, Cel. You told me that yourself—" He dug into his pockets again. He needed another game of pinball to soothe his nerves. Just talking about being sick made him feel, well, sick. He found one quarter, two dimes, and a Canadian penny. He tossed the change into the ashtray in disgust.

"You don't have health insurance," Cecelia said.

"I have enough for Maya, but none for me. So, you see, it can't be done. The system sucks. I'll take my chances."

"That was before. I can figure it out." She looked so gorgeous in the dim light of the bar. Her hair falling around her shoulders in soft waves, her eyes flashing black. If only she'd stop with the blood test business.

"You said it yourself: you're just one person. There's a whole system to fight," he reminded her.

"So let's fight it."

"Cel. Let it drop." The more Cecelia talked about this, the more he saw Sally everywhere. She was healthy and smiling. He could smell her, taste her. He could practically see her, sitting next to Maya and admiring her picture. Damn, if he were a crying kind of man, he'd be losing it now. He hated hospitals. Doctors. Sickness.

Cecelia followed his gaze to Maya. "You have to do it for Maya. She needs you to take care of yourself."

"No."

Cecelia looked so mad, he had the feeling that she was going to stick him herself with a needle when he wasn't looking. She got up from the table, pushing her chair back roughly. "I've got to go. I'm starting my new job tomorrow. I need some rest."

"Right. Maya and I will stay here tonight, so we'll be out of your hair." *Her hair.* He wanted to run his fingers through her hair, not to fight with her. But he wasn't getting mixed up with hospitals and blood tests.

"Whatever." She turned and left, stopping at the bar to admire Maya's picture and say good-bye.

Finn almost called her name, but he didn't. All this talk about sickness filled his mind with another name—his wife's name. He had two full years of hospitals before Sally died, and there was no way he was subjecting Maya to that again. The pinball machine flashed the high scores. "MAYA" held the top five spots. "FFC" held the next five.

Okay, so maybe he was being a bit childish.

Cecelia had left her quarters on the table. He scooped them up and began another game.

Chapter 37

The next morning, Cecelia started her new job at the clinic. When she came in at eight, the waiting room was already packed with people sicker than she'd seen since medical school. She had been working for six hours straight, and was listening to a previously undiagnosed textbook tachycardia in a six-year-old little girl, when she heard Amy arguing with the receptionist, Monique. Monique wasn't nearly as polite as Ellen was back at Elliot and Stan's practice. Monique had an unruly waiting room with way too many patients and not enough doctors to see them all. She had to keep order, or else.

"You can see Dr. Burns when you have an appointment," she heard Monique bellow.

Cecelia sighed. "We're going to do some tests, Ally," Cecelia told the little girl and her mother, who both nodded. It made Cecelia nuts that these people didn't ask questions, didn't ask for second opinions. None of her patients today had. But she didn't have time to teach her patients to be patients. She was too busy trying to save their lives. "Do you know what an EKG is? It doesn't hurt one bit."

The mother was trying not to cry.

Amy's angry voice continued to filter down the hall and into the tiny room.

"This is Veronica." Cecelia pointed at the nurse who had appeared at the door. "She's going to walk you through it all." Cecelia helped the little girl down from the examining table and she and her mother went off with Veronica.

Cecelia took a deep breath and went to help the receptionist. "It's okay, Monique. She's my sister."

Amy looked wilder than Cecelia had ever seen her. "C'mon back." Cecelia buzzed Amy into the maze of offices. Everything at this place was busy and messy and difficult. Cecelia was loving every minute of it.

She led Amy to her office, which she shared with three other doctors. Their desks were crammed against the wall, papers leaning precariously in all directions. She sat down opposite a buried desk and motioned Amy to take a chair.

She didn't. Instead, she paced back and forth, picked up random papers, then put them back down. "Jasmine's alive!" she blurted. "She's alive and she's the reason I lost my powers. I have to do something before she comes back to get me."

Cecelia tented her fingers and nodded her head. "Can we start at the beginning—" Cecelia couldn't help it, she was enjoying Amy's distress enormously.

"A psychic told me Jasmine's coming to get me. That she's my worst enemy. She knew her name, Cel! I don't know what to do."

"Jasmine isn't your enemy. She's your sister." Cecelia savored the irony of that statement, especially after her last month with Amy. "And of course she's alive. She just ran off like I did and you did. That was her way. All of our ways. The gypsy blood."

"I'm scared, Cel. I need your help."

Cecelia tried to take pity. But she'd just been talking to a six-year-old with a bum heart. She couldn't muster much sympathy for Amy. "Okay. Here's how I'm going to help you. I'm going to tell you that you're nuts. Jasmine is not after you. Why would she be? Even if she's in Baltimore, it doesn't make any sense that she's out to get you."

"Cel. I. Um. I—" Amy stopped. She had gone completely white.

"What?"

"I sort of stole from Jasmine. Ten years ago. Right before she took off. I never told you. Our last job together, I sort of lied about how much we took in. And I think she knew. I think that was why she left."

Cecelia threw up her palms. "Oh, Amy." This was beyond what she expected, even from Amy. "Jasmine was the sweetest little kid. She was sixteen. She was your sister." Cecelia glanced at her watch. "Look, I have to work. Just relax. No one's going to get you. Especially Jasmine. People don't just disappear for ten years and then show up out of the blue." She paused. "Except, of course, for you."

Amy didn't go back to her job for a week. She hardly left the brownstone, and when she did, she felt eyes on her from every direction. After eight days, she started to relax. After all, Cecelia was probably right, Jasmine couldn't just show up back in Baltimore after all that time.

Of course, Amy had shown up out of the blue—

She looked at the psychic's card, which the old woman had passed to her in the restaurant. It just had a name, "Madame Mesion," and a phone number. The woman was probably a fraud. But then, to come up with that name. Her skin chilled.

She dialed the number. "Hello, Madame Mesion?"

"Ms. Burns, hello," the old woman said. Her voice sounded even weaker through the phone.

The lady must have Caller ID. *I hope.* "What can you tell me about Jasmine? I need to know everything."

"Oh, I'm sorry, dear. All I get is a name. And I only get the names of the living. That's all I know."

"I can pay you."

"Dear, I sincerely doubt that. But this isn't about money. I would never extort a fellow psychic, or anyone for that matter. That's how I keep my powers strong. Anyway, I have nothing else for you. I'm sorry."

Amy hung up the phone. She couldn't keep living like this. But there was nothing she could do. If Jasmine were really out there, she'd just have to wait for her to show herself.

Finn took a break from framing the sixteenth window of the day. The work was good, the money was good, and there was no end in sight. He could stay in Baltimore if he wanted. Stay forever.

Thoughts of Cecelia overcame him and his insides stirred. Then he thought of her with a gleaming needle, and everything turned to concrete. He climbed through the empty window hole and sat on the unfinished porch. Guys were working around him, but thankfully everyone was absorbed. After hanging out with two women like Trudy and Maya most of the day, he was grateful for silence.

I don't feel sick, he thought for the hundredth time that week. In fact, he felt great. Really good sex will do that for a guy.

A simple blood test. Just do it. But every time he thought about the hospital, it brought back floods of emotion he didn't want to face.

Sally. His wife. *I'm sitting by her bedside, holding her hand, watching.* It was all the watching that killed him a little each day as Sally slowly died. Just walking into that stinking hospital, seeing those doctors. Cecelia was right about his death in the sense that a part of him had already died.

He shook the feelings away.

He was being ridiculous. He could hear Cecelia's voice, whispering in his ear after they made love: *It wasn't your fault. You did everything you could.*

But did he? Sure, in a way he had. But it wasn't what he *didn't* do, it was what he *wasn't*: rich, educated, connected. Those were the things Sally had needed from him. But those were the things he never had. Never would have.

He pulled out his wallet and flipped it open to a time-worn picture. Maya in Sally's arms.

I can't bring her back.

It's just a blood test, he imagined Sally saying. *You big wuss. Look what I went through and you're scared of a needle?*

Right. She was right.

Okay, he'd do it. He'd go to the hospital and get the test. He'd do it for Maya. And Cecelia. But most of all, he'd do it for Sally. As he stared into her eyes in the picture, he knew that she would've kicked his butt if he didn't.

"Every time I see a woman in her mid-twenties, I jump out of my skin," Amy told Trudy.

Trudy wiped down the bar without looking up. She grunted.

"I don't know what she'd look like now, but I did some sketches." She flipped open a notebook.

Trudy glanced at it from a distance and nodded.

"I can't go on like this. I can't sleep. I can't eat. I can't work. I dropped three orders last night. It was a mess. Customers walked out. I'm going to get fired."

Trudy checked the stock behind the bar. "I need more soda. I'll be right back." She disappeared down the cellar stairs.

Amy looked around the spooky, empty bar. It was the middle of the afternoon, and the dingy, pale light filtered in through the single grimy window in the front.

Suddenly the door swung open.

A woman stood in the doorway, a silhouette, framed in light.

Amy felt her stomach quiver.

The woman seemed to look right at her, although Amy couldn't see the woman's face, which was hidden in darkness.

"Amy Burns?" the woman asked.

Amy almost fell off her bar stool. She looked to either

side of her. Where the hell was Trudy? She could bolt down the stairs before the woman got any closer. But what if the woman chased her? Then she'd be *in the cellar*. And she wasn't sure if Trudy would defend her or just laugh at her. "Yes," she said, trying to make her voice strong. It sounded wobbly to her ears.

The woman began to move toward her.

"Who are you?" Amy stood up.

"You know who I am. I've been looking for you. You don't stay still long."

The woman stood before her now. She had long black hair and brown eyes—just like Jasmine. "Who are you?" Amy asked again.

"Did you miss me?" the woman asked. "I missed you."

Amy began to back away.

The woman laughed. "Sis, what's wrong? Don't you remember me?" Jasmine held out a hand, as if she wanted to shake.

Amy, trembling, put out her hand too. She took the woman's hand in hers, surprised that it was warm, alive, real. She let go quickly. "What do you want?"

Jasmine sat down on a stool. She spun around like a little kid. "What've you been up to?"

"Nothing. Working."

"Really. That's not what I heard. I heard that you lost all your powers. Now what a shame that is. Why do you think that happened?"

"I don't know."

"Oh, well I do. Because—this is really weird—I got them!"

Amy blanched.

"Surprised, are you? I don't know why? The thing is, you kept screwing up. Over and over and over again. Then, with Cecelia, that was really the last straw. Conning your sister and that nice little girl. Your powers are gone completely now, aren't they? I think they must be because I hear the voices so clearly!"

"Take them!" Amy said. "You deserve them. I think about you every single day."

"What did you think happened to me? Did you think I was dead?"

"Yes."

"Well, there you're right."

"I don't know what you mean."

"Amy, you can't be *alive* and hear the voices. Surely you know that. Don't you remember what happened when you were five? Don't you remember the bus accident?"

Amy grabbed Jasmine's arm. "What are you talking about?"

"You've been dead, honey. This whole time."

Chapter 38

Just then, Trudy came up the back stairs. Cecelia was behind her. And then Finn. And Maya. They were grinning from ear to ear, which on Trudy was not a pretty sight.

Amy stared at them.

Cecelia walked right up to Jasmine. "Nice job, Margaret. Thanks." She handed the woman two hundred-dollar bills. "I really liked the bit about Amy being dead. Very creative."

"Oh, I just thought that up on the spot. Did you see her face?"

"Oh, yes. In fact, I've got the whole thing on video. I'm really looking forward to watching it over and over. Thanks again." Cecelia was giddy with the triumph of her scam.

"Oh, no problem. It was fun," Jasmine/Margaret said. Then she looked at Amy, who was as pale as a sheet, looking at everyone like they were all ghosts. "Sorry, lady. I just needed the cash. You're a good sport." She shoved the money into her jeans and skipped out the door.

Cecelia was still grinning.

"You—" Amy began.

"Yep. Me," Cecelia said.

"And me. I helped," Trudy added. She put her arm around Amy's shoulders.

"And me," Maya added.

"I had nothing to do with it," Finn said.

Amy fell onto the stool and held her stomach as if she might throw up. "I can't believe—"

"Believe it!" Cecelia chirped happily. "Trudy, I think Amy needs a drink."

"Coming right up." Trudy went behind the bar.

"A shot of vodka. A double," Amy said. "Holy mother of God, I think I almost passed out you lousy—"

"Now, now. Don't be too angry, dear," Cecelia said. "It's not as if you didn't deserve every single luscious moment of that."

"I can't believe that I bought it," Amy said. Trudy plunked the drink in front of her and she threw it back. "That was dirty."

"That was necessary," Cecelia said happily. "If you're ever going to get your powers back, then you had to experience what it's like to be conned. Plus, I owed you."

"We owed you," Finn mumbled.

"And it was fun," Maya put in.

"You're a horrible waitress," Cecelia said, starting to feel a little sorry for Amy, who was still pale. "You have to find a way to get your powers back yourself."

Amy shook her head. "Where'd you find that old lady in the restaurant? She was good."

"On Renny Street. She had me conned a while back too. You should see her eye trick, it's really amazing.

Anyway, don't get any ideas. If you're going to get your powers back, you've got to go straight."

"I can't do it without you."

"I think you can. Anyway, I'll be around. You won't be alone."

"Why are you being nice to me?" Amy asked suspiciously.

"Because you needed my help," Cecelia said. She put her hand on Finn's shoulder. "Just like I needed yours."

Cecelia opened the new lab report on Finn nervously. She quickly scanned the results. Normal. Normal. Normal. Nice lipids. Her heart stilled and she couldn't breathe. Finn was going to live. He wasn't going to die. There was nothing wrong with his blood. The first test had either been wrong, or he had a temporary infection that his body fought off. She wanted to run through the streets, toss her hat in the air, shout for joy.

"Well?" Finn looked over her shoulder at the report, his chest brushing against her.

Forget running and hat tossing, she wanted him. "You're fine. There's nothing here." She closed the report, threw it onto the counter, and took Finn into her arms. "Don't suppose it would be such a good thing to get caught on the new job naked with you on an exam table?" She was so giddy, she couldn't stop smiling. She bit him gently on the shoulder.

"Oh, haven't you come full circle?" Finn teased, gathering her tightly. He returned the bite to her neck. "I remember meeting a doctor who was too frightened to have a picnic on an exam table, much less what I'm thinking about right now." Finn traced a line between her breasts with his finger.

"So, um, what are you thinking about right now?" She already felt breathless, already felt his rough hands running over her skin.

"I'm thinking that before you and I do one more thing, I need you to admit to me that sometimes Amy is wrong."

Cecelia felt her happiness drain out of her. She let Finn go. "Amy is never wrong."

"Thanks, but I'll trust the blood test."

Cecelia tried to ignore the shudder that raced up her spine. Why did he have to bring up Amy again?

"Cel, say that you believe I'm going to live a long and happy life. With you."

Cecelia let her head fall against his chest. The mood was gone. She didn't feel like making love to him anymore. Instead, she had an itching desire to roll him in bubble wrap and never let him out of her sight. He'd be flattened by a Mack truck on the way home, hit by a meteor, struck by lightning. Just because the blood test was fine didn't mean he was fine.

She looked into his eyes. He believed in her. She had to believe in him, not Amy. It wasn't about Amy. Focus on the healthy man before her. She sucked in her breath. "You're going to live a long and happy life. With me."

He drew her close. "Good. That's much better. Now c'mon, we don't have time to mess around. I knew I was healthy as a horse, so I've already planned a little celebration. Amy and Maya are making us dinner."

Cecelia's stomach clenched. "Amy's cooking?"

Finn shrugged. "So?"

"Oh, God, c'mon. We have to hurry. Now I know how you're going to die."

By the time they arrived back at the house, black smoke filled the hallway. "Ames? Maya?"

"In here," Maya called happily. "We're making your favorite, Dad!"

Finn and Cecelia joined Maya and Amy in the kitchen. "Hunk of burnt—" He poked at the black mass in the roasting pot. "Tire?"

Maya swatted him. "It's pot roast, Daddy. Just like Mommy used to make." She poked at it nervously.

"Except for the burnt part," Amy added. "We didn't have three hours to let the damn thing sit in there, so I figured I'd turn it up to 450 and speed things up a bit. I don't know what happened."

Cecelia noticed that Maya's eyes were filling with tears. "Hey, I have an idea." She motioned to Finn and Amy. "Why don't you two go and finish taking off that old chimney mantel like you were going to do yesterday, and I'll teach Maya how to save a pot roast. Give us an hour."

"Really? You can save it?"

Cecelia shooed Finn and Amy out of the kitchen. "Baby, I'm a doctor. I can save anything. It's my job."

An hour later, the kitchen was filled with the heady aroma of pot roast stew. Cecelia added a touch more pepper, then announced, "Perfect. Call in the troops and we'll eat."

Maya dipped her own spoon into the broth and emerged with a piece of carrot. She tasted it cautiously, ground in a little more pepper, and said, "Now it's perfect!"

A peculiar tenderness tugged at Cecelia's stomach. *Pride*.

"Daddy! Amy! Dinner!" Maya sang as she danced happily out of the room.

Cecelia smiled. Maya didn't have to know that the stew had very little to do with the original pot roast, most of which she dumped into the trash. They had made stone soup just like in the fairy tale—and it *was* good. Cecelia wiped her hands on her apron. She felt like her life was turning into a fairy tale—complete with a handsome prince.

Then, all at once, a peculiar, buzzing sensation filled her head. She shook it off and went into the dining room to check on the table, which they had elaborately set with a mishmash of mixed up dishes they had found in the basement two days ago.

She couldn't shake the odd noise in her head. It was like a crowd of murmuring voices, none of them distinct.

She went into the living room, where she found Finn half in and half out of the fireplace. Maya and Amy stood around him, Amy shouting encouragement and Maya shouting that it was dinnertime and he better come out now or else!

"I've almost got it. Hold on," he replied from somewhere inside the depths of the chimney.

The buzzing in her head grew louder. As Cecelia neared the fireplace, the sound became deafening. Was it in her head, or was Finn doing something in that chimney to make that noise?

"C'mon, dinnertime!" She addressed Finn's feet. The

rest of him was lost in the darkness of the fireplace, which was an enormous, cavernous space the size of three ordinary fireplaces.

"Minute. One. Almost got it—"

"What's he doing in there?" she asked Amy.

"We couldn't budge the mantel so he was wondering whether the chimney was even salvageable or not. He's trying to open the flue." Amy looked at Cecelia and blanched. "Weird. Do you—?"

"I know, I hear it too," Cecelia said.

"Hear what?" Maya asked. "All I hear is my stomach growling."

Amy had gone alabaster white.

"What do you hear?" Cecelia demanded.

"What do you hear?" Amy's voice was so low, Cecelia had to strain to make it out. "'Cause I just looked at you and his Name—"

"Finn!" Cecelia cried. She fell to the ground, grabbed Finn's legs, and yanked. "Get out!"

She dragged Finn out of the chimney, his arms flailing. His head clunked solidly against the slate floor just as a single loud crack rang out from somewhere deep inside the wall followed by an ominous rumble.

The chimney was coming down and it was taking the wall and a hunk of the ceiling with it.

Finn rolled away from the descending rubble like a soldier, an instant ahead of the avalanche that pursued him. He knocked Maya down as he rolled her away from the cascade, both of them barely escaping the crashing mass of drywall, brick, and stone. Cecelia and Amy somehow flew too. In less than two seconds, the entire internal structure of the chimney and the wall and a huge gaping hunk of ceiling had come down in a five-foot heap.

Dust rose around the destruction zone, billowing out in dense clouds. Light came through the ceiling from the floor above.

They looked at each other in wonder, coughing out the dust and debris that were still settling.

After a few stunned moments of silence, Maya said, "Geez. All *I* did was burn a roast."

"Guess that's one way to get the mantel down," Amy said. Then she looked at Cecelia. She froze. Then she smiled. Then she leaped at her sister. "Hot damn, you did it!" She took Cecelia into her arms and danced her around in circles.

"I did it?" Cecelia knew all at once what Amy meant and she felt as if every cell in her body had been flushed of a poison she hadn't known was there. "You mean? Really? Are you sure?" Cecelia struggled out of Amy's grasp.

"I looked at you right before it fell, and his Name was gone. Just gone. Not even the whisper I'd been hearing. And now, it's back. It's clear. It's a hundred percent."

Cecelia collapsed onto the floor, looking like a heap of rubble herself. She hadn't realized that she'd been carrying the weight of Finn's prophecy since the day Amy had shown up in Baltimore.

"Why are you all so grinny?" Maya demanded, looking from happy grown-up to happy grown-up in confusion.

Finn knelt down in front of Cecelia. "Because Cecelia saved my life." He looked into her eyes, his own eyes wide with understanding. "No more prophecy."

She nodded, unable to speak. No more prophecy.

"What's a prop a see?" Maya demanded.

Finn pulled Cecelia to her feet. "The chimney was a twenty-foot, precariously balanced pile of stones. It was ready to collapse at the slightest touch. It was meant to come down. It was waiting for the perfect time. That's prophecy."

Maya looked around her at the ecstatic adults, then at the pile of smoking rubble. "Okay. Whatever. You're all weird and the house is wrecked and I'm starved."

"See," Amy said proudly, picking up a souvenir stone from the pile. "Everything was meant to be. Every little thing."

Chapter 39

*U*m, Cel?" Finn tapped her on the shoulder. "Did you hire a gypsy?"

Cecelia turned from Maya. "Nope. It's just me and my crazy family and batty friends. That's plenty of entertainment for me. Why?"

"Well, I just wondered who those men were at the buffet wearing only G-strings."

Cecelia craned her neck.

"Made you look!" Finn cried.

"Damn. I was hoping for some action."

"Please, not in front of the children," Finn scolded.

"Or me," Maya said.

Cecelia looked around her party—her engagement party—in wonder. They were in her grandmother's house, now hers and Amy's house, soon to be Finn and Maya's house too. She was amazed that they had managed to get it ready in time for the party, but with Amy and Finn working around the clock, they had succeeded.

Maya wandered off to the buffet, leaving Finn and Cecelia alone for the first time that evening.

Finn pushed back her hair, which was loose and hung

past her shoulders. "I love your ring. It's incredibly sexy."

Cecelia looked down at her bare feet. On her pinky toe, was a tiny, delicate diamond. "I love it too."

"I'm really glad that Jack came with Sharon."

Cecelia glanced over at her former fiancé. He had gained about twenty pounds and he looked extremely happy. "Me too. They brought a great gift."

"Yeah?"

"Yeah. A three-foot-high statue of Shiva."

Finn smiled. "Well, I'm going to smash it. We're done with Shiva in this family. It's time to move on to another god." He pulled Cecelia close and she thought, *I never, ever want to leave this man*.

Then she thought, *I never, ever have to*.

"All right. All right. Enough lovey-dovey, you two." Amy came up behind them, forced herself between them, and put her arms around both their shoulders. "I always knew that you two were perfect for each other!"

"You're drunk," Cecelia said.

"Of course I'm drunk. It's no good to be sober when the strippers come."

"Amy! You didn't!" Cecelia felt her face flush.

"I thought the strippers were at the bachelorette," Finn said.

"Oh, right. That'll be next week then. Do you think you can wait that long?"

Cecelia looked Finn up and down. "I suppose I can make do."

About the Author

I love to write. That's pretty much all I do. Ask my family about the undone laundry, the unbought groceries, and the fact that I rarely find time to get dressed in the morning. Actually, if you train your family right, they won't notice any of these things. "Popcorn for dinner again, Mom! Cool," say my filthy children. God bless them, they don't know what panty hose are.

Oh, my poor husband.

What else do you want to know about me? I love kids. I love cats. I love chocolate. (Not necessarily in that order.) I live in upstate New York in paradise, except for all the snow.

I love to hear from readers. So log onto my website at www.dianaholquist.com and let me know what's on your mind!

More sizzling romance from

Diana Holquist!

⚜

Please turn this page
for a preview of

Sexiest Man Alive

Available in Fall 2007.

Chapter 1

"Hi! I'm Jasmine Burns!"

The naked man stared up at Jasmine blankly.

Great. She sounded like a cruise ship director on crack. She cleared her throat and adjusted her black teddy. "It's great to meet you!"

Ugh. This was definitely not working.

Jasmine's eyes reflected back at her in the mirror on the far (okay, not-so-far) wall of her tiny Upper West Side studio. *This only looks crazy,* she silently assured her reflection.

She looked down at the tiny naked Ken doll perched on her couch.

Okay, it was crazy. Call-the-cops nuts, even.

She paced. Seven steps. Pivot. Seven steps. Pivot. Exercise #12, page 127 in her *Goodbye Shy!* workbook had made sense in theory: *practice job interviews with a doll to focus on until the panic is gone. For best results, rehearse the interview with both parties naked to achieve optimal vulnerability.* Jasmine just couldn't get completely naked; she settled on a black lace teddy for herself. Ken wasn't so shy. He went all the way without complaint.

The mind controls the body. Let the panic wash over, then continue. Repeated exposure to the object of fear will dull the emotion.

So why was her terror growing? Her interview was three days, seven hours and twenty-seven minutes away and she was getting more panicked by the second.

She flopped onto her bed and stared at the ceiling of her shoe-box shaped apartment. The heel end was crammed with her elaborate double iron bed, centered between the door to the hallway and the door to her tiny bathroom. The toe end was dominated by a lead-glass window that stretched four feet across and from the ceiling to within two feet of the floor.

Despite her exhaustion, she forced herself off the bed and back to the "living room"—a flea-market, white-boned couch, one white over-stuffed chair, and a white coffee table rescued from a curb-side trash pile all arranged neatly at the foot of her bed.

This job was the chance of a lifetime. After all, the tailoring business she ran out of her apartment was an accident, not part of her plan. A hem here, a tuck there and within weeks she was in demand. She became known as a miracle worker who could make a cigarette hole in silk pajamas disappear, take in a suit better than anyone west of Hong Kong. It wasn't a bad way to make a living. She rarely had to leave her apartment.

But now that her graduation (M.A. in costume design from N.Y.U.) was five months past, her ex-classmates were out hitting the pavement, interning and networking, sometimes in *theaters,* sometimes even getting *paid* (she let the wonderful possibility of one day being in their shoes spread through her).

And she was playing with dolls. Naked dolls.

Maybe that was the problem. Naked Ken was too much. After all, if Ken were impersonating a famous costume designer, shouldn't he have amazing clothes?

She carried Ken to the white-washed plywood door balanced on two white wooden saw horses next to her window. Her 1949 Singer nine-stitch sewing machine gleamed in welcome. She ran her hand down it, her steel and chrome kitty. She settled at the table next to it and began to sketch.

What would Arturo Mastriani, New York's top costume designer, wear to interview her, Jasmine Burns, his next brilliant new assistant?

Jasmine jolted awake. She was on the couch, Ken in his beautiful new clothes at her side, a tiny, perfectly behaved date.

Someone was ringing the downstairs buzzer.

Her eyes jumped to the clock: 2:00 AM. Probably Susie, her best client, with a ripped seam.

Jasmine pushed the intercom button. "Susie?"

"Jas? Let me up—quick."

Jasmine fell away from the intercom in shock.

Amy, Jasmine's sister. In New York. In the middle of the night. Last time Amy showed up unannounced, Jasmine had to hide her from a guy named Rufus for two weeks.

Definitely not good.

*   *   *

Jasmine pushed the buzzer to let her sister up, then raced for the couch, tripping over the white shag throw rug. She shoved Ken between the pillows. Kicked *The Shyness Handbook* under the couch. Scooped *Living with Social Anxiety* and *Ten Steps to Being Bold* into the crick of her elbow, then fumbled them as she lunged for *Phobias and the Modern Woman*. She re-gathered the books frantically, then crammed them into one of a dozen identical 40-gallon fabric bins stacked along the wall. She was forcing the top closed when she remembered what she was wearing: the black teddy.

Oh, hell. How was she going to explain this?

The doorbell rang.

Jasmine could smell Amy's clove and cinnamon through the thin plank door separating them. Jasmine ransacked her apartment for her white terry bathrobe (24 ply, Egyptian cotton). "One sec!" She grabbed her glasses off the bedside table and slammed them on her face. There, that felt a little better.

Amy pounded on the door. "Jas? You got a man in there?"

Yeah, but it's not like he has a penis. How could she lose her bathrobe in a closet-sized apartment?

Amy pounded on the door. "Jas! Your place is the size of a rowboat. You can reach the door from the damn pot."

Could she? Well, it was close. Ah-ha. Her bathrobe was neatly folded on top of a bin of last season's cotton flannels. She pulled it on over her teddy, flipped the three deadbolts, slid free the safety chain, and stood back as Amy burst into the room.

"Jasmine. Shit." Amy went straight to the window,

threw open the curtains, and peered out. "We have to talk."

Jasmine followed her sister to the window and peered down five stories to the deserted sidewalk.

"I need cash," Amy said.

Well, might as well get right to the point. "Let me put some coffee on."

Amy pulled a two-liter, almost-empty vodka bottle out of a bulging pocket of her sheepskin coat.

"Okay. Not coffee then," Jasmine said. Amy was a social drinker, not a drunk. Jasmine's blood ran cold. Something was wrong. Amy, after all, wasn't a normal person.

Amy was a psychic.

But not just any psychic. She had one gift (besides crashing into Jasmine's life at the most inopportune moments). She could look at a person and hear a voice that spoke the name of the person's One True Love—her soul mate, her true companion, her One and Only. If you believed in such a thing. And Jasmine did. Jasmine believed completely. Not just in Amy's power, but in destiny. It made sense to her that in a world where she fit so poorly, there had to be at least one man, somewhere, who was meant for her.

But there were problems with Amy's Names. If your One True Love was named John Smith, well, too bad for you, you had to figure out which John Smith was the right one. And if the right John Smith turned out to be a married pig farmer in Iowa with seven children and you were an up-and-coming New York City costume designer, well, then, you had some tough choices to make. Amy's names rarely served up the lover a person expected. After all, who was this fate, this voice, this power? An angel? A devil? A long-dead kibbtzing old ghost, too mean-spirited even in death to mind her own business?

Well, whoever or whatever it was, it had stopped talking Friday, September 13—two years and a month ago—just days before Amy and Jasmine were reunited after a childhood apart—the ugly result of their parents' True Love-induced divorce (no, they were not each other's One True Love). Since then, Amy had been doing everything she could to get the voice to return. She ladled soup for the homeless in the moldy basements of churches (well, once, anyway, it irritated her sinuses). She consulted other psychics (who she then accused of conning her). She wore elaborate, ever-changing combinations of crystals. Now, Jasmine noted, she had turned to vodka. It seemed an unlikely fix.

Amy's eyes were closed and she rocked slightly. The bottle was empty.

Jasmine gently removed the bottle from her sister's grasp. "Is this about the voice?"

Amy's eyes sprung open and she flung herself onto the couch in a dramatic display of exhaustion. Everything about Amy was dramatic. She craved attention as much as Jasmine avoided it. "Would you get in the real world, please? I told you—it's about cash. Money. The green stuff." Amy frowned, lifted her ample hips and felt under her.

Jasmine froze.

Out came Famous-Costume-Designer-Ken, in his black wool, Hugo Boss-style suit.

Jasmine feigned surprise.

Amy dangled him from his right heel, his double-breasted jacket flapping helplessly. "Does Barbie know about this?"

Jasmine sunk onto the couch opposite Amy. She ran her hand over the flannel throw she had tossed over the couch, sensing the red through her fingertips. "Oh! There he is! I was just, um, designing costumes for a new play. He's a—prototype." The lie tasted stale in her mouth. She shrugged, trying to hide her dismay.

"Your cheeks match this throw cover, honey." Amy leaned forward and studied Jasmine closely, as if noticing her for the first time, which was likely the case. "Look at you! What are you wearing? Under your robe? It looks like—" Amy poked and pulled at Jasmine. "Something sexy."

Jasmine scurried to the far end of the couch, pushing Amy away with her bare foot. Actually, she had made the teddy in anticipation of a blind date last Thursday that she fled from following a panic attack. Twenty dollars of black Italian lace, almost wasted, until she got to the interview exercise. She tried not to think about that awful almost-date—gasping for breath, her racing heart.

Amy smoothed the creases in Ken's slacks, her eyebrows raised, waiting.

Jasmine took a deep breath. "Ken's part of an exercise to help me get ready for an interview. I'm supposed to pretend he's the interviewer. The teddy is to make me feel vulnerable."

Amy shoved Jasmine a touch too hard to be playful. "When will you stop reading those con-job self-help books and let *me* help you get over this stupid man thing?"

"It's not a man thing. It's a job thing." Jasmine rubbed her shoulder, easing out the sting of the shove. "It's a shot at an assistant position with Arturo Mastriani, the top costume designer in New York. He's—"

"He's a man."

Jasmine studied her beautiful sister. Smudged kohl rimmed her dark eyes. Her wild black hair, tangling into her legendary cleavage, seemed alive with her constant motion. Under her sheepskin coat, every inch of her clothes sparkled despite the dim light, as if lit by Amy's excess energy. She was gypsy from headscarf to toe ring.

Jasmine looked down at her own plain bathrobe wrapping her straight, thin body. The only thing gypsy about her was the blackness of her hair, as if every drop of her gypsy heritage were trying to escape through the top of her head to a more gypsy-worthy life in another body. The rest of her was pale and drained. "What's going on?" Jasmine tried again to direct the conversation back to Amy.

"Right. Okay. I'm gonna tell you straight. I need $2,000. By Wednesday."

That was just nine days away. "What about Cecelia?" Cecelia was their doctor sister who lived with Amy. The one with the cash.

"She's kinda the one I owe the money. We had a little, um, disagreement."

The sisters sat in silence. Amy surely owed Cecelia more than $2,000; she borrowed money from Cecelia all the time, with only the faintest notion of paying her back. This had to be about more than money.

"I sort of pawned one of Cecelia's rings," Amy admitted. "How could I have known it was her engagement ring? She's got so much jewelry, I thought she wouldn't miss one little bauble. Just until I got back on my feet."

"Oh, Amy." Jasmine was about to launch into a sermon on "borrowing" when she noticed Amy giving her a weird, sideways smile. "What?"

"Forget it."

"What?" Jasmine knew that smile.

"Nothing. I was just thinking. No." She shook her head, but her smile was growing. She shrugged out of her coat and stretched her arms like a cat. A sparkly, satisfied cat. Her shirt was skin-tight sheer black rayon stitched through with multi-colored glittering thread. Her skirt was shiny, black, flowing, and to her ankles. An enormous silver belt cinched her waist.

"Amy? What?"

"Okay. I'll tell you the Name of your One True Love for two thousand bucks."

A pulse of electricity shot through Jasmine. The thrill of finally knowing her One True Love's name battled with anger and disgust. How could Amy have known all along, and not told her? "You can't read the Names anymore," Jasmine reminded her sister.

"True. But I read yours two Thanksgivings ago. Cecelia had roasted that huge turkey, and you asked me to pass you the peas and—Bam!—there it was clear as day!"

Jasmine's whole body suddenly went cold. "You spilled those peas in my lap." *Was* Amy telling the truth? "You heard the name of my One True Love as Destined by Fate and all I got was a lap full of peas?" Jasmine jumped off the couch. She paced, her arms crossed. Gypsy hospitality rules mandated that she not throw Amy out—but it was tempting.

"Look, Jas, I promised Cecelia I would never, ever tell you your Named. But now that Cecelia's cut me off—to hell with her!" Amy wagged her eyebrows. "I know you want to know. It was Cecelia who wouldn't let me tell."

Jasmine considered her drunk sister. Her stomach churned with apprehension. "Why wouldn't she let you tell?"

"She thought you weren't—um, ready."

Jasmine felt her anger build. Cecelia had no right to decide something like this for her. Or Amy. Her pacing became furious. How could she not be ready? This was the moment Jasmine had spent her life preparing for. The perfect man—quiet and kind. He'd want to stay in and watch old movies, eat microwave popcorn, make soft, quiet love. And maybe, just maybe, with this man at her side, she'd be freed of her disabling anxiety—

No. Wait. Why would Cecelia have wanted to keep the truth a secret? Her One True Love was beyond awful. He was married to a woman named Melba and had seven tow-headed kids all under the age of ten. Okay. Stop pacing. Pull yourself together. Jasmine somehow made it to her kitchen—a counter, a tiny sink, a two-burner stove and a mini-fridge all shoved up against the wall.

Her Named.

Amy charging her for telling.

She pushed aside the fashion magazines and remnant books stacked on the Formica counter until she found the bottle of Burgundy she had bought for her aborted date. She poured herself a generous glass, mesmerized momentarily by the deepness of its red. She got out a glass for Amy, considered the empty vodka bottle, then put the glass back.

Jasmine took a swig of her wine. Yes, she had been waiting for this moment all her life, but now that it was here, she remembered how complicated it could be. She felt sick to her stomach. "My True Love is that awful?"

"Forget the money," Amy said suddenly. "I'm sorry. I'll tell you the Name if you want to know. I should have told you before."

Jasmine let her eyes drift between Fashion Designer Ken and Lying Blackmailer Amy. Jasmine tried to stay focused. *I want to know the name*. That was the most important thing. Amy was Amy—impossible, rude, thoughtless. But the name was the thing. "I'll find you the money if you need money. You could have just asked." Jasmine thought of the $2,324 she had in the bank. It was every penny she had made this month and she stilled owed $1,721 rent. But if she got this job with Arturo—

She was going to get the job with Arturo! If she gave Amy the money, then she'd *really* have to go through with the interview. She'd have to nail it. Going totally broke was the incentive she needed. Maybe Fate was trying to give her more than just True Love. Maybe Fate was offering up a whole new life. "Do you know him?" she blurted.

"Sort of."

"Do *I* know him?" A lump formed in her throat.

"Sort of."

"Sort of?" Pressure was building in Jasmine's head. "Are you sure you want to know?"

"Yes." *No*.

Amy knelt down regally in front of the coffee table her back upright, her head high, playing up the moment. "Your One True Love as destined by Fate. The one man on the planet destined to be your soul mate—"

Jasmine leaned forward. A flutter ran through her. Okay, it was a man. That was good.

Amy closed her eyes. "$2,000?"

Get rid of my savings. Force myself into action. Be bold. Be brave. "$2,000. But you've got to pay me back."

Amy opened her eyes. Two black coals blazed from her heart-shaped face. "Your One True Love—"

Jasmine's stomach clenched.

Amy sighed, and then shrugged. "Josh Toby, Jas. That's the thing. His name is Josh Toby."

Jasmine laughed. "Josh Toby?" Of all the men in the world, her True Love had the same name of the biggest movie star of the decade? It was absurd. Josh Toby, as any woman with a pulse knew, was the three-year-in-a-row Sexiest Man Alive according to People Magazine. His face was plastered on the wall of every thirteen-year-old girl's bedroom in America. He was married to Julie Po, last year's Sexiest Woman Alive and star of the

Agent X HBO series that made her almost as famous as her husband.

Jasmine got the shakes talking to a doll and she was supposed to go out and seduce Josh Toby?

"It might not be *that* Josh Toby. There must be others," Amy suggested.

Right. Possibly. But what if it was *that* Josh Toby? Jasmine felt betrayed. How could her One True Love be someone so unattainable, so wrong? Hell, Jed the pig farmer looked good next to this guy. Jasmine didn't have to follow the tabloids to know Josh Toby was not a stay-in-and-watch-DVD's kind of guy.

An image of Josh Toby's blue-purple eyes flashed in her mind. It was from his last movie—the one with the terrorists. Jasmine's stomach jumped. *The guy is gorgeous.*

Amy stood. "I know. He doesn't seem your type."

Could a man that sexy, practically feral, be her type?

The possibility seeped through every pore of Jasmine's body, and then drained right out. She was empty. She thought that everything would change once she knew her True Love's Name. But everything was exactly the same. She had a Name, sure, but she was still her same old self. Going out and acting on the Name was impossible. Hell, she couldn't even get up enough nerve for a job interview.

Her job interview.

What was she thinking? She couldn't just run off looking for some famous movie star. She had to prepare for Arturo. "Well, so much for that."

Amy was back at the window, staring out into the

black night. Her red fingernails tapped out Morse code for *don't be an idiot* on the glass.

"If he were the guy next door, I'd go to dinner with him," Jasmine explained. "But Josh Toby?"

Amy stopped tapping and spun around. "You wouldn't, though. You wouldn't go to dinner with the guy next door and you know it." Her eyes were blazing with challenge.

Jasmine thought of her last blind-date-turned-200-yard dash. "I would." Cripes, her voice sounded so lame, she didn't even believe herself.

"Face it, Jas. You have a man problem."

Jasmine looked at Ken. Did a grown woman playing with dolls constitute a problem? "It's just a little anxiety."

Amy put her hands firmly on her hips. "Can't you for one minute stop thinking of yourself and think of poor Josh? That sweet guy has been through a lot and maybe you're the one woman who could help him."

"Me, help *him*?" Jasmine was flabbergasted. "He doesn't need me." She pushed past Amy and yanked the curtains shut again. Maybe she could sew them shut until Amy left.

"You don't know that, Jas. The voice has spoken *for the very last time*. There must be a reason it came back one last time just for you."

Jasmine imagined meeting Josh. The lightning bolt of True Love would strike as they saw each other across a crowded, smoky ballroom. They would hurry out of the ballroom and onto the moon-dark balcony where they would swear their eternal, passionate love.

Okay, it was a little corny, but it wasn't *so* far-fetched.

Jasmine believed deep down that she was meant for bigger things than cuffs on her neighbors' pants. Somewhere in a hidden part of her soul, she believed that if she had her chance, she could be loved by a man like Josh Toby.

Or could she? What if she couldn't? What if she were just exactly what she seemed to be? A scared, timid person afraid to leave her apartment and go after her dreams?

THE DISH

Where authors give you the inside scoop!

♥ ♥ ♥ ♥ ♥ ♥ ♥ ♥ ♥ ♥ ♥ ♥ ♥ ♥ ♥ ♥

From the desks of
Diana Holquist and Kelley St. John

Dear Readers,

Pirates and gypsies, swords and prophecies, ruffled shirts and peasant skirts—all in present-day America! It is so cool that we get to write this letter about two books with so much in common. So gather up your eye patch, your crystal ball, and your handsome hero and settle in to learn what happens when two authors discuss their unique book pairing in this author-to-author interview.

Diana: So, Kelley, some scenes from your book *Real Women Don't Wear Size 2* (on sale now) take place at Gasparilla. What the heck is that? And what do your characters do there?

Kelley: You don't know what Gasparilla is? Where are you from?

Diana: I'm a northerner. Hey, you thought my book took place in Boston. It's Baltimore.

Kelley: B-cities. Whatever. They're *all* cold. But to answer your question, Gasparilla is a festival that takes place every year in Tampa, where prominent business-men dress up as pirates, board the Jose Gasparilla ship, and storm Tampa (even requiring the mayor to surrender the city each year). My heroine, Clarise, is a curvy lady who has no trouble helping other ladies embrace their voluptuous figures, but has never completely ventured out of her own shell. She heads to Gasparilla to find her wild side amid the adventurous pirates.

Diana: I love pirates! I mean, I love my husband, but I love *reading* about pirates. My book is full of gypsies.

Kelley: Gypsies and pirates are always getting mixed up. (Sort of like, you know, Boston and Baltimore . . .)

Diana: Exactly. Put on an eyepatch and a ruffled shirt, and what's the difference? (Oooh, my heroine would be mad if she heard me say that!) But the point is, pirates and gypsies can really set a modern woman free.

Kelley: Mmmmm . . . I certainly like a ruffled shirt. Though Seinfeld's puffy shirt didn't do a thing for me. Does your hero wear one? (A ruffled shirt, that is, not a puffy one.)

Diana: My hero is a carpenter, so he's a jeans-and-T-shirt kind of guy. But Cecelia, my heroine, is on the cover of *Make Me a Match* (on sale now) in full gypsy regalia. Although she could be a pirate, if you squinted.

Kelley: Love that cover! And your gypsy can tell the name of a person's One True Love?

Diana: Exactly. Imagine what would happen if you really did have One True Love on this earth—and a gypsy psychic could tell you his name. Of course, he might be your worst nightmare. Or maybe, like Cecelia in my book, you're already engaged to someone else and you don't want anything to do with your One True Love—or your gypsy heritage.

Kelley: Or what if you weren't sure your One True Love would appreciate your abundance of, er, curves. My

heroine, Clarise, is finally going to let her curves shine for her friend/boss/fantasy, Ethan Eubanks, at Gasparilla. Did I mention Gasparilla is like Mardi Gras, but with pirates and swords? Clarise wants to set her inhibitions, and her Robinson Treasures, free. (I'll let you guess about those Robinson Treasures.) So tell me, can your gypsy *really* know Cecelia's One True Love? Or is that something I get to learn when I read your fabulous book?
Diana: What? Sorry, I was busy wondering about those Treasures . . . You know, I think I've had enough of this chatting. I've got to get reading.
Kelley: Sounds like a great idea. Judging from your feisty cover, I can tell that Cecelia is ready to have a whole lot of fun and find a whole lot of love. Her One True Love, right?
Diana: Exactly. Well, maybe. Sometimes, you know, gypsies lie.

So readers, we're giving you a taste of pirates and gypsies, shapely women and psychics, and that ideal (and sometimes, not so ideal) situation when you meet that One True Love. Read them and let us know what you think! We'd love to hear from you!

Sincerely,

Diana Holquist

Kelley St. John

MAKE ME A MATCH

REAL WOMEN DON'T
WEAR SIZE 2

www.dianaholquist.com

www.kelleystjohn.com

*Want to know more about romances at
Warner Books and Warner Forever?
Get the scoop online!*

WARNER'S ROMANCE HOMEPAGE

Visit us at www.warnerforever.com for all the
latest news, reviews, and chapter excerpts!

NEW AND UPCOMING TITLES

Each month we feature our new titles
and reader favorites.

CONTESTS AND GIVEAWAYS

We give away galleys, autographed copies,
and all kinds of fun stuff.

AUTHOR INFO

You'll find bios, articles, and links to personal
Web sites for all your favorite authors—and
so much more!

THE BUZZ

Sign up for our monthly romance newsletter,
and be the first to read all about it!